# This Time, Forever

### CONSTANCE O'DAY-FLANNERY

## Zebra Books
## Kensington Publishing Corp.

http://www.zebrabooks.com

# A LOVE FOR ALL TIME

Meggie was holding up the hem of her skirt so it wouldn't get wet. Not too high, just modestly above her calves, just enough to tease him. And the sight of her shapely legs was making him crazy.

"Here," she said, turning around as they reached the small waterfall. "If you stand here, you'll be much cooler. I'll leave you now and you can . . . well, swim if you like."

She had to pass him to go back, and the mist from the fall was already getting her wet, making her clothes cling to her body. Just as she was about to pass him, his hand reached out and touched her stomach. It was so innocent, yet so intimate, that she sharply inhaled.

His back was against the falls and water gently splashed over his shoulders. Reaching up with both hands to push back the wet hair from his eyes, he gazed at her.

"Thomas." She said his name in a whisper as the cool mist enveloped them.

"Meggie. Please. Tell me . . ."

His voice was like a soft feather that ran down her spine and up the front of her body. Her thighs trembled with desire.

"I want you. Come to me, Meggie." The water ran between them, yet she could feel his chest against hers, his legs against her own. And a throbbing—a pounding so wild, so intense that it was almost overpowering.

His eyes closed for a moment and then he looked straight up, beyond the trees and into the sky. "I want her!" he shouted out in a desperate, rasping voice. "You sent her to me. Now she's mine!"

# BOOK YOUR PLACE ON OUR WEBSITE AND MAKE THE READING CONNECTION!

We've created a customized website just for our very special readers, where you can get the inside scoop on everything that's going on with Zebra, Pinnacle and Kensington books.

When you come online, you'll have the exciting opportunity to:

- View covers of upcoming books
- Read sample chapters
- Learn about our future publishing schedule (listed by publication month *and author*)
- Find out when your favorite authors will be visiting a city near you
- Search for and order backlist books from our online catalog
- Check out author bios and background information
- Send e-mail to your favorite authors
- Meet the Kensington staff online
- Join us in weekly chats with authors, readers and other guests
- Get writing guidelines
- AND MUCH MORE!

Visit our website at
http://www.zebrabooks.com

## *Acknowledgment and Thanks*

Thomas Kane, who took me on a wondrous ride through the park.

Colleen and Linda, for always being patient and never letting me give up.

My sister, Christine, for helping to create the illusion. I love you, Chrissy.

and
Pat Trowbridge, who opened up a new world and showed me how to believe in myself again.

# Chapter 1

She was trapped.

Margaret Mary Gillbride blew the stray hair away from her eyes and looked up the hill toward the Monroe colliery. It was gray, dreary, and depressing — a wooden behemoth gouging into the belly of the mountain. She hated it . . . and she was never going to get out. She would never see those beautiful places her mother had told her about. Years ago fate had stepped in and made her a prisoner. She knew, just like everyone who lived in the patch, that there was no escape.

Not in this lifetime.

What worried Meggie was that she wasn't willing to wait for her just reward in heaven. She didn't think she believed in heaven. She wasn't quite sure, but it seemed to her that God had his favorites, just like anyone else. And she, somehow, had slipped from favor. Ah, well, with her past even the priests weren't sure of her salvation. She had made a mistake once, a tragic mistake, and was forever a fallen women in their eyes. Perhaps beyond redemption. And all because she had once loved. Or thought she had loved. How foolish the young heart . . . How long must she pay?

There was no hope for her in the coal mining town. Nor was there a future for a woman who had been unmarried when she'd delivered her stillborn son. Her features hardened at the memory. And never would she forgive the church for making her bury her child outside of their sacred grounds.

For Meggie Gillbride, now there was only survival.

"I say we kill the sonofabitch, and be done with it!"

Beyond the curtain, Meggie's hands paused over the bread dough when she heard James Roarity's fierce suggestion. She knew she shouldn't be listening to the men, knew the meeting was supposed to be secret, but even a jackass had to realize that the curtain did little to hide their voices. All it served was to separate her from those who gathered in her home to discuss their next strategy for bringing down the mines.

Hearing her brother's conciliatory voice, Meggie punched down the rising dough and listened to Brian.

Now, Jimmy, let's not get carried away too quickly here. We've spent the last fifteen months on strike. Tomorrow, on the day before this country celebrates its independence, over one thousand of us are going to stop work at the mines near Mahanoy City. The breaker at Mount Carmel is going to go up in flames and send a message to the Honorable Nathen Gowen—"

Meggie was able to recognize Jack Donahue's voice as it interrupted her brother.

"The message we need to send Nate Gowen is a

bullet through his black, greedy heart! I've got three children, near starving for a decent meal, Brian. And they won't make it through the summer if this strike isn't over. I can't bear to look into their faces anymore." Donahue's voice became a whisper and Meggie strained to hear his next words.

"Your mother and father are safe with the Lord—bless their souls. And there are no children in this house, Brian. Just you and your sister. Connon Rafferty has four young ones. And this time next week they won't have a father unless we do something right away. We need a woman to plant the explosive tomorrow. That's why we're here now. What do you think? Will she do it, Brian? We've never before let a woman into the Mollie's inner circle . . ."

Meggie stopped breathing for a moment as a chill raced up her back. What were they talking about? *Her* in the Mollie Maguires! Plant an explosive? Where . . . in God's name? She wanted to tear away the curtain and confront them, demand her answers. Just then she again heard Brian's voice.

"I'm not so sure about this. Meggie's my sister. And she's a—a woman."

"The original Mollie was a woman," Roarity countered. "I'd daresay that some of our fathers dressed up like Mollie herself back on the 'ould sod' and gave the Brits a run." There was a pause, a tension-filled moment, while all waited for him to continue. "Make her do it, Brian. You're the head of this house. Just tell her she has to do it or you'll toss her out. Everybody knows she lives on your charity—"

"We're desperate, Brian," Jack Donahue quickly cut in. "You know the jury is going to come in with a hanging verdict and Connon is going swing for a murder he didn't commit. We have to make a statement and let them know that we're not going to

9

allow it. We agreed on this."

"But my sister, Jack! Meggie has—"

Without thought, Meggie Gillbride ripped back the curtain and glared at the startled men in her mother's front room. "You'll have to excuse me for interrupting you, Brian, but your sister is able to speak for herself."

Brian's eyes blazed his displeasure. *"Meggie!* Get back to your bread. You can't come in here . . . not now!"

She looked at the five men who made up this meeting, until her gaze settled on one in particular. "And how is it that you claim to know so much about me, James Roarity? You haven't even been in the patch a full year yet." She lifted her chin in defiance. "I earn my keep, sir," she stated with as much dignity as she could muster, hating the fact that every man in the room knew such personal details of her life. Dear God in heaven, would the shame never end?

James Roarity stared back at the red-haired beauty across from him. It was too bad she was already spoiled, he thought, for he would have dearly loved to have been the one to initiate her. Beyond the meek exterior she usually exhibited to others, he'd seen the true Margaret Mary Gillbride—a woman with a temperament as fiery as her hair. Wisps of curls had escaped a long braid and now framed her chiseled face. Freckles became slightly darker as her cheeks flamed with anger. And her ample breasts rose and fell with a righteous indignation. Meggie Gillbride looked like a Celtic queen surrounded by peasants. He'd noticed her the first time he'd come to the patch. Then he'd heard the stories. If Brian didn't

10

hold such importance within the Order of Hibernians, James Roarity would have made a move toward her sooner. As of now, it was enough to speak to her with his eyes and his actions. He could tell by the embarrassed flush that she'd understood his unspoken proposition.

His smile held no warmth as he watched the hate come into her startlingly light blue eyes.


Brian refused to acknowledge her anger. Almost choking on her indignation, Meggie cast her brother an accusatory look and whirled from the room. Picking up the hem of her brown skirt, she ran outside. As soon as the door slammed behind her, she leaned against the rough-planked wall and gulped in fresh air. It was as if the act could somehow cleanse her of the hate and anger she had felt in that room. But nothing, no amount of air, could make her feel clean after receiving those looks from James Roarity.

Her lower lip trembled as she slowly walked toward the clothesline. She wouldn't let Roarity make her feel dirty. She refused to give him that power over her. Even though her hands shook as she removed the linens and threw them over her shoulder, Meggie blinked furiously rather than allowing the tears to roll down her cheeks. Damn him! Damn all men!

And then, unwillingly, she pictured her Da.

Six days out of seven, William John Gillbride had worked down in the mines. The conditions were miserable, dangerously unsafe, and he'd barely earned enough for his family to live on. Yet he'd come home each night, his skin blackened with coal dust, and had gently placed a kiss on Meggie's and

11

Brian's foreheads. Every night he'd bathed in their kitchen behind a curtain while his beautiful red-haired wife tried to put dinner on the table. It was always a challenge for Meggie's mum, for there was never enough.

Lehigha was a "company" town, owned and run by the Reading Coal and Iron Company. Even the Gillbride home, little more than a shanty, was not theirs. The Reading owned everything. Many were the months that the miners were not even paid cash, but coupons that were redeemable at the company-owned stores, or used to pay rent on the company-owned house. The store prices and rents were unreasonably high and most people in Lehigha were always in debt to the Company.

It was the way the mine owners wanted it to remain.

Billy Gillbride had been one of the original Mollies in the patch, as Lehigha was called after the War Between the States. Then there weren't any killings, or bombings. Then it was enough to have a politician in the pocket, and the sheriff sympathetic. They were all immigrants back then, banding together for survival. Maybe the roads weren't paved in gold, but there was work.

The pay was often fifty cents a day, yet no one but those who labored twelve hours underground thought it was a disgrace. Sons and daughters saw their mothers grow old before their eyes from worry. Frightened girls watched their fathers and brothers, strong strapping men, grow weak from the black lung disease. Fearful boys knew the same fate awaited them. And it was that second generation, those young men born in America, that decided to fight back and change things—to right the wrongs, to end the strangulation hold of the mine owners.

Maybe their ways weren't always best . . .

"Meggie! Come in now. I need to talk with you."

Blinking a few times, Meggie turned away from the clothesline and looked back across the yard to the house. Her brother stood in the doorway—tall, dark, and suddenly threatening. He held the door open, as if in welcome, and a chill ran down her arms. For the first time in her life, she was truly frightened of Brian. Ahh, there were times a few years ago when he'd threatened to beat her for shaming the family. It had taken only one look at Da's heartbroken expression and she'd quickly lost her defiance and had yielded to Brian. She had given up her plans to run away from the disgrace of her pregnancy. Instead, she had remained in the patch. She had buried her baby, and then her father, and had kept house for Brian.

She had also turned into an old maid. A spinster.

Walking up to Brian, she had to remind herself that she was now an adult. And no one could force her to do anything. Not anymore.


She sat before them with her hands folded on her lap. She wanted to appear calm, as if their suggestion hadn't caused her heart to pound with fear and excitement. Clearing her throat, she looked directly at Jack Donahue and asked, "You want *me* to plant an explosive at the Reading Building?"

Donahue nodded. "Aye, Meggie. No one'd suspect a woman—"

"Well, I have strong suspicions," she interrupted, "that not one of you knows a tinker's heel about such things. And if you do, then God be savin' your soul because you couldn't have been up to anything good while you were learning."

13

Brian touched her shoulder, almost tenderly. "Now, Meggie. Calm down. We happen to know more than you'd think about explosives. Really. It'd be quite safe."

She turned to her older brother. "You want me to do this, Brian?" she asked. "What if someone gets hurt? How can you be sure?"

Brian looked to the fifth man in the room, as if asking for help.

Liam Dunleavy was of her father's age. He was the acknowledged head of the local branch of Mollies, and had remained silent throughout the meeting. Now, as though concentrating, he rubbed the place between his eyes and said softly, gently, "Meggie girl, this is a matter of life and death. We don't ask lightly. You know the Raffertys. You've seen Theresa and her babes. If we don't apply some pressure now, for sure Connon is going to hang. And I give you my word, the man is innocent of any crime, other than being in the wrong place at the wrong time."

He tried smiling at her. "I know what we're asking is frightening. But do you think we'd jeopardize your safety? We'll be using that new explosive, dynamite. It's so much more safe than straight nitroglycerin. And we'll be using a safety fuse. Why don't you tell her about it, Jimmy."

Meggie's gaze slid from Liam to her brother and then, reluctantly, to James Roarity. Already he was starting to explain the safety fuse.

". . . made of black powder enclosed in jute and cotton yarn. When we light it, the powder burns slowly until the flame reaches the explosive. It's the flame that sets off the charge."

"By that time you'll be safely out of the building," Brian cut in. "And then we've arranged for you to

14

spend the next two weeks in Philadelphia."

Meggie could feel her eyes widen with surprise. "Philadelphia?" Just the name sounded exotic. Her mother had told her of that city.

It was Liam who answered. "My brother Andrew will be expecting you tomorrow evening. You'll be stayin' with him and his wife and their three young ones. Mary Alice will welcome the help with the children. When it's safe, you'll return here."

*Philadelphia.* To have a chance to see it! All her life she had spent in the patch, at least all she could remember. She'd heard the stories often enough— how her Da had brought them here when his livery business had collapsed. Mining. It was only supposed to have been a few years. It had been for the rest of his life. Suddenly Meggie knew she had to get out. She didn't want to be like Da. She didn't want to die in the patch.

She swallowed several times and tried to arrange her features in a noncommittal expression. She looked from Brian to Liam and then back again. "Explain to me how no one will be hurt."

Liam tried to hide his grin. "The building will be deserted because of the holiday. A back door will be opened to you. Brian will point it out—"

"Who'll open the door?" Meggie interrupted.

Liam rubbed his chin with his wide thumb and everyone could hear the scratch of his fingernail against his beard. "Don't be askin' such questions, Meggie. Just remember what I'm tellin' you. Once you're inside, go directly to the office marked Accounting, and—"

"Why Accounting?" Meggie asked quickly, a confused expression on her face.

Liam took a deep breath and swiftly expelled it. "You ask a lot of questions."

15

Meggie raised her chin. "I believe I have that right, considering what you're asking of me."

She could see him weighing her words. And then he nodded. "Inside that office are all our accounts with the Reading. We're all in debt to the company. It's no secret. It's our way of life here in the patch. Unfortunately, Connan Rafferty's account is worse than most. We've learned from a reliable source that there's incriminating evidence against Connon being kept in that office."

"What is it?" Meggie leaned forward in her chair, intrigued.

Shaking his head, Liam said, "That I won't tell you. It's best you don't know. But think, girl. Who was it that was murdered?"

Meggie whispered, "Arthur Singer," and pictured the sour-faced man who'd kept the running accounts of all Lehigha's residents. Even if he hadn't passed away, it would not be cruel to say he'd been one of the most hated men in the town. Meggie remembered him evicting a widow whose husband had been killed in the mine last year.

Continuing, as if she'd never interrupted, Liam said, "We want you to go into the office and gently place the satchel on the floor. Then turn around and walk out the way you came." Liam brought his pipe to his mouth and puffed a few times. "It's as simple as that, Meggie. Can you do it?"

Before she could answer, Brian said in a worried voice, "She should know all of it, before she makes any decision."

Meggie watched as Liam nodded to her brother. Brian looked uneasy and cleared his throat several times before mumbling, "God forgive us, but we've stolen a nun's habit."

Unconsciously leaning closer to her brother, Meg-

16

gie asked, "What did you say?" Surely she couldn't have heard correctly.

It was James Roarity who spoke up loud and clear. "Why, you'll be dressed as a nun, girl. Meggie Gillbride in a nun's holy clothes!"

She lay in bed, listening to the song of the cicadas outside. There was no air moving on this July night and the frayed curtain at her window remained motionless. When she thought of the countless hours her mother had spent teaching her to sew a fine stitch, she sighed aloud in the darkness. There was no money now to be spent for curtain material. Hadn't it been over two years since she'd made herself the green dress? And it now looked as old as her others. On this hot endless night the future held no promises and she unconsciously pulled at the neckline of her worn cotton nightgown, praying that a breeze might enter the small room.

As she gazed at the shadow of her mother's dresser, her eyes filled with grief and loneliness. How she missed her Mum! In September it would be five years. Almost two years ago her Da had finally been taken and his pain had ended. It was then that Brian had suggested she take over their parents' bedroom. He had thought he was doing her a favor, granting her the only privacy in the small house. But it was filled with memories—painful memories of her loving parents—and she had never been comfortable.

Lying in the darkness, she wondered if her mother and father were together, looking down on her now. Would they give their consent?

"What should I do?" she whispered into the night. It was a question that haunted her and robbed her sleep. If only she knew the answer . . .

Once more she thought back to the strange meeting that had taken place earlier, hoping that this time she might come to a decision.

When James Roarity had made his hateful remark about her dressing in a nun's habit, Brian had stood up and glared at the man. It was then he had demanded that Roarity leave their home. Even while the others had shaken their heads with regret, they somehow saw the logic of Liam's hurried suggestion that it would be best for just him and Brian to remain. They would all meet at nine o'clock in Fitzhugh's Tap Room. She had ignored Roarity's attempted apology and stared at his back as he left her home. He had not apologized to her, but to Brian.

When the three of them were alone, Liam Dunleavy sat down heavily in her father's rocker.

"I'm sorry for you, Meggie, that you had to hear something like that. Jimmy Roarity's mouth will be the end of him." He smiled kindly. "I know you're a good girl, Meggie. Why, I remember the times you came all the way up the colliery to meet your daddy and me with lemonade. We used to laugh and marvel that your little legs could carry you up that hill." His expression turned mournful. "You took care of dear Billy, your father, when the damned black dust took the breath from his lungs. And you're a fine sister to your brother Brian."

She'd had to blink several times to stop the tears from forming at her eyes.

Liam cleared his throat. "But now, let me explain about why we're asking you to dress . . . differently. Every Friday night, the good sisters of Saint Aloysious pass by the Reading Building on their way to the cemetery. They bring flowers to decorate old Father Michael's grave. They've been doing it for years, ever

18

since the pastor was laid to rest. You'll be dressed like one of them—and don't be asking how we got the habit, for that's something we'll be answering for when our time comes. It'll be simple to carry the satchel under a bouquet of flowers. No one will give you a second glance. After you've left the office, walk back to Brian and he'll take you to the train."

His eyes peered into hers with such an intensity that she sat up straighter. "Will you do it, Meggie? Will you help us in this crucial matter? Will you help Connon and Theresa?"

She had yet to form an answer. Shaking her head in the dark, she let her mind wander. The faces of the Rafferty children became clear. Sweet, lovely blond-haired children, the youngest not yet three years—the same age her own son would have been . . . She quickly turned to her side, refusing to think about the poor babe who'd been born strangled by the cord that united them. To remember, to allow those thoughts, would surely drive her mad. Instead she must concentrate on her decision, for she had promised Brian and Liam an answer before morning. Could she do it? Could she help them? In turn, she would be destroying the records of debt for all of Lehigha, all those who had held her in such scorn these past years. But underneath it all, she couldn't shake the haunting face of Connon Rafferty's youngest son. She thought his name was Kevin.

Sighing, she was only sure that she wanted that tiny blond-haired boy to grow up knowing his father. God only knew there had been enough sorrow in the patch.

Maybe she could help someone . . .

Perhaps, a small child.

19

If she weren't damned to burn in hell for her other transgressions, then surely she would spend eternity repenting for this sin. Meggie kept a death grip on the satchel that she carried under a large bouquet of pink peonies and tried to ignore the scratch of wool against her skin. The nuns were surely earning their place in heaven by having to wear these habits in the hot humid summer weather, she thought, struggling to overlook the trickle of perspiration running down the center of her back.

"Are you all right, Meg?" Brian asked, his voice sounding as nervous as she felt.

"As right as I'll ever be," she answered, and was dismayed to hear the crack in her voice.

Brian led her into the alley behind the Reading Building and stopped to light a long cigar. "There it is," he whispered, nodding to the back door of the brick building across the alleyway.

Staring at the door, some fifty feet away, she whispered back, "That's it? Are you sure it's opened?" Why did her hands have to start shaking so now? Several fragile pink petals fell toward her feet.

"It's open," Brian assured her. "Though I wish I knew why Liam insisted this morning that we push up the time one hour."

Meggie turned to gape at her brother. "You don't know?"

Brian kept staring at the door. "I have my suspicions. I think he wanted the others to have firm alibis. To be as surprised as everyone else when the explosion takes place ahead of time."

Thinking of the dynamite hidden under the peonies, her shaking increased. "Brian . . . you're sure? I mean, this . . . this won't go off until it's time? Will it?"

He shook his head. "I showed you, Meggie, how the fuse is wrapped. It's measured for five minutes." With that, he checked his watch and said, "We'd better get started. Are you ready?"

She kept staring at her brother, memorizing his face, the lock of dark brown hair that fell over his forehead, just like Da. So handsome. So determined. "I'm scared, Brian," she murmured. "What if something happens?"

He smiled at her reassuringly. "Nothing will happen."

"You'll be here? You'll wait for me?"

"I'll be here, Meggie girl. Right up the corner. We can't be seen together from here on in. But I'll be watching for you to come back out and you'll follow me to the Connelly house. From there we'll go to the station. Now lift the flowers for me."

She automatically did as she was told and watched as Brian opened the satchel and lowered his cigar to the fuse. Immediately, she heard the hiss as it was ignited and smelled the acrid odor of sulfur as the fuse caught. Brian quickly brought the flowers back into place and said, "Now hurry. Remember, you have five minutes to go in, leave the bag, and get back out. I'll be watching."

Numb with fear, she nodded to her brother yet couldn't seem to move.

"Meggie, you have to go," Brian said, starting to sound desperate. "I've already lit the fuse."

She took a deep breath and said, "Pray for me, Brian, for I'm too scared to do it myself."

"You'll do fine, Meg. *Go!*"

Her legs felt as if stones were attached to them as she forced herself to move down the alleyway. She didn't dare look back to her brother. She kept moving, feeling as if the starched headpiece were strangling her. The door loomed ahead, not twenty feet away, like the entrance to a wicked, nefarious place. Would she have the courage to enter, to . . .

From the corner of her eye she saw a boy chasing a white puppy down the alley, and stopped as the child slowed directly in front of her. He stood between her and the door.

"Are ya havin' trouble, sister?" he asked, wiping the sweat from his forehead onto his shirtsleeve. "The cemetery is the other way."

Meggie could only stare at the child as she smelled the fuse burning beneath the flowers. Dear God in heaven, make him go away! Make him leave!

No longer in the patch, she had no idea as to his name. Desperate, she said crossly, "It's Friday. Have you been to confession yet today?"

The child appeared startled. "Why, no, sister. Not yet. Confessions don't start till two."

She swallowed. "Well, then you'd best be on your way, young man. I'll say a Hail Mary that you find your dog before then."

As if suddenly remembering his puppy, he nodded and swiftly ran up the alley, looking eager to get away from her.

Breathing a sigh of relief, she hurried to the door and paused before it. She looked up and down the alley, and saw no sign of the child, or for that matter, Brian. No longer hesitant, Meggie pushed it open and entered the Reading Coal and Iron Company Building. She felt almost triumphant as she gazed down the long corridor before her.

It was then she heard the low murmur of voices.

She didn't know what to do. Smelling the rapidly burning fuse, she inched her way forward, straining to hear where the voices were coming from. Suddenly they became clearer, louder, and she knew someone was walking in her direction. Frantic, she tried an office door and breathed a sigh of thanks when it easily opened. Once inside, she flattened her body against the wall and prayed that whoever was outside the office wouldn't detect her presence.

"You're sure they'll come?" a low, gruff voice asked.

"They'll be here," another answered. "They still believe there's some evidence against Rafferty in the building. I just want to double-check the door and make sure the Gillbride girl can get in. Her brother will be bringing her up the alley in an hour."

Meggie stopped breathing when she recognized the second voice.

*It was James Roarity!*

She looked about the office wildly, as if somehow there might be an escape. There were no windows, no exits besides the door she'd just entered. Then she became acutely aware of the burning fuse under the huge bouquet of peonies. She had to get out. She had to warn Brian and the others about the traitor in their midst. She also had to get away from the explosive that she carried.

Meggie had no idea how long she'd waited in that small, stifling office for the sound of the men's voices. Was it three minutes? Four? Did she only have a minute before the satchel exploded and ripped apart the room? And her along with it? Just then she heard them return from checking the door.

"You leave by the front, Jim. I'll follow in a few minutes. Needless to say . . . a good job done. Took almost a year to infiltrate those bastards, but after today we've caught them red-handed. I'd just like to see a judge and jury let one of them off this time."

Meggie heard Roarity's voice as they passed by a few feet from where she was hiding. "I'm more than ready, Nate, to get back to Chicago."

The other answered, "Well, you'll be living the good life on the fortune you've earned here. We'll only need you as a material witness at the trials and then you're free to go."

She couldn't clearly hear any more of their conversation as they moved on. Now was the time to act! Her palms were sweating as she lowered the satchel to the floor. Her heart beat so rapidly that she felt positive the men would hear it. And she knew that if she didn't get out of that office, surely she was going to faint and be blown to Hades.

Backing away from the pile of flowers on the floor, she grabbed the doorknob in her fist and turned. Even if she were caught by James Roarity and Nate Gowen, it would be a far better fate than delaying her exit. Now, there was no time to waste. Surely, it was five minutes since she'd entered this damned place.

Opening the door, Meggie didn't bother to look up the hallway toward where the men had been walking only moments ago. Now there was only time to escape. And the door, her only means of freedom, seemed so far away.

Panic, as real and terrifying as anything she had ever experienced, took over and she broke into a run.

She had to reach that door!

She had to warn Brian about James Roarity!

She had to escape—

And then it happened.

A sudden noise, loud and deafening, sounded. A fierce, vicious pain shot through her ears at the same time that a blinding white heat pushed at her back and lifted her into the air.

She experienced a moment of wonderment, a second of surprise at the ridiculous sensation of flying.

24

It was followed by another flash of pain so terrible, so intense, that she opened her mouth to cry out.

She never heard the sound of her own voice. She only welcomed the darkness that began to envelop her within its soft, numbing folds.

And then it was over.

# Chapter 2

There was no justice, no fairness to it all.

Planting his feet to keep his balance, Thomas Grey Carter looked in the small mirror and grimaced at his reflection. He looked tired, and older than his thirty-five years. Washing one's hands in the "head" of an L1011 airliner was a hell of a time to realize that life was passing one by, he thought grimly.

Who'd believe it? Here he was—a successful entrepreneur, touted as being Donald Trump's successor—as if Trump were ready to abdicate. As if he, himself, coveted the title, for that matter. It was no more than media hype, but the powerful illusion had stuck and now his life, both public and personal, was open to scrutiny . . . and gossip. It was not the life he had envisioned fifteen years ago when he'd come to New York.

Drying his hands, he crumpled the paper towel and continued to stare into his eyes in the mirror. He should have been excited, exhilarated, by the favorable outcome of this trip, for he'd just completed the friendly takeover of this country's leading computer company. It had taken over fifteen months to accomplish, thousands of man-hours, and yet strangely, he was left with a hollow feeling in the middle of his gut. He'd always trusted his instinct in the past, and now they were telling him to slow down, to stop and take a realistic look at his life before he burned himself out.

What was it his father used to say? Take your time, take a deep breath, and remember the most important thing in life: family. Everything else can be replaced. Christ! The last time he'd heard those words was a lifetime ago in Medford, Delaware. Medford seemed like a million miles away right now, and there was no more family there for him, at least no one that mattered anymore. Running his fingers through the front of his hair, he sighed to his reflection. He must be tired if he was conjuring up the ghosts of his past.

What he needed was to get into his car and drive. Sliding the latch, he opened the narrow door and walked back to his seat in first class. He would put in the Jarreau tape and blast it as loud as he could handle it. He'd start at Canal Street and take the West Side Highway south, past the New Money City across from the World Trade towers. If luck was with him, the short tunnel would be empty and he would shoot up onto FDR Drive. It lasted only a few moments, but it was always worth it, for it was then that the city of New York blasted him in the face with its brilliance.

Glad that the car would be there when he landed, he checked his watch to see how long he'd have to wait before he felt alive once more behind the wheel of his Range Rover—

It was then that he saw her.

He stopped short and checked the seat number on the overhead compartment, thinking he'd made a mistake. He hadn't.

There was a nun sitting in the previously empty

27

window seat next to his own.

Deciding she had somehow come up from coach, he cleared his throat and took his seat, trying not to acknowledge the terrified look on the woman's face. Unable to withstand her intense scrutiny, Thomas Carter turned to her and smiled. Twelve years of Catholic schooling hadn't been a total waste. It took only seconds for that black and white habit to kick back into gear and work its respectful magic. He felt fifteen years old when he began to speak.

"Is this your first flight, sister?"

*She had died!* Surely that was it, for weren't there clouds beneath her? She had seen them out the small glass window, huge billowy clouds that swiftly disappeared behind the carrier she was riding. One moment she was running toward the back door of the Reading building, and in the next she was seated here, in this large air ship on her way to—heaven? This is how you are transported to heaven?

And then he spoke . . .

The angel.

Surely he was one of God's legion sent to escort people like her. And he must be an angel, for wasn't he the most beautiful of men? Meggie stared at him in amazement, taking in his strong features, his auburn hair that was brushed back off his handsome face. Why, his green eyes were kindly, almost respectful, with lashes so thick that a woman would envy them. He wore a business suit, not unlike the wealthy men on earth, and Meggie deduced that God must not want to frighten those who'd just left their earthly bounds by letting the angels show their wings.

And this extraordinary man, this angel, was sent

28

to be her guardian, her guide. Perhaps God had decided she wasn't to be punished for her many transgressions. Wouldn't the good people of Lehigha be surprised to know that Meggie Gillbride was to be admitted into Heaven? So much for the hell and damnation that she'd—

Just then she felt a change in the carrier ship and unconsciously clutched at the sleeve of the angel.

"Nothing to worry about," the angel said. "We're beginning our descent."

Meggie's mouth opened in shock. "We're *descending?*" she whispered, a feeling of horror enveloping her as she turned to the small window. Sure enough, the clouds were nothing more than hazy vapors as the carrier dived below them. A tight knot formed in her stomach as she turned back to the angel.

"We'll be landing in less than"—the angel looked at a watch he wore on his wrist—"less than twenty minutes. Depending on how jammed up they are down there, of course."

Meggie looked back out the window to the tiny lights she could see below her. "Of course," she mumbled, then closed her eyes as she leaned her head against the seat cushion. She was doomed then, damned to pay for her sins along with a great many others.

Perhaps that was why her angel had no wings. Because she wasn't really going to heaven after all. She was going to be punished for what she had done when she was younger, for being rebellious against the Church after its members had turned on her, for listening to Brian and Liam and dressing up in this nun's garb, for wanting more out of life than mere survival in the patch. For being tempted by others. And now, God was going to demand that she pay.

29

"But she's not on the passenger manifest! Excuse me, sister, but may I have your name please?"

Meggie opened her tightly shut eyes to view a pretty woman in argument with the angel. Despite the scandalously short dress she wore, the woman looked official, as if she were in charge of the airship. Not wanting to upset anyone, lest her fate be worse than it already was, Meggie cleared her throat and attempted to speak.

"My name is, ah, uhmm, Margaret Mary Gillbride. From Lehigha, Pennsylvania." She couldn't help wringing her hands together with worry.

The woman flicked the short blond hair away from her eyes and looked down at the paper in her hand. She was shaking her head. "There's no Gillbride on here. May I see your ticket?"

"Ticket?" Meggie looked from the woman to the angel.

"Your ticket, sister," the angel repeated in a kinder voice. "The one you had when you boarded."

"But I had no ticket," Meggie insisted. "You know . . . I just happened to . . . to be here."

"This is ridiculous," the uniformed woman interrupted. "You didn't just happen to be here, sister. We check and double-check the head count, and you were never counted."

"You mean I'm *not* supposed to be here?" Meggie asked hopefully. "There was a mistake? I'm not going to be descending?" Maybe she was only going to Purgatory. Maybe the priests had been right about such a place existing. Her heart immediately felt lighter. Come to think of it, why was she feeling her heart at all? It was beating rapidly behind the wall of her chest, as if she hadn't . . . died. And the pounding headache continued. It was most surprising. Didn't death end all pain? The more she tried to make sense out of her situation, the more her head ached. "I don't think I'm supposed to be here," she said meekly, hopefully. "I think there's been a mistake."

Both the woman and the angel stared at her, as though she were talking in a different language.

"A mistake?" The official-looking woman's eyes blazed her anger, before turning back to the angel. "I'll have to inform the captain. He'll radio in to have someone meet her at the gate."

"Now, wait a minute," the angel said. "There's no need for this. Why don't I just pay for her . . . for Sister Margaret's ticket?"

Just having the young woman sitting next to him in that habit made Tom feel the guilt of not having attended church in many years. Paying for her ticket was no more than putting money in the collection basket.

"This is very unorthodox, Mr. Carter. And we'd have to charge you for a first-class seat from Seattle."

He nodded. It was a generous donation, he thought, but not excessive—considering the amount of guilt ten minutes of sitting next to a nun with an Irish accent could cause.

"They're still going to want to question her when we land. I don't see how she could have come onboard." The young woman again shook her head and Tom could see the uneasiness in her expression. Obviously she was worried about her own lack of an explanation.

"Look, have Mac Weaver call me Monday at my

office and we'll straighten this out." He opened his wallet and took out a business card and handed it to the flight attendant. "I won't have time when we land." He could see how mentioning the name of the head of security had worked. Retaining a seat on the board of Intercontinental Airlines had its advantages, and besides, he wasn't about to let anything come between him and his Range Rover. Not tonight. Tonight he needed to blow off steam, shed the corporate skin, and fill the empty void in his stomach. He wondered what Angelica was doing tonight. It was still early.

Seeing the wooden rosary beads attached to the nun's waist, he immediately cleared his mind of thoughts of his ex-wife.

Catholic guilt. It was amazing how it could rush up and hit you in the face from out of nowhere. Old habits are certainly hard to lose, he thought as he closed his wallet and slid it inside his breast pocket.


She'd seen his name on the small document inside the tiny leather case. It read: *Thomas Grey Carter, 108 Central Park South* . . . It was all she could read before he'd snapped it closed and put it away in his jacket pocket. The angel had a name, and an address. Perhaps they were assigned. Maybe he had to do so many good works before he could ascend to heaven. And then again, maybe this was all a dream. None of it was real. Yet, everything was incredible. How can people fly in this carrier? How could something this large stay in the air? She was either dreaming, or she had truly died, for only God could accomplish this miracle.

A tiny bell sounded and the angel pointed to a small, lighted sign. "You'd better put your seat belt on, sister. We're about to land."

A feeling of dread overwhelmed her as she saw the angel strap himself into his seat. Pulling up the wide belts, she held them out in front of her in hopeless confusion. Soon she was fumbling with the large metal locks in a desperate effort to connect them.

His hands appeared in front of her chest. "Here, let me show you," he said kindly, and took the belts away from her.

She watched as he easily locked her into her seat and pulled the belt to tighten it around her thighs. His fingers had been hesitant, yet gentle.

"There you are," he announced, obviously embarrassed at having touched her.

"Thank you." Her voice was a whisper as she smiled her gratitude. She had recognized his unease with her and surmised that, of course, an angel would only have the purest of minds and any embarrassment was caused only by the momentary touching of his hands on hers as she let go of the metal locks. Surely the sin was hers. She was the one who should be ashamed for the disgraceful thoughts that raced through her mind when he had leaned over to adjust the safety belt. She hoped he had no way of reading her mind, for she would be humiliated if he were to know that she found him to be the most attractive of men.

She experienced a moment of horror and confusion that her body could still react like that, especially to him. Already he had demonstrated his character. He was gentle and kind. Generous and pure of thought. Never could he think of her as anything but a charge—his mission. And soon, his mission would be over. Soon, he would deliver her to her destination.

Would she ever see him again? What fate awaited

33

her when this carrier ship landed? At this moment, it seemed unbearable that she might never meet with him again, that his hand might never brush over hers . . . She had to shake her head to drive the thoughts out, for she didn't want to add this last sin of the flesh to her numerous others. *He was an angel—Not a mere man!* And he belonged to God.

Shifting in his seat, Thomas Carter stared at the back of the cushion in front of him. He pretended to be absorbed in the stitching and the grain of the faux leather. In reality, he was uncomfortable, edgy, and reluctant to admit the brief flash of attraction that had passed between him and the very nervous nun seated next to him. *A nun!*

He wanted to get up and change his seat, but he was trapped as the plane prepared to land. He needed to get away from those sapphire blue eyes that looked back at him with something akin to reverence, to shut out the very pretty face framed by that crisp white veil, the pale skin dotted with a light dusting of freckles across her nose and cheekbones. Even her voice held a hint of an Irish accent, like someone who'd been born in this county yet had picked up the inflections from their parents. She was Ingrid Bergman, right out of *Going My Way,* and there was no escaping her until they were on the ground.

Again he shifted in his seat, impatient now for the wheels of the airliner to touch down. Damn it! He felt like a fool for being attracted to her innocence. The very best way to handle this situation, Tom thought, was to be thoroughly polite and bid her good-bye as soon as possible—which was exactly what he did.

Everyone seemed to be in a hurry as they rushed past her to their destinations. From the quiet of the carrier she had followed the angel into a large building that rang with hundreds of voices and the sound of a louder voice that seemed to float in the air as it called out names. Meggie tried to listen, in case her name was called, but she felt faint from the excitement of the landing and the heightened expectation of what awaited her now.

The angel looked around the crowd, as if expecting someone, then turned back to her and smiled. "No one's meeting you?" he asked.

Meggie shook her head in hopeless confusion.

Again, the angel smiled. This time she thought it looked strained. "Well, then, I'll say good-bye."

She could feel the tremors begin to shake her body as she watched the angel start to walk away from her. "Wait!" she called out.

He turned back to her.

"What do I do now?" she asked, an icy panic starting to set in. He really was leaving her here in this madhouse of dead people!

Tom shifted the garment bag on his shoulder and stared at the frightened woman. He sighed deeply with frustration. Was there no escaping this bride of the lord? "All right," he consented. "Come with me. I'll show you where to go."

Trying to smile, Meggie nodded as she fell into place beside him. He walked briskly, weaving his way through the strangely dressed crowds, and she was hard put to keep up with him. Several times people stopped and stared at him, yet he ignored all as he led her down mechanical stairs and out into the night. She was astonished by everything around her and felt she was swept along past each incredible circumstance, until it all blended together into one hazy, unbelievable fantasy.

Taking a deep, steadying breath, she turned her face upward, beyond the bridges with their fast-moving mechanical carriages. It was absolutely amazing. Purgatory had stars—just like Pennsylvania.

"Here we are, sister."

Dumbfounded, Meggie looked down to see her angel holding a door to one of the strange metal carriages. She blinked several times, unsure what she should do. She then recognized the impatient nod her angel sent toward the inside of the loud carriage that seemed to belch out smoke from its rear. Afraid to offend him further, she took a deep breath and entered the thing. She was sure that he would follow.

"Here's thirty," the angel said to the strange driver. "Take her wherever she wants to go."

He shut the door firmly, then added, "This has been a real pleasure, sister. Enjoy your visit."

Before she could call him back, he turned and disappeared behind the wall of frantic-looking people who were calling out for cabs.

He was gone.

And she was alone!

In purgatory . . .

"Okeey, dookey, now where do you go, ladee?"

Meggie's mouth hung open as she whipped her head around to the driver. "What?" He was dark and foreign-looking, and she hadn't understood his heavily accented voice.

"Where does the holee ladee want to go?" He'd turned around and waited for her answer.

"I . . . I don't know," she responded truthfully. "Where should I go?"

The driver scratched the cloth turban he wore over his hair and said, "You tell me. I take you." He

36

pointed to a picture over a clicking meter. "Aleem Maihir Choudhy. I have been here four months already, and I know theese city like the back of my fingers . . . yes?"

Meggie nodded. This was her new guardian angel? Aleem Maihir Choudhy? She wanted her old one back. Looking down to the cracked leather seat, she noticed a colored periodical lying against the opposite door. Picking it up, she saw the face of a young, almost feminine-looking black man on the cover with the word TIME printed in large yellow letters over his head. In smaller print was the sentence: "He's BAD . . . and he's back!" She closed her eyes and sighed. Surely this was proof. This must be a place where one pays for sins. Slowly, she allowed her gaze to return to the window where the angel Thomas had left her.

In a tiny voice she whispered, "I just want to go home."

Within seconds the vehicle shot forward and Meggie was thrust back onto the seat as Aleem pronounced gleefully, "I know just the home for a holee ladee. You will see!"

The next half hour seemed to her as though she were trapped in a living nightmare. Countless times she thought they would surely crash into the other vehicles as Aleem weaved his way through snakelike lines of the things. As they sped toward the city of lights in the distance, he kept up a constant chatter while blowing a loud horn at anyone that he thought impeded his lightning-quick progress. Once inside the city, Meggie marveled aloud at the number of people still walking the sidewalks in front of the fabulously lighted stores.

"Oh, theese is nothing," Aleem remarked in his all-knowing singsong voice. "When it is light, you can't

37

even see the streets sometimes. I know, because I have come veery close to hitting a number of people with my cab."

"You have?" The knot of apprehension in her stomach tightened and she shuddered to think of anyone who dared to place themselves in front of Aleem and a destination.

"Not to worry, holee ladee, I drove my very own cab for six, no, seven years, in New Delhi and only hit three people—with very poor vision, I must add. This is not a bad record, yes?"

She didn't answer as the cab screeched to a halt and Aleem turned around in the front seat. His grin was very wide as he said, "Saint Paderics Cadedral. We are here."

Meggie pulled herself up from the back of the cab and stared out the window. She looked upward from the huge stone building but could not see where it ended because of the night. One thing for certain, she had never seen a church this large. Surely, this must be the place.

"What is its name again?" she asked.

It took a few moments for her to translate from his heavy accent.

Meggie again looked back at the long rows of steps. "Saint Patrick's Cathedral," she breathed. Yes, of course, she thought. Where else would she belong, but in the home of the Irish patron saint?

Aleem interrupted her thoughts. "I bring many holee people to this place. Many want to see it. You go in now, yes?"

She nodded and waited for the door to open. "I can't seem to get out," she said finally after pushing on several shiny buttons and levers, all without success.

Aleem turned back to the wheel in front of him

and silenced the cab. Within seconds he opened his own door and walked around the vehicle to assist her.

"Thank you, Aleem," she said sincerely. "I . . . I should just go in now, shouldn't I?" Why had her legs chosen this moment to feel so weak and wobbly? And why was her brain so fuzzy? Her thoughts so cloudy? Why couldn't she seem to think straight? This was important. This was her day of reckoning, so to speak, wasn't it? She simply *had* to think straight now and dismiss the chills and the nausea that seemed nearly overwhelming.

She had so much to answer for, so many misdeeds to recount.

"I will wait until you go in." The driver touched his forehead in some sign of respect as she passed him, and the imposing church loomed in front of her like a colossal gray castle from a storybook. It was nothing at all like the small wooden church in Lehigha. This surely must be the house of the Lord, or of someone highly connected with him.

It was incredible to her. The doors were locked and no amount of pounding elicited a response. How could she have been brought here, and now be denied admittance? There must be a mistake. Again fighting back the nausea, Meggie managed to walk down the steps. She stopped in front of the waiting Aleem.

Shaking her head, she said, "No one's there. What should I do now?"

She hated that her voice sounded like a whimper. But really! You'd think there'd be some sort of order about dying! The angel Thomas had just dumped her into the vehicle and disappeared. One would think heaven, or purgatory, or wherever she was would provide better guidance!

The turbaned man shrugged in response to her question. "You have nowhere to go? Another place, yes?"

Meggie looked back at the darkened church and could feel an anger begin to build. Again, she was turned out. Well, this time she was going to fight back. She had nothing left to lose.

Smiling into the gentle face of her driver, she said, "Another place . . . yes! Do you know how to get to 108 Park Avenue South?"

Aleem's grin widened. "Did I not say that I know thees place like the back of my fingers?"


Most of the time Thomas Carter took for granted the luxury of his penthouse apartment overlooking Central Park. Tonight was one of those times when all he wanted was a cold drink and a warm shower—in that order. And maybe Angelica.

He was enjoying an ice-cold beer when the phone in the kitchen rang. Automatically, his eyes narrowed. It was the Towers phone that connected him to the lobby, garage, and valet service.

"Yes?" The last thing he wanted tonight was an interruption.

"Ah . . . Mr. Carter? This is the lobby. There's a—a nun down here that insists on speaking with you. I told her our policy about uninvited guests, but she says she'll wait here all night until you talk to her. What would you like me to do?"

His eyes closed briefly with exasperation before muttering, "I'll be right down." Hanging up the phone, he took a long swallow of beer and had to force himself not to slam the glass bottle back onto the tile counter.

"Damnit," he cursed. "Why me?"

As the elevator doors opened to the lobby, he felt a tightening between his shoulders as he viewed the scene before him. The nun from the airport was standing in front of the reception desk, her arms folded at her chest. She looked determined and was obviously ignoring the stares of the uniformed guards.

"Mr. Carter." One of the guards caught sight of him and spoke his name with a sigh of relief.

"What's the problem here?" Tom asked as he walked up to the group. Why was the cab driver standing at the door? And why did the young nun look ill?

"Sister Margaret Mary? Is that right?" Tom asked as he stood before her. He noticed that she was pale, nearly as white as the veiling around her face, and her lips were trembling as she nodded to him.

"You . . . you left me," she muttered, bringing her right hand up to touch her lips, as if the act might stop the trembling. He also noticed that her fingers shook.

Something was definitely wrong.

"Perhaps you'd better sit down," he offered, motioning to the large grouping of furniture in the marble lobby.

She shook her head. "No. I want you to tell me what I should do now. You shouldn't have left me like that."

His eyes narrowed. What did she want from him? He'd been used too many times in the past not to be suspicious of any woman—especially one who showed up where he lived.

"I'm afraid I don't understand what you mean," he said calmly, noticing the interested glances from the others in the lobby. It wasn't every day that Thomas Grey Carter argued with a nun. And why the hell was that cab driver still here? Was he supposed to be witness to whatever the woman was planning?

Lowering his head, he said quietly, "You don't look well. I suggest you sit down and explain yourself. I don't know what you want from me," he added as he led her to a chair. "Why are you here?"

It happened so quickly, so swiftly, that he wasn't prepared to catch her when she crumpled to the floor. One moment he was holding her arm, above the elbow, and leading her away from the others . . . and in the next she simply caved inward. Lifeless! A shot of terror spread through him when he heard the sickening crack of her forehead against the wooden table. Reacting, he immediately gathered her up and turned her over. Nothing prepared him for the horror of seeing blood trickling from her temple and rapidly staining the white headdress. She was deathly pale, her mouth seemed to have a stain of blue around it, and he didn't think she was breathing . . .

My God! He'd killed a nun!

# Chapter 3

Everyone rushed up to him and started talking at once.

"What happened to her?"

"Oh God, she's bleeding! What do we do?"

"What have you done to the holee ladee? I should never have brought her to this place."

Tom looked up at the group of men and said fiercely, "Call an ambulance! Get a doctor!"

"Right!" One of the guards ran to the telephone while the other nervously added, "What about Dr. Tankor? He came in around two hours ago."

Tom placed his palm against the woman's temple to stop the bleeding and muttered, "Call him down here. Tell him it's an emergency." She couldn't be dead! She couldn't!

He saw her eyelids flutter before again fanning closed, and he breathed a sigh of relief. She was alive! Thank God. He looked up at the turbaned cab driver and asked, "Where did you take her? What do you know about her?"

The man shrugged, yet his answers were nonstop. "She didn't know where to go, so I took her to the Cathedral on Fifth Avenue. But it was locked. She did not look happy about that and then she said to bring her here. I do not know anything about her. Do not you? Will she be all right?"

Afraid to take his hands away from her, Tom wiped his forehead on his upper arm. He shook his head. "I don't know anything about her either, except her name. Damn it! Where is everybody?"

The guard jogged back across the lobby, saying, "Dr. Tankor's on his way down. He said not to move her."

"I don't intend to," Tom muttered while taking in the number of people gathering around him. Returning residents of the tower had stopped to see what the excitement was about and Tom's jaw tightened while viewing the small crowd. What a sight they must be making — Tom Carter and an injured nun.

Looking down to his blood-soaked hand, he heard Benito Tankor's calming voice as the doctor made his way through the people.

"Excuse me. Pardon me. Will all of you please move back and give us some room?"

"Ben, thank God! I don't know what happened." Tom made room for the older man as he knelt beside him. He watched as Ben's fingers immediately went to the nun's throat to check for a pulse. Without saying anything, he removed his hand and lifted her lids. He opened his medical bag and brought out two packages and ripped them open. Taking out large pieces of gauze, he gave one to Tom for his hand and wiped away the blood on the headdress with the other.

"I'm going to have to remove this," Ben stated matter-of-factly. He reached behind the woman's neck and unbuttoned the crisp white linen.

Tom's breath caught at the back of his throat as he watched the veiling slip away and burnished red hair appear. It was so personal, almost sacrilegious, that he nearly growled to the murmuring crowd. "I would appreciate some privacy here."

He looked pointedly at several of his tenants and watched as they received his unspoken message. They turned away and headed for the elevators. He then looked back to the small, fragile woman lying at his knees. "Will she be okay, Ben? She's so pale."

"How long has she been out?"

"Minutes."

Ben Tankor was wrapping her arm to take her blood pressure when he said, "I think she has a concussion, and she's going to need stitches for that cut. We'll wait till the paramedics get here for—"

Her eyelids fluttered open and she moaned softly, painfully.

She moistened her lips with her tongue and tried to speak. "What . . . ?"

"It's all right," Ben murmured comfortingly. "You took a nasty cut on the head when you fell. Don't try to move, dear. We'll be taking you to the hospital."

She attempted to sit up. "No! You can't!"

Ben tried to calm her. "Shh . . . it'll be all right. You'll probably just spend the night for observation—"

"I won't go. You can't make me, can you?"

She was staring at her angel, terrified by the stranger's words. They were going to send her away, to a hospital. Why? If she weren't alive? And she had just found the angel again! Ignoring the pain in her head, she begged him with her eyes to help her.

Even though he knew he hadn't done anything to harm her, Tom was struck by an immediate surge of guilt when he returned her gaze. There was something about this woman, this nun, that evoked an immediate defense mechanism. He wanted to protect her.

45

"Can't you help her, Ben?" Tom asked. "She does seem much better."

The older man looked incredulous. "She probably has a concussion. She should be under observation for at least twenty-four hours. And she might need stitches — "

"You could do that," Tom interrupted, motioning to the medical bag. "You must have something in there."

Ben Tankor smiled at the woman and leaned closer to his wealthy landlord. "May I remind you, Tom, that I am a gynecologist? She should go to the emergency room for treatment."

Just then the paramedics arrived and Tom could see that Ben was relieved by their presence. Tom, however, could also see the fear return to the nun's eyes and he decided not to let his friend off the hook.

"We'll take her upstairs through the service elevator and you can examine her in my apartment," he said, noticing a new group of onlookers. "At least we can have some privacy there. If you still think she should go after you examine her, then we'll make that decision." He stood up and motioned for the emergency team. "This man's a doctor. Please assist us in bringing his patient upstairs. We'll need your stretcher." There. At least he was on more comfortable ground making decisions.

"But she's not my patient," Ben whispered to Tom as the paramedics prepared the elevated stretcher. "Do you realize what something like this can do to my malpractice insurance? What do you even know about her?

"I know she's hurt . . . and she's scared. And she needs help, Ben." He touched the man's arm and added, "I'll take full responsibility."

Chastised, Ben nodded and began talking with the men while Tom walked over to the frightened woman.

He smiled down to her. "You're going to be all right," he said gently. "Ben's a good friend and one of the best doctors in the city." He took in her huge blue eyes, the wave of red hair that fell onto her shoulder. She looked so vulnerable, so exposed . . . so humiliated by the scene taking place around her. He recognized a kindred spirit, someone else who valued privacy.

Raising his head, he ordered, "Let's get on with it. She's ready."

"Where are you taking me?" she asked in a small voice.

He looked back down at her. "I'm taking you upstairs. To my . . . to where I live. It'll be all right."

She smiled at him through the pain. He wasn't going to desert her again. She could trust him. Closing her eyes briefly, she knew it would be all right . . .

This time.


He stood in the kitchen, waiting for the water to boil. He'd already set the cup and saucer on the tray. It was quiet. Finally. Everyone was gone. Well, almost everyone. Sister Margaret Mary Gillbride was in his guest room. In bed. In one of Angelica's nightgowns. And none of it seemed real.

Ben had taken care of most of it — from examining the young nun to applying the butterfly bandages on her forehead. When she'd refused to go to the hospital, Ben had left specific instructions on how to care for the patient: what to feed her, when to wake her if she dozed, what questions to ask. What Tom couldn't figure out as he waited for the teapot to whistle was what the heck he was doing with a nun in his home. How had he let a pair of incredibly trusting blue eyes get him into this?

She was asleep now, for he'd checked on her a few minutes after Ben had left. Ben had said not to let her doze for more than a half hour. He looked at the wall clock. Five more minutes. And then he had to walk into the bedroom and wake her up.

And she was in Angelica's creamy silk nightgown. He shook his head of the image and wished he hadn't given up smoking. Reaching into the refrigerator, he had to settle for another beer.


She was dreaming.

She was back in her parents' home in the patch, but it was crowded with people. So many people dressed in black. She walked through the front room, listening to the murmur of hushed voices. Everyone's expression was sad and she tried to hear what Meghan Conroy was saying to her mother, but even that wasn't clear. Why were they all here in her home? And why was Nora Bennigan and her young sister in the kitchen arranging food onto trays? Why had these people taken over her home? If she didn't know better, she would think it was a wake, but there was no body. Suddenly frightened, she searched the room for her brother. Where was Brian?

She hurried past neighbors, yet no one noticed her. She thought she caught the sound of her name once or twice in a conversation, but paid little attention as she made her way to her bedroom.

He was sitting in the old chair by the window, surrounded by men, and she caught only a glimpse of him as she walked around the concerned-looking

48

group.

"Brian, don't blame yourself any longer," Liam Dunleavy said as he placed a hand on Brian's shoulder. "If anyone should take on the blame, it should be I. I was the one who came up with the idea of using her." Liam shook his head in sorrow. "Meggie was a brave girl. I grieve with you, lad, on her loss."

Meggie's mouth dropped open in horror and her hands came up to cover it. *They thought she'd died!* When Brian lifted his head, she gasped with regret at his grief-stricken expression. He looked older. The lines in his face that she'd barely noticed in the past were now deeply etched in sorrow. And there were tears, real tears, gathering at the corners of his eyes.

Her heart ached for him. All the love she had felt for him as a child came rushing back and she quickly knelt at his side and placed her hand on his leg.

"Brian! I'm here! See. I'm quite fine. Don't cry. Please . . . look at me!"

He didn't look at her. He didn't even notice her kneeling before him. Instead, he ignored her and stared up at Liam Dunleavy. Breathing heavily, he muttered, "I will never forgive myself. I killed my own sister!"

Amid the low murmur of denials from the surrounding men, Brian searched their faces. "What went wrong? Can someone tell me? I wrapped that fuse myself . . ." He buried his face in his hands.

"Brian, please! I'm here. Right here with you! Why won't you look at me?" She was crying with frustration when she heard the familiar voice—

"If everyone had just stayed with the plan, instead of moving it up an hour, none of it would have happened. The girl would be alive!"

Meggie's head snapped up as she searched the faces of the men. *James Roarity!* The traitor. Here, in her house!

"I already gave you the reason," Liam countered in an angry voice. "It was for your own protection. Obviously, you were as surprised as the rest of Lehigha," he added while nodding to Roarity's bandaged arm.

Unconsciously cradling his elbow, Roarity said, "I told you I was burned by a pot of scalding coffee. I'm lucky the damned thing wasn't filled."

Meggie stood up and confronted him. "Liar! Tell them where you really were, James Roarity! Tell them how you got burned and who you were with. Tell them, or by God I will!"

No one paid any attention to her. It was as if they couldn't hear her, or see her.

Brian rose to his feet and stared at Roarity. "Do you think I care about a bloody coffeepot, or your arm? My sister, Margaret Mary Gillbride, is dead because of us . . . because of me! And I can't even have her buried proper until her body is found." She watched as Brian seemed to collapse back into the old chair. "Ahh God, what have I done to you, Meggie?"

Liam quietly ushered everyone out until only she and Brian were in the bedroom. When the door was closed, Brian lifted his head and stared at the old comforter on the bed.

"You never had an easy life, Meggie girl," he whispered through his tears to the room. "And I didn't help any in the last few years. I—I never told you that I loved you. And now I can't even say I'm sorry." The sobs racked his strong body and he bent over to stop them. "I'm sorry, Meggie," he gasped. "I'm so sorry . . ."

Her heart ached to comfort him, to reach out and gather him in her arms, to tell him that she already

50

knew those things and it didn't matter. Not anymore. But she wasn't able to break through to him. He couldn't hear her, yet she could hear someone talking to her, taking her away from Brian, making his image become unclear . . .

"Sister Margaret, wake up. I have your tea."

"Brian?" Meggie blinked and shielded her eyes from the bright light of the room. The pain in her head returned and she quickly shut her eyes. It wasn't her brother. It was the voice of the angel.

"How do you feel?" he asked.

"I don't know," she answered truthfully. Her head ached. Her throat felt sore and dry. She was thirsty and opening her eyes had made her dizzy. "I — I don't feel well."

"Do you know where you are?"

"In your home?"

"That's right. And do you know what day it is?"

She didn't open her eyes. Why was he questioning her like a child? "Friday?"

"Very good. Now what's the date?"

"The date?" Why was he doing this? Was he testing her?

"Yes."

"Ah . . . July third, eighteen seventy-five?"

When he didn't answer, she sighed and said, "That's not right? Maybe I'm a little confused . . . about the time and everything. So much has happened. What is the date? The fourth?"

"July the third, nineteen ninety."

She forced her eyes open and stared at him.

# Chapter 4

"What did you say?"

"I told you the correct date," he answered, trying to stay calm. "You said eighteen seventy-five. It's okay. Ben said you might be confused. You meant nineteen ninety."

She continued to stare at him. He looked tired and uncomfortable. "I meant eighteen seventy-five," she said slowly, firmly. Why was he gaping at her like that?

Tom cleared his throat. "Yes, well, ah, here's your tea. I wasn't sure whether you took cream or lemon, so I brought both." He wiped his palms on his trousers and smiled as he backed out of the room.

"Don't leave," she whispered as she tried to sit up. The satin cover slid down to her waist and she gasped at the shamefully indecent gown she wore. Crossing an arm over her nearly exposed breasts, Meggie quickly reached for the cover and brought it up to her shoulders. She had forgotten about the nightgown that the doctor had helped her put on earlier.

Acutely embarrassed, Meggie kept her head down, took a deep breath, and forced herself to speak. "Have I died?"

"What?"

She slowly raised her head and tried to keep her lips from trembling. "Can you tell me? Have I died? Is that why I'm here?"

Tom looked at the four walls, as if something in the bedroom might have caused the absurd question. "What are you talking about? Of course you haven't died. You're here, in New York City. Listen, isn't there someone you should call? A priest? A mother superior? Isn't someone expecting you . . . somewhere?"

Meggie forgot about the cover as her mouth hung open in shock. "This is New York City?" The satin blanket once more slid down to her waist.

Nodding, Tom tried not to look at her full breasts, breasts that were completely defined by the sheer silk of Angelica's gown. Why had he ever let his ex-wife leave clothes here? Clearing his throat, he tried to concentrate on her words. "Yes, of course. Where did you think you were?"

"I—I thought . . . I mean, I wasn't sure . . ." How could she say that she had thought she was in purgatory? Now it sounded ridiculous. But still, where was she? How could she have come here? "What about the airship?"

Never in his life had he been more unnerved. He kept telling himself that she was a nun. And yes, she could have hair, thick red hair that fell to her shoulders. And just because she had committed herself to a higher cause didn't mean that her anatomy would change. Of course she would have breasts, but not graceful shoulders that begged to be touched, or kissed. Damnit! A nun shouldn't look that vulnerable, or that sexy!

Trying to bring his thoughts under control, Tom blinked several times and said, "I beg your pardon?

53

I'm afraid I didn't understand what you asked."

"The airship. Then what about that? How did I come to be on the airship?"

He shook his head. "You mean the airplane?"

"Where we met?"

He nodded. "It's called an airplane." His eyebrows drew closer together as he searched her face. Why didn't she know that? "What order do you belong to?"

"What order?" Now it was Meggie's turn to stare at the discarded habit that lay across a nearby chair. How far was she prepared to carry this lie?

"Yes," he persisted. "What order of nuns? The Benedictines? A cloistered sect?" But the back of his brain was telling him that they would've had to take her as a baby for her not to know about something as common as an airplane.

"I don't remember," Meggie said abruptly. She did recall the doctor telling her that she might be confused for a few days and it was the only thing she could think of saying after being put on the spot.

"I remember my brother Brian. And . . . and an explosion. And then you sitting next to me on the air sh—the airplane." She shook her head. "I don't think I'm supposed to be here."

He had a strange expression on his face as he nodded to her and pointed to the small table next to the bed. "We can talk about this later. I've brought tea and something to eat. I'm afraid my housekeeper won't be back until after the holiday, so there's really nothing—"

"The holiday?" she interrupted.

"The Fourth of July. Anyway, maybe you should try and eat something light. It's only scrambled eggs and bagels. I didn't know if you liked them . . ." Tom's voice trailed off. He had to get out of the

54

room. He was becoming as confused as she was. "We'll talk later."

He turned to leave but she stopped him just before he reached the door. "Thank you," she said in a quiet voice. "You're very kind."

He wouldn't look back at her, for fear of what he'd say or do. Instead, he mumbled "You're welcome," and closed the door behind him. He was losing it . . . what else would explain his irrational attraction to her? *A nun!*

Meggie turned her attention to the tray beside the bed. The teacup looked to be of fine china with tiny painted flowers at the rim. The plate of eggs matched and the knife and fork appeared to be of heavy silver. Even the crisp white napkin spoke of wealth. She didn't immediately reach for the tea. Instead, her gaze had slipped to the newspaper folded neatly at the edge of the tray. Picking it up, she unfolded it and read the headline about the violation of a peace treaty between two nations she had never heard of. And then she saw it. Right there under the title of the paper.

July 3, 1990

Nineteen ninety! This couldn't be right! What had happened to her in that explosion? Where was Brian? Where was her life?

She closed her eyes and let her head rest back against the pillow, hoping that sanity might return and end this nightmare. This couldn't have happened. It just couldn't! She was dreaming, or dying, or dead, or . . .

Suddenly her eyes opened and she stared at the closed door. It all made sense.

Why, he wasn't an angel after all.

He was only a *man!*

The first thing he was going to do was get her out of the apartment. That was it. She had to go. Somewhere. Right after the holiday, he was going to call up the Diocesan Office and find out where to send her. She knew her name. She had a brother named Brian. Surely, somewhere they kept records. She belonged somewhere. But not here! Not in his home!

He kept telling himself that he'd been working too hard. He hadn't seen Angelica in months. Tom shrugged. What else could he expect after living the life of a monk?

Christ! Everything he thought was now put in religious terms. It was an insane situation, and if anyone from the media got their hands on this story, he'd be the laughingstock of the financial community. Thomas Grey Carter had a nun for a houseguest over the holiday. A beautiful, frightened, confused nun who brought about such strong reactions inside of him that he now found himself actually taking a cold shower. A cold shower! He hadn't done this since he was a teenager.

It hadn't worked then and it was less effective now. He could still see her huge, trusting blue eyes, her red hair tousled from sleep, the outline of her body beneath the sheer nightgown. It had been too tight. He'd noticed that right away. She was shorter than Angelica, but with a more rounded figure. Sister Margaret Mary Gillbride reminded him of the women he had fantasized about as an adolescent. Women like Ann-Margaret, Sophia Loren, Marilyn Monroe . . . That was it. She was womanly, with sweeping curves and luscious mounds and—

My God! He was comparing this bride of the

Church to sex symbols. He looked down at himself and shuddered. That was it . . . she had to go. He didn't know what he believed in anymore, but an innate sense of right and wrong told him what was happening was wrong—very wrong. There was still enough leftover brainwashing to nag at him and whisper that he was going to be punished for his impure thoughts. If salacious thoughts of Gloria Pestone had brought about a decade of the rosary in eighth grade, then he was dealing in major penance here.

Deciding not to tempt fate, he quickly turned off the shower and reached for his terrycloth robe. Without drying himself, he picked up his briefcase from the hall and returned to his bedroom. He opened it, withdrew his glasses and a block of papers, then settled himself on his bed. Within three minutes he was engrossed in the financial statement of a manufacturing company he had expressed interest in acquiring. It was dry, dull reading and just what he wanted.

However less than two minutes later, he let the papers fall to his lap and stared at the opposite wall. How could she have thought it was eighteen seventy-five? A concussion would bring on confusion. Maybe you'd think it was Thursday instead of Friday . . . but this? How could you possibly mistake the *century?*

Again he unwillingly pictured the young woman who was beyond the wall. She was in there. Right in the next room. And there was no one in the apartment but the two of them. All of a sudden the large penthouse seemed far too small, too intimate. How was he ever going to make it until after the holiday?

He didn't want a wall between them. He wanted a damn fortress!

She didn't dream again. This time when she dozed, it was peaceful and healing. When she awoke once more to the bright light of the room, her body ached yet she struggled to sit upright. She waited for the dizziness and was grateful that it quickly subsided. Obviously, she wasn't as sick as everyone thought. Her gaze immediately fell to the newspaper at her side. She'd fallen back to sleep while reading the confusing reportage.

Her hand reached out to touch it, to make sure it was real. Nineteen hundred and ninety! My God, how had it happened? Now everything made a little more sense. The women in trousers, some with painted faces like those that keep house on the edge of Lehigha . . . And the men—some had hair longer than her own! Most of what she remembered was confusing, and had passed so quickly that it was difficult to sort out the strange images in her mind.

But how much of it was real?

She didn't die. At least she didn't think she had died. Well, not now. Not here, in this time. She certainly had left her own time, the time of Brian and Lehigha and . . .

But was that merely a dream? It had seemed so real. Walking in her own home amid the mourners and Brian . . .

She sat up straighter and closed her eyes. She didn't want to think about Brian now, for her brother's image brought a pain to her chest. A sharp ache of loneliness. Somehow she had to let him know that she had survived—sort of survived.

Right now, she had a more pressing issue to deal with and she hadn't the faintest idea how to solve it. She looked about the handsome room for some sign and was disappointed. Slowly, gingerly, Meggie brought her legs over the side of the bed and tested the distance to the floor. She held on to the table beside the bed until her legs were steady enough to support her. Then she began to search. Where would a man, especially one like Thomas Carter, hide the chamber pot?

After five very frustrating minutes, she decided that perhaps she should look outside. Meggie's fingers touched the silk material of the nightgown that she wore. There was a closet with several other female articles of clothing inside of it. Whose were they? she wondered once again. The housekeeper's? Could he be married? That thought made her stomach tighten and she grabbed up the rough wool of the nun's habit to cover the gown, for she couldn't go outside in such a shameful garment. The contrast of the silk and the wool against her skin made her shiver. It may have been shamefully cut, but the nightgown felt heavenly and she was sorry to don the scratchy habit once more.

It took courage to open the bedroom door and peek outside it, but Meggie was determined. She saw dim lights in the hallway that led into the huge front room. The lights in this time were strange and never seemed to be put out. The one in her bedroom stayed on whether you were asleep or awake. Deciding to peek out the window and look for the convenience, Meggie was careful as she walked barefooted through Thomas's house. Even in the meager light she could see how fine it was furnished, and she wouldn't wait until daylight to see it better. He must be a very wealthy man to live here all alone, she thought as she delicately pulled back one of the long drapes and looked out.

A low moan escaped her lips. Her hand dropped

the edge of the drape and came up to her forehead as a wave of dizziness washed over her. My God! Thomas lived up in the air!

She couldn't resist another peek and was amazed to see that his home overlooked many, many buildings. And most of them were burning lights in the middle of the night. Surely this light burning must be a custom. It looked almost like something from a fairy tale, as if someone had cast thousands of diamonds over the city. She had never seen anything to compare with it in all her life, and she stood for a full five minutes admiring the incredible view.

Despite the woolen habit thrown over her shoulders, Meggie's feet were soon cold and she gave up the idea of finding an outhouse. Not in the sky, at least. Common sense told her that she must have overlooked something in her search. Reluctantly, she left the window and went back into the bedroom to begin again.

"Do you need something, sister?"

She jumped against the wall as the sound of his voice came out of the darkness. "Holy mother of God!" Her hands were clasped in front of her chest to contain her leaping heart.

"I'm sorry. I didn't mean to frighten you. I . . . heard you. Do you think you should be out of bed?"

Meggie swallowed several times, trying to bring moisture back into her mouth. "I . . . I was looking for . . ."

"Yes?" He waited for her to continue.

She took a deep breath and was grateful that the light in this hallway was shadowed. How embarrassing. Yet there was nothing to be done to save face. This was a dilemma that only he could solve. She cleared her throat and curled her toes beneath the habit. "Well. You see, I've been unable—that is to say . . ." She looked at the dim outline of his body and took a deep breath. "Where, sir, might I find your convenience?" There. She had said it.

"I beg your pardon?"

Meggie silently moaned. How could he be so obtuse? "Your convenience," she repeated in a tiny voice, now thoroughly humiliated.

"My convenience? I'm afraid—oh! I'm sorry. I should have told you. It's right here. Right across from your room."

He moved into the hallway and Meggie could see he was dressed in a short, thick robe that ended just below his knees. His feet were as bare as hers. But what truly startled her was that when Thomas moved away from his doorway and into the hall, he was also wearing spectacles.

He opened a door and magically filled the room with light. Turning back to her, he first smiled then stared at her confused expression. On his own he realized why she was staring and grinned as he removed his glasses. "I wear them when I've been reading for some time. They ease the strain."

She nodded as he continued, "Anyway, here's the bathroom. Are you sure you're all right? Ben said you should stay in bed until morning when he comes back to check on you."

It was Meggie's turn to smile. The spectacles made Thomas more human, less perfect. "I'm feeling much better," she said.

Suddenly they were both aware that each was barely clothed. They were alone, unchaperoned in the middle of the night, and the situation was unsettling. For both of them.

It was Tom who first cleared his throat. "Yes. Well—" he motioned to the lit room—"if you need anything else, just let me know."

He started to ease away from her when she stopped him with her low, soft voice. "Thank you for letting me stay tonight. I know it's been an imposition. I'm sorry."

He shook his head. "Don't worry about it. Good night, sister."

Meggie didn't answer him as he walked back to his room and shut the door. She stood staring into the hallway after he had left. She could have told him the truth just then. Told him she wasn't a nun, merely a frightened woman who'd somehow come to this century. She'd been nearly thrown into this century. She almost laughed herself when she imagined his expression. He wouldn't believe her, and she couldn't blame him. No. It made more sense to continue the deception and let everyone believe that she was a nun. A member of the holy order appeared to be given a certain respect. At least that hadn't changed from her time. She was afraid to let anyone know that she was merely a woman, afraid that Thomas would send her away. And she couldn't bear that. Not yet. For some reason she felt safe here with him. She would let them all think she was a nun. What did she have to lose anymore?

Satisfied with her decision, Meggie closed the door and turned to look around her. "Ahh . . . now isn't this grand," she breathed while viewing the extraordinary room Thomas called a bathroom. It was almost as large as her own bedroom back home in the patch, but furnished with an elegance she could never have imagined. She touched the thick white towels that were rolled and placed in huge baskets on the matching white rug. Hanging from the forest green walls were gold framed mirrors and even the handles at the indoor sink looked to be of gold. It was by far the loveliest room she had ever seen. She turned a handle at the sink and was astonished to watch water come rushing out.

Hot water! Amazed, Meggie stooped to look under the sink to see where the water was going. She shook her head with futility. Shutting off the valve, she turned toward two odd bowl-shaped things placed to one side of the room. She walked up to them and stared. Now, what in the world could they be? She tried the handles of both. One gushed water upwards and the other contraption sounded like it took it away. She lifted the lid and stared down as the water was being replaced. Then she smiled. At last . . . and she had figured it out on her own.

Minutes later she was testing every handle and valve in the room. It was in the bathroom that she learned just how Thomas had managed to turn on the lights. It was controlled by a switch on the wall and she played with it for several seconds, enjoying the powerful feeling of creating light and then making it disappear. There was no bathtub, but a glass-enclosed room, like a large closet, that sprayed water from three walls toward the center. Without thinking, Meggie dropped the heavy habit onto the rug and pulled the silk shift over her head.

Holding her breath, she slowly walked into the very center of the fountains and gasped with pleasure as the warm water caressed her aching body from all angles. It was the most marvelous invention. Here was all the hot water one might ever desire—at the turn of a valve. Never again would one need to carry wood or buckets of water for a bath. Never more would anyone have to venture out of doors on a cold winter morning because this—this bathroom, with all its necessities, was right here within the home.

She turned her head to the built-in mirror and

stared at her reflection. Her face was pale; there were faint circles under her eyes and a white bandage covered her temple and part of her hairline.

You look terrible, Meggie," she whispered to the mirror. Spying white round balls of soap, she picked one up and lathered her hands. Bringing them to her nose, she inhaled the sweet scent of almonds and sighed with a sudden contentment. As she let her hands slide down her shoulders, she couldn't contain the luxuriant smile. "Ahh, but surely I've landed in heaven."

Down the hallway, Tom listened to the sounds of the shower. First she had turned on every single thing in the bathroom, flushed the toilet at least four times, and now she was taking a shower at three forty-two in the morning! At first he'd been embarrassed to be listening and then he'd been confused. Right now, he was doing everything he could not to envision Sister Margaret Mary Gillbride in his shower. Nude. With the jets of water surrounding her, the soap bubbles slowly sliding down her breasts . . .

Don't think about it, he chided himself. This night was unbelievable. He was never going to sleep with that woman here. Tomorrow. As soon as possible. She was definitely going.

# Chapter 5

She had never seen such an abundance of food in her life.

After she had awakened, Meggie dressed in her nun's habit—though she left the headdress off, merely pinning the white veil around her hair—and decided to explore. The living area of Thomas's home was as exquisitely furnished as she'd imagined last night. In the darkness, her bare feet had sunk into a thick carpet. This morning she'd seen it was the color of cream with a wide border of wine around its edges. Everything else had been in differing shades of white—the tables, the long sofa, and many chairs. Even the strange-looking statues had been of white material. Everything, except three wine-colored pillows and a huge matching vase on the table in front of the sofa. The vase was filled with the most beautiful pink lilies. And there were trees growing inside Thomas's parlor. Delicate trees that almost reached the high ceiling.

It was after marveling at the living area that Meggie decided to explore further. And that was when she found the kitchen. The stainless steel refrigerator was the first thing she investigated.

"Why, you would feed half of Lehigha with this,"

she whispered, while looking over the food inside the metal box. Eggs were neatly deposited in the door, along with butter, cheeses, and a strange-looking bottle of milk. It wasn't glass. She poked it with her finger. It was an odd opaque material, yet it appeared to serve the same function as the glass bottles of her own time. Shrugging, she turned her attention to the rest of the huge ice box.

She spent at least five minutes opening up containers and sniffing the contents of bowls before closing the door and looking at the rest of the room. There were many tall doors and numerous drawers along the walls. A long, narrow metal cylinder, suspended from the ceiling by metal cables, hung parallel over the entire counter area. There were two sinks. One on each end of the long counter . . . that obviously served as the cooking area. It was in the center of the bright, sunny room, standing alone, and Meggie ran her fingers down the fifteen feet of clean counter until she touched two switches at the end. She stared down at them, then looked up and spied many valves and buttons. It was confusing, but if the bathing room could be conquered then surely a kitchen would be a much simpler task. A kitchen was where she had spent most of her life in Lehigha. Nothing at all like this, but still . . .

Taking a deep breath, Meggie turned one switch and breathed aloud her appreciation as the long metal cylinder immediately lit up. Suddenly she smiled. It was Saturday. Perhaps she could pay Thomas back for his hospitality. Besides, she silently admitted, she was starved!

It couldn't be too hard to make a simple breakfast. Thomas had done it himself last night. Hadn't he?

He smiled in that hazy brief period of awakening. He could smell the bacon cooking and his tastebuds came alive, yet he only smacked his lips together and turned over on his side. He didn't want to get up. It felt too good to just lie here. He'd wait until Mom came up and forced him out of—

His eyes immediately opened and he stared across the empty bedroom. Damn, he was thirty-five years old and he was dreaming about his mother! And suddenly, it all came back to him. Neither of his parents were alive anymore. He wasn't in his bedroom in Delaware. This was New York City. This was his home—far removed from the upper-middle-class neighborhood of his parents. This was his home overlooking Central Park, the penthouse that he'd retained ownership over when Angelica divorced him. So who was cooking the bacon?

The nun.

Immediately his jaw tightened as he threw off the sheet and hurried out of bed. Within a few minutes he had brushed his teeth and combed his hair. As he slipped into a comfortable pair of khaki pants, he glanced at the round gold clock by his bed.

It wasn't even eight o'clock. And it was Saturday. It was also less than five hours since he'd left her at the bathroom. Didn't the woman ever sleep like normal people? She'd had a concussion, a possible concussion. Ben said she was supposed to sleep. This was not sleeping. This was insane. Picking up his robe, he put it on as he left the bedroom to find out exactly what she was up to this time.

Nothing prepared him for the scene taking place in his kitchen—his previously spotlessly clean kitchen. Wait until Celia came back from vacation and saw this . . .

Sister Margaret Mary was in the middle of a culinary disaster. Pans were everywhere. Food was scattered over the tiled work counter, cupboards were open, and she was muttering something as she searched a cabinet. He listened closely, not quite sure that he had heard correctly.

"Now where could the damned thing be?" she asked herself. Her head was almost inside the cabinet as her hands searched the shelf. "There's more bloody cupboards in this place than—"

"What are you looking for?" he interrupted, confused, and a little embarrassed to have heard the good sister swear.

She gave a little scream and swung around to face him. Unfortunately, her wide sleeve caught the handle of a wooden spoon and the flour mixture beside her rolled off the counter. When the bowl hit the floor, puffs of airborne flour surrounded her and she coughed while waving her arm. "Look what the hell you've made me do!"

"I made you do that?" He couldn't help grinning, in spite of the mess she'd created. He'd never heard a nun curse before. They really had changed since he'd gone to school. Hurrying to the stove, he slid the pan of now burning bacon off to one side. "Damn it!" He inhaled through clenched teeth and popped his burnt thumb into his mouth.

He shrugged his shoulders. "Sorry," he mumbled when he saw that tears were forming at the corners of her eyes.

She shook her head. "Look at this mess. I thought I could handle everything. I just don't know . . ." She let her words trail off as she swallowed down the tears. Taking a deep breath, she rolled up her sleeves and said, "Well, I'd best be cleaning this up. I've made a fine mess now, haven't I?"

"What were you looking for?"

"What?" She glanced up at him with almost impatience. Where would they keep a broom in this place?

"When I came in, you were searching for something. Maybe I could tell you where it is."

She wiped the flour off the front of her habit. "Lard."

He stared at her. "I beg your pardon."

"Lard. You asked what I was looking for. I couldn't find your lard."

He wanted to laugh, but resisted. It was unnerving how adorable she looked. Her red hair was escaping the wilted veil and her face was heavily smudged with flour, along with her habit. Her cheeks were flushed and her freckles were shining with perspiration. She looked wonderful, and nothing at all like a nun.

"I'm afraid I don't have lard. I don't think Celia, my housekeeper, uses it."

"Then how does she make biscuits?"

Tom shrugged. "I don't remember her ever making them. I don't usually eat breakfast. Just coffee and fruit. Nothing . . ." He looked around the kitchen at her efforts and stopped speaking. "Except on weekends," he lied. "Then I fix myself a more substantial meal." He began nodding as he took in the disaster. "Maybe I could help you."

"You?" Meggie was shocked. A man offering to cook and clean! A wealthy man, no less.

He smiled. "You look like you could use some help."

She brushed at the front of the habit in a futile effort to clean it of flour. It was hopeless, for she managed only to smudge it further into the dark wool. Frustrated, she looked back up at him and almost smiled at his sweet expression. She would have, too, if she weren't so angry with herself. Thomas almost appeared younger, with his hair falling onto his forehead. She could see the silky hair on his chest where the robe gaped open, and she quickly lowered her eyes as a flush crept up from her neck to cover her face. It was then she noticed his bare feet. "Don't come any closer or you'll be tracking the flour all over your home. If you'll tell me where your broom is, I'll get right to it." She cleared her throat. "I'm—I'm very sorry about the mess. I'm just so clumsy since yesterday."

"You shouldn't even be out of bed. Ben's coming over this morning to check on you—"

She issued a small yelp. "He'll be coming here?" she demanded.

He nodded, confused by her expression of horror.

"Well, then tell me where the broom is, Thomas. I can't be having him see this calamity."

"Sister Margaret, there's no need to get upset. I'll help—"

"The broom. Where is it?" she again demanded, and Tom swore she sounded exactly like his fifth grade nun.

The answer was just as automatic as when he was a boy. "In the pantry, just behind that wall."

Meggie lifted the hem of her skirt and walked over the mess on the floor. Opening a door that led into another room, she raised her hand to search for the hidden light switches that seemed to be everywhere. She was quickly rewarded by flooding the space with light. Lining three walls were shelves and most of them were filled with cans and boxes of food.

"Sweet Jesus," she whispered in awe. "I swear there's more food in this house than in Martin Dunlap's store!"

"Who?" He'd come up behind her and she swung

70

around to him.

"Martin Dunlap. He runs the Reading's general store."

His eyes narrowed. "Are you saying you come from Reading? In Pennsylvania?"

She shook her head. "No. The Reading is the company, and it owns everything—"

Suddenly she stopped speaking. She was telling him too much. He would make inquiries and send her back. But back to where? What was waiting for her in Lehigha? Afraid of the answers, Meggie picked up the broom and assumed a nun's voice that seemed to work so well in the kitchen. "Put your shoes on, Thomas, before you get hurt by any glass. We have to hurry before the good doctor comes."

She brushed past him with the broom and left him contemplating her words as he stared after her.

What glass? Tom swore the bowl had been stainless steel. Something was very strange, he decided as he left the pantry. It wasn't until he was standing before the door of his bedroom that he stopped and realized that he was doing exactly as she had instructed. He was going to find his shoes! He was brainwashed. It never ended. All one needed was the sight of a habit and that tone of voice. Overnight he had mentally regressed from a highly successful businessman to . . . to an obedient, insecure youth.

She had to go.

Soon.


They sat at the kitchen table, each awkward with the other. Tom had taken a quick shower and his hair was still wet and slicked back off his forehead. He was comfortably dressed in pants and a lightweight sweater . . . and shoes. He waited politely as she

71

sipped her tea.

"Breakfast was delicious. Thank you." She, too, had cleaned up. Gone was any trace of flour, save the smudge on her habit. Her face was clean and she had left the veil off to pull back her hair in a bun. Tom thought it was too severe a style for her face, but he reminded himself that it wasn't any of his business how she wore her hair. He wished he didn't have to see her hair at all. He thought the dark shade of red brought out the roses in her cheeks. Stifling a groan, he almost shook his head to drive away the foolish thought.

"Thank you," Meggie answered. It hadn't gone all that bad, now that it was over. Bacon, cold and a wee bit overdone. Eggs, hot. And tea. The tea was perfect, even if it had come out of tiny paper bags with strings on them. Too bad about the lard. She would have dearly loved to make biscuits and show him how well she could cook. Well, you can't have everything, Meggie, she told herself. It was enough that she had cleaned up the kitchen and put a breakfast on the table—one that he could eat. Though cooking with that gas had proved a tricky business, indeed. But she had done it and could congratulate herself on making it through the morning. Now if only she could convince Thomas that his friend the doctor needn't come. Surely, he would tell Thomas that she was better and could leave.

And she didn't want to leave. Not quite yet.


He was sure she'd been part of a cloistered sect. Nothing else could explain her fascination with the dishwasher, her bewilderment when asking for tooth powder and given toothpaste. She had even told him how much she liked the sharp, minty taste. And now he sat watching her watch cartoons on television.

Saturday morning and he had a nun in his living room watching "The Smurfs!" He couldn't take his eyes off her. She was mesmerized. She hadn't said a word when he'd turned on the TV and handed the remote to her. He'd picked up the paper and sat in a nearby chair to enjoy last night's news. He had been about to start reading an article on the Japanese trade deficit when he'd heard these high, whining voices. Annoying voices. Folding down the top portion of the paper, he stared at the adult nun completely absorbed in the ridiculous adventure taking place on the screen before her.

She looked so young, so captivated by the silly cartoon, that he smiled in spite of himself. She sat primly in a chair, her hands neatly clasped together in her lap, her old-fashioned shoes peeking out from under the soiled woolen habit. It was as if she were hypnotized and he nearly jumped when she finally spoke in a low voice.

"Why are they blue?"

"I'm sorry?" He tried to sound as though he had been engrossed in the newspaper, and not enchanted with her.

"These people—creatures. Why are they blue?"

He'd heard her the first time. He'd only been stalling for a little of it himself. "It's a cartoon. Haven't you ever seen one?"

She shook her head.

Tom shrugged his shoulders. "I suppose they thought they'd look—cute."

"Who are *they?*"

"They? The creators—"

"Creators?" Her eyes widened with fear and he realized his mistake at once.

"No, no. That's not what I mean. The people who

73

designed this show for television. The artists who draw those things," he finally muttered with frustration. He could actually quote complete statues on corporate law, yet he found himself stumbling over a simple explanation for a stupid cartoon!

"Why don't you use the remote control I handed you," he said a little impatiently. "I'm sure there are others that you'd enjoy." Well, one thing was certain. She wasn't a teaching nun. She was like a small child herself in many ways. And he'd swear she'd never seen a television before this morning!

It was unbelievable! Staring at the colorful screen in front of her, Meggie had to remind herself to breathe. Television. That's what Thomas had called it. To her, it was the most wondrous thing she had ever seen. It was like a magic box, and she was the magician. With the slightest touch of her finger, she would call upon it to serve up those cute little strange blue creatures, or comedy, or drama — whatever she wished to view. How fortunate were the people of this time, she thought. Only once before had Meggie seen a play, and that was a religious play at the church. Even though she had been very young, no more than twelve, she had never forgotten that Saturday. But this . . . this television was magic, and she was enchanted. Breathing deeply, she allowed herself to be swept away.

He'd been watching her for over ten minutes, fascinated by the wonderment in her expression. When the phone rang, she gasped and Tom was sorry for the intrusion. He had no time to reassure her as he quickly picked up the receiver to silence it.

"Ahh, you're back." The invitation was clear.

Taking off his glasses, he glanced at Sister Margaret switching channels. "This isn't a good time," he whispered.

74

The voice that answered him sounded annoyed. "It's been a while, Tom. I need to talk to you."

Once more he looked at the pretty nun, now seated on the rug in front of the screen. "Just a minute," he muttered into the phone. He stood up and excused himself, though he didn't believe the good sister had heard a word he'd said. Her attention was centered on something called "Pee Wee's Playhouse." She looked confused. With good reason, he thought, as he took the phone into the dining room. That show confused him as well.

He sat in one of the twelve chairs that joined the table. He still wanted to be able to see Sister Margaret; he just didn't want her to hear him.

"Angelica?"

"What is going on there?" his ex-wife demanded. "Are you all right?"

"Yes. I'm fine. Now, what is it you have to tell me?"

"You don't have to ask in that bored, corporate tone of voice, Tom." There was a pause. "If I'm bothering you, just tell me. I haven't forgotten our agreement."

He immediately regretted snapping at her. Angelica had been a good friend over the last few years. They just couldn't live together, nor agree on a lifestyle that suited them both. "Sorry," he muttered. "It was a hell of a flight in from Seattle. Now, what's up?"

He heard her earthy laughter. "Well, why don't I just tell you my dilemma? You see, Kurt insists on leaving for Vienna tonight. On the Fourth of July—"

"That's what you get for marrying a German count. They don't give a damn about American tradition."

"Stop it, Tom. Kurt is very sweet . . . usually. He

75

has this thing in his head about JFK being empty because all Americans are shooting off fireworks in the streets."

It was Tom's turn to laugh, but it wasn't a pleasant one. "Is it still worth it?" he asked in a tired voice. "How much society and nobility does it take to obliterate the fact that you've married a seventy-one-year-old pseudo-intellectual thief who calls himself the Count of Monte Crisco?"

"Stop it, Tom," she repeated. "He's the Count of Monteva, and you know that. And he's not a thief. He's a businessman."

"He earns eighty-five percent of his money in the United States, but he'll only stay in this country five months so he doesn't have to pay any taxes. That's not profit, darling. That's profiteering." Tom shook his head, as if the act might take back the words. He was jealous as hell at the tax dodge, since his own contribution to the IRS was staggering. He rubbed the place between his eyes to stop the headache that was forming. What was wrong with him this morning?

"Are you finished?"

He took a deep breath and said, "Yes, and I'm sorry. I didn't mean to get into that again. Are you going to Vienna with him?"

There was a long moment of silence. "Actually, that was my dilemma. But now I don't think I want to be around you. You sound dreadful. I might just go on holiday after all."

"I'm sorry. I'm not in a very good mood. You'd probably have a better time in Europe."

"You're apologizing a great deal this morning, Tom. Are you saying you don't want to see me?" He could hear the surprise in her voice.

Glancing up, he looked into the living room and

saw the nun. No. He might regret it tomorrow, but right now he didn't want Angelica. Even if it was safe. The count was impotent and looked the other way when she met with her ex-husband. Very European of him. The meetings were infrequent. Perhaps once every two, three months. And it didn't always end in bed. Sometimes, they actually enjoyed each other's company. One would wonder why they ever divorced, for Tom was worth more than the aging count. It wasn't money that made Angelica leave him. It was loneliness. And Tom's refusal to play the society game. He valued his privacy. Angelica craved the notoriety of opening night at the theater, dinner at Maxim's, gala balls at the Museum, weekends in Connecticut or Massachusetts with the right people. It never ended. And there was too little of it that he enjoyed.

They'd parted friends and had remained so. Now, how was he to tell her?

"I don't think this is a good time, Angelica."

"Are you serious?" She sounded disappointed, as though she'd planned on his acquiescence.

"I—I have work to finish. Someone has to clean up the residual paperwork from the takeover."

"I don't believe this . . ."

"Look, it's going to be a busy weekend. I'm sorry."

"There. You did it again. Why are you apologizing? Something's not right. I can hear it in your voice. Maybe I should come over and see for myself. You aren't sick, are you? I've seen you work through a fever before—"

He sat up straighter, and felt a knot form in his stomach when he saw the red-haired woman in the other room. "No. I'm fine! I'm busy, that's all. This is an open relationship. We aren't married to each other, Angelica. I can work when needed."

He could hear her deep breaths. "If we were married, I'd divorce you again for acting like such a shit! Fine. I shall be forced to explode fireworks over the Danube. Not exactly the Hudson River. And a day late, no less."

He grinned. "Think of the publicity, Angelica."

She issued a very unladylike curse, especially for a countess, then hung up.

Tom felt a tremendous weight lift from his shoulders as he disconnected the portable phone and stood. He couldn't wait to get back to watching Sister Margaret. It was sick, obviously brought about by his near celibate life. And he had just sent Angelica off to Europe for weeks! Granted, it had been his own choice, but something very strange was happening to him now, something very hard to ignore. He couldn't remember feeling like this about anyone, even Angelica. With Angelica he had wanted to show her his ability to provide a fortune for their future. He had loved her, loved what he'd thought she was, but it hadn't lasted. That love had mellowed into a deep friendship. Now he felt like a bumbling, young schoolboy, flushing when the good sister smiled at him; mumbling answers that he should have known. She was an unnerving houseguest.

She was also the loveliest creature he had ever seen.


An hour later he was bringing tea to her in the living room when the doorbell rang. They were both expecting Ben Tankor and Thomas smiled while placing the tray on a nearby table. "I'll be right back," he said in a reassuring voice. He knew she was nervous about meeting again with a doctor.

78

Nothing prepared Meggie for what followed.

"Ohh . . . don't look so upset, darling. Did you actually think I was going to leave the country without checking up on you? I'm meeting Kurt at the terminal, but first I had to—"

The woman stopped speaking when she saw Meggie, and Meggie's heart sank when she saw the beautiful woman, dressed in trousers and shockingly high heels. Thomas stood behind her, running his fingers through his hair.

"I . . . seem to be interrupting you," the woman said evenly. And then looked at Meggie's habit. She cleared her throat. "I can see now why you were busy this weekend, Tom. Costumes? I never saw this side of you—"

"Angelica," Tom interrupted before she could say anything else, "I'd like to introduce you to Sister Margaret Mary Gillbride."

The woman turned to him. "Are you serious?"

He nodded and Angelica raised her eyebrows while shaking her head. As if coming to a decision, she threw her purse onto the sofa and walked in Meggie's direction.

Without any notice, she extended her hand and said, "How do you do, sister? I'm Tom's wife."

*His wife!* Meggie could do no more than let the woman pump her hand as Thomas groaned loudly. He was married! She had coveted another's spouse.

My God, how many commandments had she broken thus far?

# Chapter 6

Thomas quickly walked up to her and grimaced, as though in pain. "Angelica is my ex-wife," he explained. Meggie watched as he turned and glared at the tall, beautiful woman.

"Oh . . ." Meggie was humiliated and miserably confused.

"We were divorced several years ago," he added.

She felt her face flush. "You were divorced?" As soon as the words had left her mouth, she wanted to take them back, yet she was curious to know why he had left this lovely woman with short blond hair that curled around her head, and bright inquisitive eyes that seemed to be laughing at both of them.

Angelica spoke up. Waving a hand, she said in dismissal, "We weren't married in a church, if that's what is worrying you."

Meggie shook her head, thoroughly bewildered. "I'm afraid I don't know—oh . . . you were talking about excommunication. Because of the divorce . . ." She was babbling, making no sense at all. She felt awkward and ugly next to the elegant woman and wanted nothing more than to run out of the room, leaving the two of them alone.

Clearing her throat, she said, "Excuse me," and

tried to move away from them. Angelica stopped her with her voice.

"How did you hurt your head?" she asked, staring at the bandage.

Meggie turned back to her, wishing that she possessed more courage. How was she to explain anything to this cool, poised woman? This woman who had been married to Thomas . . .

"Sister Margaret fell downstairs in the lobby," Tom offered. "Ben Tankor and I thought it best that she remain here for the night."

Angelica looked at her ex-husband as if he'd lost his mind. "Why didn't she go to a hospital? I find it hard to believe that Ben would agree to this."

"Angelica. It's fine. Sister Margaret is a member of a cloistered sect. She's never been inside a hospital before. We didn't see any reason to subject her to a possibly frightening experience. That's all there is to it." Tom forced a tight smile.

Angelica lifted her chin and her eyes widened. "A cloistered sect?"

Nodding, Tom said, "And because of the circumstances, she's my houseguest. She's staying here until we can get some information on Monday. The holiday," he reminded her.

"This doesn't make any sense," Angelica countered. "You and a nun?"

Thomas looked angry. "Angelica . . ." He said her name with a warning. One that she ignored. "Sister Margaret is my houseguest."

"Well, it is funny when you think of it," Angelica continued, her eyes reflecting her merriment. "Just how did the two of you happen to meet?"

Meggie continued to stare at the lovely woman who had been married to Thomas. Angelica's cheeks were rouged, and her lips were painted a dark pink.

For some reason she had more color on her eyelids, and her nails were also painted in the deep pink shade. She had never seen anyone quite like her before. More than ever, Meggie felt like a plain spinster. And more than ever she wanted to flee, to run away from a sophistication that only made the comparison more painful. Never could she hope to achieve such grace, such an illusion of ease . . . as if this grand lifestyle were due her. Thomas's wife possessed such qualities. Angelica was a lady. And Meggie wasn't. Perhaps that was why the difference was so painful, for Meggie had been enjoying pretending otherwise with Thomas. But now, that too was over. She was just Meggie Gillbride, from the patch, and she'd been a fool to think it could ever be any different.

"Do you have any other clothes, sister?"

Meggie merely blinked at Angelica. It was obvious the woman had been speaking to her. "I beg your pardon?" she asked awkwardly.

"No, Angelica, she doesn't have anything else. Not with her. I thought I had just explained that." It was Thomas who answered. He was beginning to sound annoyed. Again. And Meggie was afraid she had caused more strain between the couple. They were, after all, divorced, and must not be on the best of terms.

The woman turned away and faced her husband. "Well, Tom, I would say that she needs a few things. Something to replace that robe until it's cleaned. I happen to know from experience that clothing is not a top priority with you. You did say she'd lost her luggage, didn't you?"

Tom looked at the nun. Her habit was soiled from the flour. And it couldn't be that comfortable. Wool in July? If Sister Margaret remained until Monday when the Diocesan office opened, then they would have to do something about clothes. He looked back to Angelica.

She appeared amused, as if reading his mind. "Darling, I don't think we're the same size."

He silently agreed. Angelica was tall yet small boned, in contrast to Sister Margaret, who was shorter and fuller and softer— Damn! He almost shook his head to stop the thoughts. From the corner of his eye, he caught the good sister backing up toward the hall and he stared at her. He could almost feel her unease with the situation.

"If you'll both excuse me, I'll see if the rest of my . . . my habit is dry." Meggie unconsciously touched her hair where the veiling should have been, before turning toward the hallway and quickly moving down it. Once in her room she shut the door and leaned quietly against the painted wood.

She had seen their looks of pity and it was obvious they had sensed her confusion. What had they been discussing while she was daydreaming? It was about her, that much she knew.

"Ahh, God," she murmured, "what am I doing here? Do you have a plan for me? Is that it?" Looking up to the ceiling of the bedroom, she blinked away a tear and added in a rebellious voice. "If not, then be good enough to send me back to the patch. At least there, I knew where I belonged. I'm lost here. I don't fit in with these people."

She couldn't believe they were meant for her. There were two nightgowns made of the softest white cotton and a long pale yellow robe, a light brown skirt, a cream-colored silky blouse, and a pair of gray trousers that said RALPH LAUREN inside the waistband. There were also several "unmentionables" in the shiny white boxes that had been delivered that afternoon. It had been the most unusual day.

She had stayed in her room until Dr. Tankor came and examined her and proclaimed her to be healing rapidly. The lovely Angelica had peeked her head into Meggie's bedroom and announced that she was off to Europe and hoped Meggie enjoyed her stay in New York City. It had been hard not to like the vivacious woman, and again Meggie wondered why Angelica and Thomas were divorced. Neither one seemed particularly scandalized by their situation. Within an hour of Angelica's departure, a small, pleasant-looking man arrived with the shiny white boxes — all different sizes. And all for her. She had felt like a child at Christmas as she opened each one.

It seemed everyone had registered a protest. She had told Thomas that he shouldn't have bought her the clothing. It was far too extravagant. Thomas had shrugged and sweetly protested that it was obvious she needed clothes until Monday. And the shop owner declared that it had been no trouble to open the store on the holiday, once Angelica had called and explained their problem. All three of them had smiled at each other, until Meggie had taken the boxes into her room and spread them out on the bed.

Secretly pleased with the beautiful, modern clothes, Meggie couldn't help feeling a bit guilty when she thought about Angelica. It was through Angelica's intercession that the clothes were here at all. Meggie had thought not to like any women who had been married to Thomas, especially one who had divorced him. But this situation was nothing like the priests had lectured at Sunday mass. Divorce. There was no horror, no scandal that she could see. Thomas and Angelica had seemed friends, not ene-

84

mies. And it was hard to think of either of them being condemned to hell because they couldn't live together. But then, everything was confusing now. Nothing was the same as in the patch.

She picked up a delicate French-cut bikini and turned it several ways, trying to figure out how to wear the undergarment. *This tiny silky wisp of material simply could not have replaced a pair of decent drawers. Could it?* She remembered seeing pictures in the newspaper, advertisements for clothing—some of them quite risqué—and she reached for the periodical that Thomas had brought to her last night. Maybe if she studied the pictures and drawings of women in the paper, she could determine just how to solve this problem—for the accompanying garment, obviously meant for the breasts—looked like something one would use in torture. Beyond the silk material were wires! She had felt them. Not bone, as in a corset—actually wires that surrounded the breasts. Who would wear such a thing?

She was all alone, there was no one that she could go to for advice, and her resolve and determination were quickly fading as the afternoon progressed into evening. It was also becoming painfully clear that she needed help, if she was to remain here for any length of time. The transition was not going to be as easy as she'd thought. And that admission hurt.


He tried not to laugh. Biting his lower lip, Tom nodded to her and held out her chair. She was wearing slacks underneath her skirt!

"Is something wrong?" Meggie asked as she sat at the long glass dining room table. Already sensitive, she had caught the look of amusement on his face.

Sitting down opposite her, Tom smiled. "No.

Nothing is wrong. You look—very nice," he said while handing her the bowl of salad. "I hope you don't mind soup again. I forgot to defrost something for dinner." His grin widened. "I'm afraid it wouldn't have mattered if I had remembered. You see, outside of this Caesar Salad, for which I've gained a considerable reputation, I'm not a very good cook—"

"You should have let me cook dinner," she interrupted. "Now that I know how everything works, I wouldn't have made such a mess this time. I could still cook you something, if you'd like . . ." Meggie quickly looked toward the kitchen. "Exactly—what is defrost?"

He laughed out loud. "To defrost is to let something thaw that has been frozen—"

"Frozen in July?"

He nodded. Again that look appeared on his face, the one that said she should have known such things.

"In the freezer. Don't they have a freezer at your convent?"

She hated the lies. They seemed to be building up. Trying to avoid another falsity, she shook her head and said, "I don't remember anything about a freezer."

"I'll show you one after dinner. It's in the kitchen. I'm surprised you didn't find it this morning. It's the bottom half of the refrigerator."

"Ahh . . ." She nodded her head with understanding. She knew about the refrigerator. "Is that why everything is so cold? Because of the freezer?"

He offered her the minestrone soup that was imported from Italy. "It's very complicated, but motors take in the warm air and exchange it for cold. It keeps the food fresh for longer periods if it's frozen."

"Is that why this hotel is so cold in the summer?"

He put his spoon down and stared at her. "This

isn't a hotel. People live here on a permanent basis."

"There must be so very many living here." She gazed out the window to the darkening sky. "It is a very large building. And cold. I find it hard to believe that it is actually July."

"Are you talking about the air-conditioning? Is that why you're wearing the pants under your skirt? Are you cold?"

She blinked rapidly, trying to make sense out of his questions. "I, ahh, the pants? I wasn't supposed to wear them?"

He shrugged his shoulders, more confused than she. "Well, I don't know. Usually women wear either one or the other."

"But the skirt is so short," she protested. "And a woman . . . a lady wouldn't wear trousers. Would she?"

He smiled. He couldn't help it. "Yes, she might. Angelica does. And the skirt doesn't seem short at all. It's well below your knees." He stabbed the lettuce with his fork. "But then, I suppose you should wear what you feel most comfortable in . . . to hell with fashion." His head jerked up and his face turned red. "I'm sorry. I keep forgetting—"

She raised her hand, as if in dismissal. "That's quite all right. Strong language doesn't shock me."

He simply didn't get it. Strong language docsn't shock her, but she'd never heard of a freezer and hasn't the slightest knowledge of fashion! She was unlike any woman he had ever known. And she was driving him crazy, now more than ever. She looked positively lovely in modern clothes, even if they were as plain as Paul could find. She looked less like a nun. And more like a woman.

It was a frightening thought.

They ate in silence, each filled with questions that

neither had the courage to ask. Suddenly, a noise sounded from outside and Meggie nearly rose from her seat with fear.

"Fireworks." Tom stood up and motioned for her to follow. They walked into the living room, and leaving the lights out, he came to the wall and pressed a button.

The drapes were magically swept away from the window, revealing a spectacular view. Above the thousands of lights that sparkled over the city, the night came alive like a fountain of glittering jewels, spraying shimmering colors down from the sky. She had never seen anything so beautiful in her life. It was like a gift from heaven, a perfect show of power and beauty.

She made an appreciative sound with each burst of light and color that lit up the sky. "It's beautiful." Her words were whispered and filled with awe.

Tom couldn't help smiling. It was a magnificent view and he was glad she was with him to appreciate it. Her excitement was contagious and he found himself talking like a tour guide, wanting to impress her, entertain her . . .

"If you turn around, over there beyond Wall Street, is the Statue of Liberty. You can't see them, but the barges in the East River are setting off the fireworks. Look, see—they actually light up the Brooklyn Bridge. Now, look this way." He touched her arm while pointing to the west. "You can see the fireworks from New Jersey."

They both turned and stared at the spectacular vista, from the George Washington Bridge down the coast of New Jersey. You could actually see the fireworks set off in individual towns, each trying to be more majestic than the next. It was a showy, garish way to celebrate freedom, yet it grabbed the soul and stirred up feelings of patriotism. It was a glittering celebration, and it was a sight to behold.

*I'm dreaming,* she thought. I must be, for surely this doesn't happen in real life—to stand so close to the sky and watch the sparkle and glitter of fireworks, so near that you might open a window and quickly gather a handful of fading stars. Ahh, Meggie, remember this, she told herself, for soon you'll wake up back in the patch and this'll be just a distant memory. She unconsciously touched his arm as another rocket exploded right in front of them, spraying white and blue and pink diamond lights into the night. Her sigh of appreciation was low and soft and filled with reverence.

But what a grand memory it would all make, for this was a night to memorize each exciting detail. A night of magic . . .

His breath caught at the back of his throat. His heart pounded behind his rib cage. He stared at her profile, her beautiful profile, and tried to bring himself back under control. It had only lasted seconds, but it'd been enough to terrify him. For a brief moment, a span of time that could only be measured in seconds, he had actually leaned closer to her—for he'd been about to gather her in his arms and taste her mouth under his. Like a real woman. Like the warm attractive woman that she was. He ached for it, deep, in the very fiber and muscle of his body and it frightened him. Thank God he'd stopped himself in time, for Sister Margaret would surely have fainted dead away again. This time from shock.

Why did she have to be so pure? Of heart and mind pure. The tightening in his belly was almost painful, like the denial of a man who had fasted. Well, tonight had proved to him that he was starved. But for a nun? The thought terrified him and he ran

89

his fingers through his hair and concentrated on the fireworks.

God help him, but his gaze was drawn back to her. He simply couldn't help it.

She felt his stare. It was as if he'd grazed her, so very softly, yet commanding a reaction, a response. Without thought, caught up in the enchantment of the night, Meggie lifted her face and looked back. It was bold; it was also impossible to deny.

They were both in the dark, in the silence, waiting for the next explosion of light. And when it came, through a burst of brilliance, they both saw something astonishing in the other.

It was hunger. Raw. Undeniable.

And unbelievably real.

She was stunned, reluctant to allow any logical thoughts to enter her mind, but they crept in like thieves, swiftly stealing away the moment. He's divorced, she thought. He can't be attracted to you after being married to a woman like Angelica. He feels sorry for you. You can never be like her. You will never have that sophistication or grace. You are a spinster, from the patch, and he is a man of wealth and quality. You're to be pitied, Meggie Gillbride, for believing anything else — even for a moment.

She cleared her throat and crossed her arms over her chest. "I . . ." Oh God, why was talking such an effort now? "That is, I think I'll clear the table if you're finished."

He felt awkward, like a teenager. "No. Don't bother. I'll do it. There's only a few dishes." Why didn't he just walk over to the lamp and turn it on? Break the spell. Deep down he knew the reason: he didn't want her to see him, was afraid of what his face would reveal.

She didn't question him. She pushed from her

mind the outrageous thought of a man, a wealthy man, washing dishes. Embarrassed by what he must be thinking of her, Meggie nodded and left him. Maybe he hadn't seen her expression, she hoped. But maybe he had. The possibility was humiliating.

He watched her leave the room, leave him, and felt a painful hollow begin to spread in his belly. She must have seen his hunger and was repelled. What was happening to him? Looking back out the window to the fireworks, Tom felt the hollow begin to fill with a strange mixture of fascination and damnation.

He wanted her.

# Chapter 7

She tried not to listen to the sounds of distant fireworks. It was late, and they should have stopped. She wanted to sleep, to erase the embarrassing episode with Thomas from her mind. But the celebration continued and the sudden noises frightened her, reminding her of another explosion. Of another time . . .

It felt easy in the darkness. If she closed her eyes and relaxed, letting her body feel almost weightless, she could actually sense something pulling her. Gently. Yet steadily. She knew she should stop, shake herself awake, but there was Mount Carmel Church in the distance. So real . . . And wasn't that old Teddy Haynes walking past it?

"Teddy!" She wasn't sure whether or not she'd yelled his name aloud. She was there though — Standing in a field of dried clover back in the patch. In Lehigha. It felt so real. It smelled of the indoor fires, of baking, of coal. Without further thought, she ran toward Teddy, hoping to talk to him, to touch him, but he turned the corner and disappeared.

She slid to a halt at the crossroad and looked beyond. He was gone. She felt like crying out her frustration, but knew she was only dreaming. As real as it seemed, it couldn't be happening. She could *not* be back in Lehigha. For if that were true, then Thomas never existed, nor his magical, confusing world of the future. And that thought brought a sudden pain into her chest, like grief.

Standing before the old church, Meggie looked up to its wooden steeple. She allowed her gaze to lower until she stared at the dark green painted doors. She was not welcome inside. Oh, no one had thrown her out, nor was it stated that she was not to return, but it was understood that she was no longer one of them. It was in the looks of disapproval, the lack of warmth in their presence. She may have made a mistake once, but she wasn't so dense not to recognize a shunning. She had pretended that it didn't hurt not to be included any longer in activities. The sporting events and church-sponsored dances were the only entertainments in the patch, and she had shed too many tears alone at home while others laughed and took pleasure in life. There was a reason why she would never enter those doors again. The hurt ran too deep.

Shaking her head, Meggie turned away and slowly walked toward the cemetery. It was where she'd had her own private services every Sunday. While the others were inside, listening to Father Andrew, Meggie had been just outside the cemetery, tending a tiny grave, listening to her heart. And that was where she had found her peace.

Anxious now to reach the small grave, she hurried past familiar markers until she was beyond the white picket fence. Reaching her destination, Meggie slowly walked up to the small stone she and Brian had placed for her son. She felt the customary wave of grief and guilt. Patrick John Gillbride. So tiny. So tragic . . .

She stopped suddenly, as if grabbed from behind. Her mouth opened in shock when she saw an even smaller headstone next to it. Her throat felt strangled with fear as she read the newly carved name by her son's:

MARGARET MARY GILLBRIDE  1849-1875
BELOVED DAUGHTER AND SISTER

She looked to the ground. There was no newly turned earth. No grave. What was happening? Who had done this? Desperately frightened, Meggie reached out her finger and shakily traced the letters.

It was real! She could feel the grooves made by the chisel as it had carved out her name. *Her name!* My God . . . she had died!

"No! No! It can't be . . ."

The scream tore out of her throat and she clawed at the air, as if to stop herself from drowning in the insanity of the moment. She wasn't dead! She wasn't. She was alive! Alive!

"Help me . . . someone . . . please!"

"It's all right. I'm here. Shh . . . It's all right now. You were dreaming."

She felt herself gathered into his arms, strong, safe arms, and started to sob in relief when she heard his steady heartbeat. She couldn't be dead and hear the beating of a man's heart under her ear. "Ahh, Brian, I was so frightened. The dream . . ."

"I'm not Brian."

She lifted her head and stared into the darkness. The faint moonlight allowed her to see his face. "Thomas," she breathed, a sudden joy closing around her when she recognized him.

Without thought to consequences, she immediately replaced her head to his chest and wrapped her arms around him, hugging him to her, as if to reassure herself that he was actually there. "Thank God," she exclaimed. "I—I was so afraid. It's all so confusing. I don't know what's real anymore."

She would have been all right if he hadn't brushed back her hair and whispered, "It was only a dream. You're safe now."

She couldn't help it. The very last thing she wanted to do was cry, but the hot, burning sensation crept up her throat and before she could stop it, she was quietly sobbing against his chest. To be safe . . . with this man, would be a gift from heaven. Even if fate decided to snatch it all away, she would selfishly keep this moment.

"Please. Stay with me . . . until I fall asleep." She could feel his body tense under her hands. She sniffled back another sob. "You see, I have these dreams and—and I'm afraid to close my eyes, to sleep."

He seemed to hesitate for a moment, as if thinking it over, then he relaxed. "Here, let me rest against the headboard. I'll stay with you until you fall asleep."

He shifted himself against the pillows and gathered her back into his arms. Meggie didn't care what he thought of her, she didn't want to be the nun. All she wanted was to stay here in his arms and rest. Safe. Secure. It had been so long since she'd felt this protected. Not since her Da had held her. And then she'd been a very young girl. It had been so many years since she could relax and let someone else do the worrying. She didn't care what happened in the morning. Nothing else but the moment was of any importance. She could finally relax, and close her eyes, and know where she'd wake up.

In Thomas's arms.

He told himself it was innocent enough. He was

only holding her, a frightened woman, nothing more. It was innocent, yet something stirred within him as he rested against the pillows and held her to his chest. It was warm and soothing, like the brandy he'd been drinking when he'd first heard her cries. He didn't care what or who she was. Now she was a woman. That's all. Frightened and shaking in his arms. And she felt so right. Maybe in the dark they could both pretend . . .

"You know I used to be frightened of the dark myself," he whispered down to her. "I was eleven or twelve before I could fall asleep without the hall light. Crazy science fiction movies. Alfred Hitchcock stories on television. My imagination was vivid. I can remember moving my bed against the wall, so I'd only have to watch two sides, instead of four." An unexpected chuckle bubbled up inside of him. "I was convinced *The Crawling Hand* was making its way to my bedroom and to me."

He let out his breath and relaxed. "You're not alone. Everybody, at some time in their life, fights the night." When she didn't answer, he added, "It's okay, I'll take care of you."

And right then, at that moment, he wanted it to be true. It made no sense at all. It wasn't sexual; it wasn't even desire. It was the acrid burning in his chest when he'd said he'd take care of her. It rang so true that he'd wanted to force her to look at him, to give him a reaction. But she hadn't even acknowledged his words.

She was falling back to sleep in his arms when he heard the first indiscriminate murmurings of her jumbled thoughts. Holding his breath, he listened.

"Brian . . . the babe . . . betrayal . . . I can't save him. I can't!"

He heard a moan of anguish so heartbreaking that

he tightened his arms around her as whimpers jerked her body. And then just as quickly the tension was released as she softened against him.

What was she talking about? Her brother, Brian? What about a baby? And betrayal? Who did she want to save? Brian, or the baby? She sounded as if she was in a lot of trouble. Was she escaping from the convent? That was ludicrous. No one could hold her against her will. But what had happened to make her forget everything modern? What had she done? Who was this woman in his arms . . . Sister Margaret Mary Gillbride? And why did he want to protect her so? Just thinking about anyone hurting her made him lower his lips to her hair. He had never felt this protective of anyone in his entire life.

Confused and tired, he swallowed down the burning lump that had risen to his throat and closed his eyes. He could feel her breath against his chest, soft and warm through the material of his shirt, and steady. Already she was falling back to sleep and he let himself relax with her, wanting to remember exactly how it felt . . . for he knew that after tonight it would never take place again.

He refused to acknowledge the small warning that said he was being a fool. It felt too damned good to be wrong.

The first sensation that registered was one of weightlessness. It was pleasant, like falling asleep. Only now he was waking. A chill ran down his back and he gathered the soft warm body closer to him. It felt natural—

*Warm body!*

He jerked awake, blinking several times as Sister Margaret made soft moaning sounds, stretching her arms above thick red hair, as if reluctant to relinquish sleep. As astonishing as that sight might be, what really captured his attention was the sky and clouds above his head. He was outside. He and Sister Margaret had been sleeping outside! What the hell was going on?

As if just realizing that she had spent the night against him, Sister Margaret gathered the cotton nightgown closer to her neck and pulled away in embarrassment.

"I'm . . . I don't know—"

"Where the hell are we?" he demanded, sitting up and noting the mountains behind him. Birds were chirping and he could hear dogs barking in the distance. He looked toward the sound and saw a town. An old-looking town.

She followed his line of vision and suddenly jumped up. Pointing to the town, she said, "It's Lehigha. I'm back!"

"You're back where? I'm afraid I don't understand. How did we get here?"

She turned around to him and smiled. Even though he was bewildered, he was still moved by her natural beauty. It was morning and she was lovely, without any artifice. Clear pale freckled skin seemed to blush under his scrutiny.

"This is Lehigha. This is where I live."

He shook his head and stood up, tentatively placing his bare feet on the rocky ground. "Wait a minute. Are you saying this is where your convent is located?"

"This is where I'm from."

"How did we get here? Is this a dream? Am I dreaming?"

Again, she smiled. "I don't know. If you are, then I'm having the same dream." She looked back to the town. "Will you come with me? I would like to see my brother."

He didn't know what to do. Of course it was a dream. What else could explain the absurdity of it? One does not fall asleep in a penthouse overlooking Central Park and wake up in . . . in Lehigha— wherever that was. Outside, no less. He'd had some brandy last night, that was it. He'd just follow her into this town, complete the dream, and then wake up back in his apartment in New York City. But why did he have to dream with bare feet? The small stones and rocks were killing him.

"Keep to the grass," she advised after hearing him curse again. "We'll be on the dirt road soon."

A dirt road. This could not be happening.

"What is that?" he asked as they neared the town of wooden buildings.

She looked up toward where he was pointing. "That's the colliery. It's not very pretty, is it?"

"A colliery. To process what? Coal?"

She nodded. "The men have been on strike now for over a year. These are bad times."

"Where are we? In Pennsylvania? Ohio?"

"Pennsylvania. Come, here's old Bridget Humne. Let me just ask her what day this is. If she answers, then we're not dreaming. Dear God, look at the way I'm dressed!" She crossed her arms over her chest, as if that made her look more respectable.

Tom watched as a wizened old woman carried a basket up the path. Her dress was long, brushing the tops of her worn black shoes, and in the rising sunshine she wore a wide straw hat.

"Good morning to you, Miss Bridget. Would you be on your way to picking berries?"

The woman ignored Sister Margaret's greeting and nearly yelped in fright when she saw him standing at the side of the path.

"Saints be praised! Ya nearly frightened me into me grave." She looked him over, noticing his feet, and held her basket tighter to her waist. Lifting her chin, she added, "Are ya lost, boyo, or have ya just misplaced your shoes out here?"

Tom looked down at his feet. "I, ah, I think I misplaced them," he answered.

"Miss Bridget, are you going to say good morning to me?" Sister Margaret asked, a worried look on her face.

Again ignoring her, the woman shook her head and said, "These are bad times to be lookin' for a handout, son. Ya aren't plannin' to look for work, are ya? 'Cause there's none to be found."

"No work?" Tom asked. "What about the colliery?"

"The men are on strike." The old woman and the nun said the same thing almost in unison, yet only the nun seemed to hear the other.

Tom looked at both of them, an idea starting in his head. "Would you look here," he asked the woman. "What do you see?"

The old one appeared confused but did his bidding. He watched as she seemed to look right through the nun and beyond, as if the lovely young woman with striking red hair weren't there.

"I see a fine summer morning. And what do you see?" Bridget asked.

Tom looked at Sister Margaret and saw the shock on her face. "She can't see me!"

Tom blinked a few times and then turned his attention back to the old woman. "A fine summer morning. Do you know of someone called Sister Margaret?"

The nun shook her head. "Don't ask her that. She

wouldn't know me."

"Sister Margaret, ya say?" The old one frowned. "I can't say that I have. Are ya lookin' for her? Is that why you've come?"

He glanced up to the younger woman. Quickly, she said, "Tell her that you're looking for a place to stay and that you heard she runs the best boarding house in two counties."

Tom smiled down to Bridget. "I'm looking for a place to stay."

Bridget cleared her throat and gave his feet her attention. "I wouldn't think a man without shoes would be havin' the means to pay for a room."

"Tell her the part—"

Tom gave the nun an impatient look, as if to say that he was getting to it. "I heard that Bridget Humne runs the best boarding house in two counties," he added, not believing that he was buttering up this old woman. And for what?

"No man comes in my house without shoes."

"Tell her you'll have them."

"I'll have them."

The woman nodded, allowing a small smile to touch her lips. "Nor without money. You won't be charmin' Bridget Humne out of boardin' money."

"I'll have that also," he quickly added before Sister Margaret could tell him. Though for the life of him he hadn't the slightest idea of how he was to obtain money. Or shoes. Or why he'd be needing a room in the first place.

The old woman moved past him on her way toward the hills and thickets ripe with berries. "And who would I be talkin' to, sir?" she asked.

"Thomas Carter," he answered, surprised by the lack of recognition his name produced. He was definitely dreaming.

The woman stopped. "Carter? You're English?"

"I'm American—"

"Tell her you're Irish, on your mother's side," Sister Margaret quickly whispered.

He sounded annoyed. "I am," he muttered to the nun, then turned back to the old woman. "I am . . . Irish. On my mother's side. McKenna."

The woman smiled. "Well then, Thomas Carter, when you find your shoes, and proper dress, you'll be welcome in my home."

He smiled. "Thank you." Even though it was only a dream, Tom felt as if he had passed the first test. Now *that* was crazy.


Old Bridget couldn't see her! Meggie tried to stay calm and help Thomas, who was obviously quite visible to the old woman. But why couldn't she see her? It was the possibilities that frightened her. After Bridget walked up the hill, Meggie turned to Thomas.

"I think I'm dead." She tried not to let her voice crack, but wasn't successful.

"What do you mean? Of course you're not dead." He sounded impatient, as if her comments were childish, and not desperate.

"Then why couldn't Bridget see me? I'm telling you—I'm dead!"

"This is nonsense." He ran his hand through his hair as he looked toward the town. "You are not—dead. Everyone saw you in New York. How many people spoke with you?"

She thought about that. "You're right. Several."

"And what about your head? Ben Tankor even treated you. Dead people don't bleed and then heal."

"Then why couldn't Bridget see me now?" she

demanded. "Maybe I'm only dead in this time, and not in yours." Dear God, please don't let me cry again, she thought. It wasn't going to be easy, for she could feel herself once more filling up with tears.

He let his breath out in a frustrated rush. "Look, Sister . . . Sister Margaret . . . we are only dreaming. None of this is real. Don't be so—"

"Stop calling me that!" Honestly, the man was being so dense. Didn't he know this wasn't a dream? Couldn't he feel it? "My name is Meggie."

He became very still, very quiet. "What do you mean?"

She sniffled and pushed the hair away from her eyes. "I mean that I want you to stop calling me Sister Margaret. I'll be paying for enough sins— wherever I'm going—and I'll not be paying for that one any longer. My name is Meggie. Meggie Gillbride."

His eyes widened, then quickly narrowed. She sensed a deep anger swiftly coming to the surface. "Are you saying you are not a nun?"

She could actually feel his breath on her as he exhaled and she stepped back against a rose of sharon bush. For the first time, he frightened her. "I'm—I—I haven't yet taken my final vows," she blurted out in a rapid stream of words. *You're damned to hell for sure now,* she told herself, a feeling of doom settling in.

He seemed to rein in his anger—a bit. "You're a novice then?"

She nodded, not trusting her voice. Let him think it. Let him believe anything, but that she'd deceived him. Instinct told her that was one thing Thomas Carter would not deal with easily. "I think I can get shoes for you," she offered in a small voice. "Since it seems no one can see me, I suppose I could lift them from the Reading's store."

"Lift them? You mean steal?" He looked surprised.

She shrugged. "I wouldn't call it stealing. Not exactly. Not if this is only a dream. And neither one of us is exactly dressed to go into town."

She could see he was thinking about her answer. Finally he said, "I guess you're right. You in your nightgown, and me . . ." He looked down to his wrinkled pants and opened shirt.

Buttoning up his collar, he continued, "Well, anyway, how are you going to go about it? I mean, suppose you take the shoes—you can't be seen, but what about the shoes? Do they just float in the air? What are you going to do?"

She thought about it for a moment. As if coming to a decision, she picked up a nearby rock and hid it in the folds of her nightgown. "C'mon," she said. "Let's see if anyone in the patch notices a floating rock."

He followed her the short distance to the edge of town when she stopped and turned back to him. "You wait over here, behind the well. I'll be back in a few minutes. Either with the shoes, or a crowd of people following them." She started in the direction of the store then turned and said, "You know, this might not be such a bad thing after all." Giving him a grin, she left him and he could swear there was a near skip to her walk.

She was enjoying this!

It had worked. No one in the store had noticed the rock and she'd let it drop to the wooden floor between two bolts of unfinished cotton. Martin Dunlap looked up when he'd heard the soft thud and had walked over to investigate. Meggie had had to cover her mouth not to giggle as she moved away and watched him examine the good-sized rock.

"Now how in the world did this get in here?" he'd demanded of no one in particular. Several shoppers glanced up but gave no comment. And it was then, while he was pondering her rock, that Meggie slipped the size nine boots into the pocket she had made of the front of her nightgown. The cold leather made her shiver, yet she kept them close as she looked over the store. Now, shouldn't Thomas have a jacket? It was only proper that a gentleman wear one, especially if he's new in town. Thomas was going to get the once-over from the patch, and she was going to make sure he passed with flying colors. That brown gabardine would look just fine.

Smiling at the others in the store, she reached out her foot and knocked over a small barrel of raw sugar. Delighted, she laughed outright when Martin Dunlap ran toward it, muttering a few choice words under his breath. It was easy pickings to stuff the jacket in with the boots.

No one had heard her laugh. No one could see her. She could do whatever she wanted . . . and get away with it. Suddenly she looked at the filled shelves of the store with a new light. She could have anything at all.

Five minutes later, Meggie Gillbride prepared to leave the Reading company store. The front of her nightgown was filled and she bumped into Maeve Hagan on her way out, pushing the town gossip into a stack of apples.

The old woman looked shocked as she watched the apples scatter to the floor. "I didn't do it," she protested to Mr. Dunlap, who came running to pick up the fruit. "I swear. Something came up behind me and—and pushed me!"

Everyone in the store stopped and stared at the woman. Meggie laughed outright.

"I'd be careful, Maeve," Meggie whispered, although she knew no one could hear her, "or they might just start talking about you. And you know how vicious wagging tongues can be. Or do you?" Thinking about the pain Maeve Hagan had caused her over the years, Meggie wasn't all that careful about swinging the front of her nightgown as she left the store.

She didn't look back, only grinned, as she heard Maeve's shriek of surprise as the woman landed in a bin of flour. Yes, Meggie thought, being invisible had definite advantages.

## Chapter 8

He waited for her to return.

He had no idea why he was waiting, why he didn't just get up and walk on to something else in the dream. For some strange reason, he was content to sit on the edge of the woods and hide behind a large stone well. Unlike Sister Margaret, he could be seen, for a dog had warily approached him, sniffed him, and then quite haughtily dismissed him, as if he wasn't worth the notice. And then there was the encounter with the old woman, Bridget — a real character from the past. The old woman had the same slightly accented voice as . . . What did she ask to be called? Meggie?

He shook his head. It was a very bizarre dream. He had actually projected her into his sleeping thoughts, a sure sign that he was becoming obsessed with the woman. She had looked so lovely when he had thought he'd awakened this morning, that he'd been tempted to lower his head and kiss her. Kiss her! But then all too soon she had realized the situation and pulled away from him. He would be furious with her, if any of it were really happening. Imagine letting him believe that she was a nun? A full-fledged, oathtaking nun with divine promises of poverty, obedience, and chastity. Funny how he remembered those oaths, especially the one about chastity. But then again, the woman was driving him crazy. Wasn't this dream proof of it? He couldn't even remember the last time he had dreamed, yet now he was so influenced by *Meggie*, that he was doing so in living color. He could even smell the summer morning scent, that satisfying mixture of grass and dirt and clean air. He could hear the wings of insects as they inspected wild flowers, or created a strange symphony of nature beneath the tall, dried grass. He inhaled deeply and could detect the aroma of freshly baked bread and—maybe cinnamon. Salivating, Tom felt his stomach immediately tighten with an unexpected hunger.

And that made him stop and think.

Why was he hungry? He was only dreaming. Wasn't he? He tried to think back, to recall other dreams, but it was impossible. However, he didn't think he was ever hungry in any of them, nor was he so attuned to the senses of smell and hearing. It all seemed so real, so authentic, that when he heard the girlish giggle, he wasn't surprised to see her standing in front of him.

"Wait till you see what I have for you," she promised in a happy voice.

He didn't look up. He couldn't. He was fascinated by the sight of Sister Margaret's legs. She had gathered her booty into the front of her nightgown and held the material together to form a large pouch. He blinked several times as she released the cotton and showered him with her plunder. Shoes, apples, a jacket, socks, and a small metal tin fell and surrounded him, like presents on Christmas morning.

"Ohh, Thomas, you should have been there!" she giggled. "No one could see me. I was free to lift whatever I happened to choose." She collapsed in a fit of laughter. "Poor Martin Dunlap—I'm sure he thinks he's losing his mind. And that old bitty, Maeve Hagan . . ."

"What did you do to her?" He was afraid to hear the answer, for the woman in front of him was nothing at all like the meek little nun who had entered his life and turned it upside down. This woman of his dream was full of life. Her cheeks were flushed from laughter and her incredibly light blue eyes were filled with mischief. She was vivacious and charming and . . . and he was fascinated by her. He also couldn't stop his lips from forming a smile. Her happy mood was that contagious and irresistible. It was obvious that he had invented this animated woman, for Sister Margaret Mary Gillbride would never be so uninhibited as to pull her gown up to her knees and slip on a pair of shoes in front of him.

Meggie shook her head as she tied the buttonhooked shoelaces. "Why, when Maeve was inspecting flour, I merely helped her get a closer look, that's all." Again, she was unable to stop the giggles. "I believe she lost her balance."

He looked sideways at her. "She fell?"

Meggie shrugged. "The last I saw, she was covered with flour." Her smile widened. "I hope her mouth is as dry as this dirt."

She could see his surprised expression and she defended herself. "Maeve Hagan is the town gossip. You can't begin to imagine the number of people she's hurt with her vicious tongue. She's the self-appointed judge and jury in the patch. I have never known such a judgmental, condemning woman—"

"You sound as if you've experienced her wounds firsthand." Tom had watched as Meggie's face was transformed to loathing while she spoke of the

109

woman.

Again Meggie shrugged, as if the idea wasn't important. "What's done is done. You can't always take back what you say about another. Someday it'll all come back to Maeve." Finished with her shoes, she flipped down her nightgown and filled her lungs with fresh air as she stared up at the cloudless sky. "I believe you get back what you give out to others . . . eventually. It all comes around."

He was staring at her, watching the pain come into her eyes and then quickly disappear. It was as if long ago she had refused to allow the hurt any more power over her. He actually saw her banish it, struggle to put it behind her, as she took another deep breath and stood up.

"Put your shoes on, Thomas," she said in a quiet voice. "I want to find my brother, Brian."

Doing as he was told, Tom fought with the old-fashioned shoes. They were too large, too stiff, and they had high tops, like basketball sneakers. Walking proved awkward, but as he slipped on the gabardine jacket, Tom promised not to complain. She had gone through a lot to get him these clothes. And anyway, it was only a dream. He was merely going along for the ride.

Even in summer when it should have appeared at its best, the town looked bleak and dreary. The paint on the small wooden houses seemed to be blistering and peeling in the morning heat. Flowers and plants that lined porches were drying up by the lack of moisture. He got the impression of something dying . . . and he thought it was the town. Tom realized what he wanted to blame on nature was really the effects of poverty and apathy. There was no point in painting a house that didn't belong to you, when you had no money for paint. And water was too precious, not to be wasted on such frivolous things as flowers. There was cooking and washing, and bathing on Saturday night in preparation for Sunday mass. He shook his head, not knowing where the strange thoughts were coming from. How would he know such things?

Suddenly bells started ringing and both Meggie and Tom stopped in the middle of the street to stare at each other.

"Is it Sunday? They are church bells, aren't they?"

She shook her head. "The store wouldn't have been open on a Sunday. Come on. Let's see what's happening."

They walked together up a small hill. No one seemed to pay him much attention. Everyone, dressed in old-fashioned clothing, was too intent to reach the wooden church at the top. It was obvious by their murmurs that something of importance was about to take place.

Tom and Meggie picked a spot off to the side, the better to observe. As Meggie named each one, tired-looking women carried babies closer to the church while keeping well-behaved, silent children near to their skirts. Tom was appalled by their condition. Although clean, the worn material of their clothing showed numerous patches. Yet it was their faces, especially their eyes, that told the story. He couldn't find even a glimmer of hope that anything would change for the better. He wondered how long these people had been on strike, for the men looked haggard and serious as they stood together behind the women. Everyone's attention, except his, was centered on the green door of the church.

As if on request, it opened and a priest came outside, followed by two men in old-fashioned double-breasted suits.

"Father Andrew," Meggie whispered, as though anyone could actually hear her. "And that short, mean-looking man is Nathen Gowen, president of the Reading Coal and Iron Company. I don't know who the taller one is."

Tom had the impression she wanted to spit, for her mouth curled up with distaste as she named the mine owner. He was fascinated by this woman who called herself Meggie, this woman who was so totally different from the nun, and he watched as her eyes searched the crowd for her brother. It was only moments, however, before their attention was caught by the deep resonant voice of the priest.

"People of Lehigha, I have good news. Mr. Nathen Gowen has come to me with what I think is a very good offer of reconciliation, to end the discord that has ruled our lives these many months."

Those around Tom made unflattering noises, as if not believing the statement, yet the priest raised his chin and continued.

"We are all aware of the unfortunate accident that took place at the Reading's offices. Not only were important records destroyed, but from eyewitness reports we must believe that we lost one of our own in the explosion. How many more people must die because of this strike?" He looked around at the faces in the crowd. "Mr. Gowen has come to me with an offer to release Connon Rafferty . . ."

Amid the sudden cheers, someone yelled, "Now ain't that generous? Might that be because he lost his trumped-up evidence in the fire? Gowen's back is up against the wall!"

The priest ignored the cries and raised his hands for quiet. "The statements of record for all debts incurred as of May of this year have also been destroyed . . ." An even louder cheer began, and the priest had to shout to be heard. "However, we are all aware that everyone in Lehigha owes money, especially to the company store, and that debt will have to be settled."

"How?" An anonymous voice demanded. "Even Dunlap has no idea how much each of us owes."

Father Andrew drew in his breath, an action that even Tom could see meant the priest was going to impart something of great importance.

"Each family will be levied with a thirty-dollar debt—"

The uproar was expected and Father Andrew again shouted to be heard. "This is all subject to negotiations. Mr. Gowen has agreed to a discussion of this matter if you agree to return to work . . . at one dollar a day, plus—"

"And what of the charges for breakage? For renting of the picks? For the oil for our lamps? That dollar would soon be less than the fifty cents that we're strikin' against now!"

Meggie said his name aloud. "Brian . . ." And stretched her neck to see him. He stood with Liam and Jack Donahue and Bobby Hannigan. Her eyes devoured only her brother. Tall, with brown hair and blue eyes, Brian set a grand style. Even if his shirt was in need of a button or two, Meggie noted.

Nate Gowen leaned closer to the priest and whispered something. Father Andrew nodded and cleared his throat, ready once more to address the crowd. "Brian. You and Liam Dunleavy will represent the miners of Lehigha. Along with James Roarity."

Everyone seemed pleased by the selection, except Meggie. "It's a fix!" she shouted, though no one could hear her. "James Roarity is a bloody traitor!"

Tom's mouth opened in shock as he stared at her. Her cheeks were flushed with anger and she looked

113

ready to cry, though not from sorrow. Sister Margaret, or Meggie, seemed prepared to do battle with the priest, the mine owner, and anyone else who got in her way.

"Calm down," he whispered out of the corner of his mouth. "No one can hear you, you know."

She sniffled. "Then you tell them. They can hear you."

Tom shook his head.

"Tell them about that cur, Roarity."

He crossed his arms over his chest and again shook his head, hoping no one was paying him any attention. "I will not," he muttered. "I don't know any of them. Be quiet and listen." Why was he arguing with a dream?

She cast him a smoldering glance. "Why are you actin' the high-up gent here? I come from these people and I know them. James Roarity is a traitor and he's going to get Brian killed. Why won't you believe me?"

As the priest continued to talk and introduce the mine owner's negotiators, Tom took the opportunity to slowly back away from the crowd. She followed him, just as he had hoped.

"Now you listen to me," he said when the rest of the townspeople were behind him. "You're not going to be telling me what to do here. This is my dream. I don't even know why you're in it. You may be acquainted with these people, maybe you're supposed to be my guide, but you won't be giving me orders. Don't you realize they would have turned on me, even your brother? I'm the outsider here. I can't tell them that there is a traitor without any proof, except the word of an invisible woman!"

Her bottom lip ceased to tremble. "Then you're going to have to get to know my Brian, earn his trust so he'll take your word. I can't save him, Thomas. Only you can."

It was too dramatic for a dream, yet he found himself saying, "What do you want me to do?"

She smiled at him and his heart melted with the sweetness of her lips.

"You're a fine figure of a man, Thomas. The first thing you have to do is get through Fitzhugh's Tap Room. And I'll be helping you there."

"Keep walking."

He could feel the suspicion in more than a dozen pairs of eyes as he made his way through the old-fashioned bar. There was a barber shop in back, yet most men wore hats as they sat at long tables and played checkers or dominoes. Even though it was summer, the old men's rounded shoulders were wrapped in shawls. They were gray-looking, as if little life remained inside them, and he tried very hard not to stare as he listened to Meggie's command and walked up to the long wooden bar.

"Tell him you'll have a pint," she said, looking over the bar to Timmy Fitzhugh. "Don't drop your gaze, Thomas, that's what he's waiting for. Go ahead, tell him you'll have a pint of his best ale."

Tom tried to smile. "I'll have a pint of your best."

Fitzhugh glared at him. "My best what?"

"Your best ale," Tom said, beginning to get annoyed by the attitude of the bartender.

"A man ought to say what he wants then. I've never been known to read minds before."

"And tell him you didn't expect it now," Meggie answered, anger creeping into her voice. "Tell him you didn't mean to put him out none."

"I didn't mean to put you out none," Tom repeated

115

in a much calmer voice. "I was merely thirsty." He wanted to tell Meggie not to be so upset, for she was confusing him. He was finding it hard to tell what was said in an earnest attempt to help, or what was a reaction to her anger.

The bartender drew a pint of ale and placed it before him. Tom picked it up and sipped at the brew. It was far stronger than the beer he was used to and he had to stop himself from deeply exhaling.

"You're new here."

It wasn't a question, yet Tom nodded. "Came in this morning. From the discussion in front of the church, it seems I showed up at a good time. Looks like the mines will be open again."

Timmy Fitzhugh kept staring at him, as if he was ready to pick a fight. "Aren't you the lucky beggar then? They'll be hirin' for sure now."

Tom noticed two men slowly walk up on either side of him and nod to the bartender. Without a word, the man brought two more pints and set them before the newcomers. Chancing a glance toward Meggie, Tom could see the adoration as she gazed up at the taller one. So this was Brian, the one looking at him with such suspicion, such distrust. He could see the resemblance to Meggie now that he looked closer. It was in the eyes and around the mouth.

"Where are ya from then?" Brian asked while staring into the mirror behind the bar.

Meggie said, "Tell them you're from Ashland."

"Ashland," Tom repeated.

"Then you'd be knowing the O'Flarretys?"

Meggie grinned up at her brother. "He's trying to trick you, Thomas. Tell him you know the Doyles, Michael in particular. Go ahead. Just shrug, as if —"

Tom shrugged and interrupted Meggie, "I can't say that I know them." He picked up his mug of beer

116

and took another sip. "It was Michael Doyle that suggested I try Lehigha."

"Michael, huh?" Brian asked. "As red-haired as a fox, I remember."

Again Meggie smiled at her brother. "Tell him Michael is as gray as a badger."

Tom also grinned. He found that he was enjoying the challenge and answered with an infectious lilt of an Irish accent, "Why I believe old Michael is as gray as a badger. You must be thinking about someone else."

Great dream, he thought. Maybe it could be fun at that.

Suddenly, without any warning at all, the man on Tom's left grabbed him from behind, pinning his arms back as he laced his large hands around Tom's neck. "Hey! What's this?"

Brian captured Tom's right hand in a deadly grip and examined it. "Hands as soft as a woman's. Never been in the mines in your life. Your shoes are brand new, and the thread on your coat is still wet. Now why would Michael be sendin' ya? Or are you perhaps sent by another? Maybe in the employ of Mr. Nate Gowen? Be right useful to find out what the little people are plannin', now wouldn't it?"

Tom had no time to form an answer as Brian's huge fist connected with his cheek. Arrows of pain shot through Tom's nose and eyes as if stabbed by a hot poker. His legs buckled and he heard Meggie's moan as he slowly crumpled to the floor.

"Ahh . . . Jesus, Mary, and Joseph, Brian! Do ya always have to be using your fist? Will you never use your head first?" Glaring at her brother, Meggie shook her own head in dismay as she reached down to assist Tom.

"I'm sorry about this, Thomas," she apologized as

she helped him to stand. "He's really a sweet boy, a wee bit pigheaded, but then all the Irish are."

Tom looked about him wildly, unable to believe that any dream could hurt as much as his face did. The other patrons of the tap room had left their games and were observing him, only mildly interested in the obvious outcome of the altercation. His gaze fell upon Meggie and he whispered, "Just shut up and get me out of here."

"What're ya mumbling there, boyo? Ready to tell us the truth yet?"

"You'll have to fight him, Thomas."

He stared at her as if she'd lost her mind. He hadn't had a fist fight with anyone since high school! Wasn't that what maturity was all about? Finding reasonable solutions to such problems? How the hell do you get out of a dream? This one's becoming too real, too—

He never had time to finish his thought as another huge fist smashed into his belly, doubling him over until he was down again on one knee. This time he thought he might throw up, but his face hurt too much.

"You've got to get up, Thomas, and fight back. I'll help, if I can . . ."

He wanted to murder her. She was the one who had gotten him into this. It was her idea to enter the damn place. Suddenly, from somewhere long buried, Tom felt a rage begin. The adrenalin started pumping, the heart started pounding, and the wealthy gentleman of Wall Street was lost as the kid from Medford, Delaware, took over. He was seventeen again, powerful, potent, and this time he had a secret weapon.

"Hold his fucking right arm," he muttered to Meggie as he stood up and faced her brother. Waiting until she had done as she was told, he saw the surprise on Brian's face. It was all he needed.

With everything in his power, Tom summoned his strength and pulled back his fist. He felt a growl in his throat as he released his arm and smiled as his knuckles smashed into Brian's nose. He hoped he broke it, but was afraid that his own fist might be damaged by the impact.

Brian staggered and Meggie stood at his side, her hands over her mouth as blood started to seep out of her brother's nose.

"Ahh, Brian," she moaned in a sorrowful voice, "forgive me . . ."

Tom sputtered in anger. She wanted *him* to forgive her? It was unbelievable! He looked to the other man who had held his arms and saw that the fight was to be between him and Brian. Satisfied that there would be no further interference, Tom pulled back his arm and hit Meggie's brother in the gut. A feeling of supreme satisfaction permeated his system as Brian Gillbride was brought to his knees beneath the bar.

"Woman's hands, huh?" Tom straightened his jacket and would have wiped his palms together in the age-old gesture of finality, except his right hand hurt like a sonofabitch. It had to be broken! He could see a green bruise already starting beneath his knuckles.

"Why did you hit him again? You already bloodied his nose. Wasn't that enough for you?" Meggie was wringing the front of her nightgown together in frustration. "Now just look at him. And here I am, like some ghost, unable to even help."

He wanted to tell her to leave him alone to savor his victory, but too many eyes were watching his every movement. He couldn't have cared less if her

119

brother never breathed through his nose again. Slowly, carefully, he sidestepped Brian and the man who was helping him to stand, and picked up his pint. Using his left hand, Tom brought the ale to a table and sat down. This time his back was to the wall.

"Now," he said in a deceptively calm voice. "I've come from Ashland to look for work. Does anyone else in here have a problem with that?"

"I have a problem," Mcggie said as she tore her gaze away from her brother. Brian was using his handkerchief to stop the flow of blood.

Tom ignored her as he stared back at the men in the tap room. She was a nag. He almost felt sorry for Brian, if he'd had to listen to her constant interference.

"There you sit," she continued, "actin' the high-up lord because you've broken a poor man's nose. And you, that has the mouth of a corner boy. In my life, I've never heard such filthy expressions. You'll be minding your mouth around me from now on." She had one hand on her hip, as if she were his mother giving him a severe reprimand. Or an eighth grade nun . . .

Meggie Gillbride, or Sister Margaret Mary? It made no difference to him. Right now she was an annoyance, and he wanted her to know who was controlling this . . . dream. He gave her his fiercest glare and watched with satisfaction as her hand dropped to her side. She stood up straighter, though her chin still lifted in defiance. He'd allow her that.

Looking beyond her to her brother he said, "If you pinch the bridge of your nose and hold your head back for a few minutes, it'll stop bleeding."

Brian didn't answer him, but he could see that the taller man was taking his advice. Tom tried flexing his right hand and winced at the pain. Again using his left, he sipped the ale. It actually tasted good now. Just took a little getting used to the bitter taste. Despite the fact that his cheekbone felt shattered, his hand seemed broken, and his midsection was still burning, Thomas Grey Carter had never felt better in his life — Especially when Brian Gillbride got up, walked over to his table, and pulled out the chair opposite him.

Still holding the sodden handkerchief to his nose, Brian reached out across the unpolished wood and held out his hand. "You never did say what your name was."

Tom returned his glance. "Tom. Thomas Grey Carter."

"English?"

Tom smiled, even though it hurt. "Irish, on my mother's side. McKenna."

Meggie's brother grinned. "Brian Gillbride. Welcome to the patch."

Standing off to one side, Meggie sniffled and wiped her eyes with the sleeve of her nightgown. She couldn't remember a lovelier sight. Her brother and her angel. Never were there two finer men in all of Lehigha. And they were both hers.

It was a grand display, indeed.

# Chapter 9

"You're drunk!" Supporting his shoulder, Meggie helped him walk behind the row of houses on Center Street. He was leaning on her so heavily that she was sure Thomas must appear deformed to anyone who happened to look out their back windows. All they'd see is one very drunk man, stumbling along, with one shoulder much higher than the other.

"Did you see how poor everyone is, Meg?" he muttered. "I saw children today that hadn't any shoes. Imagine . . ." Tom shook his head with sorrow, while trying to disguise a drunken belch. "It's the children," he went on, "always paying for the mistakes of adults."

"Did you think I was struck blind in the last day?" she demanded. "I've lived my life in this patch. Besides, it's summer. The children will be saving their shoes for Mass tomorrow morning."

She tightened her grip on his waist. "Now for you . . . shame on you, Thomas. Drinking yourself to the edge with Brian. As if either one of you was in any condition to begin with. The two of you — like two old sots! And me, havin' to hear the braggin' and —"

"Leave off with your nagging, woman," he slurred, sharply inhaling from the ache in his cheek. He'd heard a man in the bar tell that to his wife and it sounded like the right thing to say now. "Can't you understand I'm in pain."

"You're too ignorant to feel pain."

He stopped abruptly and tried to focus his eyes on her. "Ignorant? I'll have you know that I graduated summa cum laude from a very prestigious school. Ahh . . . ? Wait a minute, it'll come to me."

She clucked her tongue in disgust and prodded him further. "Oh, you're a fine educated gentleman, all right. And how are we supposed to get you into Bridget Humne's with that ale on your breath and you actin' the fool?"

"It was Dartmouth! I knew I'd remember." He was grinning at her, the silliest expression on his bruised face. "Meggie? Isn't your brother a terrific guy?"

She gazed up at him. Despite the black and blue mark on his swollen cheek, he looked young and happy. And she fought with herself not to lift her mouth to his. Maybe he wouldn't even remember. Instead, she took a deep breath and said, "Isn't that just like a man? First you break someone's nose and then you treat him like he's your boyhood buddy. I'll never understand the breed of you."

"I don't believe his nose is broken," Tom offered, bringing his fingers up before his eyes. "But I think my hand is." He winced as he tried to flex it.

"Go on with you," Meggie said as she dragged him another few steps. "You'd better take a couple of deep breaths and watch what you say because here's old Bridget's. And if you don't want to sleep under the stars tonight, you'll straighten up."

The mention of sleep made Tom stand more erect and push the hair back from his eyes. He wanted that bed in Bridget's. Desperately.

They stood before an old home and Meggie said, "Now knock. Lightly. And be polite. I'll tell you what to say. Stand up straight."

Tom smiled when the old woman opened the door.

"Tell her good day. And you've come about the room."

He blinked several times. "Good day. I've come about the room."

Old Bridget looked down to his feet and said, "I see you've got yourself a pair of shoes. Do you have the money also?"

"Tell her you do."

"I do."

Bridget nodded. "Will you be payin' by the night or by the week?"

Tom waited until Meggie said, "Tell her you'll take it for the week."

He looked to Meggie. "The week?" He didn't expect the dream to last that long.

The old woman opened her door wider. "The week then. It'll be one dollar and fifty cents for room and board, paid up until next Sunday. I already spent this morning cleaning up the spare room. You've missed lunch, you know. But I'll be makin' a stew tonight for supper, since you'll be paying me in advance, thank you very much."

"I will?" He felt totally confused.

"Lordy Jesus!" Meggie hissed. "Reach into your pocket and get out the dollar and fifty cent pieces. Must I do everything?" Without another warning, she did just that.

Tom quickly inhaled at the touch of her hand

124

fumbling around in his pocket and he immediately reached down to stop her. She placed the money in his palm and swiftly withdrew her hand from his trousers. Her cheeks were flaming with embarrassment as she looked away from him. Breathing heavily, he handed the money to Bridget, who was looking at him as if he'd just had some sort of fit. It didn't help matters that Meggie again called him a drunken sot and he stumbled into the house as she pushed him from behind. She was far more polite in his New York City apartment, he thought as he braced himself against a wall and glared at the younger woman in the nightgown, while trying to smile at the older one. In this dream, Margaret Mary Gillbride was a real pain in the—

"Follow me up the stairs," Bridget ordered in her kind, yet firm voice. "I'll be givin' you my John's room."

"John?" Tom asked. He didn't want to be sharing a room with another.

"God rest his soul. He was killed in the breakers when he was but twelve years old."

"Her son," Meggie whispered. "She's grieved ever since."

Bridget opened the door to a small, but surprisingly cheery room with a window that overlooked the mountain. "I trust you'll be comfortable here," she said. "There'll be no shoes on the bed, and you'll wash up outside if you're even thinkin' about workin' the mines. Which might be soon, now that Father Andrew is helpin' to settle this strike." She smiled. "Maybe you brought us luck, Thomas Grey Carter McKenna."

"My last name is Carter, not McKenna."

"No offense. I like your mother's name better."

He was finding it hard to stay upright with the

bed so near, yet he straightened his shoulders and said in a surprisingly sober voice, "But my name happens to be Carter."

"Ah well, we can't all be blessed with proper names, now can we?" Without waiting for an answer, she added, "Would you like me to bring your supper up here?"

He nodded.

Bridget grinned and made a point of looking at his bruises for the first time. "I can see you've had a very busy day gettin' acquainted and all. I thought you might want to rest."

"I would," Tom agreed, casting a longing glance toward the bed. "Thank you, Bridget."

"I just want you to know that I don't hold with any fisticuffs in this house, or in my yard either. While you're here, you'll act the gentleman or you'll be lookin' for a room elsewhere."

Feeling twelve years old, Tom answered, "Yes, ma'am."

He didn't even hear the door shut behind her. Just Meggie's soft whisper . . .

"You can lie down now. She's gone."

He collapsed onto the soft mattress and groaned in pain as his hand once more throbbed. "I know it's broken." He cradled his fingers to his chest and shut his eyes.

Sitting on the edge of the mattress, Meggie said, "Not if it's as thick as your head. Here, let me see it." She gently took his hand in hers and examined it.

"Well, it's bruised all right, but I don't think it's broken." Without looking at him she gently laid his hand back on his chest and added, "Would serve you right, though, for what you did to Brian."

He opened his eyes. "That was survival. Your

126

brother was beating the hell out of me."

She grinned. "He was, wasn't he?"

Tom scowled at her then lowered her lids, as if they were too heavy to keep open. He heard the sound of material being ripped and of water being poured, but was too exhausted to investigate. It wasn't until he felt the soothing coolness on his cheek that he looked at her.

"I don't know what else to do for you," she said in a soft voice after placing the cold compress on his bruised cheekbone.

He watched her rip another length of white cotton ruffle from the bottom of her nightgown and dip it into the water that Bridget had left. Wringing it out, she leisurely walked over to him and sat at his side.

"It's a good thing tomorrow is Sunday, for you'd never be able to work with this hand," she said as she wrapped it in the cold linen.

"What are you talking about? I'm not going to work here."

She looked up at him with surprise. "But you said— You told everyone that you were looking for work in the mines."

He issued a weak, tired laugh. "That was just the story you made up, Meggie. You couldn't have seriously thought that I would work down in a mine. This is a dream. It isn't reality."

"You think it's a dream, do you?" she demanded, a look of disappointment crossing her face. "What about the pain you feel? How about your hand, blowing up as it is like a dead fish? Or the way you can feel hunger? And what about getting as drunk as a Dublin sotty? When was the last time you were inebriated in a dream, I ask you?"

Closing his eyes, Tom shook his head. "Why

won't you leave me alone? I just want to sleep. I can't make sense out of this. I did everything you told me to do, now I need rest." His voice became more low as his words trailed off.

Quickly opening his eyes to make sure she was still there, he muttered, "Don't be angry with me, Meggie." His lips formed a silly, drunken smile. "You're much nicer like this, you know. More human." He released his breath in a tired sigh. "I wish you weren't a nun."

"I told you. I'm not."

His eyelids fluttered closed. "I'm glad. Glad you're not a nun. "You're too pretty . . . too . . . ornery . . ."

His breathing slowed and she could see that he was asleep. Now it was safe. Her fingers reached up, hesitantly at first, then more bravely, as she slowly brushed back the soft auburn hair from his forehead. She had wanted to touch it from the very first time she had seen him in the airship. Then he had been in charge, full of authority and wisdom, knowing how to handle every situation. But here, in her time, he was near lost, and she felt protective toward this man. She smiled as she gazed at him. He looked so young, almost innocent. "You've had a very full day—haven't you, Thomas?"

She didn't expect an answer. He was fast asleep from exhaustion, with a bit of help from the buckets of ale he and Brian had downed. Brian liked him and Meggie was glad, even if both men would wear bruises for days. She slowly let out her breath and shook her head in dismay. Men! She would never understand their ways. And Thomas thought it was all a dream. Maybe he was right, for there was no answer forthcoming as to what had happened. But whose dream was it?

Hers?

Or his?

It had to be hers, for the longer she looked at him, the more she realized that only in her imagination could this man come into her life. Maybe she was dreaming now, in her own tiny home on Maple Street. Maybe Brian was in the back room sleeping and none of it had happened—not the explosion, nor any of the incredible things she'd experienced from the future. And maybe this man wasn't even real and they weren't here together in Bridget Humne's upstairs bedroom.

What if none of it were real?

A tightness began in her belly that had nothing to do with her hunger. She couldn't have imagined it all! He was real! The tips of her fingers traveled down his temple and traced the outline of his mouth. His lips twitched, as if tickled, then again relaxed as he settled back to sleep. When was the last time she had touched a man so intimately? A mental picture of Terry Nolan entered her mind and she quickly shook her head to drive him out. She didn't want to remember him, had promised herself never again to do so, but he crept back in and she found herself caught up in a web of painful memories.

Terrence Nolan had the most beautiful smile she had ever seen. And she used to see it often. He was a young man blessed with an even temperament and a quick sense of humor. And Terry had loved to make her laugh . . .

Meggie's eyes began to burn as she thought back to the man she had first allowed into her heart. He was twenty-six when she met him, and he had just come to Lehigha as an inspector. It was a fine job, above ground, and Brian had been impressed. Brian had put in a good word for him at home and even the old fellow, sick though he was, welcomed the newcomer at their table. Meggie had known right away that Terry's interest in her was more than friendly, for he pursued her with a vengeance. All with the approval of her father and brother. She couldn't turn around when he'd come to visit without finding him in front of her, telling her silly stories about the places he'd been and making her laugh. She thought she was in love, though she wasn't truly old enough to see it for what it really was. She thought he was going to marry her. So did Brian and Da. Everything was taken for granted. Nobody expected Terry Nolan to disappear into the night when she told him she was pregnant. Especially Meggie. Left alone to deal with her brother and father, she withstood the condemnation. She'd dealt with her family, defied the town biddies, endured the ridicule, and closed her heart to any other man. For who would want her? She had brought disgrace to her family and she could bring nothing of any value to a man. She was forever to remain barren. She had nothing to offer anyone.

Except now, as she watched Thomas sleep, something long buried began to stir once more. Who would it hurt? Who would ever know? And the years had been so very long, and lonely . . . Bending down, she softly allowed her lips to touch his. It was so forward, almost bold, that she could sense a blush creep up from her throat. Yet it was only a mere grazing, a moment when she felt his breath upon her like a soft caress. It was as she'd expected and she permitted herself a few seconds of pleasure as the sweetness raced through her body. Lifting her head, she stared at him and smiled. He would never know, but for this moment in time she

130

would admit it to herself.

She was falling in love with her angel. As she wiped the tears away from her eyes, her gaze took in his bruises, her nose picked up the scent of ale, and her smile became tender. A tarnished, slightly drunk angel? No. Meggie knew she was falling in love with the man.

And that frightened her.

She had no idea how long she remained on the edge of the mattress, staring at him, memorizing every feature, for fear he'd suddenly disappear. It was only when she heard Bridget's soft knock that she stirred and turned to the door as the old woman peeked her head in to look.

Meggie smiled, although she knew she couldn't be seen. Bridgi had been good to her over the years and Meggie could never remember a harsh word directed toward her by the woman.

When the old one saw that Thomas was asleep, she placed the tray on a nearby table and quietly walked out while muttering something about the similarity between grown men and children. Meggie loved the impertinent and cheeky way that was all Bridget Humne. The woman didn't fear a single soul, including Father Andrew, and that had endeared her to Meggie. It wasn't that Bridgi was anticlerical, far from it. It was just that the woman had strong opinions and considered hers to be as important as any man's. Maybe it came from living on her own these many years.

Sniffing the air, Meggie's stomach grumbled. Suddenly it came to her that she'd had nothing to eat except an apple this morning. She was starved. And Thomas was asleep. He probably wouldn't waken until morning.

It really would be a shame to let the food go to

waste. And then, everyone knew what a fine cook old Bridgi was . . .

Her mind made up, she walked over to the table and lifted the linen away from a small basket. The delicious aroma of freshly baked biscuits rose through the air and it was all Meggie needed. She was surprised her moans of pleasure didn't wake up Thomas, for who remembered the last time anyone had the luxury of this much food? Bridgi was lucky to cook for the men who guarded the mines during the strike, she thought, licking her lips as she tasted the stew. The strike had made beggars out of more than one family. It was a good sign that Gowen himself wanted a settlement. It seemed the explosion had accomplished something after all.

She looked back to the man sleeping on the bed and listened to his snoring. What was it he had said? Something about the children and their shoes. She remembered. His heart was touched by the sight of the young ones and the deprivation they had to endure because of the strike. She looked at the new boots she had lifted for Thomas and the glimmer of an idea started in her brain. She continued to eat, letting her thoughts grow, until finally she threw back her head and laughed.

She'd be making a few more trips to the Reading's General Store. Poor Martin Dunlap. Wait until he tries explaining his suddenly depleted shelves to his superiors. Her grin widened as she imagined his plight.

She couldn't wait. She'd make this night special. It would be like Christmas in July.

Five hours later Meggie wearily made her way back into the bedroom of Bridget's home. She was exhausted from her adventure, but what a time she'd had. Shoes were secretly placed by children's beds and clothing distributed to needy families. Even a few frivolous items were included, such as books and pictures and faux jewelry. She had been surprised at the amount of goods kept in the back storeroom and had felt less guilty by disposing of some of them.

Just as she had thought, Thomas was still sleeping as sound as a babe. Meggie looked down to her nightgown and grimaced. She was a mess, but there was nothing to be done. Refusing to sleep on the floor, she eyed the mattress. Did she really care about what was proper anymore? Too tired to do anything else, she crawled over to the bottom of the bed and folded her arm under her head.

It was peaceful and dark, and even the warmth of the summer evening didn't bother her. Closing her eyes, Meggie allowed a smile. She couldn't wait to hear how the patch was going to handle their unexpected windfall. There really was going to be a Christmas in July. And she'd made it happen.

It was the headache that woke him. That and the fact that his mouth tasted like an army had done precision drills inside it. Blinking in the sunlight, he groaned as he turned over onto his side. The last thing he needed was the glare of the sun off the mirror.

The mirror? But why was he in the guest room? Immediately his eyes opened as he felt the presence of another in the bed. Taking a deep breath, he ignored the shooting pain behind his lids as he looked toward the bottom of the mattress.

"Oh my God," he whispered, staring at the mass

of red hair, the long curving expanse of thigh and calf. She was there, curled up by his feet. He'd slept with a nun!

Maybe he could slip out of the room before she woke. Desperate, he tried to push himself off the mattress, but gasped aloud at the sudden pain in his right hand. It didn't help matters that Sister Margaret stirred, purred, and stretched her arms over her head as she woke up.

They stared at one another in confusion.

Of course, he thought, he'd come in last night to comfort her after she'd had that nightmare. It was the fireworks.

What are we doing here? Meggie silently questioned as panic began to set in. Why were they back in this room? In New York City?

"I must have fallen asleep," he muttered, not sure why she was looking at him with such horror.

"We both did," she whispered. "But look where we woke up!"

His eyes narrowed. What was she saying? It was as if she was talking about his crazy dream. And that was impossible. As real as it had seemed, it was merely an embarrassing episode that had taken place in his subconscious.

"I don't understand," he offered. "I came in here last night because you were having a nightmare. Don't you remember? It was the fireworks."

She sat up and pushed herself off the bed, as if suddenly aware that her gown had ridden up her legs. "You don't remember?"

"Remember what?" he asked, wondering why his face hurt so much.

She pointed to him. "Look in the mirror."

He glanced toward the mirror and then back at her. It was only to satisfy himself as to what was causing the tightness in his cheek that he walked over to the glass. Standing before it, his heart suddenly started hammering inside his chest, his mouth opened in shock as he brought his hand up before his face. It was swollen and bruised—just like in the dream!

"My God! What the hell is going on?"

# Chapter 10

He stared at her through the mirror. Her expression showed her fear. Again, he looked back to his own reflection. He was battered. The left side of his face was swollen and black and blue. No wonder it hurt even to speak. He glanced down to his hand, cradled at his waist as if broken.

"What happened to me?" His head ached and something told him it was from drinking. But if that were so . . .

"Don't you remember?" Her voice sounded frightened.

He stared back at her. "You tell me." There wasn't any way she could possibly tell him about the dream.

"You fought with my brother. Brian."

He swung around to face her. "What are you saying?" he demanded. "How could you know that? I dreamt—it was all a dream . . . a subconscious—"

"I was there, Thomas."

He didn't care that she backed away from him in fright. This was insane. This sort of thing didn't happen in his life—didn't happen in anyone's life that he knew about. It wasn't possible that she should know what took place in his dreams!

"What do you mean you were there? Who are you?" He advanced on her until her back was against the wall. She looked like a cornered rabbit, and it didn't matter that she was shaking with fear. "What are you?" he demanded with a low growl, "Some sort of witch?"

She stared back at him, wanting to cry but refusing to do so. Swallowing down her fear, she attempted to speak. "I—well, you see, I'm not sure how it happens."

His face was inches from her own and she could see the fury building up in his eyes. "How what happens?" he challenged.

"How we—we went back to Lehigha and Fitzhugh's tap room and met Brian and—"

"My God!" He nearly yelled at her before turning away to pace in front of the bed. "Wait a minute. My cheek feels shattered. What happened?" he hissed while waving his good hand. "There has to be an explanation here. You told me about those places, didn't you?"

"I don't think so—"

"You must have," he interrupted, running his fingers through his hair. "You just don't remember, but you had to have told me. I mean—how else?" He shrugged, as though any other explanation wasn't worth discussing.

"Thomas."

She said his name and watched as he abruptly stopped pacing. Standing quite still, he slowly turned around to face her, a look of astonishment on his features.

She smiled, suddenly feeling more secure. After all, this was the first time it had happened to him but she had done this before. It wasn't quite as frightening for her. "Thomas, we woke up in a field outside of Lehigha. On the way into town we met Bridget Humne, and you later rented a room from her. We heard Father Andrew at the church talk about an end to the strike. Then, you went into Fitzhugh's and met my brother Brian."

She nodded to his hand. "You also nearly broke my brother's nose and then proceeded to get drunk with him."

His mouth hung open in shock, yet she continued, determined to get it all out. "You made it to Bridgi's and then passed out. I went back to the Reading store, distributed some things to a few people, then fell asleep at the bottom of your bed. When we awoke, it was here. I don't know how it happens. I only know I can't control it."

"What do you mean you went back to the Reading store? Are you saying that you went back there to steal more things?"

She shrugged, not prepared to answer that question. She had thought he would have asked about something else, like Bridgi or Brian's nose. "You wouldn't believe how much they have in the storeroom. Besides, wasn't it you that said the poor children could use new shoes and such?"

It was his turn to back away from her. "You are a witch! How else could you know those things. It was only a dream."

"It wasn't a dream, Thomas."

He pointed his finger at her, as if in accusation. "You—you're either a witch, involved in voodoo and spells, or . . . or you drugged me." He started nodding rapidly, suddenly satisfied with a logical answer. He was an intelligent man, after all, and unexplainable happenings were just not acceptable. There was always an answer. Like drugs. "That's it, isn't it? You put something in my food."

"You prepared the soup and salad for dinner last night. I didn't touch it."

She could see his mind was searching for another explanation.

"Then what about breakfast? You had my kitchen turned into a disaster area. You could have slipped something into—"

"I didn't do anything like that, Thomas," she interrupted. "And you know it. I am not a witch, and I know nothing of spells or potions to drug someone. I'm lost. Can't you understand that?"

He didn't answer her. Somehow, she knew he couldn't find any words to express the fear in his heart. Hadn't she felt the same way on the airship? Maybe it was time to reveal a few things; she decided to keep speaking.

"I was in an explosion, in my time, and the next thing I knew I was sitting beside you in that airship. I actually thought you were an angel, sent to guide me and that's why I followed you here. I thought you had deserted me. That's why I didn't know anything. Weren't you curious? Didn't you wonder why I seemed so in this time?"

She could see he was at least attempting to consider her words, as if the idea, the very notion might be possible. He kept blinking, staring at her and waiting for her next sentence.

She took a deep breath and continued, "You were in my time. Eighteen seventy-five. In Lehigha. You met my brother, my friend, Bridget Humne. Don't you see? *You* returned, instead of me! They can't see me there. To them, I'm dead! I don't exist in my own time . . . only in yours."

He kept staring, blinking rapidly and taking deep breaths. Finally, he said, "I think you'd better leave.

I don't know how you did it—I don't know if you brought someone in here to beat me to a pulp and I don't want to know. I just want to be left alone. I want you, Sister Margaret, or whoever you are, to go back—"

"I can't! Don't you think I would if I could? Don't you think I'd want to be with Brian?"

He seemed to gather his strength about him. "No, I don't. Why would anyone want to live there? Maybe it had its charm when there wasn't a strike, but right now the patch is depressing—"

And then he stopped, his mouth still open, yet no sound coming out.

"How would you know that if you weren't there?" she asked quietly, her eyes filling with tears. "It was your words about the sorry plight of the children that made me think I could do something for them by slipping back into the store. You were there, Thomas. In the patch. The same as me."

He was shaking his head, not wanting to believe her. How could it be possible? How could she have entered his dreams? There was something else to this, something that terrified him. He was either drugged, or . . . *It can't be possible!* But what other answer was there? He'd been injured in a fight, a fight with her brother. And he had a hangover from drinking with her brother. He remembered . . .

"You're called Meggie," he said slowly. "And you aren't really a nun, are you?"

She wasn't sure what to say. "I'm called Meggie," she said, trying to look him in the eye.

"But you're a novitiate, right?"

He sounded so earnest, as though trying to remember her words. She only had moments to question whether or not she should give him an honest

140

answer. But he already had so much to absorb . . .

"I haven't made my mind up yet about final vows," she said in a low voice, hoping God wasn't going to strike her for continuing the lie.

Thomas seemed satisfied by her response. "I also remember you saying that you thought I was going to work in the mines. With your brother."

She smiled, glad to be on another subject. "See," she remarked, "you are remembering. We were there, Thomas, back in the patch. We fell asleep in this time and woke up in another."

"And you can't be seen in your time. I wonder if . . ." He tore out of the bedroom and she followed, not sure what he was about to do. He seemed determined and didn't stop until he'd reached the all-white drawing room where they had watched the fireworks. And then he picked up that apparatus. The one that had made the ringing noises.

"Ben? Sorry to call you so early on a Sunday morning but do you think you might come up here?" She listened to his hurried words and knew he was talking to the doctor. "What? No, she's fine. I think. It's me. You see, I was—that is, I was in a fist fight and I—" He winced, as if being scolded. "Yes, Ben. You heard correctly. A fist fight, with a huge person. If I remember correctly, when I retaliated, it was like hitting the trunk of a tree, a big tree." He glanced down to his cradled palm. "I think I broke my hand." There was another pause. "All right. Thanks."

He turned to her. "He's coming." Without waiting for an answer, Tom resumed his pacing—this time in front of the window. "I've established that he can hear me. Now if he can see me, as well, then I'm okay."

"Do you know what you're saying?" she asked,

141

studying him, noticing the speculative glint in his eyes. "You're saying that you believe me."

He stopped pacing and stared at her. "I'm not saying anything," he stated in an emphatic voice. "Not yet. Not until I've checked up on a few things."

She nodded, understanding perfectly why he was waiting to pass judgment. She just wondered what kind of checking up he was going to be able to do. Did they have information on this sort of thing? And did she really want to know?

"Are you sure you weren't mugged?" Ben Tankor asked while wrapping Tom's hand. He'd already treated the bruised cheek and he had to admit Tom Carter looked like hell. For the first time the dynamic entrepreneur appeared less than in control. On the one hand it was reassuring that Tom was human. On the other, it was intriguing, to say the least. Who, or what, had Thomas Gray Carter come up against?

"I wasn't mugged. I told you. I was in a fight." Tom watched as his friend taped his hand. "You're sure it isn't broken?"

Ben sighed in exasperation. "If you would come with me to the hospital and have it x-rayed, then I would be completely sure. Since you've refused, I can only say that I'm almost certain it's just badly bruised." Ripping off the end of the tape, he added, "between you and Sister Margaret here, I've practiced more general medicine in the last two days than I have in the last two years."

"Her name is Meggie."

Ben looked up at his friend, then glanced across the room to the shy woman who was clutching the front of her robe, as if embarrassed to be the subject of discussion. He smiled at her. "How does your head feel . . . Meggie?" He felt a bit foolish calling her by her first name. After all, he was the one who had unbuttoned her headdress when she was injured. And she had most certainly looked like a nun to him.

"Meggie is in her novitiate year at the convent. She hasn't yet made up her mind about her final vows." Tom lifted his chin and looked across the room to her. "Have you?"

She shook her head and appeared embarrassed by the question. "No, I haven't. Not yet."

Tom Carter had numerous acquaintances throughout the world, but Ben Tankor counted himself among Tom's small circle of friends, people that could be trusted. He'd watched Tom end a marriage and bury himself in his work. But he'd never seen that look of hunger in his eyes as when his young friend had been staring at the woman across the room. Closing his medical bag, Ben could almost feel sorry for them both. Clearly, whatever Tom felt for this woman, Meggie, was obviously too new for him to hide. He doubted if Tom was even aware of it yet. Glancing at the lovely Irish-looking woman, Ben smiled and wondered if it wasn't a totally helpless situation. They were nothing alike; there was no common ground between them. One was worldly, maybe even jaded, and the other was sheltered and naive. But then she smiled back, a lovely brilliant smile, and Ben found himself silently cheering Tom on. He hoped his friend could talk her out of becoming a nun. Watching her walk up to Tom, Ben thought it would be a shame to hide a woman such as Meggie.

"C'mon. Let's go."

Meggie pulled back from him, all the while conscious of the uniformed guards watching her. "I'm afraid, Thomas. Everything is . . . so strange," she whispered. Once more, she peeked at the splendor of the lobby. "I don't know if I can do this."

She was self-conscious, dressed as she was in the modern clothes, and she felt masculine wearing the trousers. Even if they were meant for females, they were still a man's attire—not a woman's. And Thomas, well, Thomas looked to be blind with those large dark spectacles that hid his eyes—even if they did partially conceal the bruise on his cheek. None of it felt right. She hated to admit that she felt more comfortable in Lehigha, safer. Even if she couldn't be seen.

Taking hold of her elbow, Tom quickly ushered her outside and into the sunlight. "There," he pronounced. "You've done it. And you didn't melt."

"I don't understand, why would I melt?"

"It's a joke."

"Oh . . ." Meggie's mouth opened in shock as she saw in the daylight what she had only glimpsed on the night she had come to this time. People dressed in the strangest costumes brushed past her. Some women were in attire that looked more suited for bathing than walking on a street. Their legs were showing clear up to their . . . Well, anyway, one would think that a lady would dress more modestly. Unless, of course, they weren't. She gasped, clearly fascinated by the possibility.

"They're called shorts." He nodded to the retreating figure of a woman and bit his lip to keep from smiling. "And I agree that they are more appropriately worn outside the city, unless, of course, you're exercising or . . . never mind."

Meggie had already forgotten about the women as she gaped at the passing crowd. Men in garish clothing were carrying large boxes on their shoulders, and the boxes blared a strange-sounding music that seemed to influence the way they walked. It was odd.

Laughing, Tom pulled her across the lanes of traffic, past the cars on Fifty-ninth Street, and toward the Grand Army Plaza. He stopped in front of a large bronze statue and waited as she read the inscription.

"Isn't it grand?" she breathed, looking up at a statue of General William Tecumseh Sherman. The great general was seated on a horse, looking out over the city. A winged woman held a palm leaf in her hand, as if leading him toward peace. "February 8, 1820, to February 14, 1891," she read aloud. "This was erected after—"

Tom gazed down at her. "After your time."

"I don't understand. Do you believe me now?"

He took her wrist and led her past the memorial. "I don't know what to believe anymore. And until I can check out a few facts—"

"What facts?" she interrupted as they came up to a long expanse of books displayed on tables that bordered the sidewalk. A sign said STRAND BOOKSTORE. Striped canvas awnings hung over the books for protection, and Meggie was reminded of a gypsy caravan that would close up and disappear with the night.

He didn't let go of her wrist as he searched the tables, turning books on their sides as he read the titles. "I'd like some information on parapsychology," he said to the old man behind a table piled two feet high with publications.

Nodding, the man with rounded shoulders escorted them three tables down and entered into a discussion with Thomas. Meggie, not knowing what parapsychology was, or what they were talking about, let her gaze take in the spectacular vista before her. Young boys were walking dogs, some holding as many as six leashes, yet somehow keeping the animals under control. Women passed her in beautiful dresses, light, airy, flowery creations ending a good measure above dainty shoes with elevated heels or delicate lower heels—mere strips of leather that reminded her of the picture of sandals from the Bible. It was exotic and fascinating. Sighing, she stared after them with envy. If only she could look so pretty. Just once.

Books under his arm, Thomas watched her gaze at the wealthier women of the East Side as they briskly walked down Fifth Avenue. "Let's go for a walk," he said.

She glanced up at him. "A walk?"

He smiled. "Let me introduce you to Central Park."

"The park? You'd like to walk in the park?" She glanced at the books tucked under his arm. "What about your research?"

He shrugged. Tom thought she looked lovely, though he would never say so aloud. It was one thing to have these thoughts in a dream—what he thought was a dream—but now was reality. And in reality it would never do for him to tell her that she was by far more attractive than the pampered women around her. Meggie was real—she wasn't perfect, nor did she need to be. She was healthy-looking. She didn't wear a gram of makeup, and outside of slight circles under her eyes, her skin was

146

flawless. And when she smiled . . . well, no amount of lipstick could enhance that smile.

He wanted to see her as happy and carefree as she'd been in Lehigha. Stopping short, Tom couldn't believe his own thoughts. He was actually thinking he'd been there. Back in time. Her time. He shook his head, as if the gesture might drive out the ridiculous thought, and steered Meggie back toward the park entrance. It was then that he became aware of the stares from those who recognized him, or thought they recognized him. Sighing, he realized that he was definitely back in New York City, and privacy was something to be appreciated.

"I know just the way for you to see the park for the first time," he said while pulling her toward a line of carriages. "Pick one," Tom offered.

Meggie looked to the row of carriages that waited for passengers. Her gaze kept returning to a shiny black vehicle. A black horse stood in front of it, flicking its head, as if impatient to leave the noisy city street and return to the park. The seats of the carriage were of red leather and some sort of white flowers had been placed in a brass vase that was attached to one side. It was beautiful, like something out of one of the tales her Mum used to tell her when she was a young girl.

"Well? Which one is it to be?" Thomas asked.

How her heart yearned to sit in that carriage, to fulfill a dream, for never was there anything so grand in the patch. Even Nate Gowen, president of the Reading, didn't own such a fine carriage. But her upbringing rose to the surface and she realized how extravagant it would seem. "Why, there's nothing wrong with our feet, now is there? We can walk through the park, if you'd like."

147

He shifted his weight and pushed the dark spectacles back up his nose. "Listen, I would really like to show you the park, but I'd rather not walk." He glanced around him, as if uncomfortable on the street.

It suddenly dawned on her that Thomas must still be suffering from the fight with Brian. He was probably afraid that. someone might see him and question his bruises. And that created a wonderful excuse. "Yes, of course," she answered in an excited voice. "I had forgotten about your—your injuries. Certainly we can ride in a carriage . . . if you think it's best for you."

His mouth opened, as though he was going to say something, then he changed his mind. Instead, he led her to the nearest carriage.

"No. Wait." She pulled back from him and once more glanced up the line of vehicles toward the shiny black one. The liveried driver in his black and red uniform was staring back at her. When their eyes met, the old man lifted his tall hat and bowed his head—as if in respect. The small gesture tugged at her heart and she smiled back. "That one, Thomas," she whispered, and pointed to the black carriage. "Why don't we take that one instead?"

"Fine." He touched her elbow, escorting her through the people on the sidewalk. After making a hurried arrangement with the driver, Thomas turned and assisted her into the carriage.

She ran her fingers over the leather seat, noting its superior quality. Smiling at Thomas when he joined her, Meggie sat back and decided to enjoy the ride.

It was to be an afternoon she would never forget.

"It's a fine day you've chosen," the old driver

said in a heavy Irish accent. "Puts one in mind of spring, rather than summer."

Her face lifted toward the sound of his voice. He sounded just like her Da when he'd said that. If she closed her eyes and imagined . . .

"Are you from Ireland?" Thomas asked as the man flicked the reins and the carriage pulled forward into the park.

"Aye. That I am. Gerald Kane."

Thomas looked suspicious as he glanced at the driver's back and then at her. "I've heard too many Irish accents recently."

Meggie ignored him and smiled back up at the driver. "How long have you been here, Gerald?" she asked.

"Well over three years now. Left the farming back over there. This," he said, while half turning in his seat and gesturing toward the park, "this is as close to it as I'm about to find here. I love horses and the sun on my face. And I can breathe in here. I can also indulge in my hobby . . . history. This park is filled with it."

Meggie looked around and noticed the sun shining through the lacy rooftop of trees. The scenery was lush and green. Rocks of all sizes dotted the landscape, and for a moment, she felt taken back to another time, maybe her time, when the sounds of birds and the clip of horses' hooves filled the air. It was peaceful.

For the next hour she was treated to sights that would remain with her forever. Gerald proved to be the perfect guide. Even Thomas had been surprised by the places Gerald had chosen for them to explore. He had stopped to let them get out of the carriage and watch the human chess pieces move inside a pavilion. Meggie felt foolish, yet rubbed the head of a statue of a dog when Tom told her it was good luck. She marveled at the many stone arches and bridges; the fountains and sculptures. A wide grin appeared at her lips when she watched grown men sailing their miniature boats, as if on the high seas. Her mind was filled with so many questions about the strange sight of men and women riding bicycles, or running for no apparent reason through the paths in the woods. It was odd, for they didn't seem to be in any great hurry, nor did they appear to be running away from anyone, or in any danger. They were just running, slowly, methodically, and with great concentration. It was truly an odd sight to behold.

Gerald took them past the band shell and told them there would be a concert later that evening for all to enjoy. He stopped for them to climb the stone steps of Bethesda Terrace and look down on the lake with its many rowboats. Seeing the graceful fountain, the bright banners softly waving in the breeze, Meggie smiled. It really felt like stepping back to her own time. Watching those people rowing over the lake made her think of when her Da had taken her and Brian and Mum to Mount Carmel and had rented a rowboat. All four of them had crossed the Schukyll River to lunch on Braver's Island. It had been a grand afternoon, and she wondered now why they had never done it again.

"Are you unhappy?"

She turned to him and smiled. Shaking her head, she said, "No, Thomas. I'm not unhappy. I'm just thinking—about my own time. About the day my father took us out on a rowboat. We had great fun that day. I was just wondering why we never went back."

She looked up at him, and even though he wore

those dark spectacles, she could tell that he was staring at her. That knowledge made her feel warm inside, even a little uncomfortable. All through the tour of Central Park, Thomas had been a perfect gentleman, patiently explaining certain customs and answering her questions. He didn't make her feel foolish for not knowing; he made her feel intelligent for having the curiosity to ask. Today they had shared laughter. Today they were on a common ground. But right now was different. Now she felt the overwhelming need to place her head against his chest, to feel his arms close around her, to—

"I'll take you out on the lake," he said in a low voice, one that ran down her spine like the soft brush of a feather. "Whenever you want . . ."

She swallowed several times, unsure of how to answer. Something was pulling her to him. It was an invisible force, a power so strong that she literally had to shake her head to break it. Surely she was imagining it, this exciting pull, for Thomas would never expect Sister Margaret Mary, even a novitiate, to respond like this. Was she a fool to want him? She knew the answer, for her lies were quickly catching up to her.

Forcing herself to smile, she said, "Thank you, I would enjoy a boat ride, but I'm afraid your hand isn't up to the task of rowing. Perhaps another time."

He nodded, as though he hadn't really expected her to accept his offer. He led her back to the carriage and Meggie found that she had to concentrate as Gerald took them past some place called Strawberry Fields and spoke to them of someone called John Lennon. None of it made any sense to her, yet Thomas appeared interested, as if he'd completely forgotten that thrilling moment back at the lake. It was as if she'd just imagined it.

Determined to present an intelligent appearance, Meggie straightened her shoulders, lifted her chin, and looked out to the woods. Her eyes weren't really focusing on anything, nor was her mind actually concentrating. If Thomas could forget so easily, then so could she. So could— Her eyes narrowed at the movement in the woods and she tried to make out what had caused the noise and interrupted her thoughts. And then she saw.

Her mouth opened in shock and her hands came up to cover it. Two people, a man and a woman, were actually engaged in . . . were right there in the woods, in front of God and everyone, performing . . . surely she was mistaken. It simply could not be so, but the woman was leaning against a stout tree, her skirt pulled up to the tops of her legs, the man so close against her. And she was holding him to her, grabbing at him as if she would fall without his support. And his hands . . . Dear God!

"Gerald," Thomas said in a strained voice, "I think Meggie would like to see Sheep's Meadow. Why don't we hurry? You think Old Walfy there might pick up the pace?"

"Yes, sir," the driver announced and flicked the reins over the horse's rump.

Thomas and Gerald, it appeared, had also seen the incredible sight. Both men looked mortified.

Imagine, Meggie thought as a hot blush crept up her neck and settled on her face, people making love outside, in a park—a public place.

What had the world come to?

She barely heard Gerald as he spoke in a nervous voice about various points of interest, and she didn't dare look at Thomas. Maybe she had been wrong, she thought. Maybe the man and the woman weren't . . . But she wasn't that naive. And perhaps that was what embarrassed her the most. Perhaps it was the knowledge that she wasn't as innocent as Thomas thought. How would he react if he found out that she'd known a man and had delivered a child? Here was another answer that was hard to admit. Thomas would be disgusted. He believed her to be a woman of purity, and thinking of giving her life over to the Church. She had known that he'd respected her decisions. He had told her about growing up with the teaching nuns. He actually believed her to be an honorable woman. If the truth came out, she would lose that respect forever. Thomas Carter would never understand her many lies.

He glanced at her from the corner of his eye. She was very quiet, sitting next to him with her hands folded on her lap, staring at them as if afraid to look elsewhere. Tom shook his head with frustration. Damn it! Why did that have to happen? She'd been enjoying herself, actually laughing. She didn't seem the crazed nun at all. She seemed quite sane, almost carefree, until she'd seen that couple. Damnit all, even if it was New York City, that kind of behavior was outrageous. He could just imagine thoughts of sin and wickedness filling her mind. She would condemn this time, the entire city, him included.

*This time?* Why, he was even thinking like her now, as if she came from another place—long ago.

The patch. Lehigha.

The names swirled around in his head until they created an actual ache, and he quickly let out his breath. What was happening to them? Which one of them knew reality? For if she was sane, then what did that make him? He genuinely believed her.

153

At least he believed that she believed . . . Hell, all he knew was that Sister Margaret—*Meggie*—had had the same dream last night. And that he had hurt his hand, and someone had given him a beating. Why was it that in the back of his brain he knew the answer? And why couldn't he bring it forward and admit it? Admit what? That he and a nun, a novitiate, had traveled back to eighteen seventy-five? That he'd spoken to people long dead, fought with them, drank with them, shaken hands with them? It was too bizarre.

But what were the answers then? How could any of it be possible?

"It was our pleasure to have shown you this fine park. We, Walfy and me, would be honored if you would return with us soon."

Tom and Meggie looked up at the white-haired driver and both gave him an answering smile. The old man's craggy face positively lit up with friendliness.

Helping Meggie out of the carriage, Tom asked, "Would you like to come back? You've only seen a small part of the park."

She looked at both men and her smile widened. "I would dearly love to come back."

"Then you certainly should. Shouldn't she, Mr. Carter?" Gerald gazed at the younger man and waited for an answer.

Tom's eyes narrowed. "You know me?" he asked suspiciously.

"Ahh . . . now who wouldn't be knowin' the man that led the park restoration when the city kept draggin' their, er, took forever. Besides, I point out your building at least ten times in a single day. Yes sir, Mr. Carter, I do know you."

"But you didn't let on earlier," Tom mentioned,

thinking the man was holding out for a bigger tip.

Gerald looked him straight in the eye and said, "I figured if you wanted the attention, you would've told me right off. A man's business is a man's business. Which has nothing to do, you understand, with that shiner you're sportin'. Like I said, a man's business is his business."

Surprising everyone, Tom laughed. "So, if Miss Gillbride again wishes another carriage ride in the park, then I assume I can trust you to escort her . . . without the benefit of the press?"

Gerald tipped the front of his hat. "Aye. That you can, sir."

"You realize certain newspapers would love to know about today? And pay you well for your information."

Shrugging, the driver said, "I never held with gossip. It's for old women, bored with their crocheting."

Meggie could see that Gerald's answer pleased Thomas and she felt glad when the younger man held out a bill of money to the old one.

"How can I contact you, Gerald, if Miss Gillbride wants to further explore the park? Through the Claremont Stables?"

Impressed with the fifty-dollar bill in his hand, Gerald nodded. "Yes, sir. You can find me there. And I'd be more than happy to show Miss Gillbride any number of sights. Not just the park, you know. I've also acquainted myself with the rest of the city as well. I'm fairly conversant with its history."

Tom grinned. "Well, then thank you, Gerald. I'm sure we'll contact you soon."

"Yes, thank you," Meggie added in a sincere voice. It was obvious that she found the old driver delightful. "I have never enjoyed a ride so much as

155

this one. I hope we can do it again."

Gerald Kane nodded and smiled as the handsome couple walked away from him. He watched as they crossed Fifty-ninth Street and walked toward Carter's famous apartment building. Just before they entered, the woman turned back to the park and looked for him. She waved and he held up his hand in response, to let her know that he was watching. Yes, I'm still here, he thought as he saw them disappear inside the revolving doors. He wasn't going anywhere. Not now.

He had waited so very long for this day.

# Chapter 11

"This is ridiculous! Listen to this: Can astral travelers get lost? Suppose they forget the time? Astral Projection is natural. Soul Sculpture! My God, and people actually believe in this!" Surrounded by books, Tom looked up at her and shook his head. "Crazy, huh?"

Meggie shrugged and brought her robe closer to her chest. He'd been at this for over five hours, reading from the books, calling out to her when he'd come upon something upsetting. It was late. She was tired. And confused.

"I don't know, Thomas." Taking a deep breath, she tried to keep her voice patient as she added, "All I can say is that *something* happened to us. It isn't just me anymore. You were there. If you would just admit it—"

"Admit what?" he demanded. "That we went back in time over a hundred years? That we *astrally projected* ourselves into Lehigha? Believe me, Meggie, if I were going to do that, I'd pick a better place."

She looked offended.

"I mean, wouldn't it be more exciting to travel back in time to, say, the time of George Washington . . . watch Thomas Jefferson write the Declaration of Independence . . . listen to Lincoln's Gettysburg

Address? I hardly think, if I had my choice, that I would pick a bar room fight with your brother in the town of Lehigha."

She shifted on the couch and looked at him more directly. "Thomas, why are you refusing to see this? It doesn't have anything to do with what you're reading or talking about. What you've read to me maintains that someone consciously projects themselves somewhere else. I had no control over coming to this time. And you had no control over returning to mine—"

"Well, this is just great," Tom interrupted, as he stood up and walked away from the table where he'd been engrossed in books on parapsychology. "According to you, this—this phenomenon could happen at any time. In other words, I could be addressing a board of directors and suddenly appear in Fitzhugh's Tap Room . . . without my doing anything."

Again, she shrugged. "I suppose it could happen."

"Damn it." He started pacing. "Well, I don't want it to happen! I don't need this in my life. I didn't invite it. I was doing just fine. Do you understand that?"

She nodded. "I didn't do anything intentionally. You don't really think I wanted to come to this time? Who even thinks about life one hundred years in the future."

"But it's you. You brought this—"

Her chin lifted in defiance. "It isn't the plague."

"It is to me. Do you think I want to be popping in and out of centuries?"

"Do you think I do?" She stood up and faced him, no longer afraid. She was too tired. It wasn't her fault, and she'd be damned if he would make her feel

158

any more guilty than she already did.

It was a mistake. She knew that immediately. Standing this close to him. Face to face, like that couple in the park. My God, when was the last time she had felt her blood thicken so swiftly? It was as if she were in a trance—her limbs felt heavy, her breathing became deeper, and she couldn't tear her gaze away from his. The sane part of her brain told her to break the spell, look away, and tell him good night. The lonely part of her subconscious, the part that remembered all the solitary years when love was denied, urged her to look deeper—see the hunger in his eyes and recognize an emotion that went beyond that, beyond lust. It was a yearning. As strong as her own. A need to contact another, and cling together against the universe until you found your place within it.

Almost of their own volition, her fingers moved up to brush back the hair at his temple. "Thomas," she whispered in a shaky voice, "I don't think we can control what's happening. And I'm frightened . . . for both of us."

He made a noise, almost as if in pain, and flinched his head away from her fingers. "I guess we should say good night," he said uneasily, and cleared his throat. "Ah . . . tomorrow, perhaps tomorrow we'll think more clearly and—"

She didn't hear any more. When he'd pulled away from her touch, she had experienced such embarrassment and pain. She had to get away. Somewhere. Anywhere. But not here, not where he could see her humiliation. "I—I think you were right this morning. I think I should leave," she muttered as she turned and walked away from him. She couldn't face the rejection. How could she have been so foolish? So—

He caught her arm and turned her around. She could see he was confused, and when he looked down to his hand on her arm, he dropped it, as if he were burned. "Don't. I mean . . . where would you go? What would you do? You don't know anyone in the city."

She shook her head and forced her lips into a tight smile. "I'll be all right. I can take care of myself. Maybe someone could use a housekeeper, or a cook." She folded her arms over her chest, wishing he would just let her leave quietly, before the blush creeping up her cheeks turned her face a deep, humiliating red. "I'll manage."

"You'll manage?" he repeated, his voice sounding incredulous. "Do you have any idea just how dangerous this city is? It isn't as peaceful as your ride through the park this afternoon. That was a fantasy in the middle of what can be a very ugly city."

He ran his fingers through his hair in frustration. "You can't go out there alone. You'd be swallowed up before the night was over. You're too—too trusting, too kind. People aren't always good, Meggie. There's evil out there, too. Stay here. I need a housekeeper. And you can cook—dinner tonight was delicious. Stay here," he repeated with an urgency. "Work for me."

Her mouth opened in shock. "But you said you had a housekeeper. I remember. You said she was off for the holiday."

"You're right," he admitted, while searching the room with his eyes. "But I forgot to tell you that Celia has been . . . has been wanting to see her grandson in Phoenix. Yes, that's right," he said, almost to himself. Nodding, he continued, "Now she can go. She was reluctant because I hadn't found anyone to replace her. But"—and he swung his hand in her direction—"you've already proven you can take over. If you want it, the job is yours."

She didn't know what to say. It was a generous offer. And also false, if she were honest with herself, for it was obvious that Thomas was making it up. For some reason, he wanted her to stay. Perhaps, it was pity. Then again, she had nowhere else to go. And he was right. New York City in the year nineteen hundred and ninety was a frightening place. Maybe, just maybe, she could prolong the time she spent with this man. This time she would remember it all and cherish each memory, for she had no doubt that he would be taken from her. Didn't she lose everyone she had ever cared about? Yes, Thomas would be taken from her sooner or later. And she wanted to make it later.

"Are you sure about this?" she asked, hope growing inside her like the opening petals of a flower. "What about your housekeeper? Celia? What if she isn't prepared to make a trip? You're not giving her any notice—"

He snapped his fingers and pointed to the machine she now knew was a telephone. "You know, you might be right. Let's call her and find out."

As he was dialing, Meggie came back into the room and stood next to him. Maybe . . . Her hands came up to her chest as her heartbeat increased while she listened to his words.

"Hello? Celia? This is Tom. How are you?" He paused for the woman to answer. "Listen, Celia, I know how much you've wanted to visit your daughter and grandson out in Phoenix. So how would you like an early Christmas bonus?"

Meggie could hear an excited chatter as Tom held

the listening part away from his ear and smiled. "Wait," he interrupted. "Of course, you're not fired. Yes. I do. I have someone here that's perfect. Never mind how. Just know that everything will be taken care of while you're in Phoenix. Now what do you say? I can have you on a nonstop flight tomorrow afternoon."

His smile increased. "No. It isn't any of your business, but I'll tell you anyway. Her name is Meggie." Thomas glanced over to her and grinned. "You'll have to see for yourself when you return in two weeks. Take three if you want. No, that's all I'm going to tell you. Now I'd better let you call your daughter. I'll get back to you early tomorrow morning and let you know what time the car will take you to the airport." He looked down at the rest of the telephone and said in a low voice, "You're quite welcome. Have a wonderful time, Celia. You deserve it."

Replacing the receiver, Tom took a deep breath and glanced up to her. "Well. It's all taken care of. Now, if you say no, I'll have no one. I'll have to survive on canned soup and Caesar's Salad for two weeks."

She smiled. He could be such a dear man. Did she dare do this? Perhaps it was time to think about herself, to be good to herself for a change. Maybe it was time to be brave and take that first step. All she had to do was say yes and she could stay with him. For a little while . . .

"Thank you, Thomas," she said sincerely. "You've already been more than generous—with your hospitality, the clothes, and now a job. I'll try not to disappoint you."

Tom kept staring at her, unable to form an answer.

162

A brief nod became his reply and she smiled at him before saying good night. He'd come close to losing her tonight. He'd offended her, injured her pride, and she had wanted to run away from him. How could he tell her what her touch had done to him? She would never understand how her gentle fingers at his temple had produced a searing heat that had quickly spread through his body. That he wanted her more deeply, more fiercely, than he had ever wanted a woman. And she was afraid of disappointing him?

He watched her walk out of the living room and muttered to himself, "I don't think you could, Meggie. I don't think you ever could."

She tried to stop the smile from spreading over her face. It would never do to go grinning like a fool as she crossed the street. Alone.

Today was an adventure. Thomas had said this morning that he'd made the arrangements with Gerald. She was to meet the carriage driver in front of Sherman's monument and he would take her wherever she wanted to go. Spying the old man, she let the grin on her face have its way and hurried her step. She couldn't contain her pleasure at seeing the Irishman. There was something about him, something so friendly, so familiar . . .

"Ahh, aren't you prettier than I remembered? I'm glad to see you again, Miss Gillbride," Gerald said, taking her hand and holding it out so he could see her outfit. It was a very lightweight cotton blouse and skirt, of the palest yellow, and her shoes were of the softest leather, like dancing slippers. She had to admit that Thomas had very fine taste indeed.

"And I'm glad to see you, Gerald. Please, call me

Meggie." She could hardly contain her excitement, but made an effort as she said, "What do you think we should do today? Thomas said we'd be walking."

Gerald brushed an imaginary speck of lint from his jacket sleeve. Even though it was July and the heat was significant, Gerald wore a crisp white shirt under the navy blue jacket. A red bow tie and white linen trousers completed his attire. He looked surprisingly cool, and every bit a gentleman. "Our Mr. Carter was correct. We shall be walking, taking in a few of the nearby stores and attractions. I must say our friend certainly did a thorough investigation of me. My employer at the stables says Mr. Carter's men spent over an hour asking questions. I believe they attempted to fingerprint me before allowing you to spend the afternoon in my company."

Meggie turned to him. "Oh, please don't be offended," she said, touching his arm. "Thomas is so very protective. Sometimes he treats me like a child. He's constantly lecturing me on being careful."

Gerald smiled. "I'm not angry, my dear. Far from it. I have nothing to hide. Not from your Mr. Carter, nor anyone else. Now, come. Let's see what we can discover today."

He offered his arm and Meggie smiled as she inserted her own through his. It was a fine day to explore her new freedom.

They went through the Central Park Zoo and Meggie marveled at the many animals who lived so close to Thomas's home. Every one of them was foreign to her. She laughed at the monkeys, marveled at the beautiful and exotic birds, and cringed at the reptiles. She fell in love with a polar bear that floated on its back to cool off, and giggled until she cried at the playful antics of the seals. It was wonderful. She felt filled with questions about other lands where these fantastic creatures lived. Confined to the patch all her life, her world had once seemed so very small. Now, this world, Thomas's world, seemed almost too vast to comprehend. This was an exciting time, and she vowed to ask Thomas for maps. Maybe he could help her to better understand this fascinating era.

Leaving the park, Meggie and Gerald crossed over Fifth Avenue. As they walked up to Madison, she looked in the windows of the elegant shops. She read the signs of the foreign embassies and Gerald explained that other countries bought houses where their representatives could live while in this country. As he was talking, a strange, exotic-looking man walked out of a building.

"He looks like Aleem."

"Who?" Gerald asked.

"Aleem Choudhy, I think his name was. He brought me here to the city."

"An Indian cab driver?"

Meggie stopped walking and looked at her companion. "An Indian? No. He had on one of those odd cloth hats —"

"A turban," Gerald interrupted.

"A turban," she repeated, listening to the sound of the strange word. "Not feathers. I've seen pictures of Indians."

Gerald laughed. "Dear child, you are a joy. These men are from the country of India. I'm not speaking of American Indians."

She looked confused. "Oh."

He took her arm and led her down the street. "Come. Let's have lunch and then I'll show you some of my favorite places in the city."

Gerald insisted she taste something called a hamburger. She found it delicious, though it was very messy to eat with one's hands. After a quick lunch, her guide took her through *Stair and Company,* an antique dealer that seemed like nothing ordinary on the outside, but inside reminded Meggie of an English manor house with its beautifully decorated rooms. Gerald appeared to know everyone and all greeted him as a friend. Delighted with her tour, she quickly agreed to accompany Gerald to another dealer. In *Florian Papp* she was fascinated by the many Filigree Paperworks of Art. This lost art of rolled, scrolled, crimped, and folded strips of colored paper formed many pictorial patterns. Gerald and the owner showed her an advertisement from an eighteenth-century magazine *The New Lady's Magazine,* which described filigree work as "the art which affords an amusement to the female mind capable of the most pleasing and extensive variety . . ."

Amused, Meggie entered a tiny elevator with her friend and was then deposited on another floor. There she saw a casket, a small decorative filigreed box that contained an intriguing array of eighteenth- and nineteenth-century life.

She listened with rapt attention as Gerald explained each item. One was a small oval portrait of King George the Third, worn over the heart of gentlemen attending a Thanksgiving service for His Majesty in seventeen eighty-nine. A small paper unfolded to reveal a tiny piece of bark with the written words: "piece of the tree under which Wellington stood while writing his dispatches at the battle of Waterloo—eighteen hundred and fifteen." Another envelope contained a piece of vine that had grown over the house where Peter the Great dwelt while studying the art of shipbuilding. Dried flowers came from a wreath placed by Queen Victoria on Prince Albert's grave.

Meggie was touched, for she remembered her mother telling her of the prince's death, and how Victoria never really recovered from her grief. A strange sensation came over her as she stared at the many articles from the cabinet. She felt light-headed, dizzy. Some of the things were from her time, and some were older. An overwhelming need to touch the dried flowers grew within her and she lifted her hand.

Before she could reach the faded blossoms, Gerald took her fingers and squeezed them. "We must be getting on now, Meggie dear. We've kept our host too long from his business."

She listened to Gerald thanking the proprietor of these many treasures. Smiling her appreciation, she allowed her new friend to lead her outside.

"Well, what do you think? Are you up to another? Or would you like to quit for today?" When she didn't answer, Gerald offered his arm and added, "You have seen quite a bit. Perhaps it's too much to assimilate at one time. Why don't we just walk and see how you feel."

"Thank you," Meggie murmured, placing her arm through his and letting the old man slowly lead her through the people on the sidewalk. She felt strange and had no idea what had just happened inside that shop. What odd, peculiar feelings!

Giving herself over to her friend, she listened as he directed her attention to various points of interest. Soon she forgot the incident and was enjoying herself. Yet just as they crossed the street, Meggie looked into the window of a shop and stopped walking. She squinted against the glare of the sun off the window, trying very hard to see inside the antique shop. As if on request, the sun receded behind a cloud or perhaps a building.

And then she saw it.

Her jaw dropped in astonishment; she felt weak and her heart raced inside her chest as she leaned closer to the window.

"What is it, Meggie?" Gerald asked, concern in his voice.

She didn't look at him. She couldn't tear her gaze away from it. She was told there was only one like it, only a single one had been made in that exact way. How often had she heard the story when she was younger? She grasped the front of her blouse with one hand and touched the window with the other.

She felt the glass, warmed by the sun, under her fingers. That was the only thing separating her from her mother's sewing table.

My God, it was here. In this time! In New York City!

"I think we should go now," Gerald said, pulling on her elbow.

She tugged her arm away from his hand. "I want to go inside," she said in a voice that sounded strange even to her own ears.

"It's closed, child. There's a sign on the door. They won't be back for three more days. They must have taken a long holiday. What's wrong with you, Meggie? I think we should get you back to Mr. Carter's."

She wasn't listening. Not anymore. She was staring at her Mum's sewing table. It had to be! She read the tiny white card that described it: *George III Mahogany and Satinwood Inlaid Sewing Table circa 1790 $6500*. George the Third, mahogany and satinwood

168

inlaid. Yes! If only she could get inside. Touch it. Inspect it. Look for her Mum's initials that had been finely carved under the lid and her own initials that she had scratched in the delicate wood when she was a child. Lord in heaven, how her Mum had let in to her when she'd discovered what Meggie had done . . .

*"Oh Meggie, how could you? You know what this table means to me. We've sold everything, but I can't bear to part with this. And now you've scratched it."*

*"But Mum," her tiny voice had piped, "I only wanted to add my name to yours. You said it will come to me one day. I wanted to make sure my name was there for all to see. One day it'll belong to me. You said so . . ."*

Meggie felt the same odd sensation enter her when she thought back to that conversation with her Mum. Something was happening; something was pulling her. Away. Away from the street outside the antique shop, away from Gerald. Away from Thomas!

Terrified, she looked in the window and saw her own reflection. Behind her the scene of the busy street was rapidly changing. Instead of the fast automobiles, she saw wagons drawn by horses. Horse-drawn trolleys clanged down the street. There were freight wagons, brewery wagons carrying kegs of beer, sleek black broughams and landaus with uniformed, liveried drivers sitting tall at the reins. And everything was moving. The wagons. The people. The window became like a living picture. She could smell the manure of the horses mixed with the scents of leather, roasted almonds, and baked bread. It was crazy. Insane. Her fingers closed into fists of terror as she shut her eyes and shook her head against the bizarre scene. It couldn't be happening again. Not here! Not now! For it wasn't Lehigha that she was seeing in the window.

She felt it inside of her, that queer dizziness, and knew just what was taking place—for it wasn't the first time. Afraid, she forced her eyes open, terrified of where she would find herself.

Her hands came up to cover her mouth; her eyes widened past the point of comfort. It couldn't be! It was Bridgi's room in the patch. And . . . she couldn't even think as she continued to stare across the room in disbelief.

He stood near the dresser; his legs wide apart. His arms were out in front of him, as if to keep from falling. And he was dressed in the fine suit he had worn this morning before he had left for work. Slowly, upon recognizing her, his arms fell to his side and his expression changed from terror to astonishment. Then looking about the room, he let his gaze fall on her. The anger of his glare rooted her to the floor.

"Sonofabitch!" Thomas exclaimed in a strangled voice. "How the hell could this happen?"

# Chapter 12

She was afraid to answer. Unable to speak, Meggie could only shake her head.

Tom stumbled against a dresser and held on. "I . . . I'd just come back into my office after speaking with the board and . . . and suddenly I felt strange—dizzy," he muttered in a dazed voice. "I was . . . I was trying to reach the chair behind my desk when I felt myself falling. That's what it felt like—falling—that sickening feeling you get when you know nothing is going to break your fall . . ."

She nodded. "I was with Gerald," she said slowly. Swallowing deeply after every few words, she added, "I was looking into a shop window and . . . and it started."

He stared at her, suspicion in his eyes. "You must have been doing something to cause it. I can't believe this has happened again. And this time I know I'm not dreaming!"

She felt like crying. He was so angry with her, as if she could stop this—

A knock on the door interrupted her thoughts. "Mr. Carter? Are you awake then?"

"It's Bridgi!" she whispered to Thomas. Her eyes widened again, this time with horror as she looked at the door.

"Mr. Carter?" Bridgi again called. "You've only thirty minutes before the whistle blows and no man that slept at Bridget Humne's has ever been late for work yet. Now, up with ya!"

"What is she talking about?" Tom whispered to Meggie, a look of dread replacing his anger.

Meggie shrugged. "Tell her you're up," she suggested.

"I, ah, I'm up, Mrs. Humne," Tom repeated, and waited for her answer.

"I have your breakfast here on a tray. Just tea and some of last night's rolls. The one's you said you preferred. You'll have no time to join me as usual downstairs. Now open the door and take it from me hands. It's gettin' heavy for an old woman."

Tom and Meggie stared at each other. What was the woman talking about?

"You better open it," Meggie said, nodding to the door. "She's not going to go away."

Hesitantly, as though opening the door to bedlam, Tom reached out and turned the knob.

"Well, about time," Bridget Humne muttered as she brushed past him and placed the tray on the wooden table by the window. "I believe I'm getting a touch of old age in my bones . . ."

Her words dropped off as she turned around and faced Tom. Her mouth opened in surprise and she smiled in an astonished way. "Well, well, and what are we dressed for, may I ask?" she questioned, looking him up and down. "Don't be telling me you forgot today was Monday. This is your

172

second week of work. You won't be using them fine clothes down in the mine."

Tom looked at his gray suit and touched his blue striped tie. "Down in the mines?"

Bridgi shook her head slowly, as if bewildered. "You're a strange one, Thomas McKenna Carter. That you are. Need I be remindin' you that today marks your second week down under? How could you forget, son? And pray tell, why are you dressed for church?"

"Ahhh . . . ?" He looked to Meggie and shrugged in a hopeless gesture. "I forgot?" He felt ten years old answering this woman.

"It's got an odd cut to it, that much I'll say," she remarked while continuing to eye his suit. "Well, you'd better hurry. Like I said, you've over-slept and have little time for conversation. I'll be packin' you a good piece of that leg of mutton you professed such a likin' to last night. Ought to keep you satisfied until you come home again." Leaving the room, she added, "Let this morning be a lesson to you, Thomas. Stay up late, carous-ing with the likes of Brian Gillbride and that crowd of buckos, and you'll be facing another morning just like this one.

"Imagine, not even rememberin' the day," she clucked, while shaking her head. "I'll see you downstairs. Oh, and I've washed your shirt. It's folded here, right in the hall. How many times do I have to tell you that's where you'll find your laundry?" She tucked a stray gray strand of hair back into her neat bun and then reached for the doorknob. "I told you I never enter my boarder's room without permission. And that goes for tak-ing care of your clothes. Now shake a leg, or

173

you'll be late for sure."

When the door was shut, Tom turned to Meggie and demanded, "What was that all about? Is that woman crazy?"

Meggie shook her head. "I don't know. Bridgi's been grieving for many years over her son, but her mind has always been sound—"

"She acts like I've been here all along," he interrupted. "She actually thinks I'm working in a mine!"

"Keep your voice down," Meggie reminded him as she began pacing the small room. "It's me Bridgi can't hear, not you. She's going to wonder who you're yelling at."

He looked as if he was about to say something and then stopped. His face became even more red; his eyes turned angrier and Meggie was afraid he might explode if he didn't say something.

"I suppose you'll have to get dressed for work," she suggested, knowing the proposal would surely bring a response.

*"Work!"* He glared at her. "You heard the woman. She thinks I'm a miner!"

"Is that so terrible?" Meggie demanded. "My father was a miner. And so is my brother. Some very fine people are miners—"

"That's not what I'm talking about," he hotly interrupted. "I haven't the slightest idea how to go about working in a mine." He looked almost as if he were in pain. "How could I have been here in Lehigha and also be in New York City at the same time?"

"It wasn't the same time, Thomas. There's a hundred years difference."

"You know what I mean," he countered in an

174

angry voice. "I'd like to know what's going on. Why don't I remember being here last night. Drinking with your brother, like Bridget says. How is this happening to me?"

"To us," she added, and her words stopped him.

Staring into her eyes, he asked, "What are we going to do, Meggie?"

She didn't say anything for a few seconds then smiled sadly. "I think you're about to go to work. I don't know what else to do, except to go along with it and see what happens."

His expression spoke volumes. Clearly miserable, Thomas yanked at the formal tie and pulled it away from his neck.

"Unless you intend to be completely shocked, I'd suggest you leave the room," he said, while placing his suit jacket on the bed. "Why don't you find the shirt Bridget was talking about. In the hallway," she said.

Watching his fingers push each button through its hole, Meggie unconsciously licked her lips. He was undressing. Right here. In front of her! She almost had to force her eyes to blink. Finally, she tore her gaze away and nodded. "Yes, of course. I'll find it." And she quickly left the room. Breathing heavily in the hallway, she tried to bring herself back under control. Why could she not stop wanting him? On top of everything, this could not be happening . . . again.

Standing at the bottom of the stairwell, Bridgi Humne was about to once more shout up to her boarder when she saw the strangest sight. Rubbing her eyes, she blinked several times in astonishment as she watched the bedroom door open by itself. But what truly astonished her was seeing Mr. Carter's shirt floating in thin air and disappearing into the room. Sweet Jesus! That was the very last time she was going to have a jigger of whiskey before bed. It was time to admit it. She had more gray hair on her than sense, and she was gettin' too old for this kind of foolishness.

Clearing her throat, she yelled, "Mind the time, Mr. Carter. My reputation's at stake!" For added measure, she quickly crossed herself for protection then hurried back into the kitchen.


He felt ridiculous wearing the strange clothes and equipment. A wide hat had a metal band around the brim that held a container of oil. Meggie had told him that he was to light the wick once underground. That thought certainly gave him chills, even though it was a warm and humid summer morning.

Underground. Like a mole. He didn't know if he could do it. He didn't even know *why* he had to do it. In fact, he had been arguing his case to Meggie as they left Bridget's house when Meggie's brother had come up behind him and slapped him on the back.

"You're not looking your best there, Tom," Brian had remarked with a grin. "You survived the first week and that's always the worst. Most don't, you know. Especially outsiders. They're usually on a train before the week is out."

Tom had nodded. "Hello, Brian." He hadn't even been surprised to see the man. He felt like a fatalist, as if someone else was running his life and it didn't do any good to fight against it. He had glanced at Meggie and could see tears forming

176

at the corner of her eyes when she looked at her brother. He knew she was hurting and he had wanted to comfort her. All he could do was smile with understanding.

"I guess I just wasn't prepared for the life of a miner," he said to her brother. "It still seems confusing." *What an understatement!*

Brian patted him on the back and urged him farther onto the street, where they fell in behind dozens of others making their way up to the colliery. "Not to worry. I'll help you out again, if you need it."

Tom looked down at the pick axe and shovel in his hands, the tin lunch box that hung from a leather strap over his shoulder, and the can of oil that clipped onto his belt with a short metal chain. He had no idea what to do with any of the equipment, except the lunch box. "Thanks, Brian," he muttered, more to himself than anyone else. "I believe you'll be hearing from me sooner than you think."

He fell in line behind the others, feeling like a prisoner being led off to hard labor. It didn't matter that he'd been at the top of his class at Wharton. No one here cared or had heard of his latest spectacular acquisition. His reputation as the number one leveraged-buyout specialist meant absolutely nothing to these people, or anyone in this town. He'd spent the last twenty years developing his mind and right now the importance of that could be fitted in his tin lunch box. Now, at this moment, he would need a strong back, not a strong mind. Somehow, he had a feeling that his workouts at the Athletic Club weren't going to be enough to get him through this.

Lehigha's colliery was a huge wooden building. From a distance, it appeared to be something out of a bizarre amusement park, with its many tracks running in and out of it—like a giant roller coaster gone haywire. Only when you came closer could you make out where the wooden carts were going—into the ground through a large tunnel, out again filled with coal, then through a winding passage to another building to be sorted and finally deposited into waiting railroad cars.

It was his job, Meggie told him, to bring the coal out from under the ground.

"Just follow Brian," she advised as they came closer to the place where a large cart would take them into the belly of the mountain. "I'd go with you," she said in a nervous voice, "except once I tried and it—well, it didn't work. When I was little, my father tried to show me how it was all done and I—I panicked. Not to say you will, you understand. The old man said it can happen to some people."

"Claustrophobia," Tom mumbled.

"What?" Brian asked as he sat down on the cart and made room for Tom.

"Nothing," Tom answered, feeling doomed as he tried to sit on the flat wooden bed and not injure himself or someone else with the damned pick axe. "Just talking to myself."

"You do that a lot, don't you?" Brian teased as the cart started its descent.

It didn't help matters to see that the only thing holding it back from dropping to the bottom of the mine was a single rope. It really was like an

178

amusement park, like the top of the roller coaster, right before it was ready to take that first plunge.

As he left daylight behind him, only he heard a woman call out with false brightness, "Good luck to you, Thomas."

He knew her voice was really filled with pity.

His body felt the steep angle as they descended into the mountain and he caught his breath as he heard the screech of the cart's wheels as it strained against the rope pulley. Whistles were ringing and bells were clanging and Tom felt he had been lowered straight into hell.

All too soon the cart reached the bottom and abruptly stopped. The men around him quickly filed out and Tom followed Brian, unsure where to go or what to do. All he could think was that hell was sure cold, for it had to be a good thirty degrees cooler than above ground. Looking around him, he couldn't believe that anyone worked under these conditions. The ground was made of crushed, flaked coal sprinkled with hay. Already he could see the dust being kicked up from it by the men or the mules who dragged carts behind them. It was dusty and filthy, and he could see now why no one spoke to each other unless it was necessary. No one wanted to breathe it in.

Several men nodded to him, as if they knew him. He recognized a few from Fitzhugh's bar, and assumed the rest were Brian's friends, so he returned their brief greeting. Without warning, Brian turned to him and held a match to his head. Startled, Tom jerked back.

"Hey, I'm only lighting your head lamp," Brian said, once more putting the match to Tom's hat.

"Sorry," Tom mumbled, feeling more out of

179

place than ever.

Brian stood back and looked at him. His grin was sympathetic. "It's terrible hard work down here, isn't it?" Without waiting for an answer, he continued, "You did good last week. I know you didn't get paid much, less than two dollars, wasn't it? But that's going to change with these negotiations. This time we're not giving in."

Tom didn't know what to say, so he nodded his agreement. That seemed to please Brian.

He clamped Tom on the shoulder and added, "You've been a big help with all your suggestions, but I think you should get some rest tonight. You look a mite peaked." His voice lowered. "If you feel like it, though, we're meeting at Liam's house. Ten o'clock."

"Ten o'clock," Tom repeated in the same secretive voice, not knowing what Brian was talking about. Suddenly, he wondered just what he'd been doing, what he'd been up to with Meggie's brother this past week. He could have done anything. It was too confusing, too frightening to think about.

"Carter!" Someone shouted his name and Tom turned in the direction of the gruff voice. A stout man with a heavy handlebar mustache glared at him. "You'll be working this week at the new vein," he said, indicating that Tom was to follow him. Giving Brian a nod, he fell in behind the man and was led off into one of the many passageways.

"After you break for lunch, see John Smithen. He said he needs extra men to tunnel." The man waited for him to respond, then gave him a disgusted look. Tom read it correctly. He was the rookie, the inexperienced one that held the rest of them back. This man wasn't a miner. This man was management. And having an apprentice in his crew was only a liability.

"See if you can manage not to break anything this week," the man sneered. "At the rate you're going, you'll never see a three-dollar week. How much did they deduct from your pay?"

Tom didn't answer. He was beginning to lose his fear of underground. This man was oppressive.

"Eight thirty-five, I'd heard."

"Is this where you want me to work?" Tom asked, ignoring the taunt.

The man kicked at the flooring, creating a small black storm of dust that swirled around the both of them. Leaning closer, the man whispered, "I'd be more careful about the friends you choose, if I were you. A tenderfoot like you can get real hurt down here. No telling when a load of coal might come loose. Happens all the time."

Tom willed himself not to cough because of the thin black dust that was settling all over him. He refused to look away from the man and his jaw hardened in anger as his hand tightened on the pick axe. "Are you threatening me?" he asked in a deadly calm voice that drew the attention of those around them.

The man took a step backward. "I'm warning you. You're new down here. Just want you to be careful," he added, looking around him to the other miners. Glancing back to Tom, he whispered, "Watch your step, Carter. I don't like you — coming into this town and creating trouble. I heard all about your activities. Talk is you're real smart . . . a brainy, bookish man that ain't got no business interfering with the lives of others. You

181

leave these negotiations to the people that was appointed. You mind me, boy, 'cause you just made yourself one powerful enemy."

Tom's gaze never faltered. "I'll remember that," he said with a coolness that he didn't feel. He was looking at the hate in the foreman's eyes, recognizing it, and not knowing exactly what he had done to deserve it. It didn't matter, though, for as he watched the man walk away, he knew that it was all about power. Hadn't he dealt with other forms of it for twenty years? It was only slightly different here. The players were different. This time the play for power was between the mine owners and these men down here. The struggle was always between them on top and them below, but never before had it been more clear to him than right now.

The capitalist, the super-powered manager of the past, receded in this underground hell and a new side of him emerged. What these men needed was a union. And an organizer.

Holding up his pick axe, he spied the shiny gray vein in the mountain and took a swing at it. Coal broke off in chunks and hit the floor. Although his hand still ached, he felt pretty good about himself as he bent down and picked it up. The black coal was heavy and cold. Tossing it into a waiting bin, he wiped his palms on the legs of his pants. It was useless. Already the skin on his hands was coated in black dust.

"I'd be careful, Carter, about mixing it up with Ben Creedon. That's one mean sonofabitch."

Tom looked over to a young man who was working eight feet away from him. The boy looked no more than eighteen.

Tom smiled. "What's your name?"

"Andy Larkin." Even his voice sounded dull, as if at his early age he knew life wasn't about to get any better.

The expression on Tom's face was friendly as he said, "That was Ben Creedon, huh? Well"—and he took a deep breath—"looks like it's going to be a long day."

"Ten hours," Andy muttered sarcastically as his own axe dug into the wall of the mountain.

Coughing on the inhaled dust, Tom could only stare at the boy. *Ten hours? Underground?* His earlier determination quickly vanished. He'd already put in a five-hour workday before he'd been zapped to this time! How would he ever make it? Just to see daylight again . . .

If working underground was hell, then the sight of Meggie waiting at the entrance of the tunnel was pure heaven. He kept his eyes on her as the pulley drew the trolley out of the mountain. No one bothered to talk; no one had the energy. He wanted to shout out to her, but his mouth was too dry and he was too tired, yet it seemed incredible that he was the only one who could actually see this beautiful woman. Even though it was fading in the early evening, the sunlight hurt his eyes and he squinted to see her better. She looked wonderful. Her hair was pulled back into a braid and wisps of red curls surrounded her face. She was still dressed in the pale yellow clothing from his time and the skirt caught a slight breeze and lifted away from her long, straight legs. Spotting him, her smile was wide with welcome. And he wished

. . . oh how he wished she had never thought of becoming a nun.

When the trolley came to a complete stop, he fought with his body to make it move out of the cart. He needed to get to her. He had thought today that he was going to die down there. There were times when his body simply couldn't lift another mound of coal or swing another axe. He forgot how often he'd wanted to yell out from the constant sound of trickling water that grated on his raw nerves. How many times had he swung his shovel at rats the size of small dogs? But he'd survived, because he knew at the end of it all, at the end of the day, she would be there, waiting for him. And he wasn't wrong.

Ignoring his screaming muscles, Tom pushed his body upward and dragged himself away from the tunnel. Quickly, she rushed up to him.

Oh God, Meggie thought as she looked at him, it was like seeing Brian or Da. His face was completely black, only his eyes and his mouth showed color. Every inch of skin, or tuft of hair that was exposed, was covered in coal dust. Only this time it was worse because she knew this wasn't his way. Thomas's way of life was that of a gentleman. She had seen the pride he had taken with his appearance, always spotless clothing, always neatly groomed. This poor man walking toward her was barely recognizable as the same soul who'd gone into the mines this morning.

"Let me get you home," she whispered into his tortured eyes. "I'll take care of you." She placed her arm through his, and feeling his weight leaning heavily against her, she led him down from the mountain.

# Chapter 13

"Are ya awake then, Mr. Carter? Your supper'll be ready in a few minutes."

Meggie looked at the door and wanted to stop Bridgi from saying anything more. But then she remembered that Bridgi couldn't hear her. Quickly, she glanced at Thomas, asleep on the bed. He was exhausted and needed his rest.

"Will you be comin' down?" Again, Bridgi called through the door.

Startled, he half sat up in bed. His eyes were wide with alarm. "Huh? Wha—"

Meggie came back toward him. "It's all right. It's only Bridgi asking you down to supper. Tell her you'll eat in here."

Tom could only stare at her. He'd thought it was all a dream. But it wasn't. All of it was really happening . . .

"Mr. Carter?"

"Answer her, Thomas. Ask her to bring you up a tray. Tell her you're too tired to come downstairs."

Confused, Tom did as he was asked. "Could you

please bring me my dinner on a tray. I'm"—and he looked at Meggie, who was nodding her encouragement—"I'm exhausted."

There was a pause and then Bridgi replied, "I suppose I can. But don't you be makin' a habit out of this."

Both he and Meggie listened to the woman's heavy footsteps on the stairs. Slowly, Meggie looked toward the bed. Thomas was staring at her, a confused expression on his face.

"How do you feel?" she whispered, noting that the hair on his chest was much darker than the tousled hair that fell onto his forehead.

"Like a truck ran over me," he answered, swallowing down the dryness in his mouth. "What happened?" Before she could answer, his expression changed. *"The mine!"*

She nodded. "You were down there for nine hours."

He closed his eyes with a heavy weariness. "When was it? Yesterday?"

"This morning."

Appalled, he looked at her and let his body fall back against the pillow. "This morning?" he repeated in disbelief. "My God!" Suddenly, his eyes opened and he asked in a strangled voice, "Did I bathe outside in a wooden tub?"

Meggie smiled. "You did."

"In a tub? Outside?"

"All the men do. It's always been that way. And Bridgi's so fussy, she would never allow you in her home covered in coal dust. Besides, we don't have your beautiful bathing rooms, with water coming out of walls." Her smile increased. "We're more old-fashioned, and it may take a bit longer, but we do manage to get clean."

His eyes slowly shut. "And did Bridget take my clothes away?"

This time Meggie couldn't help laughing. "Yes, she did. Although you weren't too tired to argue with her about it. She only washed them."

"I seem to remember her giving me new ones. But where did I get them? I think she said they were in here."

Nodding, Meggie mumbled, "I got them."

"What?" he turned his head and looked at her. "Where did you—" His mouth opened in surprise. "You didn't! Not again!"

"I did," she said defensively. "While you were working. The company store has more than enough to go around. If I can't be seen, then I might as well make the best use of it."

He leaned up on one elbow and the sheet dropped down to his waist. "But you can't keep appropriating whatever you want, Meggie. People are going to recognize these things and know they're stolen."

"It isn't really stealing," she countered, "so don't be givin' me that woebegone look. I only take what is needed."

"Listen, I was too tired to tell you what I'd heard down there in the mines. There's going to be an investigation about all the missing articles from the Reading store. Some men were joking about a patron saint, or something. Others are worried that the mine owners will use it against them in the negotiations."

Trying to keep her eyes away from his bare

187

chest, she crossed her arms and walked toward the window. "I never thought anyone might get in trouble," she whispered. "I was only trying to help."

"I know that. And you did help. But it has to stop. From what I gather, everyone has to be careful now, until these negotiations are over."

Looking out at the mountain, Meggie said, "Do you really think anything will change, Thomas? Nate Gowen will win. He always does. He's even planted a spy in our midst."

"What are you talking about?"

She looked at him. "James Roarity, damn his black heart."

A picture of a tall, thin, dark-haired man came to mind and Tom said, "Roarity is a traitor? How do you know this?"

She looked back out the window. "I know. Right before the explosion, I heard him and Nate Gowen speaking. Roarity is from Chicago. He's been planted here to spy on us. *That's* why I was trapped in that building and the dynamite—"

She stopped speaking, aware that he was staring at her in the most peculiar way.

"What are you talking about?" he demanded. "What building? What dynamite?"

Meggie could no longer endure the horrified expression on his face. Clearing off a small area on the table, she said in a falsely calm voice, "Oh, just the Reading office building. But that's where I heard it. James Roarity was hired by the Reading to become one of us. I tried to tell you this before."

Keeping the sheet around his waist, Tom sat up.

188

"Wait a minute. What are we talking about here?"

A knock on the door saved Meggie from answering.

"Mr. Carter? I have your supper."

He looked frustrated by the interruption and motioned for Meggie to turn around. Pulling on his trousers, he called out, "I'm coming, Mrs. Humne. Be right there."

Bridget walked in, deposited her tray on the table, and turned around, as if searching the small room. "Thought I heard you talking up here," she remarked.

Shrugging, Tom tried to smile.

"Come to think of it," Bridget continued, "I might as well be honest. I've been hearin' you talkin' up here for some time now. Seems a bit strange, to say the least."

Tom felt guilty, as if found out, yet when he looked at Meggie, he could see her innocent expression. Knowing he wasn't about to get any help from her, he cleared his throat, pushed his hair back off his forehead, and said, "Sometimes, when I'm thinking, I like to talk out the solutions."

"Solutions to what?" Bridget asked, her eyes narrowing as she looked back at him.

"Ahh . . . like the problems with the mine," he fumbled, "and the negotiations. Sometimes I think aloud about that." He felt like an idiot, and it didn't' help that Meggie was grinning like a fool behind the old woman.

"That's what happens when you keep company with Brian Gillbride and the likes—"

"Why don't you like Brian?" Tom interrupted, noting the quick anger that came into Meggie's eyes.

Bridget poured cool tea into a large glass and said, "Oh, I always liked Brian, to be sure. He was a good boy, and now he's a good man — I suppose."

"What do you mean?" Tom saw the old woman was trying to tell him something, maybe even warn him.

"There's some that say Brian Gillbride is a hero, and then there's some that say him and his crowd are part and parcel of all the trouble that's been happening around here. Most don't think he'll ever make old bones the way he's going."

"*Stop it!*" Meggie demanded. "Tell her to stop it!"

Looking at Meggie's frightened expression almost made Tom change the subject, but something was nagging at him, something that didn't make any sense until now. Turning his attention back to the older woman, Tom asked, "What do you mean about Brian and his crowd? Are you saying they're . . . they're terrorists?"

"I don't know about that," Bridget remarked. "Though the Mollies have certainly brought terror to many . . . mostly the mine owners and — "

"Did you say the *Mollies?*" Tom quickly interrupted, while he heard Meggie groan across the room.

Bridgi looked around her in a secretive way. "You've been spending all your time with them this past week, don't tell me you don't know who they are. Listen to me, Thomas McKenna Carter, I'm tellin' you this because I don't want any trouble in this house. When I fall asleep at night, I

190

don't want to fear who'll come barging into my bedroom and shoot me while I sleep."

"They did that?" Tom asked in disbelief.

"Don't listen to her," Meggie begged, tears forming in her eyes. "She doesn't know it all. She doesn't know the reasons behind their actions—"

Bridgi shrugged. "I'm only telling you what I've heard through the years. I don't know who's done what because it's a secretive society, you know, and women are supposed to pretend it doesn't even exist. Hah! As if we'd lost our reasoning."

"What do you think, Bridget?" Tom asked. "You live here. Is Brian a hero, or a terrorist?"

Smoothing out the cloth napkin, she took a deep breath, as if trying to form a correct answer. Finally she said, "I lost both my husband and son before their time. It didn't have to be that way. The mine killed them. If it wasn't the damned dust takin' the breath out of my man's lungs, then it was my poor Robert, just a child, workin' in the breakers for eight to ten hours a day. Until he didn't come home one horrible May afternoon. They say his back was broke from the fall."

She took a handkerchief out from her waistband and wiped her eyes. "My little man never had his chance at life. And there wasn't a one of them, Nate Gowen included, that came to see him off." She raised her head and Tom could see an anger that went far beyond the hurt in her voice. "You want to know what I think, Mr. Carter? What they gave me was pity and thirty-one dollars. How did they come up with the exact figure, I've asked myself a hundred times over the years. Was that what my Robert was worth in their eyes? Thirty-

191

one dollars? I have no husband. I have no son. But I bought this house and it's mine. And I'm here, a reminder of what thirty-one dollars of conscience money will buy."

She blew her nose and sniffled back more tears. "So I take in boarders and cook for the guards and keep my eyes and ears open, because I have a debt that has yet to be paid. In my eyes Brian Gillbride is a hero."

"A hero?" Tom was surprised. He quickly looked at Meggie and saw she was smiling, despite her own tears. "But then why did you say those things about Brian?"

Bridget lifted her chin in defiance. "I thought you should be warned because it isn't really your fight. You're new here and you seem to be drawn into this. And Brian used to be more level-headed. Since his sister's death, he's taken to drinkin' more often than's wise. He should be more careful, especially now. I only hope he stays alive long enough to make a difference."

"His sister?" Tom looked up to Meggie and their eyes locked. "What was her name again?"

"Meggie," Bridget answered.

She was shaking her head, silently asking him to stop questioning the old woman. But he felt so close to a discovery of something important.

"And how did she die?" he asked, seeing the sorrow return to Meggie's eyes.

"It was when the Reading building went up. Some say Brian sent her in there to plant a bomb and that's why he won't forgive himself. Although I can't imagine Meggie doing such a thing."

"Why?" Tom asked, finally breaking Meggie's

gaze and looking back to the old woman. "Because she was a n—"

Suddenly one of the chairs at the table fell over to the floor, interrupting Tom and scaring Bridget so that the woman jumped back and held a hand over her heart.

"Lord! Did you see that?" Bridget demanded in a frightened voice. "It was like someone flung it down in anger." She crossed herself.

That's exactly what happened, Tom thought, as he looked into Meggie's angry eyes. "I must have leaned it up against the table incorrectly."

Bridget gaped at him. She wasn't convinced. "Yes, well, I'm sure your dinner is past cold now. I'll warm it up for you."

"Don't bother. It's too hot for that." Tom wiped his forehead with his palm, as if just noticing the July heat and humidity. Or was it Meggie's incensed expression that made his body react?

"Well, then, I'll let you eat. I'll be back later for the tray."

"Don't bother. I'll bring it down for you," Tom offered while walking Bridget to the door.

The old woman turned around to him and smiled. "I'm glad we had this talk," she announced, "but be more careful about the furniture, if you will. Too many strange occurrences." She hesitated for a moment. "I hope I didn't make a mistake with you, Thomas McKenna Carter."

Tom smiled back. "You didn't."

Even before the door was completely closed, he heard her angry voice, "How dare you? If you have any questions about my life, you can ask me!"

193

"I thought you were too quiet during that discussion," he remarked dryly while pulling out the chair and sitting down to his dinner.

She wouldn't let up. "You questioned her, prodded her. What were you trying to do?"

"I was trying to find out some information," he answered in a calm voice. Not seeing any knife, he picked up a piece of chicken and took a bite.

"Information? I could have told you anything you wanted to know," she countered while looking at the chicken. Unconsciously, her tongue ran over her lips in hunger. How long had it been since she'd eaten? Was it that hamburger with Gerald? Just thinking about sinking her teeth into that delight made her actually salivate. It didn't help matters that her stomach reacted to her thoughts by rumbling loudly.

"Please, join me. Sit down," he offered. "There's plenty."

She didn't need a second invitation.

He lifted his plate toward her and she took a piece of chicken. "Thank you."

"I should thank you. I don't know how I would have gotten through all this without you." He smiled and waited for her to react.

She was still upset and ignored his plea. "You had no right to do that, Thomas," she said reprovingly.

"What? Ask about your brother? You heard her, Meggie. She practically said Brian was a terrorist."

She quickly swallowed, needing to reply to that accusation. "Sometimes you use strange words . . . like terrorist. You make it sound like Brian is a criminal. Well, he's not. He's fighting to make

194

things better here. All of them are. And it isn't a crime to want change. It's survival."

"But shooting people in their beds . . ."

"She never said Brian did that. That didn't take place here. No one in this assembly of Mollies has ever killed—"

"Do you mean to say there are others?" he interrupted.

She nodded. "Of course. There's divisions all over the state. We're all fighting for justice. All we want is to be treated decently, fairly."

"You won't get that with violence."

"Tell that to Brian," she whispered fervently. "Make them all listen. And tell them about James Roarity. You have to do it. I can't."

Tom held up his hand. "Wait a minute. Why are you so involved in this? And why did you throw that chair just when I was asking about you? You're hiding something. I can feel it."

She laughed, as if his suggestion were comical. "Don't be ridiculous. I was annoyed because you were questioning an old woman, instead of asking me."

"Then I'm asking you now. What were you doing in the Reading building? And why does Brian feel guilty about it? Did he really send you in there with a bomb?"

She didn't say anything. She continued to eat while stubbornly ignoring him.

"I thought you said I could ask you anything. What are you hiding?" He put the chicken back on his plate and stared at her. "You're one of them, aren't you?"

She looked away.

"Why won't you look at me?" he demanded. "I can't believe it! How could Brian ask you to do that? He had no right to involve you . . . a nun."

"Oh, stop it!" she said in disgust, more for herself than anyone else. "No one made me do it. I thought about it, long and hard, before I made my decision. You don't know what it's been like here. Oh granted, you've just spent your first day underground and gotten your first taste, but that's nothing compared to the years the Reading's been bleeding us dry. And what happens when we're too old, or too sick? Or too poor to pay off our debts? We're cast aside, or put in jail, because we're no longer productive."

"Meggie . . ."

"No, you listen. You don't know. My father was a strong man. He prided himself on loading eighteen cars of coal in a week. If it was a good week and nobody was maimed or killed, if there wasn't a cave-in or some other disaster, then maybe he would make around fifty cents a car. That's nine dollars, and it wouldn't be bad pay except now you'd have to deduct five dollars for two kegs of powder, a dollar fifty for two gallons of oil for the head lamp. Maybe two or three broken drills would cost another dollar. Then take out two more dollars for ground rental on that sad piece of land. Deduct groceries and clothing and what do you have left?"

Tom did a few mental calculations. "You wouldn't have anything left. You'd owe money."

"Exactly. Most of us were in such debt that we couldn't leave, or run away from it. The Reading owned us. That's why I was willing to plant the explosive. That and Connon Rafferty."

He was looking at her as if he was seeing her for the first time. "Who's Connon Rafferty?" he asked with a feeling of dread.

"Connon Rafferty was unjustly accused of murder. It's a long story, but he was innocent. There was evidence in the Reading building that was going to help convict him and I wasn't about to stand by and let them hang an innocent man. A family man with young children. This time I could do something."

"This time? You mean they've done this before?"

Suddenly she looked older than he, wiser in a way that spoke volumes. He felt naive, gullible, as if he were the innocent in the conversation.

"Thomas. That's what we're fighting against. That's what we want to change. You have good ideas. You're educated. You can help Brian in these negotiations."

He briefly looked out the window. Dusk was settling on the patch like a light summer blanket, and he could feel the oppressive heat bearing down on him, just like Meggie's suggestions. Taking a deep breath, he shook his head. Why not, he thought, he might as well go along. Maybe this was the purpose to all this craziness. Perhaps this is why they kept popping up in this time.

Looking at her, he smiled. "There's a meeting tonight. At Liam's. I think I'll go."

Her smile was filled with promise. *"We'll* go, Thomas. Together."

# Chapter 14

They sat around the scarred wooden table, all five of them — Liam Dunleavy, Jack Donahue, James Roarity, Connon Rafferty, and Brian. Thomas sat by the door, merely an observer, not yet invited to enter the discussion. As the men began arguing once more, he stared beyond them to Meggie. She looked tired, and sad. Tears were forming at her eyes. Being around her brother and not being able to speak to him was tearing her apart. He wished they were alone right now. He'd take her in his arms and hold her, comfort her . . . Why couldn't he stop that fierce wanting? His body still reacted to her, even now, in this small wooden house with its multitude of doilies, fragile lace that reminded him of his grandmother. Meggie. He still wanted her. It was like a sickness that had no cure. As he watched a tear slowly slide down her cheek, Tom fought within himself to find a remedy, for he was swiftly losing the battle.

She stood behind her brother's chair, staring at the back of his head. How she longed to touch the dark strands, to let him know that he wasn't to blame for anything. Brian, she thought his name, as if somehow he could hear her thoughts. How she loved him, her only family. And she was proud of him. She had always thought that Liam was the head of this group. Somehow, at some unknown time, that responsibility had shifted to Brian.

Ignoring that black-hearted Roarity, she looked at the faces of the other men. They were listening intently as Brian spoke.

"I say we all remain calm. There's nothing to be gained right now from overreacting. There's too much at stake and Connon would be the first to agree."

"How can you let this go by without striking back?" Jimmy Roarity demanded. "They beat the bloody hell out of Connon before they released him. Show them, Connon. Show them the bruises—"

"There's no need for that, Connon," Brian interrupted, touching the shoulder of the quiet man to his left. "We're all aware of what happened."

Poor Connon, Meggie thought, as she looked at the man next to her brother. It seemed as if the life had gone out of him since his arrest two months ago. But that didn't give Roarity the right to provoke the others. She looked across the room to Thomas.

"Say something. I told you Roarity works for the mine owners. He's trying to incite them. Can't you see it?"

Thomas shook his head to quiet her. He'd already told her that he wouldn't get involved unless he was asked.

"If you're aware, Brian, then how can you just let it pass?" Jack Donahue asked. "Maybe Jimmy, here, is right. Who's it going to be next time?"

"Listen to me," Brian commanded in a passionate voice. "That is *exactly* what they're expecting. The hotheaded Irishmen are going to retaliate. And then this time they have all of us. And that's the end to the negotiations. We're already back in the mines. They know it's only temporary. For the first time we have some power, something to negotiate with."

"And what is that?" Roarity asked.

Meggie saw the gleam in Roarity's eyes and something broke inside her. *Nobody* believed her! Without further thought, she walked up behind the traitorous bastard and, with all her strength, yanked his hair.

Roarity yelled out as his head was jerked back and then thrust forward until it nearly hit the tabletop. Everyone at the table looked at him, as if he'd just had a fit.

"Are you all right, James?" Liam was the first to speak while the others continued to stare.

Tom rose to his feet, too startled by Meggie's actions to say anything. To him, Roarity seemed more frightened than hurt. He continued to stare at Meggie as if she'd lost all reason.

"I had to do something," Meggie said in her defense. "Brian was about to give all his plans to the bas—to the traitor."

Shaking his head, Tom ran his fingers through his own hair. He was powerless to stop her now and she knew it. He couldn't even answer her in

200

front of the others.

"It—it was like something grabbed hold of me and shook me," Roarity mumbled, his face white as a sheet. "I could feel it."

Meggie grinned. "And I'll do it again," she threatened to Tom.

Tom tried shaking his head, warning her not to carry it too far, but she ignored him. He could see she was feeling her power over her enemy.

"Maybe you should go on home, Jim," Donahue offered. "You're not looking well."

"No," Roarity insisted. "I want to hear what Brian has to say."

Meggie looked at Tom and shrugged her shoulders, as if to silently convey that she had given Roarity a chance. "What can I do?" she asked aloud.

Tom didn't answer as Brian began to speak and Meggie reached out for Roarity's hair. As the man was again thoroughly shaken, those around him backed away in fright.

"My God, man. What's happening to you?"

"Jimmy!"

"Sweet Lord, somebody get help!"

Holding his forehead, Tom shook his head and looked toward the wall. "I can't believe this!" he mumbled to himself. "It's like being in a Stephen King novel."

Laughing at the scene she had caused, Meggie turned to him. "Who's Stephen King?" she asked between giggles.

Again, Tom shook his head, though no one would notice if he were to stand on it. Everyone was staring at Roarity. And Meggie, she was reigning over them all. With her auburn braid hanging down her back and her chin held high, she looked like an ancient queen dealing with her inferiors. She was definitely enjoying this, and he realized that he would have to put a stop to her punishment. Walking over to the table, he ignored Meggie's last question about Stephen King and said, "I think you should go home now, Roarity. Get some rest. You don't look well at all."

The others agreed with him and even Roarity couldn't argue with his wisdom. Truly, the man was convinced he was ill.

"I'll see you home, James," Connon offered. It was the first time Tom had heard the blond man speak and he looked relieved to leave the meeting.

"We'll talk later then, Brian?" Roarity asked.

Brian nodded. "Tomorrow, after the mass to bless the negotiations."

Roarity motioned to Connon and the two men quickly left. Thoroughly pleased with herself, Meggie sat down in the empty chair next to her brother and smiled at Tom.

"Come," she said, indicating the place vacated by Roarity. "Join us."

He had a hundred things he wanted to say to her, and most of them weren't fit for her ears. Knowing he couldn't say any of them right now, he turned his attention to her brother.

"Brian. I've been over there listening and I wonder if I might say something."

Brian nodded. "I know you told me you didn't want to interfere, but you've been helpful before and I don't think any of us will object to you speaking now."

202

Brian looked around the table and all shook their heads, including Meggie. Again, forcing himself to ignore her, Tom began. "I think Brian's right about staying calm. You're not going to win this by violence. If you're thinking retaliation for what's been done to Connon, it doesn't matter whether it's justified or not, you're still going to be outside the law. And that's the weapon the mine owners are going to use against you. Right now, if I understand correctly, there are no records of your debt to the company."

"They were destroyed in the explosion," Jack Donahue offered. "That was before you came to the patch."

Glancing at Meggie, Tom nodded before continuing. "That's what you have to hold over them. All of you know you owe money, but they can only guess at how much. Right now, you could all walk away, free and clear. They might try to stop you, but without proof of your debt you can't be held responsible."

"Why would we walk away?" Donahue asked. "This is the only work we know. This is what our fathers did."

"And died for it," Meggie added, though none but Tom could hear her.

"Then if you want to continue working here, you'll have to come to an agreement with Nate Gowen. And there's a way to start."

He looked at the expectant faces and wondered whether he was making a mistake. Should he stay out of it? Not interfere? For the life of him, he couldn't understand why the whole town didn't just pack up and leave. But Donahue was right.

This was their life, their way. And maybe that's why he was sent here to this time. Whatever reason, he knew instinctively that it was right.

Taking a deep breath, he wiped the perspiration from his brow onto his shirtsleeve. Why was it so damned humid? He was nervous enough. Knowing there wasn't any other way, he just said it. "You're going to have to form a union."

"What?"

"A union?"

"Here? In Lehigha? That's for the big cities," Liam said over the voices of the others. "Besides, everyone knows they don't last. Old Billy Silvis tried it in '59, down there in Philadelphia. Called it the National Labor Union. Completely gone now."

"Wait a minute," Brian called out. "Let's think about this before being in such a hurry to say no. What do you know about unions, Tom?"

Tom swallowed, took another deep breath, and plunged in. "A union, workers standing together, can lobby for the important issues like hourly wages, safety measures, getting those children out of the mines. And getting rid of the company store with its inflated pricing. Allow free enterprise. This is America. Why shouldn't, say, Jack, here, be allowed to open a general store and compete with the Reading? Then the prices would be more in line. Just to stay in business, the company store would have to lower its prices to compete with Jack."

"They'll never go for it," Jack announced. "Why should they? Right now they've got a stranglehold on us and they know it."

204

"But the hold isn't quite so strong," Tom countered. "This may be summer, but the company is already thinking about winter. How many months behind in production are they because of the strike? If Pennsylvania can't fill its orders, then there's always West Virginia, or Ohio . . . another coal mining region. Believe me, the strike has hurt them. They want an end to this as much as you do, or they'd never have agreed to negotiations."

He looked around the table and was pleased by the interested expressions. At least they were listening and not shouting about retaliation. "Now here's what I think you should do: I think we need to make a trip to Philadelphia. Find this Billy Silvis person and see what he has to say. But most important, we're going to talk to a few newspapers. What if we could interest a couple of reporters in coming up here? Let them see what's really going on. See the kids on the breakers, the old men sick from the mines, the hopelessness of never being able to get out from under. I think it's time the country hears your side of the story. And don't ever underestimate the power of the word. The right reporter and the right story will give you more strength than a hundred men swinging shovels at guards. The right coverage will gain you sympathy. That's when you're going to get the politicians in your corner because they always want to be on the popular side come election time. And *that,* my friends, is the kind of pressure, the leverage, you're going to need going into negotiations. Take this fight out of the patch and make it a national one."

They looked at one another and smiles slowly

began to show on their faces.

Lifting her head, Meggie gazed at him, her eyes filled with admiration. "And no one has to lift a hand in anger," she whispered to him in an awed voice.

He didn't care if the others thought him strange, he couldn't look away from her. She stirred something so primitive, so male, that he was glad she'd forced her presence tonight. He had wanted to impress her. But it was more than that now. Much more.

He wanted her.

"You gave them hope, Thomas. For the first time, I could see it in their faces." Her voice was soft, almost shy.

Walking with her through the patch, he looked out to the dimly lit street. Just walking next to her was unbearable. There was something about the night, the heat, the darkness . . .

"I just told them about procedures that are very successful in my time. If I helped, I'm glad." He could barely speak. All he wanted was to press up against one of these old buildings and kiss her, taste her . . .

"Oh, you helped, Thomas. I've never seen Brian that enthusiastic before. Thank you for that. He seemed like himself tonight."

Tom nodded, not trusting his voice. What the hell were they going to do when they got back to Bridget's room? He wasn't going to make it.

"Is something wrong?"

"Wrong?" His voice sounded like a squeak.

Could she tell?

"You're quiet. I don't know. I thought maybe you were—"

"I'm hot," he interrupted, again using his sleeve to wipe his forehead. "I mean . . . it's so humid! Is it always like this?"

Even in the moonlight he could see she looked confused. "Well, it is July. You must be missing your home . . . the way you can make it cold."

"The air-conditioning. Right. I could certainly use an air-conditioner tonight," he mumbled while thinking a cold shower would be more welcome.

As if reading his thoughts, she stopped and touched his arm. It was like a hot poker searing his skin.

"I know a place where you can cool off, but you'd have to walk."

He looked at her, feeling desperate. "Where?"

"A mountain spring. Nobody would be there this time of night."

He didn't think twice. "Show me." It was as close to a cold shower as he would get.

Within twenty minutes Meggie had led him through the woods to her favorite spot in all the world. Her mother had taken her there many times when she was a child. She had come alone when she was older, especially when she had lost her baby and was truly alone. She felt the love of her mother here. Few people came, for many years ago some of the old ones told the story of its being haunted. Meggie didn't believe in such foolishness. Her mother would never have brought her if it were true. For Meggie, it was a special, almost magical place.

She stopped and looked out over the small pool. She could see the reflection of the moon over the still water and hear the soft musical sound of the waterfall. "In the spring, it's much larger and you can barely stand under the force of the waterfall," she said, feeling someone should speak and fill the silence. "It's very cold because of the mountain. But that's in the spring."

Tom looked at the water and felt little relief. Following her through the woods had been torture. How many times had his hands almost reached up to stop her, turn her around . . . "Looks great," he muttered, pulling at the starched collar of his shirt.

She glanced at him from the corner of her eye. "I can, um, wait for you over there," she mumbled, pointing to a spot in the darkness.

"How do you get to the waterfall?" Tom asked. "It's hard to tell at night."

She looked out to the water, as if struggling within herself. Finally, she said, "I suppose I could show you. But you'd have to be careful."

Neither of them said anything for a few seconds. It was Tom who broke the silence in a low voice. "I'll be careful."

*Ahh, God* . . . Meggie moaned inwardly. How was she ever going to manage this? It was a mistake, bringing him here. This was her special place, her secret spot. This was where she had dreamed of a man . . . a special man who would want her, and love her. A special man like Thomas. And her Mum had said this was a place where dreams could come true, if you wished and you worked hard enough.

Her heart beat furiously against her breast, and warm rivers of blood pounded through her veins as she said, "We'll have to take our shoes off."

"Our shoes?" Tom looked down to his feet.

"Yes. Of course."

Self-conscious, they both removed their shoes. Meggie's toes curled under as her bare feet touched the ground. It was cool. But not cool enough. Why couldn't she be wearing her own clothes? Clothes that were heavier than this pale yellow cotton Thomas had picked out. These were as light as a nightgown. Don't think, she told herself. Just lead him to the waterfall and leave him there.

"Come," she said in a strained voice. "And remember, be careful."

He didn't answer. He was too busy concentrating on placing his feet on the same wet stones that she was using before him. And in truth, he was afraid to say anything. She was holding up the hem of her skirt so it wouldn't get wet. Not too high, just modestly above her calves, just enough to tease him. And the sight of her slender ankles and calves was making him crazy. It was embarrassing.

"Here," she said, turning around as they reached the small waterfall. "If you stand here you'll be much cooler. I'll . . . leave you now and you can . . . well, swim if you like."

She had to pass him to get back and the mist from the fall was already making her wet, making her hair curl around her face, her clothes cling to her body. Any moment now, he was going to see the front of her blouse, the way her nipples were reacting to the cool water, to him . . . and she would never survive that embarrassment. How was she ever going to do this? And why was he staring at her like that? Didn't he know what he was doing to her? Please make him stop it!

Bringing her fingers up to her face, she wiped the mist away, anything to break that spell. Just as she was about to pass him, his hand reached out and touched her stomach. It was so innocent, yet so intimate, that she sharply inhaled. Rapidly blinking from the mist, she could only stare back at him.

"Don't."

He said it quietly. It wasn't like a plea. It was more of an admission. And he waited . . .

His back was against the falls and water gently splashed over his shoulders. Reaching up with both hands to push back the wet hair from his eyes, he blinked away the mist and gazed at her. Still, waiting . . .

"Thomas." She said his name in a whisper as the cool mist enveloped them. She was burning inside and leaned her head back against the rocks, as if for support.

Immediately, he placed his hands on either side of her shoulders, his arms pinning her against the rocks. "Meggie. Please. Tell me . . ."

His voice was like a soft feather that ran down her spine and up the front of her body. Her breasts ached for his hands; her thighs trembled with desire. She couldn't answer him. What did he want her so say?

"Tell me, Meggie. Say it." His voice was almost hoarse and he sounded as if he was in pain.

Staring back at him, she cried, "I can't . . . I don't know . . ."

His strong hands took hold of her face and he gently pulled her close to him, drawing her beneath the waterfall. She gasped as the water saturated her clothes and ran over her body.

"I want you. Come to me, Meggie." The water ran between them, yet she could feel his chest against her breasts, his legs against her own. And a throbbing . . . a pounding so wild, so intense, it was almost overpowering.

"Thomas. I don't know . . ." she repeated. "I . . ."

His eyes closed for a moment and then he looked straight up, beyond the trees and into the sky. "I want her," he shouted out in a desperate, rasping voice. "You sent her to me. Now, she's mine!"

Breathing heavily, he looked down to her, a tortured look on his face. "I don't care anymore, Meggie. I don't care about any of it. I need you." His fingers caressed her face in a silent, urgent plea. "Say something."

It was so clear now, and the answer so simple.

"Ahh, Tommy . . ." She lifted her hands to his hair and wound her fingers through the wet strands. Gently, yet firmly, with a purpose, she pulled his face down to hers.

The kiss started out as a gentle grazing of lips, an innocent touch, a hesitant tasting, but soon it became so much more. He quickly demanded a response; she gladly gave it — clinging to him, her heart silently singing with joy. It was astonishing how she craved him, and soon overwhelming. They separated, gasping for breath, and stared at one another. Without words they again came together, their lips meeting in a fierce duel. They were hungry, starved for each other, and the barriers started to quickly dissolve.

"Oh, Meggie . . ." Tom kissed her over and over—her lips, her cheeks, her eyelids. "You'll never know how much I've wanted to do this. You'll never know . . ."

She held him to her, savoring the sweetness of him. Never had she dreamed that he would want her like this. Never had she thought it was possible.

Kissing her neck, he unbuttoned her blouse and she reveled when he freed her breast and she could feel his skin against her own. His mouth traveled down, capturing her nipple and teasing it beyond endurance. She tugged his shirt away from his back and ran her nails down its center, causing him to arch against her.

Quickly, as if in silent communication, they pulled away and stared at each other.

His breath was short and rough. "Come into the pool with me," he softly commanded as he unbuttoned his trousers. "Come with me, Meggie."

She never took her eyes away from his. "Aye, Tommy," she whispered, running her fingers over his cheek. "I'll come with you." The decision was so easy, so natural.

Clothing quickly became a barrier that needed to be removed. There was no embarrassment, no hesitation. Each knew it was their time, their destiny.

And then they entered, slowly—two separate

people, holding hands until the water was deep enough and they could hold each other. Her body slid over his, creating such sweet heat that she cried out with pleasure and he threw back his head and laughed, enjoying her discovery.

"Meggie." He said her name softly, endearingly.

Her eyes filled with tears when she heard the tenderness in his voice. Her name had never before been said with such feeling, such warmth. To cover her emotion, she swiftly kissed him and he willingly responded.

The water did nothing to cool the passion between them. It was feverish, frantic, and seething with a craving kept too long under control. He entered her slowly, not wanting to hurt her, yet she grew impatient and pulled him to her in one swift, breathtaking moment. Her face lifted to the sky and Tom watched her in the moonlight.

There were tears on her cheeks.

"I'm sorry, Meggie," he said softly, kissing her arm. "I didn't mean to hurt you."

She looked down at him and smiled. "Don't ever be sorry. You didn't hurt me, Thomas. You couldn't. These are tears of joy." Her legs tightened around his waist and he held her closer. "Joy . . ." she repeated as he began a slow, ancient ritual. A ritual older than time, yet part of the universe.

Something happened to him then, something that thrilled yet frightened him, for he knew with a certainty he could never give her up. Not now. Not ever. She filled that emptiness inside him and made him whole. She made him feel strong and protective and part of something bigger than him-

213

self. He was filled with wonder as he stared at her beauty, and his throat burned raw with emotion as he whispered her name into the night.

"Meggie . . ."

# Chapter 15

"Mr. Carter, time to get up. Are ya awake, then?"

Their eyes opened at the same time and they stared at each other, each trying to frantically remember why they were in bed together. Realization dawned simultaneously and relief was quick to wash over them.

Tom smiled in remembrance and moved his lips toward hers. After briefly kissing her, he grinned. "Yes, Mrs. Humne. I'm awake," he called out.

Meggie returned his smile, shyness beginning to take over. Lord, she hadn't thought about waking up this morning in his arms! She hadn't thought about anything last night, except loving him and accepting the love he chose to give her. Last night. It was magical.

"I just wanted to remind you," Bridget called out, "about Mass this morning. The high and mighty Nathen Gowen will even be in attendance. The whole of the patch is turnin' out for this one."

"Mass." Meggie said the word in a shaken voice.

*"Mass,"* Tom repeated, the word coming out like a whispered proclamation of doom. "Oh, my God."

"Do ya hear me, Thomas?" Bridget yelled. "Everyone is expected to attend. It's the blessing for the negotiations." There was a pause, as if she was waiting for an answer. "Now up with ya. I won't be havin' it said that Bridget Humne can't get a man to Mass on time."

He stared at the woman still in his arms. Only moments before, Meggie had been warm and smiling, her red hair tousled around her face. Now, he could see the shame enter her beautiful blue eyes, feel the embarrassment in her stiff body, and he tried to stop it.

"Don't," he whispered. "Last night was—"

She closed her eyes, unable to look at him. "Last night was wrong," she interrupted. "Please . . . let me up."

He watched her, hoping she would open her eyes and look at him. She turned her face toward the wall. "Please, Thomas," she repeated. "Let me get up before Bridgi comes in."

"She can't see you—"

"Mr. Carter?"

*"I'm up!"* Tom shouted, annoyed by the woman's nagging. He was desperate; he could feel Meggie's shame, and he wouldn't allow it.

"Meggie, you didn't do anything wrong. It wasn't your fault. I should never have let you take me to the pool. You have nothing to feel ashamed about. Let me finish," he added, seeing her mouth open in denial. "I accept the responsibility for last night. And I'd do it again."

216

Her eyelids snapped open and she stared at him. "You would?"

He nodded. "Meggie, last night was—was magical and a little frightening. I'm sorry. About your vows, I mean . . ."

As soon as the words had left his mouth, he knew it was the wrong thing to say. He could see the horror in her eyes. Her vows. Now *he* felt ashamed. How could he have done that to her? He had taken away her choice. Could he live with that? "It wasn't fair of me, I know, but you have to believe that I wanted you so much. Meggie. Last night I would have dared anything for you, even God."

"Oh, no. Don't say that . . ." She held her temples, as if in pain, and shook her head. "Please. Let me get up!" Something snapped inside her and she shoved him away, enough to grab the blanket at the bottom of the bed and wrap it around her before she stood. "Get dressed, Thomas," she said in a chillingly calm voice as she pushed back the hair from her eyes. "After what you said last night, Brian and the rest of them will be expecting you at Mass."

"I don't care about that. I care about you, and how you feel." He sat up, the sheet barely covering him. He could sense her pulling away. And even though he should have expected it, the morning after, he refused to give her up without a fight. "Maybe you should think about what you want to do. I mean, it was in this time that you thought of becoming a nun. In my time, where you belong, you haven't made that decision. You can start over. Think things through—"

"What do you mean *belong?*" she interrupted. "I don't belong anywhere! Not here. Here, I'm like a ghost, unable to be seen, to touch my brother, to let him know that I love him. And I don't belong in your time either, or I wouldn't keep coming back here. Maybe I'm doomed to never stay in one place. Maybe I'm being punished. So don't talk to me about belonging!"

"Why would you be punished? For planting an explosive? I don't believe that violence solves anything, but think of the good that was accomplished when that building went up. Granted, for a permanent solution, you'd—"

"The good?" She stared at him as if he'd lost his mind. "*I* went up with that building. That's when this insanity began. Of course, I'm being punished, and not only for that. We all have to pay for our sins eventually." She wrapped the blanket closer around her shoulders and turned to the window. Pulling the curtain to one side, she stared out to the patch. Already people were in the street, making their way to the church for mass. "You'd better get dressed," she said in a disillusioned voice. "Or you're going to be late. Wear your suit," she added. "Bridget will be pleased."

She could hear him leave the bed.

"Meggie?"

She wouldn't turn around. She couldn't face him right now. He felt sorry for her! How could she ever tell him the truth now? What would he do if she told him that she had never entertained the thought of becoming a nun? That it was all a disguise? A ruse to commit a justifiable crime, if there was such a thing? And how would he feel to

218

find out that she had let him believe her, only for her own protection? And that now it had become so complicated that she had no idea how to get out of the lie anymore? He would never forgive her for not telling the truth before last night . . . before he had challenged God for her and put his soul in jeopardy. Swallowing down tears, she knew in her heart that this lie, this deception, would come between them. It would always be there.

"Are you coming?"

Turning, she looked at him and smiled. "You look handsome in your suit. Bridgi will be the talk of the patch."

Now he was embarrassed. How could he have made love to this woman, shared such an overwhelming experience with her, and now be uncomfortable with her compliments? He had to say something; she was staring at him. "Bridgi mothers me to death," Tom said while straightening his tie.

"She needs to mother," Meggie answered. "It was denied her for too many years. Be patient."

Just then they heard Bridget Humne's voice from the bottom of the stairwell. "Will you be fastin' for Communion? There'll be no time for anything but a cup of tea, and if you don't get down here, you'll be doin' without that."

Meggie and Tom looked at each other and smiled. It broke the tension in the room. "Go ahead," she said. "Have your tea. I'll get dressed and then walk with you and Bridgi to church."

He looked as if he wanted to say something more, but changed his mind. Nodding, Tom left her alone in the room.

I will not cry, she told herself as she quickly dressed in the yellow skirt and blouse. Without the benefit of an iron, it was wrinkled. But at least it was clean from the pool last night. Don't think about it, she silently argued. What good will it do? He thinks he's disgraced a nun, and he's having a terrible time of it. To tell him the truth would stop his guilt but he would hate her for her many lies. There was no easy answer to it. She would lose him either way. And so she'd take the coward's way out and do nothing.

Brushing her hair in front of the mirror, she couldn't look herself in the eye. It was too painful.


"Just look at them," Bridget muttered out of the corner of her mouth as they approached the church. "Like the royal guard, they are, standin' before the door and greetin' all who enter."

Meggie grinned at Tom as if to silently ask him to be patient. Smiling, Tom looked down to the gray-haired woman at his side.

"I don't know, Mrs. Humne, maybe they're just trying to be friendly."

"Hah!" The old woman straightened her hat and glared up at him. "You'd be a fool then, Thomas McKenna Carter. Nathen Gowen and his henchmen are only interested in money and power. Look, there's Brian. See, he's waiting for you. Good for him, he's not up there with Gowen and the likes."

Meggie looked at her brother and smiled. He was waving at Thomas, motioning for Thomas to join him. She saw Thomas wave back and then he looked at her, waiting for her to come with him.

She shook her head. "I'll be here when you get out."

He glanced down to the older woman by his side and said, "Why don't you go on, Mrs. Humne? I'll meet you inside."

Meggie watched Bridgi walk toward the green door of the church. She greeted Father Andrew, but curtly dismissed the Reading's president and the men who surrounded him. Meggie smiled.

"Why aren't you coming to the Mass?" Tom questioned, holding his hand up to Brian to ask him to wait.

Meggie shook her head. "I'd rather not. You go ahead. Brian's waiting."

"You can't go in because of last night. That's it. Isn't it? You feel—"

"Good God, man," Brian said behind him. "What're you doing? You're talking to the air." Meggie's brother laughed, as if amused.

Tom didn't say anything as he glared at Meggie. Once again, she had managed to avoid an answer. She was quite good at that.

The silence was dreadful and she felt she had to say something. "It has nothing to do with last night. I haven't entered that church in years, Thomas."

"Come along," Brian said as he took Tom's arm and led him away. "They're waiting. You know, Tom, I've been doing a lot of thinking about what you said last night. I believe you've got something there . . . a trade union. I like the sound of that."

Tom turned around twice to look back at her and she knew he was thinking about her words.

Maybe she shouldn't have said it, about how long she'd been away from the church, but at least it was the truth. And perhaps, that was the beginning. The truth . . .

Just as she was thinking it, something odd began happening. As Thomas and Brian reached the door of the church, Thomas suddenly started to fade, to disappear. Slowly, a little bit at a time. She blinked rapidly, as if to clear her vision, but he continued to diminish before her eyes. It couldn't be happening! Not now!

*"Thomas!"* she screamed, and he pulled from her brother and turned to her. He looked as frightened as she felt. Brian kept walking, proceeding through the green door of the church, as though nothing was happening, and Meggie knew she had to move, had to reach Thomas. She ran to him, desperate to get to him before he was gone, but he was too far away and she knew she would never make it . . . she would never stop it from happening!

*Oh, God, don't do this!*

Her fists pressed against her temples, trying to push away the terrifying vision, but he was disappearing right before her eyes! "Thomas!" His name came out as a forlorn cry, but it was too late.

He had already vanished.

He heard the noises, the sound of car horns, telephones ringing, computers printing out reports, and it all annoyed him. His heart was swiftly beating behind his chest, drumming in his ears, reminding him that he was alive, yet he fought

222

against opening his eyes.

Slowly, forcing himself, Tom lifted his lids. He knew before he even looked and saw the green lamp on his desk. He was back.

Without her.

His shaking hands covered his eyes. "What have I done to her?" he whispered in a frightened voice.

Who was being punished now?

The intercom buzzed and he stared at it, as if it were something alien. Again, even more insistent, the noise continued and he reached out his hand and pressed a small button.

"Mr. Carter?" a female voice asked.

He cleared his throat. "Yes . . . what is it, Janine?" It was odd that everything was familiar, like the name of his secretary, yet it was all so strange.

"Mr. Carter, it's Mac Weaver from Intercontinental on line three. He said you were expecting his call."

Mac Weaver. Head of Security for the airline. Meggie. Shaking his head, Tom tried to piece it all together. "All right. I'll take it."

Knowing he had to stay calm and not think about what had just happened, Tom pushed the line button and said, "Hello, Mac. What can I do for you?"

There was a short laugh from the security man. "I'll take that up at another time, Tom. Right now, I wanted to let you know that I've straightened out everything concerning the ticket for your religious friend."

Meggie. Yes, Tom thought, he remembered now

223

asking Mac to clear it with the airlines. He also remembered asking the man for another favor. "And of the other matter? How did it go there?" Tom closed his eyes and waited.

"Sorry, Tom. It's the craziest thing. There's absolutely nothing on a Sister Margaret Mary Gillbride. Checked with social security, IRS, even the federal agencies we use to check out our own security . . . and nothing. It's like this woman doesn't exist. Sure it's the right name?"

Trying to stay in control, Tom held his forehead and stared at the phone. "I could've been wrong, Mac. As it turns out, it doesn't matter anymore. Thanks for trying. And Mac," he added, knowing somehow that it was expected of him, "send me a bill."

By the time he hung up the phone, his palms were sweating so badly that he wiped his hands on his pants. "What am I going to do?"

Unable to handle the impossibility of the situation, the businessman, the logical side of him, kicked into gear. He needed a plan. And then he'd know where to start. Taking a deep breath, he pressed Janine's line and said, "Please call the Claremont Stables in the park and have them contact Gerald Kane. It's urgent. Tell them I'll meet him at my apartment. I'm leaving now, Janine."

"But the ICS contracts are nearly completed and you have a four-thirty appointment with Rick Peterson—"

"Let Morris handle it," Tom cut in. He'd always meant to relinquish some of the responsibility and now was the time to test his second in command. "I'm leaving. I don't know when I'll be back."

"Yes, sir," Janine answered in a subdued voice. "Will you be in tomorrow as usual?"

*Usual?* What was usual anymore? His whole life had turned upside down. "I don't know when I'm coming back. Tell Morris . . . never mind, I'll write him a note and tell him myself." There was a pause. "And thanks, Janine. Help Morris out, will you?"

"Of course."

He smiled. Pulling a pad of paper to him, Tom felt a tremendous weight lift from his chest. At least he was about to do something. He'd get her back. Somehow. He had to.

There had to be a way.


She sank to her knees in front of the church, watching Nate Gowen and his men file inside. Tears were streaming down her cheeks and a terrible feeling of emptiness began to settle inside her. She was alone. Finally. It had happened. So this is what hell is, she thought, this horrible, hollow feeling . . . where there is no one to speak with, no one to listen, no one to see you or touch you or love. My God, it was too much to bear!

*Thomas.* She had lost him, just as she knew she would. Why was it that happiness was always to be denied her? What had she done that was so horrible? She had loved. Last night she had felt blessed by Thomas's love. It was so precious. She had not expected to ever feel that way and thought surely God had forgiven her. Surely she had paid for any transgressions, or she never would have received the gift of Thomas's love.

It was unfair to have let her taste it and then snatch it away. She raised her chin and stared up to the blue sky. "It's unfair!" she repeated aloud, her chin quivering. "Why didn't you just let me die in the explosion?"

In the silence that followed, she freely let the tears roll down her cheeks. She had no idea how long she sat in the road. What did that matter anymore? She was doomed to wander unseen, unloved. The doors to the church opened and the townspeople started to come out. Men, women, children, Brian, Liam, and . . . Thomas!

*"Thomas!"* She wasn't sure whether she had opened her mouth or whether it was her mind that was screaming his name. Scrambling to her feet, she ran up to him, wiping away the tears, allowing a smile to come to her lips. It had been a mistake. She hadn't really seem him vanish as she'd thought. None of it had happened. How very silly, how foolish . . .

"Thomas. If you only knew what I've been going through—Thomas! What's wrong with you?" In deep conversation with her brother, he walked right past her. "Listen to me, Thomas, I was wrong about everything. I have to tell you the truth. You see, I'm not a nun at all. It was only a disguise. Please, don't be angry—talk to me. What's wrong with you?"

He kept walking with Brian, involved in a discussion. The others joined them and they all left together for the mines. Without her. It was as if he couldn't hear her, or see her. Running up to him, she reached out to touch him, but as with Brian, something held her back. What tragic irony.

Why was it that she could shake James Roarity's hair, but she couldn't touch someone she loved?

She pulled her hand back and covered her mouth as she watched him walk away. *Loved?* Of course, she loved him! And what better punishment than to realize that love when it was too late . . . never to say it . . . never to share it . . .

An anger started deep within her. For too long she had let fate rule her life, punishing her, taking from her everything that was important. Nothing mattered any longer. She had nothing left to lose. What could be worse than seeing Thomas, loving him, and always being shut out?

Now it was time to fight back.

She followed Thomas to Bridgi's house, where he would change into his work clothes. She entered the bedroom with him and watched as he removed the fine suit and pulled on the dull clothes of a miner. There was no embarrassment, for this wasn't her Thomas. It had come to her as she followed him. This was the side of Thomas that the others had seen back in the patch, while they were in New York City. This was the Thomas that had started working in the mines and had been meeting with Brian, but it wasn't the man she had fallen in love with. This man had never met her, laughed with her, or loved her. There was a part to him that was missing.

She smiled.

And so she would watch out for this man, guarding him from any harm, until that part of him that was her Thomas returned. And he would come back to her. She believed in the love they had shared last night. It had been too beautiful, too precious. He had been tender, yet demanding, and she had gladly given. When they had returned to Bridgi's house, there was no embarrassment, for the night was enchanted. Again, he had loved her and taught her to love him. She had never known that love between a man and a woman could be so sweet, yet comical; soul stirring, yet wild. And she had finally fallen asleep in his arms, strong, tender arms that encircled her in safety. Yes, last night had been a gift to treasure, to remember. No longer was she afraid. They had shared a special love last night and that was what would bring him back. Love.

She had waited her whole life for him. She could wait for his return.

He simply *had* to come back to her.

# Chapter 16

He wasn't home more than fifteen minutes when the doorman downstairs called to say that Gerald Kane was in the lobby and asking to speak with him.

"Send him right up," Tom answered, and hung up the phone. He stared at the door, waiting for the bell to ring. He pulled his tie off and flung it over a chair, next to his jacket. Still, nothing. What was keeping him? Impatient, he went into the foyer, threw open the door, and watched the elevator.

It seemed like an eternity until the steel doors opened to present the man. Gerald Kane was dressed in a suit and looked more like a wealthy, retired banker than a carriage driver. But the expression on his face told a different story. Something had happened to this old man. Something frightening.

"Is she here?" Gerald asked, looking beyond Tom. He brought a handkerchief out from his pocket and dabbed at his forehead.

"I was hoping she was with you," Tom answered, disappointment in his voice. "Come in."

Tom led the man into his home and offered him a cold drink. Gerald gladly accepted the chilled beer and sat on the edge of a chair in the white living room. Tom wasn't sure who was more upset — he or the driver.

"What happened?" Tom asked, pouring himself a stiff drink. He had a feeling he was going to need it.

"We were having such a fine afternoon," Gerald began. "Miss Gillbride . . . Meggie . . . was enjoying herself tremendously. We went through the zoo. I introduced her to my friends, people who own antique shops on Madison Avenue. She was clearly enjoying herself, until . . ."

"Until what?" Tom demanded. "What happened to her?"

Gerald took a deep breath and continued, "After lunch, we were passing another antique shop when she suddenly stopped and looked into the window. She became . . . well, transfixed."

"What do you mean?"

"She was staring into the shop, looking at something. It was as if she were seeing a ghost. And then she demanded that we go in. But it was closed for the holiday. There was a sign. The owners wouldn't be back for two more days."

Tom gulped his drink, stared at the man, then asked, "And then what happened?"

Gerald looked confused. "It was odd. She was looking in the window, saying something about a sewing table, when the strangest expression came over her face. She was pale and trembling. The sun came out from behind some clouds and the glare on the window was so strong that for a second, a few at the most, I couldn't see her. When I moved away from the glare, she was gone."

"Gone?" Tom asked. "You didn't see anything else? You didn't see her leave?"

Gerald shook his head. "I looked for her. I thought she might have become lost." He shrugged his shoulders. "I'm sorry, Mr. Carter, I was hoping she had made her way back here."

Tom swallowed down his drink. "Not yet," he muttered. "Not yet."

"Pardon me?"

Tom blinked several times, remembering who he was speaking with—poor Gerald. He felt Meggie's disappearance was his fault.

"Don't worry," Tom said. "I'm going to find her." He stood up and took Gerald's glass. "Would you like something stronger?" he asked the old man.

Gerald nodded. "That I would. Thank you." Folding his handkerchief and placing it back in his pocket, the man accepted the scotch whiskey and nodded to the books on the white stone coffee table. "They yours?"

Tom looked down to several volumes on parapsychology that he had bought at the Strand. He shrugged. "I thought they might be interesting."

Gerald picked one up and read the back cover. "Interesting, yes," he noted, an amused tone to his voice.

Tom heard the amusement. "Do you know anything about the subject?" he asked, suddenly very interested himself.

231

This time it was Gerald who shrugged. "I have a curiosity about such things." Gerald looked up at his host and smiled. "Who doesn't?"

Tom gazed down to the old man. He forced his lips to form a smile. "You're right. Who doesn't?" he repeated. "I, ah . . . I read about some curious things."

"What things?" Gerald quickly asked.

"Like out-of-body experiences, astral projections."

Gerald looked even more amused. "I've heard of such things."

Tom had the feeling that the man was laughing at him, and he had to admit that he felt foolish talking about these subjects with anyone but Meggie. "Yes, well. What do you think?"

Gerald raised his bushy, white eyebrows in a question. "I think anything is possible, under the right circumstances."

"What circumstances?"

"The state of mind, for instance. There are those who say that such things are schizophrenic in nature. I, myself, tend to think of it as exploring the possibilities."

Tom's gaze met Gerald's and held. There was something about this old man, Tom thought. Something peculiar, beyond the quaintness of his Irish accent . . . something compelling. "Will you help me find her?" he heard himself asking.

"You love her that much?"

"Yes." The answer was immediate and surprising, although it shouldn't have been. Taking a deep breath, Tom realized that it was somehow comforting and strengthening to admit it aloud.

232

He loved her. He loved Meggie!

Gerald's smile was warm. "Then I'll help you, lad. Now, tell me everything you know about her."

Tom took a deep breath and stared at the man. "You know the media would pay a small fortune for what I'm about to tell you? How can I trust you?"

Gerald sat back in his chair and laughed. Threading his fingers together over his ample belly, he noted, "You're a very suspicious man, Thomas Grey Carter. With all this"—and he waved his hand out toward the penthouse—"I can see why you're cautious. But it's more than that, isn't it?"

Realizing Gerald hadn't answered his question, just asked another, Tom decided it wouldn't hurt to test him. "I don't like the media. I consider it necessary, but thriving more on gossip than news. There's a fascination in this country for information about successful people—"

"Maybe those who aren't successful think they might discover something about those who are, and make use of it," Gerald interrupted. "Everybody's lookin' for the magic, lad. Don't you know that?"

"The magic?" Tom asked.

"Aye. The magic answer to why some of us are successful, with abundance to spare, and why some of us will spend the night on the sidewalk tonight." There was a pause and then Gerald continued. "I know you've asked yourself that question. The number of charities that you support tells me you aren't an unfeeling man."

"How do you know that? About the charities?"

"I can read, can't I? Do you think you're the

233

only one that can investigate a person? That media you have such a dislike for can sometimes carry the truth along with its gossip. You're a private person, that's for sure, and until recently not a very happy one. Is that when Meggie came into your life?"

Tom could only nod. What was it about this man that made him admit things about himself? Did he dare to trust him?

"Then we're back to my first request, aren't we? Tell me, Thomas, everything you know about her. Tell me about Meggie."

Maybe it was the way Gerald said his name, just like Meggie did, or perhaps it was the feeling of relief he felt in the old man's presence. And then again, maybe it was time to trust someone. He needed help, and this time he had nowhere else to go. This time his money, his connections were of no help.

"I was on a flight from Seattle to JFK when I first saw her . . ."

It took well over an hour to tell the story. Tom paced in front of the old man, gesturing with his hands to make a point, pouring drinks for both of them when his mouth became dry from speaking. Gerald was a good listener, barely interrupting throughout the long narration. When Tom was finished, when he had told the part about leaving Meggie behind and coming back to his office, he sat down on the edge of a chair and looked across to the older man.

"It sounds crazy, doesn't it?"

Gerald only smiled and shrugged his shoulders.

"I'm telling you, Gerald, if it hadn't happened

to me, I wouldn't believe it either. But I didn't make this up. It all *happened,* just like I told you." Frustrated, Tom rubbed his temples and whispered, "And I left her back there. All alone . . ."

"How do you know this alternate time isn't happening right now?"

Tom looked up at the man. Gerald was peacefully sitting back on the couch. He didn't look like a man that had just heard the insane ramblings of another. He looked . . . peaceful. "What?" Tom asked. "What did you say?"

Again Gerald smiled. "I said, how do you know this alternate time, 1875, isn't happening right now?"

"But how can it be?" Tom looked around the penthouse and waved a hand. *"This* is happening now."

Leaning forward, Gerald reached out and picked a small leaf from a ficus tree. He held it in the palm of his hand to show the younger man. "There's life here in this leaf, life you and I can't see with the naked eye. And if I were to do this—" Gerald picked up his glass and let a tiny droplet of condensation slide onto the leaf, creating a small bubble of water right in the center of the green. "Even your science will tell you there is a whole other existence right there in that drop, a whole other life taking place in that water. You and I can't see that other world, but we know it exists. Don't we?"

Nodding, Tom continued to stare at the leaf while imagining molecules and bacteria. His imagination grew fertile as he continued to listen to

Gerald's voice.

"Just look at the drop of water, Thomas. You and I are about sixty-five percent water. So is a mouse. An elephant and an ear of corn are about seventy percent. A potato and an earthworm are more. We live in a world of water; it's in our blood and our tears and our sweat. Do you know there's as much water on the earth today as there ever was—or ever will be?"

He didn't wait for an answer, and in truth Tom was too mesmerized by his voice and his words to respond.

"Almost every drop of water that we use, maybe even this one, finds its way back to the oceans. There it's evaporated by the sun and then falls once more back to earth as rain. Water, just about all of it, is used and reused over and over again. Water changes only from one form to another, and moves from one place to another. The water you bathed in last night might have flowed in the Danube last month or in Russia's Volga River. Or perhaps Augustus Caesar might have drank it well over two thousand years ago. It is never used up, Thomas. It's only recycled over and over again."

He smiled, while looking down at his hand. "What if this drop of water, this one on the leaf, is the same drop that Alexander the Great offered his Persian princess on the banks of the Tigris River? It was real for her. It quenched that young woman's thirst in the hot Persian sun as she looked up at her new husband, the King of Macedonia, the conqueror of Egypt and Asia Minor. And you're looking at it now, Thomas. It's certainly real for you now. But even your scientists will tell you that this drop of water existed in another form, at another time."

Gerald took a deep breath and asked, "So which time is real, Thomas? The time in this micro world, in this drop of water, the one you can't see but you know exists? Or your time, here in this luxurious apartment overlooking the city?"

Tom couldn't immediately answer him. He was still thinking about the possibilities. Finally he said, "Couldn't they both be real?"

Gerald was pleased. "Exactly! Who's to say, Thomas, that two different worlds, your time and Meggie's time, couldn't be happening in what you think of as the same time?"

Tom shook his head. "I'm confused. Are you talking about parallel time?"

Gerald nodded. "I am."

Tom sat back in his chair and closed his eyes. His breath left his lungs in a slow, steady exhale. "You believe that?" he asked without opening his eyes.

"I believe anything is possible," Gerald answered.

Tom wondered why it was beginning to make sense to him. Was it the alcohol that had clouded his brain? He didn't feel drunk. He felt more alive, more alert, and more frightened than he had in many years. "So what do I do, Gerald?" he asked, opening his eyes and staring at the older intelligent man. "How do I get her back?"

Gerald smiled broadly and held out his glass for a refill. "We talk, lad. You've got a lot to learn."

Tom took the glass from his hand. "Who are you?" he asked, looking deep into the old blue eyes.

Gerald laughed lightly. "I'm a friend, Thomas. That much you can take for truth."

"I don't know what's happened. The story should have appeared last week. This week at the latest." Jack Donahue turned away from the Philadelphia newspaper and looked at Liam. "That reporter person spent three days here talkin' to just about everybody in the patch. We had a helluva time hiding him, but he promised to tell our story!"

Liam shook his head. "Now, lads, let's not give up hope. It was a good idea, and it still might work."

"That's right," Brian added. "None of us knows how long it takes to get a story in the paper. There's still time."

"Not enough," Tom Carter interjected. "Gowen's not going to wait much longer for an answer. He might just call off the negotiations all together."

"I say we send another letter," Jimmy Roarity suggested. "Let's find out what the holdup is."

Jack Donahue and Connon Rafferty both nodded, while Liam shrugged. Brian said nothing, yet looked to see Tom's reaction.

"What do you think, Tom?"

"Why're you askin' him, Brian?" Roarity demanded. "Aren't you and Liam the ones who make the decisions?"

Brian deeply exhaled, as if trying to keep his patience. "Look, Jimmy, this was Tom's idea to begin with—"

"Yes, and look what's happened!" Roarity inter-

238

rupted. "We've wasted all this time. I still say we should have shown them we meant business and went after Saul Raskin."

"You can't solve this with violence," Tom stated in a heated voice. "You go after the superintendent of the collieries and Nate Gowen will pull away from any negotiations and we'll all be back on strike."

"So we're just supposed to sit here and wait?" Roarity asked, a sneer appearing on his face.

"I've had it," Meggie muttered to herself from the corner of the room. Without waiting any longer, she rose from a chair and walked up behind Roarity. It was with great pleasure that she reached up and pulled back on his hair.

Roarity, a tall man, reared back like a bucking horse and let out a yell of pain. The men around him stared at him as he tried to regain his balance.

"Lordy Jesus, Jimmy! What's wrong with you?" Jack Donahue demanded.

Before Roarity could answer, Meggie again reached up and pulled his hair, this time in a forward direction. When he lowered his head and followed her to ease the pain, Meggie let him go past. As he sailed by, she lifted her leg and planted her foot on his behind. Grinning, she let him have it in the rear.

More frightened than hurt, Jimmy Roarity let out a fearful shriek that brought Liam's daughter into the front room.

"Merciful God in heaven," she whispered. "What's going on out here?"

Brian, shocked by Roarity's behavior, rushed up

239

to Noreen. "Jimmy's havin' some sort of fit, I believe. We'd better get him home." He nodded to Jack and Connon.

Roarity pushed their helping hands away. "Leave me be!" He demanded. "Something did that to me! Something shoved at me and pulled at me. *I felt it!*"

Jack and Connon again reached out to help the man to his feet. "C'mon, Jimmy. Let's go home," Connon said, while nodding to the others. "Me 'n' Jack will get you settled and fetch Doc Tanner."

"I'm tellin' you I don't need a doctor! *Somethin's* after me! I can feel it!"

Everyone looked embarrassed and Roarity stumbled to his feet. Without saying anything more, he allowed Connon and Jack to lead him outside.

Noreen crossed herself. "God help him," she muttered.

Brian said, "I think I heard once about a falling sickness. I'm not sure what it is—"

"Epilepsy," Tom cut in.

Brian shook his head. "How do you know that? I don't recall that being the name of it."

Tom shrugged. "I don't know. The name just came to me."

Liam cleared his throat. "Be that as it may, we still have a problem, lads. Do we send another letter, as Jimmy suggested? Time is running out. If something doesn't happen then we'll be forced to settle for Gowen's meager proposal. And that's little better than what we had when we began this strike those many months ago."

"I suppose we could write another letter," Brian said while looking at Noreen from the corner of

240

his eye.

"Noreen," Liam asked, "do you think we might have a spot of tea? I think we'll be doin' a bit more talkin' before this night is over."

Shyly smiling at Brian, Noreen Dunleavy nodded to her father and left the room.

Watching it all, Meggie smiled as she wearily sank back into a chair. Poor Noreen, with her long black hair, pretty smile, and sweet disposition, was helplessly in love with Brian—and had been for years. Was it only now that Brian was taking any notice? she wondered. Ah well, Meggie thought, shifting on the seat to make herself more comfortable, she had her own problems to think about. She watched Brian's gaze follow the lovely Noreen from the room and sighed. If she could manage to throw the two of them together, she would. It was time. Brian needed someone in his life and Noreen Dunleavy was just the person. And then that would be one less thing to worry about.

She brushed the curls back from her face and stared at the men in the front room of Liam Dunleavy's home. Taking a deep breath, she settled against the back support of the chair. She was tired, more tired than she should have been. She wasn't doing anything except following Thomas, this version of the man she loved. This Thomas was a good man, a hard worker in the mines. He was blessed with good humor and a keen wit, but he wasn't her Thomas. Her Thomas was all that and more. He was highly intelligent, compassionate. He laughed more easily than this man. It was as if this man was an ancestor—he resembled

Thomas, spoke like him, yet it wasn't. It was too hard to explain, even to herself. It was something she felt deep inside her. All those qualities that made up the man she loved were precious memories that she took out at night. It really was so unfair to compare this man to her Thomas.

Both were good men.

One she felt great affection for, not unlike a brother, or a cousin. The other touched her heart and took possession of her soul. She loved the other with a fervor that was almost frightening. Perhaps that was why she didn't feel well. In the three weeks that she had been abandoned here in the past, she had nearly lost her appetite. Despite the fact that she could have anything that she wanted, walk into any store, any kitchen, and eat whatever she wanted, she found that she wanted very little.

She wanted her Thomas back.

That ache in her middle was becoming more and more unbearable with each passing day. It didn't help that she could cry at the drop of a hat just thinking about him. It was almost too much to endure. And not for the first time she thought that perhaps this was to be her punishment, her hell, for loving again without the blessing of marriage. Was she to wander after this version of her Thomas? A man enough like Thomas to make her heart ache each time she looked at him?

She wanted to believe in a God of love, one that would love her in return and want her happiness, not punish her again. But she was in this limbo, this place where she couldn't be seen or heard or loved, and this was a punishment far worse than the fires the priests talked about.

Sniffling, the tears once again fell down her cheeks and she brushed them away with the back of her hand. "Please," she whispered, "bring him back to me. Or let me die. I can't go on this way . . ."

Just then she heard Brian say, "I think that's a grand idea, Tom. But can you afford to stay in Philadelphia? We can't help much with money, but we could give you names—"

Thomas waved away Brian's suggestion of help. "I've nothing to spend it on, but my board and a few tankards of ale. Tell that miserable Ben Creedon that I'm sick and will be taking a few days off."

"And you'll contact the newspaper and find out what's happened to our story?" Liam suggested.

Tom nodded. "I'll look up that reporter fellow and see just what is the problem in publishing it. We should have some answers in a few days."

"Should I still send another letter?" Brian asked both men.

Liam looked to Tom. "Send it," Tom said in a low voice. "I didn't want to say anything earlier, but I think it's highly suspicious how our letters are never answered. I don't say this easily, gentlemen, but there just might be one of us that isn't what he seems."

Brian and Liam looked shocked.

Meggie stood up and grinned. Maybe this Thomas had memories he could draw upon, vague remembrances tugging at the back of his brain. Whatever had caused him to speak up, Meggie was thrilled.

James Roarity was not going to win.

She followed behind Brian and Thomas. When they entered her home, Brian's home now, she stopped and stared at the wooden house. Not much to show after all those years of working for the Reading. Her poor Mum and Da . . . how they had struggled. Memories, swift and painful, flooded over her and Meggie sniffled back another tear. Lord, but she was never far from tears these days. Ever since she had left this house with Brian the morning of the explosion, she hadn't come back. Not really. Perhaps it was only self-preservation that had made her avoid this encounter, but now she knew it was time.

Taking a deep breath, Meggie gathered her courage, opened the door, and entered.

"I'd swear I just closed that," Brian said, walking over and giving the door a shove. "How about a bit of whiskey before you take off?" Brian asked his guest as he came back into the small front room.

Thomas, this Thomas, smiled and nodded. "That sounds fine, Brian. Thank you."

Meggie paid very little attention to the two men. Her gaze was moving about her mother's front room. Never elegant to begin with, it looked far worse than she had left it. The once polished tables were heavily ladened with dust; the only imprints were of hands that had slid across the surface. It was obvious that a rag hadn't touched them since she'd left. Articles of clothing were strewn about, as if the man hadn't known there were dresser drawers in the next room. Shaking her head in dismay, Meggie made up her mind to come back and tidy up. Her poor Mum would be turnin' in her grave if she were to see this. They might have been poor, but they were always decent. This . . . this was inexcusable.

She turned her attention to Brian as he swept away unwashed dishes and searched for glasses. "Don't mind the mess," he said to Thomas, and Meggie clucked her tongue against her teeth in derision.

"I mind very much," she muttered, resisting the urge to start cleaning. "What a lazy sot you've turned into, William Brian Gillbride!"

Immune to her insult, Brian made an appreciative sound when he found two clean glasses. "Here we are," he said, pouring out a measure of whiskey into each. Handing one to Thomas, he held his up in a salute. "To success," he toasted.

Thomas held up his glass. "To success . . . in Philadelphia and at the negotiations table."

Both men took deep drafts of the potent whiskey and then smiled at each other. "Come," said Brian, bending down to pick up a shirt off a chair and throw it onto the floor. "Sit down."

Thomas sat at the wooden table, resting his elbows on its edge. Brian joined him, his fingers playing with the rim of his glass. "You're the first person I've had in here since the funeral," Brian said, studying the glass in front of him.

"Your sister?" Thomas asked.

Brian nodded.

"I'm sorry for your trouble. I had heard about your loss when I came to the patch."

"She was a good girl, our Meggie. And I killed her."

"Brian!" Thomas put his hand on his friend's shoulder. "Don't say that."

"It's true. I was the one that talked her into helping us. She never would have done it, if it wasn't for me." Picking up his glass, Brian swallowed the remaining whiskey. "Never even found her body, that's how bad it was. Me and Jimmy Roarity double-checked everything. I still don't know how it could have happened . . . and all I could do was put up a small stone for her next to her baby boy's grave. Not even in the church cemetery, it is. It's pathetic, the two of them. Outside . . . just like poor Meggie's life those last years. If only I was more understanding, more kind. I was just content to let her take care of things—me, this house. I tell you, Thomas, I miss the sound of her voice when I come in that door." He paused for a moment, trying to regain his composure. When again he spoke, his voice was cracking with emotion. "I truly miss her . . ."

Meggie stood behind his chair, silently crying. Dear, sweet Brian. How she longed to reach out and touch him, to run her fingers through his hair and let him know he wasn't to blame. When he had started speaking about her, she had frozen, afraid of what he would say. The mention of her baby had shocked her, for it was a first. Never before when she lived in this house had Brian talked to her about her child. She had always felt it was something shameful, something he could not bring himself to discuss. And to think that he had done it now, with Thomas. Thank God the man sitting across from her brother had reacted only with sympathy, for this man didn't know her. Her secret would be safe and remain hidden. Never did she want her Thomas to find out about that shameful part of her past. She wanted to forget, to go on . . .

Brian lifted his head and, looking about the room, grinned. "She'd have a right conniption if she ever saw this place. I used to call her a nag." He reached down and picked up the shirt he had thrown earlier. "She used to call me a drony, shiftless lout." He glanced down to the shirt in his hand. "She was right, too. If I had earned a proper wage, I'd never have had to sell Mum's sewing table for Meggie's headstone. Megs set such store in that table." He shook his head in sorrow. "Damn that strike!"

Meggie covered her mouth in surprise and looked to the empty corner where the table had stood all those many years. It was gone. For a moment she keenly felt its loss, then she turned back to her brother.

"Ahh, Brian, you fool you. Bless your heart."

# Chapter 17

Nothing was happening.

"They'll be back tomorrow?" Tom asked as they stood in front of the antique shop on the corner of Madison Avenue.

Gerald, gazing in the window, nodded. "The sign on the door says tomorrow."

"Is that it?" Tom was looking at the sewing table nestled among other antiques for display.

"It is," Gerald confirmed. "That's the one."

Tom tried to see it better. It was a handsome piece of furniture, in remarkable condition. If you looked closely, you could see the actual sewing basket of pale green velvet underneath the top of inlaid mahogany and satinwood. Sixty-five hundred dollars. Not outrageous, but overpriced nonetheless. He'd come back tomorrow and make an offer, one he was sure the owner would take. Now was not the time to bargain, as much as these Madison Avenue shops loved the game. Tom only wanted the sewing table. It was his link to Meggie.

He had thought something would happen when he came here. How foolish of him to think this was the way back to her. Just because it had happened to her in this spot didn't mean it would also work for him. He nearly grinned. It was hard to believe that he was almost looking forward to going back in time to the patch . . . to her. She was the reason. Since admitting to Gerald that he loved her, Tom was torn up inside from the separation. He needed to talk to her, to tell her how he felt. Somehow, he'd find the words, the right words to explain it all and put her at ease about her vows. Somehow, he'd make it right and take away the guilt. For both of them.

"Nothing's happening," he said to Gerald.

The old man sighed loudly. "I think you're trying too hard. I told you to clear your mind. I can tell by your face that you're thinking of her. It won't work if you won't cooperate."

Tom cursed. "This is ridiculous! I don't know why I'm even going along with this." He shook his head with frustration. "I don't even know why I listened to you. Don't be too offended, Gerald, but this is all starting to sound like a bunch of hocus pocus garbage. Nothing's going to work."

Gerald was definitely offended. "Well, I can see I've wasted the best part of the evening with you." He lifted his chin, smoothed down the side of his moustache, and added, "I hope you won't be insulted if I say that you are a stubborn, impatient jackass, and if you'd take your head out of the steel skyscrapers that you insist on building and concentrate on what's right around you, you might just have better luck in this endeavor."

Tom's jaw hung open in surprise. It had been a long time since anyone had had the courage to tell him off.

Before he could form a reply, he heard Gerald add, "Now I'm off across the park for P.J. Carney's, the one place in this city that can make me forget where I am and let me dream. After a few pints, I swear it's Dublin."

He left Tom to stare after him as he headed toward Central Park. Seeing him hastily making his way through the light evening crowd made Tom react.

"Gerald, wait!" He couldn't lose the old man! Gerald believed him. He was the only one he could talk to about this. If he lost him . . . "Wait up, will you?"

Finally catching up to the white-haired man, Tom smiled. "I'm sorry. It isn't garbage. It's confusing. And frightening."

Gerald looked up at him and, after a few moments, returned his smile. "Of course it is. That's because it's all new to you, but these ideas have been around for thousands of years . . . and they don't go away, Thomas. There's been too many unexplainable happenings throughout the centuries to dismiss." Placing his hand on the younger man's shoulder, he added, "I forgive you. Now, come along. I'm going to take you to a real bar, with real pub food. You may think you've died, lad, and gone to heaven."

Leading him into Central Park, Gerald actually giggled at his own joke.

Three hours later Tom left the pub, and Gerald singing with his Irish cronies. It had been a good night and he'd slipped out unnoticed while the old man was giving an emotional rendition of some obscure folk song. True to his word, Gerald had fed him steak and kidneys, had poured glass after glass of ale into him, as if it were no more than fruit juice, and had slapped him on the back more than once when he'd remembered the second verse to "Galway Bay." Gerald had treated him tonight like a son or a nephew, and he'd come away feeling good about their friendship. But then he'd seen a woman with red hair, not an unusual occurrence in an Irish bar. It had been enough to make his stomach tighten with a sudden pain and his chest ache with an emptiness. He'd had to leave, to get away as the memories became more sharp, more painful . . .

Standing at Columbus Circle, he debated walking through the park again. It was late now, and the crazies would be out, but there wasn't a cab in sight. He could easily walk home, but it wasn't home he wanted.

He wanted Meggie.

And there was only one place, one way, that he knew of to get her.

Why not, he thought as he walked past the Maine Monument and entered the park. He was already half drunk from the ale. In the mood he was in, he'd kill the first sonofabitch that even looked at him wrong.

What did he have to lose anymore?

He'd already lost her.


He stood in front of the window, staring at the sewing table. Could it really be connected to Meggie? Gerald seemed to think so. But then Gerald

251

had some very strange ideas. What did he say? That over sixty percent of the world's population had undergone some sort of psychic experience? Some unexplainable occurrence in their lives? Jamming his fists into his jacket pockets, Tom stared into the window and shook his head. Words such as extrasensory perception, déjà vu, and retrocognition raced around inside him and cluttered his brain. What did he know about such things? Only a short time ago he was just like the people who passed behind him on the sidewalk. Blissfully ignorant, and considerably happier.

No. Not happier. Not before Meggie came into his life. He could picture her as she looked that night at the small pool. Her head thrown back toward the sky, tears of happiness sliding down her cheeks as he made love to her . . . and later, back in his room, she had lain beneath him, warm and loving, eager to please, full of life and laughter . . .

Oh, just to hold her again.

What had Gerald said to him? Something about taking his head out of the skyscrapers and paying attention to what's around him? Normally, in most cities, there weren't too many people walking at night, but this was New York City and night only meant more adventure. Well-dressed couples returned from dinner to their choice homes on the East Side. Young kids, wearing jeans and T-shirts, walked hand in hand and window-shopped at the elegant stores that lined Madison Avenue. One block over was the Metropolitan Museum and they must have had a costume ball for weren't there couples, dressed in period clothing, men in

252

formal suits with elaborate ties and hats and women in gowns, wide gowns that swept the sidewalk . . . My God . . .

He was afraid to move, to breathe, for fear it might all go away. He smelled the horses, heard the sounds of carriages. These people, these things, were not ethereal, not shadowy.

They were real. Slowly, still holding his breath, he turned around and was startled by the appearance of an older man who, in passing him on the stone sidewalk, touched the tip of his tall hat in a friendly gesture and smiled. They had made eye contact, him and the man.

He had done it!

Ecstatic, Tom took a deep breath and stepped forward. In that instant, that fraction of time, the scenery changed, whirling around him until he became dizzy. Trying to stay upright, he held his head and closed his eyes against the blur of colors. Suddenly it was dark and he was lying on something soft. He could hear his heart beating furiously against his chest wall as he opened his eyes.

She was there, before him. Outlined in moonlight, she stood in front of the window in a white nightgown, a gauzy shawl thrown over her shoulders. Her hair was unbound and falling down her back. She was gazing out into the night, and the moonlight highlighted an expression of intense sadness on her face. Still, she looked lovely. Like an angel.

Not knowing if he was dreaming, he sat up and called her name.

"Meggie?"

She thought it was cruel to imagine his voice calling to her. Why was it that her mind played such merciless tricks? Was it not enough to want him every waking moment? And especially on endless nights like this, when sleep eluded her and images of Thomas tormented her imagination. Now she was hearing his voice. Sure, but this punishment was never ending . . .

"Meggie? Is it you?"

She spun around to face the bed. Her heart started beating faster and her ears were ringing. Clutching the cotton gown at her chest, she whispered his name. *"Thomas?"*

He stood up and she cried out before running across the room to him. She threw herself into his arms and held him close to her, as if to meld his body into hers so he might never again escape. "Thomas . . . Thomas . . ." The tears that were occurring with such frequency returned, only this time they were tears of joy as she repeated his name over and over again. "Thomas . . . Thomas . . . you're back!"

He was kissing her, burying his face in her hair, holding her to him to keep her close. "Meggie! I thought I'd lost you!" He didn't know if the tears were hers or his. He had her back! "I'll never let you go. Do you hear me?"

She was crying, kissing him, and laughing. "Aye, love. I hear you. I'm yours forever."

"Forever," he repeated, just before his mouth came down on hers in a hard, possessive kiss that branded her as his own.

His kisses were feverish, searing her skin as his lips moved over her body. She felt dazed and held on to him for support as he removed her night-gown and swept her up in his arms. He brought her to the bed and gently placed her on the mattress, looking at her, loving her with his eyes. She stared back at him, her gaze following his fingers as they unbuttoned his shirt and pulled it away from his chest. He quickly removed his belt and trousers and she moaned when he stood before her, naked and powerful.

Slowly, as if in a dream, she extended her hand, palm up — as though in invitation. When he came to her, enveloped her in his arms, she knew she had invited him into her life. Forever. And it was right. She felt it as his mouth again began to play over her with a thrilling mixture of astonishing gentleness and overwhelming heat.

It was frenzied and passionate, frantic and inflamed.

He was relentless, teasing her with his mouth and his hands, licking, rubbing, tasting; stroking her to a feverish pitch until she was seething, aroused to an exquisite point of near pain. Unable to endure much more, she wrapped her fingers through his silky hair and pulled him up to her face. Breathing heavily, she whispered into his mouth.

"Please, Tommy . . ." Her eyes blazed her passion and her need.

Kissing her trembling lips, Tom whispered back, "Yes, love . . . now."

And then he filled her with his heat, wrapping his arms around her, holding her close and talking to her of his fear that he had lost her, telling her how he had dreamed of this moment together, this

255

joyful reunion. She trusted him with her life, and with her love. Slowly, as if summoning the tide, her blood became thick, and hot, and heavy, rushing toward the center of her body. She held on to him, moving with him in an overpowering ritual. Neither talked, yet communicated in a language as old as the universe.

It was moment to stir her soul. She entered him, becoming a part of him as vital as any organ. And she knew that from this moment on, she would never again be alone. No matter where the morning found her, she would carry him within her heart.

Always.


She felt at peace, for the first time in so very long. She watched the dawn break over the mountain and sighed with contentment. Had it only been hours earlier that she had stood here and despaired of ever again being happy? Meggie allowed her smile to widen. He'd come back to her. What she had thought of as a dream, the cruel imagining of her mind, had turned into an exquisite memory to be cherished.

He loved her.

He must, she thought. Surely a man doesn't act like that unless it is out of love. But what did she know of men's reactions? Once before when she was little more than a child, she had thought a man loved her, loved her enough to marry her and give her child a name . . . But that was long ago, she chided herself, and that man that had abandoned her wasn't anything at all like Thomas.

Thomas was a man of honor. A man to be trusted. Hadn't he told her last night how he had suffered over leaving her . . . and that he had done everything he could think of to come back to her? What other proof did she need? He had left his time, a time in which he was wealthy and respected, to come back here, here where he was a coal miner, fighting to make things better for so many less fortunate. She inhaled the soft morning breeze and smiled.

This time she had been blessed. This time, for as long as it lasted, Meggie Gillbride was going to be happy . . .

"You look just like the cat that ate the canary," he said in a sleepy voice.

She turned away from the window and smiled. "I'm happy."

"I'm glad. Now, come back to bed."

She went to him and sat on the edge of the mattress. His hair was falling over his forehead and she reached out to push it back. Thomas caught her hand and brought it to his mouth.

Kissing the pulse point of her wrist, he whispered, "That isn't what I meant when I said to come back to bed." He glanced up at her. "I want you back in my arms, Meggie."

She sighed, fighting within herself. It was so tempting. Picking up his silver pocket watch, she read the time. "Thomas, you're catching a train for Philadelphia in little more than an hour." She looked back at him and said with regret, "You'd best be getting up."

Tom took the watch out of her hand. "Where did you get this?"

Meggie shrugged and realization came to him. "You didn't? You took it?"

She grinned. "Well, he needed a watch. He was forever late—"

"What was he like, Meggie? Was he like me?" Tom brushed the sleep from his eyes and sat up.

She nodded, noticing the way the sheet fell to his hips. The hair on his chest curled in dark auburn waves and tapered over his muscled stomach. Lord, but she would need a strong will to resist him. She inhaled deeply. "He was . . . and he wasn't. I kept calling him *this Thomas,* to make him different from you. He was . . . like a brother. I watched over him, keeping him safe until you came back."

"And you knew I would." His eyes were warm and inviting.

"I wasn't sure of anything. I would talk to you at night, as if you could hear me. It sounds silly now, I know. While he slept, I told you what was happening back here in the patch. Somehow, someday . . . yes, Thomas, I knew in here"—and she touched her heart—"that you would come back to me. For if you didn't, surely I would perish. I would not have been able to bear the loneliness."

He gathered her into his arms. "Shh . . . don't think about it anymore. I'm here."

She sniffled. "But what you left in your time—"

He tightened his hold on her. "I found out that what was more important was what I'd left in *this* time."

She lifted her head and looked into his incredibly green eyes. Should she tell him what was in her heart? That she loved him with an intensity that frightened her? Or should she keep it secret awhile longer? Protect it. Nurture it. And when it was strong, present her love to him. It made sense. For still, in the back of her brain, was the nagging, traitorous thought that she must also protect herself from pain. She would not survive another rejection. Not this time. This time he was her life.

"You're going to be late," she whispered as his mouth moved closer to hers.

"I don't care."

"Yes, you do. The train . . ." She could feel his breath on her. His lips were so close. Waiting.

"There'll be another," he muttered, already making love to her with just his eyes.

*Be happy, Meggie.* Hadn't she just promised herself that? "You're right. There's one at noon," she murmured against his mouth. "But still—"

"But nothing," he interrupted, letting his lips gently graze over hers. "Come back to bed, love."

Groaning, she gladly allowed him to pull her against him. "Ah, Tommy," she whispered against his mouth, "I'm afraid I'm lost in ya . . ."

He smiled and kissed the tip of her nose. "Do you know your Irish accent becomes more pronounced when your passions are aroused?" he teased.

"I do not have an accent," she answered, feeling a blush creep up her throat. "And if it did, it wouldn't be doing anything of the kind."

"Yes, it does," he countered with a grin as he pushed a long curl behind her ear. "Either when you're angry, or passionate, or frightened. But, Meggie, you don't ever have to be afraid. Not ever

259

again."

She sighed, deeply and happily.

She was lost in him.

# Chapter 18

"Oh, Thomas! Isn't it grand?"

Looking out the window of a two-horse omni-bus, Tom nodded and smiled. Philadelphia. Eight-een seventy-five. It was *unbelievable*.

He was fascinated by the people they passed on the cobblestone walks. Even in summer, almost all the men wore somber black suits, carried walking sticks, and sported high silk hats or derbies. It appeared that nearly all were either mustached or bearded. The women were more colorful, adorned in summer pastel gowns with matching umbrellas to protect their faces from the sun. Like the men, all wore hats, elegant creations, and almost all had their hair swept up inside of them. Several even had servants walking behind them carrying pack-ages. This wasn't the patch, dismal and oppressive in its poverty. This was Philadelphia in the late nineteenth century, over one hundred years into the past.

And it was amazing.

Having gone to the Wharton School, Tom was familiar with the city—the city of the late twentieth century. But certain parts hadn't changed all that much in the last hundred years. He could tell they were traveling through Society Hill, a historic section that looked much as it had during colonial times.

Yes, he thought, remembering Meggie's exclamation. It was grand. How he wished he could answer, to tell her what the city was like in his time, but that would have to wait. He had learned that speaking out loud to her only caused those around him to shrink back in horror. The train trip from Lehigha had been a lesson well learned. He was sure the old lady and her daughter who were seated across from him would take days to recover. In trying to make the women leave their seats so she could sit down, Meggie had played at her usually innocent tricks for over two and a half hours — picking at the women's purse strings, plucking at their hat pins, and finally, pushing the hats down until they rested on flaring nostrils. As much as he had tried, he'd been unable to contain his laughter. Eventually, he had to tell Meggie to stop harassing the women. She was enjoying it too much. But the women had looked at him as if he were insane. Their frightened expressions had quickly stopped his laughter.

He simply had to remember that his Meggie, this incredible woman that he loved, could not be seen by others. That she didn't belong in this world of bustles and brooches and umbrellas any longer. Somehow, after he had helped Brian and the others, he had to find a way of getting her back to his time.

And keeping her there.

He was shown into the suite of rooms and grinned as he heard Meggie's exclamation of approval. "I'm so glad you changed the plans," she sighed, looking about the rooms. "This hotel is so — so luxurious."

Once he had seen where Brian and Liam had told him to stay, Tom had quickly turned about and led Meggie to this establishment. He wanted this time with her to be special, and a room overlooking an alley in an obscure rooming house wasn't what he had in mind. Just one look at her face told him he'd made the right decision. The suite was a fine display of pink and pale green Victoriana. Tiffany lamps, a heavy mahogany bed, stenciled wallpaper, and pink marbled-topped dressers graced the bedroom. The same was carried into the sitting room, with its burled walnut table and chairs and twin sofas. There was even a bouquet of silk flowers under glass to complete the picture.

"Can we afford it, Thomas?" she asked, a hopeful look in her eyes.

"I think we can at least stay overnight," he teased.

Grinning, she reached inside the pocket of her skirt and took out a handful of bills. She let them spill onto a table before looking up at him. "Let's stay longer."

"Where did you get that?" he demanded, coming closer to her.

She shrugged. "I don't think you really want to know. Let's just say the Reading Coal and Iron Company would be very surprised to find out they've contributed to this trip."

Shaking his head, he gathered her into his arms. "Meggie . . . what am I going to do with you? You can't keep stealing from them."

She pouted. "And why not? They've been stealing from us for over twenty years."

Although he knew it was wrong, he could see her logic. "So it looks like we're staying a bit longer," he said with a smile.

"Aye, that we are. But first, I want to go shopping. Did you see some of the dresses those women were wearing? Weren't they lovely enough to melt your heart? I think I shall begin looking — "

He kissed her into silence. Pulling back he whispered in a husky voice, "No, Meggie. *First* I want to show you something in the other room."

Her gaze held his. "Thomas Grey Carter, you're a shameful layabout. You do realize that it's only afternoon? Broad daylight, it is."

His hands traveled up her back and neck and reached into her hair. Unpinning it, he watched the red curls fall about her shoulders like a rich shawl of fine velvet. "Meggie, we're here. Alone. No Bridget Humne to worry about. Did you see the size of that bed?" he demanded softly. "It's twice as large as the one at Bridget's."

She smiled and reached for his hand. "I've already seen it, Tommy. And did ya notice the lovely pitcher on the washstand? It's filled with lilac-scented water. Don't you think it's very nice of them to have that for their weary travelers?"

His blood grew thick and heavy and he started to feel his desire for her grow with each of her words. "Your accent again," he muttered. "I told

264

you it gets more pronounced."

She returned his smile and led him into the bedroom. "That's something I'll have to work on then. Don't you think?"

She turned to him inside the room and he groaned as he viewed the large bed behind her.

"Don't you dare," he commanded, pulling her against his chest. He stared into her eyes, memorizing her features in the late afternoon light. "Don't change anything."

She sighed. "Ahh, yes. I do think I'm going to enjoy Philadelphia."

It was nothing at all like a big city newsroom. But then again, there were no phones, no computers, no teletypes—nothing that would remind him of the frantic newspapers of his time. Everything was relatively quiet as he and Meggie walked up to the male receptionist.

"Yes? May I help you, sir?" The young man's heavily starched collar seemed to bite into his neck as he looked up at his visitor.

Tom cleared his throat. "Harry Korson, please."

"Is he expecting you?" The young man looked over the cut of Tom's suit and decided him to be of little importance.

Trying to ignore the man's superior tone, Tom said, "Well, no. He isn't. Not today. But if you would tell him that Thomas Carter is here from Lehigha, I'm sure he'll see me."

The receptionist lifted his eyebrows, to show he doubted Tom's words. "Wait here. I'll see if Mr. Korson is in."

"Isn't he actin' the high-up lord? You'd think he owned the place," Meggie muttered as the young man walked back behind swinging doors to the interior of the newsroom. "How dare he treat you like that?"

Tom smiled. "It doesn't matter," he whispered out of the corner of his mouth.

"But it does," Meggie objected. "Why, you could buy and sell this place ten times over in your time. And that . . . that young pup treating you like you weren't worth the time of day!"

Tom sighed. He couldn't answer her and she knew it. Hadn't they just had that talk before coming here? The one about her not asking him questions in public that he couldn't answer? He should remember though that when Meggie felt deeply about something, she was incapable of silence. He smiled as the rude man returned. That was part of what he liked about her. She was an honest woman, honest enough to say what was on her mind.

"I'm sorry, but Mr. Korson is unavailable." The man sat back down at his desk and ignored Tom.

Disappointed, Tom asked, "When will he be available?"

"Try tomorrow," the man said without looking up.

Tom placed his hand over the paper the man was reading, forcing the man's attention to turn to him. "Please go back in and tell Mr. Korson that this matter is of great importance."

Finally, the man looked up.

"Please," Tom repeated. "I've come a long way to speak with him."

"Mr. Korson is unavailable. And if you don't remove your hand from my desk, I'll be forced to summon the police."

Very cool, Tom thought. He hadn't expected someone this young to be so sure of himself. Placing his hand in his pocket, he said, "Please tell Mr. Korson that I have no intention of leaving the city without seeing him."

He turned to leave, expecting Meggie to be at his side. When he approached the stairs, he glanced back in time to see her push the swinging doors apart and enter the inner sanctum of *The Philadelphia Gazette*.

My God, he silently groaned. There was no controlling her.

After looking over those men in the room, she saw the reporter who had come to the patch. He was speaking to an older man in a glass-enclosed office. Meggie quickly made her way through the newsroom, causing more than a few papers to fall to the floor in her wake. If she hadn't been so angry, she might have been amused by the surprised remarks that followed her. If only they knew it wasn't an unexpected summer breeze passing through the window that made their papers flutter. But she was in a hurry to get to that office. How dare that young man insult Thomas? Where were his manners? They had come too far to be turned away like that! She couldn't wait to reach him and teach him a lesson, yet from the look on Harry Korson's face, something very important was being discussed behind those glass walls. Something that was causing his face to turn a deep shade of red.

And she was about to find out just what that was.

"I'm telling you, Harry, leave it alone. Let it be."

Opening the door just a fraction, Meggie held her breath as she listened to the reporter's answer. "I don't understand. One of those miners came here to find out when my byline is going to appear, and I'm pretty interested to hear what you have to say."

The older man, balding yet sporting a thick mustache, took out a handkerchief and mopped at his high forehead. "I've already explained to you that I'm also under pressure not to print your story of these miners. There are people, Harry, important people in this state that don't want this publicized."

"But you read it," Korson argued. "There are children, not yet ten years old, that are working twelve hours a day sorting coal. They sit in those breakers, on top of huge mounds of coal, and pick through it. Their faces, Mr. Shotwell, would break your heart. They don't look ten, more like thirty. And their fathers and brothers have it worse. These men have been on strike for almost a year, and no one's paying any attention. No one cares about their struggle."

Mr. Shotwell paced in front of his desk. "You could find children right here in the city that work as hard—"

"But it's not right," young Korson interrupted.

Shotwell smiled grimly. "No, it's not. It's the Gilded Age, my boy. Don't you know that? Twain had it right when he used that term to describe this culture. So many newly rich. Lacking any tradition, they've become showy, flamboyant boors. Look at the mansions they build to imitate and compete with European palaces, and look what they fill them with—gaudy, ostentatious decorations." Shotwell shook his head. "It's a damn shame, I agree. In 1850 there were maybe twenty millionaires in this country. I'd guess to say that twenty-five years later there are at least two thousand more. That are a whole lot of people getting a whole lot of rich, son."

"But they made their fortunes on the labors of men who worked in the factories, in the mills and the mines," Korson contended. "Men who will never share the benefits. You can't ask a man to work sixty hours a week for an average pay of twenty cents an hour. There's too many of them starving together in the slums of the city or in the patches outside the mines while the rich ignore them. Mr. Shotwell, has everyone forgotten the French Revolution? Are we going to wait until the masses unite and rise up against the wealthy?"

Shotwell patted the younger man's shoulder. "I think you're overexaggerating things, Harry. Oh, it's bad. I agree. Overcrowding. Overwork. Inadequate diet. Little or no education—all of that. But there's one thing that this country offers that they didn't have in the one they left. Hope. That's what makes their lives tolerable. Hope that someday they'll find a better life."

"But that's what these miners are striking for," Korson argued. "They're only back to work conditionally now. They need these newspaper articles. They have a mine owner ready to sit down and actually discuss working conditions. It's almost unheard of."

"I can't do it," Shotwell answered. "It isn't me, you understand. I, too, have to answer to someone, and by the highest authority of this newspaper, I have been told to drop the Lehigha story."

"But —"

Shotwell shrugged. "Harry, for your own good, I repeat — let this be. It's politics. It seems this mine owner, Nathen Gowen, is highly connected to some powerful people. Neither you, nor I, want to go up against them." He looked at the man in front of him. "You're young. Maybe you could start over out West, some small paper in Denver. But not me. I've spent twenty-three years of my life working for this paper. And I've learned when not to push back. This is one of those times."

"Are you saying that we should compromise ourselves?" Harry appeared shocked.

Shotwell grinned. His eyes looked older and his expression was sad. "I'm saying that those two thousand millionaires control this country. They let the rest of us think we have something to do with it, but we don't. They have all the power. And, Harry, they don't want to give any of it up. The reform movement will die a quick, sudden death."

"I refuse to believe that."

"You're young," Shotwell said. "Talk to me in another ten years."

"But it's not right," Harry protested.

"That may be; nevertheless, your story is dead. I'm sorry."

Harry didn't answer. He merely stood up and walked out of the office.

Meggie followed him to his small desk and then left. Harry Korson. How interesting. And what a nice young man . . .

She met Thomas outside the newspaper building and explained everything she had overheard. Together they waited for the young reporter. It was Meggie who spotted him and pointed him out to Tom. "There. There he is. The one with blond hair."

Tom didn't waste any time. Moving quickly, he called out, "Mr. Korson! May I speak with you?"

The young man turned around, a look of recognition on his face. "Mr. Carter. I'm sorry about this afternoon." He glanced back to his newspaper building. "I was told not to see you."

"Why?" Tom asked. When the younger man hesitated, Tom quickly added, "Look, is there someplace where we can talk? I'm staying at the Shermark—"

Korson nodded his head. "Follow me."

He led him into a nearby bar. Seated at one of the many small tables, Tom looked up at Meggie and had to hide his grin. She was staring at a nearly nude painting of a woman over the long polished bar. He cleared his throat, bringing her attention back to Harry Korson. "What's happening? Why didn't you answer any of our letters?"

After ordering a beer, Harry shook his head. "I don't know how to tell you this, but it doesn't look like anyone will be reading that story. I'm—sorry. Really sorry, Mr. Carter."

"I don't understand."

Harry leaned closer and said in a conspiratorial voice, "There are people that don't want you to gain any sympathy. Powerful people."

"And who might these powerful people be?"

"Mr. Nathen Gowen is one of them."

Tom nodded, pleased that the younger man wasn't going to withhold important information. "Can you tell me what you know, Mr. Korson? Anything would help."

It took less than ten minutes to relate the same conversation that Meggie had overheard. Clearly, the man was upset. When he was finished, Tom smiled and said, "You've been a great help. Obviously we didn't do as good a job in hiding you as we thought. It's really too bad."

"I don't know how they could have found out," Harry said. "We took every precaution."

*"James Roarity!"* Meggie spat out. "That black-hearted traitor knew everything and informed on us."

Tom silently agreed with Meggie. Looking at the man across from him, he asked, "And what about our letters? Did you ever receive them?"

"No. Never. I wasn't aware that you had sent any."

An idea started to form in Tom's brain, but he put it on hold until he could do more research. Thinking of the encyclopedia that he had used in his own study, Tom said, "Have you ever heard of a man named William Silvas or Terence Powderly—"

"Sure," Harry interrupted in an eager voice. "Bill Silvas organized the National Union of Iron Molders in . . . I think it was the fifties. He was doing pretty good, from what I've read, until '72. It's been dissolved." Seeing the disappointment in Tom's face, Harry added, "I'm sorry."

Tom nodded. "What about Terence Powderly?"

"The name doesn't ring a bell. But have you ever heard of Uriah Stephans? You've got a better chance there. He organized the garment workers in this city. He called it The Noble Order of the Knights of Labor. Everybody just calls it the Knights of Labor now. Nobody thought it would last as long as this, but I hear he's actually going to try to take it national. If he succeeds, it'll be the first national labor union in this country."

"And this Uriah Stephans and his Knights of Labor are here, in Philadelphia?"

"That's right."

"How can I contact him?" Tom asked.

Harry Korson smiled. "I'll find out and let you know."


For the first time in her life she felt beautiful. She ran her fingertips over the silky material of the nightgown and robe and sighed with pleasure. This gift from Thomas was both unexpected and delightful. Grinning, as she picked up the thick brush and pulled it through her hair, Meggie recalled how shocked and surprised she had been when Thomas had walked into the small elegant woman's shop. She had followed, begging to know what he was doing, but he'd refused to answer her questions. Men just did not enter such establishments and take over, she had told him. It was shocking. The women in the shop reacted in like manner, for most fled, but a few lingered—their curiosity as strong as hers. When the shopkeeper had approached him, Thomas had smiled and asked to see something called a peignoir set. Meggie hadn't known what that was until he was shown several beautiful dressing gowns.

And this one, she thought, gazing at her reflection in the oval mirror. This gift was almost too lovely to wear. The color reminded her of the aged patina of heirloom silver. The intricate lace at the collar and sleeves was thick and heavy and surely as fine as the old women of Dublin could produce. Its matching *negligee,* and she repeated the foreign name in her head, was shockingly revealing, being held together from thigh to breast by tiny satin bows in the palest shade of silver. She felt elegant, feminine, almost like a bride.

*Don't think of it,* she lectured herself. Be happy with what you have. Be joyful that Thomas was returned to you. Find your happiness in now, not in what could be. Placing the brush back on the dresser, she took a deep breath and then turned toward the door that led into the sitting room.

She would accept this gift of time together and be thankful for it.

He had waited while she bathed and it had seemed like an eternity. Several times he had been tempted to step into the other room and put an end to his ordeal, to gather her wet body to him and make wild, passionate love. But he knew she needed this time. No. She deserved it. Their lovemaking had always been frantic, as if the next moment might be snatched away from them. She had never been courted, to use an old-fashioned term. But Meggie was an old-fashioned woman, and it would be something that she expected. He never wanted her to feel lacking, that she had missed anything. He wanted her to feel the way he saw her—beautiful, warm, intelligent, funny, and unbelievably sexy. All that, and more . . .

She came through the door like a Celtic goddess, her thick red curls falling like waves over the satin robe, and desire for her quickly rose up inside him. Smiling, Tom held out her chair.

"Your place, madam." He waited until she was seated before bending and kissing her shoulder. She smelled of jasmine, and a heat rose from her body that had little to do with her recent bath. The very air was charged with a sensual electricity that passed from one to the other and then back again, causing them both to stare at the other in wonderment.

When he was seated, Tom said, "You look beautiful, Meggie. Absolutely beautiful."

Her reaction was immediate. No one in her entire life had ever said that to her and she saw herself in the reflection of his eyes. She felt beautiful for him. "Thank you," she whispered, her throat burning from unshed tears. She would not ruin this moment by blubbering. Lord, but she must control herself. She was *happy.* Even knowing that didn't matter, for she could cry for any reason. Lowering her head, she somehow managed to say, "The peignoir is what's beautiful. Thank you . . ."

He reached across the table and picked up her hand. Bringing it to his lips, he gently kissed her fingertips. "Look at me, Meggie," he softly com-

275

manded, and she was helpless to resist.

"You are what's beautiful."

"Thomas . . ."

Whatever she was going to say was cut off by the sound of a knock on the door. Smiling at her, Tom rose to answer it. A waiter pushed a cart into the room and Meggie had to remind herself that she couldn't be seen in the revealing robe. Relaxing, she inhaled the delicious aromas that entered the room and was suddenly very hungry. Whatever was beneath the silver dome covers was making her mouth water.

"Service for two, sir?" the waiter asked Thomas.

"Yes. I'm expecting someone to join me for dinner." He grinned at Meggie as the waiter placed a large china plate in front of her. Very efficiently, the man set the table with elegant china and crystal and silver. The snow white napkins were so heavily starched that they stood up like fans on each plate. Completing the picture was a lovely small vase of summer flowers.

Satisfied with his work, the waiter returned to the cart and addressed Thomas. "I wouldn't remove the covers, sir, until your guest arrives. As you requested, we've included a sampling of what our kitchen offers. I'll point out each for you now. This is the Maryland terrapin, a maraschino sorbet for between courses is here on ice. The canvasback duck . . ."

Meggie barely listened as the man completed his recitation. She was staring at Thomas. He had done this for her, all of it. From the lovely clothes he'd purchased to this elegant dinner. What a treasure he was, she thought. She watched as Thomas gave the man a tip and closed the door behind him.

He turned back to her and grinned. "And how would you like to begin, madam?" he asked, assuming the voice of the waiter.

She smiled. "Ahh . . . perhaps with the Maryland terrapin?" she said, trying to recall the name of a dish before she had started daydreaming.

"Wonderful choice," he commented, wheeling the cart closer to the table. Picking up the proper lid, he inhaled with appreciation as he served her.

She was starving, yet she waited until he was seated across from her to taste it. It was delicious and she told him so. "I've never had anything quite like it before. What is it?"

"The terrapin?"

She nodded.

"Tortoise."

"Tortoise?" she repeated, reaching for the crystal goblet. It couldn't . . .

"Turtle." Thomas continued to eat, obviously pleased with the dish.

Very slowly she replaced her glass and sat back, willing her stomach to settle. She fought with it to stop churning, pleaded with it not to ruin this special night, yet she could feel it turning over and threatening to do just that. She tried to concentrate on other things, but her body rebelled and she broke into a cold sweat.

He was talking to her about Delaware, about growing up in a small town in that state. He was telling her that he hadn't had this dish since he was a young boy. She tried to listen, tried to concentrate on his words, but her gaze kept sliding down to her own plate. And instead, she was envisioning those moving mounds of mud that spent the spring and summer living at her secret pond. They were ugly, unfriendly creatures . . . and now she had eaten one of them.

Unable to help herself, she pushed back her chair and ran from the room. Please God, she silently prayed, save her this embarrassment! She barely made it to the basin on the marble washstand.

"Meggie!" Startled, Thomas called out her name as he ran after her. "What's wrong?" he demanded, concern in his voice.

She couldn't answer him. She was mortified. No one else in this time could see her. Why, she miserably wondered, couldn't she be invisible to him right now? Instead, she was forced to lift her head and apologize. Some fine, elegant lady she turned out to be. It just goes to prove you can't be what you aren't. She was Margaret Mary Gillbride from the patch. But still. Just for one night? One night to pretend that it was all going to work out for them. Was that asking for the impossible?

## Chapter 19

"How do you feel?"

He came into the room after letting the maid out and sat on the edge of the bed. Reaching up, she touched his cheek and allowed her fingers to graze his lips. "I'm so sorry. I've ruined everything."

"Shh . . . don't talk about it. And you haven't ruined anything." He grinned. "I thought you knew about . . . about that dish. I'm the one who should apologize. I wanted to surprise you and I wound up making you ill."

He looked so sincere, so earnest, that she couldn't help laughing. "All the trouble you went to. And I haven't the courage to match. I'm afraid I let my imagination play tricks on me. The next thing I knew I was beating a path to this room." She took a deep breath and smiled. "Come to think of it, I feel much better. Let's go back. I'll sit with you while you eat."

"No. You stay here and rest."

"Don't be silly," she insisted, and swung her feet over the side of the bed. "Maybe we can still salvage something of this evening yet."

He helped her up. "Perhaps you'd like a little of the sorbet. It's cool and it might soothe your throat."

"Sounds wonderful," she said truthfully. Strangely, her appetite had returned. How odd. Slipping an arm around his waist, she led him back into the sitting room. "Come. I refuse to let anything ruin the remainder of this night."

The sorbet was perfect, calming her stomach, and she was so glad that she had insisted upon returning to the table. Thomas was the most fascinating conversationalist, telling her what the city of Philadelphia was like in his time. She listened to him, watching his lips move, seeing the excitement in his eyes. A lock of auburn hair fell onto his forehead and it took a supreme effort not to reach out and lovingly push it back. He was handsome in a classical sense, like the heroes in her Mum's old books. He poured wine for them both, but she barely touched hers as she continued to watch him. She didn't know how this was happening to her, how this man had come into her life and become such an important part, but she knew she wanted it to continue. The trouble was she didn't know how to ensure that. Thinking about their problems, that at any moment they might once again be separated, frightened her so that she quickly interrupted him.

"Thomas, tell me about Gerald. You started to in Lehigha, but we've been so busy since then and—and we haven't had that much time alone."

He put down his knife and fork and stared at her. "It's so strange, Meggie. I hardly know where to begin."

She reached out her hand and held his, gaining warmth and strength from it. "Tell me what he said to you. Maybe together we can make sense of it."

For twenty minutes Tom related the events leading up to his reappearance in Bridget Humne's house. He tried to remember everything, from the sounds in his office to the people on the street in New York City. After finishing his wine, he shrugged. "That's it. Not much to go on, is there?"

She leaned into the table and rested her arms. Trying very hard to understand, she asked, "But what does he mean, *parallel time?* Two times running together?"

"Not exactly together," Tom explained. "And not just two times, my time and yours. According to Gerald and even some noted scientists, everything that has ever happened or will ever happen is taking place right now. Right as we speak. It's only separate by where we place our reality . . . what dimension we're in."

"I don't understand."

"Neither do I," he admitted. "It goes against everything I've been taught, everything I've believed. But then look what's happened to us. I never would have believed that either. I'm more confused than ever, Meggie. And I thought Einstein's Theory of Relativity was difficult to comprehend. At least that was mathematics. This"—and he shook his head—"this is like being at the mercy of an unseen Time Coordinator. One that has his signals short-circuited."

Her expression was confused. "What do you mean? I stopped following when you began talking about someone's theory."

"Einstein," he said. "A genius. Some say he even believed in time travel."

Her sorbet had melted and she pushed the dish to one side. "Well, I'm not a genius, and I certainly believe in it. You and I are living proof. But that's not enough, though, is it?"

He shook his head. "There's just you and me. I'm telling you, Meggie, I'm afraid to let you out of my sight. I only know what happened to me in front of that antique shop. I had to clear my mind of the modern things that were around me. I couldn't even think about you, or I would be trying too hard. It just happened. When I thought I was wasting my time, that the whole thing was foolish, it happened. I can't explain it, or understand it."

He reached across the table and took her hand. Holding it tightly, he said, "So we won't think about my time. All right? Not now. I want to help Brian and the others. I'm not sure what I can do for them, but I want to try. After that, though, I want to go back."

"Back?" Her heart sank to her stomach.

"To my time. And I want you to come with me. We'll do what we can here and then we have to let it go. Stop thinking about it. If something happened, if we were lost, I don't know if we would find each other again. And I don't want to take that chance."

"You don't?" She was so confused. What was he saying? That he wanted her with him forever?

He shook his head. "I found out something when I thought I had lost you, when I thought I might never see you again."

He stared into her eyes. "I love you, Meg. I can't imagine my life without you."

She made a tiny sound in the back of her throat and brought her hand up to her lips. "Oh, Thomas . . ."

He looked anxious. "I had to say it. I'm sorry if it frightens you, Meggie, but it's how I feel. I know neither one of us expected it to happen. My God, both our lives were going in different directions. But maybe, just maybe in time you could—"

She left her chair and leaned over to silence him. Thoroughly kissing him, she wrapped her arms around his shoulders and melted into his embrace. When she pulled back and looked up into his eyes, it was her turn to appear hesitant.

Tom, at first elated by the depth of her kiss, suddenly felt it was his turn to be sick. There was something in her eyes, something that actually scared him. "What is it?" he asked, not really wanting to hear her answer.

She swallowed several times, as if working up her courage. It was the convent thing, he thought. Her vows. She's going to tell me she can't love me. She's going to say—

"I'm not really a nun."

He blinked a few times. That was not what she was supposed to say. "I beg your pardon?" he heard himself ask.

She tried smiling. "I know this is going to come as a surprise, Thomas, but I'm not really a nun." Her weak attempt at a smile faded. "Not even a novitiate, I'm afraid."

She felt the muscles at his shoulders tighten and he pulled away from her. His eyes, only moments ago a deep, warm, inviting gray, had turned a cold green.

"What are you saying, Meggie?"

She felt desperate to hold on to him and reached again for his shoulder. "Thomas . . . listen to me. I was dressed as a nun for protection. First to get into the Reading building, and then . . . later . . ."

"Later, what?" he demanded, pulling her hand away from him. "Later you lied to protect yourself from *me?* Is that what you were going to say?"

It sounded so terrible. "It wasn't like that," she protested. "You—you assumed I was a nun and I let you. Think about where I was, what was happening to me! What would you do if you were in my place? If you were terrified, thinking you had died, and someone treated you with respect and kindness because of a costume you were wearing? Would you take it off?"

"You deceived me!" He stood up and looked at her as if she were a stranger. "You let me go on thinking you were a nun. Even after you got to know me; even when you knew I was falling in love with you!" Running his fingers through his hair, he stared up at the ceiling. "To think of the misery I went through because I thought I was taking you away from your God, your vows! I thought you were honest—"

"I'm trying to be, Thomas. That's why I had to tell you the truth before I could tell you what was in my heart. That I loved you—"

284

He stared down at her, a look of intense pain on his face. "Why doesn't that mean as much now as it would have two minutes ago? My God, Meggie . . . I don't even know you." Shaking his head, he muttered, "I guess I never did!"

He turned, picked up his jacket from a nearby chair, and walked toward the door.

*"Thomas!"*

He never answered her.


She had lost him.

She stared at the door, not believing what had happened. Hadn't he just said he loved her? Had she only imagined it? How could he wrap her in love one moment and snatch it away in the next? She'd known he was going to be upset when she told him the truth, but this was insane!

She kept blinking, thinking that it would stop the tears. Instead, it only made them run faster down her cheeks. Brushing them away with the back of her hand, she looked down to her elegant robe. It was all so false. They were both living a lie. He didn't know her. If he did, if he knew all about her past, then he wouldn't love her. A man like Thomas couldn't love a woman like her. Not with her secrets. She had let him fall in love with this more innocent version of herself—maybe it was the way she wanted to be for him. And maybe that was why she had let it continue so long. She should have told him the truth, but she couldn't. She didn't want to see his face when he found out that she was only Meggie Gillbride, who lived in the shadow of Monroe colliery. She had never done anything remarkable, anything noble. She was just a woman who had ruined her life when she was little more than a young girl. And she kept paying for that mistake. Over and over again . . .

She wasn't the nun Thomas thought her to be. She wasn't even the woman he had fallen in love with. She was Margaret Mary Gillbride, a survivor, a woman who would tuck away the hurt, just as she had done so many times in the past, and wrap herself in her pride.

But this time . . . dear God, this time it was going to be so much harder.

"It's not fair!" she said aloud to the empty room. Silently, she cried out her love for him while covering her face with her hands.

"How do you stop loving?"

The truth of her words hit her with such force that she buried her face in her arms and sobbed deeply and heavily. Enveloped in grief, in the loss of a beautiful, innocent love, Meggie rose from the chair and slowly walked back into the bedroom. She let the robe fall from her shoulders onto the flowered rug, and barely paused to look as it crumpled in a soft pile. It didn't matter. She felt empty, like the ghost of the person that she once was. It was as if part of herself, an important part, was closing itself off. And it wasn't just for protection. It hurt too much. She simply didn't want to care. Not about anyone . . . or anything.

Not anymore.

The Claymore House.

It sounded innocent enough to Tom, just a place where he could get away from her and think. To his surprise, upon entering the establishment, he was immediately surrounded by noise coming from men of all ages and sizes—men who made room for him at the bar, nodding to him in acknowledgment, or ignoring him in turn. It was no place to think, yet he didn't make a move to leave. Perhaps this was just what he needed, noise and enough people to obliterate her from his head. How could she have done it? How could she have lied like that? He was heartsick and tried to get the bartender's attention, desperate for something strong, something that would make him forget.

"Now you look like a man that could use a drink."

Tom glanced to his left, in the direction of the voice. A woman was standing next to him, her elbow resting on the bar. She wasn't attractive, not exactly. Dressed in a high-collared lace blouse and a long straight black skirt, she was of average height and far from being thin. She had thick brown hair that was pulled back behind her ears into a bun with a thin white ribbon woven into the strands. Wisps of curls had escaped in the summer heat to circle her face. When she smiled, her lips revealed a crooked incisor. But it was her eyes. They were a warm, friendly blue, and when she smiled, for some strange reason, Tom felt comfortable—as if he'd known her for many years.

It was a ridiculous notion, yet he couldn't help grinning at her friendly expression. "I'm trying to get the bartender's attention," he said, looking back at the busy man.

"What do you want?" she asked, lifting her hand to signal the bartender. Less than ten seconds passed before the man was standing in front of them.

"What can I get you, Miss Alice?"

She looked at Tom and smiled. "This gentleman would like . . . ?"

"Brandy," Tom filled in, not able to stop himself from grinning.

"Brandy, Leon. And I think I'll join him."

The man nodded and turned away to fill their order.

"Do you work here?" Tom was impressed by the quick service.

She laughed and threw back her head, as if enjoying the question. Gazing around the bar, she smiled. "I own the place."

"Really?" Now he was definitely impressed. A woman owning a bar in this time was no small accomplishment.

She nodded. "I try to take care of those who walk through that door. You looked lost."

"I am." The words slipped out before he could stop them. "I mean—not really. I know where I am."

She handed him his brandy. "Sure you do."

He looked at her, not knowing what to say.

Instead, she spoke. "I'm Alice Tate. Would you like to sit down? Get away from all this?" She indicated the crush of men around the bar.

Suddenly it seemed as if they were closing in on him and he could think of nothing better than to sit down with this woman and talk. "Thanks for the invitation," he said. "My name's Thomas

288

Carter."

He followed her through the crowd of men, noticing how several actually flirted with her and more than a few gazed after her with longing. He couldn't understand it — men were actually looking at him with envy, as if he had somehow captured a prize. In his time she would never be considered a beauty, nor did he think she would be the recipient of such attention. It was unusual, to say the least. Could the perception of beauty have changed so in the last one hundred years? Or had modern society placed such importance on it that the value of a woman, the real value, had somehow been lost over the years? These men more than appreciated Alice Tate and Tom was curious to know why. He had little time to ponder over it as they reached a small table in the rear of the bar. It was in an alcove, one wall holding back the onslaught of male voices.

Settled in a comfortable chair, Alice Tate sipped her brandy and smiled. "So, Thomas Carter . . . what brought you to my door tonight?"

"I'm not sure," he answered. And it was the truth.

She grinned, her crooked tooth appearing. "I'm over forty years old, Mr. Carter," she said with an amazing honesty. "I've been a wife, a mother, a mistress, and now I own Claymore House. Very little surprises me anymore, and I'm rarely shocked. You look like a man with woman trouble. Now I have six very pretty, clean girls upstairs that could make you forget for a few hours, but that wouldn't solve your problem, would it?"

He didn't answer. What was she? A mind

reader?

Her smile grew warmer. "No. I don't think you need any temporary solutions. Why don't you tell me about her?"

"Her?" Tom could feel his throat closing on him.

Her smile continued. "The one that has put such pain in your eyes."

How could he tell this woman about Meggie? Even thinking her name caused his stomach to tighten.

She sat back, waiting for him to begin. When she recognized his inner struggle, she leaned forward and whispered, "I want nothing from you, Thomas. I'm here to help. You see, someone helped me once and now it's my turn to give back. I've been waiting for you."

"Me?" He pulled back, suddenly afraid.

She shrugged. "Someone like you, someone in such obvious need. It's all right. Really. You see, I'm not important to you. You can tell me anything and never see me again after tonight. It's your choice. Or you can hold it all inside of you, until you're choking on it, until it eats at you and takes away all the joy."

"Who are you?" His voice was almost a whisper.

Very slowly, she reached across the table and patted his hand. "Don't be afraid. I'm a friend."

"A friend?" Gerald had used those same words to him. "But I've just met you."

"It doesn't matter," she answered. "When I saw you walk in tonight, you looked lost. I remember that look. I used to wear it myself." She sipped her brandy and then replaced the glass on the table. Staring at the amber liquid, she continued, "Anyway, when things got better, and they have, I made a promise to myself that if I ever recognized that kind of pain in someone else, I would try to do something about it. You see, I've felt it, Mr. Carter, and it does go away." Her lips moved into a warm smile. "Sometimes all you need is a friendly ear to listen."

"This isn't something I can talk about," he said, wondering what it was about her that made him sit here across from a stranger. "I don't think talking would change anything." She waited for him to continue and he felt the power of her eyes, the persuasion of her smile. "Let's just say tonight I found out that I loved the wrong woman. The woman I loved didn't even exist."

"That sounds serious, so final. Can't you forgive her for whatever she's done?"

Tom felt the burning in his throat return. He hadn't felt this vulnerable, this bruised, since he was a young kid. "It isn't a matter of forgiving," he muttered. "It's a matter of trust. And I don't have any left to give."

She felt the movement of the mattress as he sat on the edge of the bed. Opening her eyes, she saw his silhouette in the moonlight. His back was toward her, yet she could sense more than see the sadness that enveloped him. He struggled with his shoe, finally removing it and letting it drop with a thud to the carpet beneath his feet. She didn't have to see him to know he was drunk. There would be no talking to him tonight. And in truth

291

she was too tired. He wouldn't hear her explanations; he would only hear that she had knowingly deceived him.

And she couldn't deny it.

She closed her eyes and willed her mind to release thoughts of him. The last time he had looked at her, his face had reflected what was in his heart. And it wasn't love. Not anymore. It was shock, despair, and a pain so vivid that she couldn't return his gaze. *You had to have known it wasn't to last, Meggie,* she told herself. Nothing good for you ever does.

Yet as he rested his head against the pillow, she opened her eyes. Staring at his profile, she listened to his heavy breathing and felt a stinging behind her lids. It would be so easy to cry, to let the tears come and take relief in them. But that was over. From somewhere, a small speck of pride had emerged during the night and had taken root in her heart. She would not beg his forgiveness, nor would she cry for his lost love. She had only done what she had to to survive. They came from two different worlds, she and Thomas. In his, he was confident and secure, never wanting. She'd been born into wanting, into the struggle to survive. It had been bred into her through centuries of strife. One did whatever one had to do to survive, to make it through. And you held your head up because of self-respect, if nothing else. She didn't know any other way to endure.

Listening to the sound of his steady breathing, she closed her eyes. Yes, she thought wearily, she had her pride.

It was all she had left.

292

"I originally started it as a secret fraternal lodge, back in '69." Uriah Stephans sat back in the chair behind his desk and smiled. "Anyone could join and become a member, except bankers, stockbrokers, lawyers, professional gamblers, or anyone who bought or made liquor. Those were the rules, and they still stand."

"And your goals?" Tom asked, seated across from the man and holding the silly straw hat he had bought that morning. "What did you hope to accomplish, sir?"

The old man steepled his fingers over his stomach. "We're still hopin', son. We haven't given up seeing equal pay for equal work, the abolition of child labor, and an eight-hour workday, instead of ten or twelve."

It sounded too good to be true. "This is exactly what the men of Lehigha want, but they need help in organizing."

"I thought you said the mine owner had already agreed to sit down and negotiate with them."

Tom sighed. "The mine owners have no intention of doing anything more than lulling them into a false sense of security and getting them back to work. The men are already working with the promise that these negotiations will see a decent raise in pay, enough so that the children don't have to work the breakers. What we need is someone who can take them through the process of collective bargaining, someone who can work out a compromise between the company and the miners."

Stephans was nodding. "And I like that idea about getting a newspaper's support. You picked the wrong one, though, Mr. Carter. You should have gone to *The Inquirer*." He smiled. "Let me handle that for you."

Tom moved closer to the heavy desk. "Does that mean you're willing to help us?"

Uriah Stephans pushed himself up from his chair. Holding out his hand to the younger man, he smiled. "I have to admire them, staying out of the mines for almost a year. And everyone knows what a bastard Nathen Gowen is. Hell, if I didn't have to deal with a boycott down here, I'd go myself."

He led Tom to the door. "C'mon. Let me introduce you to Terry Powderly. He'll handle this one."

Despite everything, Tom felt a shot of excitement to meet the man he had read about when he'd researched labor unions. Terence Powderly had beaten Jay Gould himself in a strike against the millionaire's railroads. It wouldn't happen for another ten years, but he sure couldn't get a better man to lead the miners in the patch than the one standing up to shake his hand.

"How do you do, sir?" Tom said with all the respect he could muster. "It's a real pleasure to meet you."

It hurt too much to look at her, so he let his gaze return to the scenery outside the window. As the train made its way back up the Appalachians to Lehigha, Tom tried to concentrate on the spindly pine trees that lined the hillsides already gray with coal slag. He didn't want to think about her, how she had quietly accepted his decision to leave Philadelphia early and return to the patch. She had barely said a word, as she'd changed into the modern, but much cooler, yellow skirt and blouse. As they left the hotel and rode to the train station, the tone of her voice was so low that he'd had to strain to hear her. She was so subdued that one would think *he* had deceived *her!* That he was the one who had perpetuated the lie! Well, he wouldn't allow her to play these mind games.

He had a plan.

Terence Powderly was coming to the patch in three days' time. As soon as Tom got back to Bridget's house, he was going to write everything down — maybe even sooner if he could find some paper on this train. He'd detail all his plans. So that if he shouldn't be there, Brian would know how to proceed. He would do everything he could to help the miners settle this strike fairly. It had come to him last night, as he had talked to Alice Tate in her comfortable bar. He'd been brought back to this time for a reason. Before he had thought it was just Meggie, finding the one woman he could love even more than himself, or his life's work. He would have done anything for her. Anything, if she had been honest. He could not tolerate dishonesty, for painful experience told him that only led to other disloyal traits. He had opened himself to her, given up everything to find her . . . and she still felt she had to deceive him. She was a stranger to him, and it hurt too much to think about. Last night, he had realized that he'd been brought back to accomplish something, for a reason. Helping Brian and the others had to be it. Now, he only wanted to get on with his *mission* and get back to his own time. His own life. He needed his own reality. Not this.

Life in the nineteenth century could be charming, but it was also crude and rough, and particularly cruel to those who needed the most kindness.

He didn't belong here.

He wanted a normal life—the one he'd had before she'd shown up on that plane and turned his world upside down. Looking at her from the corner of his eye, he mentally cursed as the pain returned to his chest. She looked so sad, so dejected. She also looked beautiful. Damn her! How could she have done this to them?

He had to get away from this insanity.

He belonged in the future.

# Chapter 20

She was exhausted.

Walking behind Thomas and Brian, Meggie wanted only to place her head upon a pillow and sleep. The train ride had been bleak and disheartening. She'd wished that the car had been crowded, so that she wouldn't have to sit across from Thomas and endure his sidelong glances. But it was a price she had to pay, and she would keep on paying. Now she only had to wait until Brian and Thomas finished their business and then she would tell him that she was going to her brother's. She wouldn't remain with Thomas, for neither of them could abide living together and yet becoming more separate than if they had remained in their own centuries. Had it only been two days ago that she had left for Philadelphia thinking that the world was a beautiful place? That he would love her throughout eternity? How foolish to believe in all the fairy tales of everlasting love. That was for children; today Meggie felt older than Bridgi. Thomas . . . Listening to him as he talked to her brother, she felt the heavy sadness increase and settle on her heart.

". . . he'll explain a process called collective bargaining. You, Brian, have to get Gowen to agree to a mediator, a neutral third party who can suggest solutions to both your problems and The Reading's. That's where *The Inquirer* comes in. Once this gets coverage and the public sees you are trying to fairly negotiate, you'll have their sympathy. And that's what you're going for. Nate Gowen's business depends on those people. He's not going to offend them and possibly risk a boycott by refusing to sit down with you and a mediator. But Powderly will explain it all. Trust him, Brian. He knows what he's doing."

His face still black from the coal dust, Brian shook his head in wonder. When he smiled, his teeth stood out like white beacons behind the dark soot. "I don't know what to say, Tom. I can't believe what you've accomplished. And you mean to tell me that the newspaper and these . . . these Knights of Labor are really coming here?"

Tom nodded and brought a folded sheet of paper out of his pocket. "Day after tomorrow. I wrote everything down for you while I was on the train. I was going to wait until tomorrow, but I thought you might want to go over it a few times before they arrived."

"This is great. I can't wait to tell the others—"

"Don't."

Brian looked at Tom. "I don't understand."

Taking a deep breath, Tom said, "Don't tell anyone about this, except Liam."

"Why?"

"Someone," Tom began, "has been informing on

298

us every step of the way. *The Gazette* never even received one of our letters. Gowen and his men have known all along every single move we've planned. This has got to be kept secret, Brian. Or it will fail."

Brian's expression was filled with alarm. "But . . . who? Ah, Tom, it can't be—"

"James Roarity," Tom said bluntly. "Have someone follow him and I think he'll lead you right to Nate Gowen."

"What proof do you have? Listen, I've known Jimmy for near a year. Him and Connon are fast friends. Connon took him in when he came to the patch—"

"He probably set up Connon and then turned him in to the authorities," Tom interrupted. He looked at Meggie. Something had broken through her shell of indifference. Her eyes were filled with tears, yet a smile touched her lips. He couldn't be affected; he wouldn't allow himself. Turning his attention back to her brother, he said, "Someone overheard him saying he was from Chicago. He's not one of you, Brian. My bet is he was hired to spy on the Mollies and bring all of you down."

Brian's face was darkening with his anger. "If you're right . . . my God!" he muttered. "I'll kill the sonofabitch with my bare hands and send him back to Chicago in a box."

Tom clamped his hand on his friend's shoulder. "Brian! You must do nothing! Do you understand? *You* have to lead the others. They look up to you; they'll follow you. Don't you know that Gowen is expecting you to react with violence? Damnit, he's counting on it. Think about it. With you arrested, they've broken the Mollies and the others will go back down to the mines without a fight."

Brian looked tortured and Tom shook his head. "I'm sorry, but you have to realize what's at stake here. You must be careful. Don't you remember Roarity trying to convince you to go after that superintendent? What would happen to all of them, the men depending on you to bring about a fair settlement, the kids, who are too young to be working in the first place? What would have happened if you'd listened to Roarity?"

He didn't even wait for Brian's answer. "Gowen's men would have been waiting for you, that's what. You have to protect yourself, Brian. You're at the center of this."

"There'd be others," Brian protested. "This fight won't end if something happens to me. You, Tom. You've done all the work on this. You'd take over."

"No. I wouldn't," Tom said. "Don't depend on me. This isn't really my fight. I may not even be here that long."

"Where would you go? You're one of us now."

Smiling, Tom said, "Thanks, Brian, but you can't depend on me. I wandered into Fitzhugh's bar and I'll probably wander on to another place soon enough. Now, go on," he added, while stopping at Brian's street, "go on home and think about everything I've said. We'll get together and go over it again tomorrow. Just remember . . . *be careful.*"

They both watched Brian walk up the dirt road toward his house. Tom glanced at Meggie then turned away. Sighing loudly, she followed.

"Thomas. I must speak with you."

He didn't stop until he was in front of the church. "Why?" he demanded. "I think we've said just about enough to each other. I'm so tired."

"So am I," she agreed. "But this has to be said. "I'm not going with you to Bridget's. I'm going to stay with Brian."

He continued to stare at her until she felt so uncomfortable that she added, "I think we'd both prefer it this way, don't you?"

Her voice was still low, as if what was happening to them didn't really affect her. "Do whatever you want. Go back to Brian's," he said angrily. "I don't care."

She would not cry in front of him, she silently vowed. Swallowing several times, she managed to say, "I think I will stay with Brian, then. The place is near falling down around his ears."

Tom nodded, as if remembering. "The night I was there—" He stopped speaking and stared at her. He was never in Brian's home. Never. Yet he could remember what the front room looked like. He could see in his mind's eye the clutter of clothes scattered around the place. They were drinking, and he could hear Brian talking about his sister, about Meggie. He could hear the pain in his voice when Brian said that he missed her; the sorrow when he spoke about placing a headstone on her grave . . . a grave next to—

"Thomas! What's wrong?" Suddenly, she was frightened. His eyes widened and a look of shock replaced his anger.

"Where's the cemetery?" he demanded.

"Why?" Her heart started pounding behind her breast. He couldn't know! He couldn't!

Impatient, he looked behind the church. He searched the surrounding area until he saw it. Giving no explanation, he walked past her and headed for the graveyard.

"What are you doing?" she called after him. Fearful, she broke into a run and caught up with him as he paused beside a wooden gate that led to the cemetery.

"Where is it?" he commanded. "Tell me!"

Breathing heavily, Meggie thought she would faint as she said, "I don't know what you're talking about."

The anger came back to his eyes; the fury curled at his mouth. *"Liar!* Tell me, where it is?"

He knew! How could he? That wasn't Thomas who was in her brother's house. How could this be happening? She was crying, gasping for breath, desperate to stay upright and not collapse at his feet. Dear God, don't do this to me, she silently pleaded. "Don't do this to me," she repeated aloud. "Please, Thomas. Don't . . ." She grabbed his arm as he turned to search the graves.

"That's right, it isn't here, is it?" he demanded. "Brian said it was outside the cemetery . . . There!" His voice was filled with a bitter satisfaction as he pulled his arm away from her and walked toward the two tiny headstones under the willow tree.

She followed, begging him not to continue. "Please . . . why are you doing this to me? Please . . . *stop it!*"

He, too, was breathing heavily as he stood be-

302

fore the graves. One was hers, newly carved:

MARGARET MARY GILLBRIDE 1849-1875
BELOVED DAUGHTER AND SISTER.

And the other . . . the other . . . He blinked
rapidly, trying to stop the burning behind his lids,
the intense rage that was building inside of him.
The other simply read:

PATRICK JOHN GILLBRIDE
GOD LOVE HIM AND KEEP HIM

He felt his shoulders heaving from emotion and
his voice was almost hoarse when he demanded,
"Why didn't you tell me?"

She shook her head, incapable of answering.
There was nothing left to her . . . nothing.

He spun around. "How *could* you?"

In that moment, that instant, she hated him.
Quickly, she found her voice. "Don't you dare talk
to me like that! I've spent years listening to them
talk about me behind my back. And I took it,
first for Da and then for Brian. But I refuse to
take it from you! This is my life. The child that's
buried here is mine—do you understand? The
memories are mine! I don't choose to allow anyone to share them. Not even you."

He was furious. "How could you keep this from
me? How could you not tell me about it?" He
issued a bitter laugh. "And I thought you were so
innocent, so naive. Oh, I knew you weren't a
virgin. But this? You must have really been
amused by how gullible I looked. My God, what

303

an actress you are—"

She hit him. Without thinking, she pulled back her arm and slapped his cheek. Immediately, she saw the red imprint of her hand and brought her fingers to her mouth. "I loved you," she whispered, forcing the words to go beyond her sobs. "Damn you for being so perfect! So . . . so self-righteous—" She stopped speaking when she saw the look of terror on his face.

"What's wrong? Thomas!"

It was happening. He could feel it, just like before. The dizziness was returning with such a vengeance that he could barely stay upright. His heartbeat raced; he could feel the adrenalin rushing throughout his system. Oh God, he thought in a panic. Now. It was happening now . . .

In a span of time too brief to measure, he stared into her eyes and saw his own panic and terror reflected. It came upon him then, the flash of white light, so blinding, so intense that he had to turn his face away to shield it. And in that mere crack of time, he instinctively reached out and thrust his hand through that exquisite radiance.

Until he touched her.

Felt her.

And pulled her to him.

# Chapter 21

The first thing he became aware of was the music blaring in his ears. It was vaguely familiar . . . like something from his childhood. Herman's Hermits. Strawberry Alarm Clock. Donovan. Jefferson Airplane. Each distinct for a moment and then jumbled together in an absurd mental concert. But that loud, drawn out, almost strident chord could only be produced from Jimi Hendrix's guitar. More than confused, Tom opened his eyes and stared at the incredible scene before him.

They were somewhere in the park, Central Park. Maybe Sheep Meadow. Yes, he thought, as he turned his head. There was the Dakota. But what . . . ? All around them were young people dressed in strange clothes. Music was blaring from numerous radios. Some people were carrying signs with peace symbols, or slogans protesting the war. The women wore flowing tie-dyed or flowered outfits. Their hair was straight and long, and several wore beaded headbands. The men looked almost the same as the women—long hair, or Afroed out beyond any reasonable proportion. Wide pointed collars and equally wide bell-bottom pants could only mean one thing.

They were not in 1990.

"What's happening?" Meggie whispered, an expression of fear on her face. "Where are we?"

"I've got a good idea," Tom muttered, pulling away from her to question a thin young man who stood by him.

"Excuse me," Tom shouted over the music coming from a nearby radio. It was late summer, and as usual, the Meadow was taken over by young people with blankets and radios. Each one was louder than the next, as if the noise might mark a territory.

The man turned to him and smiled. "Hey . . . beautiful day, man. Lift your face up to Daddy sun, I say—"

"Could you tell me what year it is?" Tom interrupted what seemed to him the beginning of a speech.

The younger man looked at him and shook his head, causing his long hair to fall over his shoulder. He wore multicolored beads over a Janis Joplin T-shirt. Love beads, Tom suddenly remembered.

"What year? Bad trip, huh?" The man gazed at them with pity.

"Yes," Meggie answered. "It was terrible. Where are we?"

Tom shot Meggie a frustrated look. "He's talking about drugs!" Tom muttered to her out of the side of his mouth. "Let me handle this, will you?"

"I don't touch that stuff. Droppin' acid really messes up your mind," the man advised.

Nodding, Tom asked, "Could you just tell me the year?"

"Nineteen sixty-eight."

*"Sixty-eight?"* Tom said it more to himself than anyone else.

Meggie tugged on his sleeve. "Where are we?" she whispered. "I've never seen anything like this." She stared, open-mouthed, at the scene before her.

Tom answered her unspoken question. "They're called hippies. It looks like there's going to be a protest here soon. Damn it! How could this happen? Why aren't we in 1990? Like we're supposed to be!"

"Far out!"

Tom turned to the man beside him. He could be no more than twenty-two, yet he looked like a relic from an old newsreel. *Hippies!* This couldn't be happening.

"That must have been some trip!" the man exclaimed. "What'd you take? Mushrooms? Brownies? And I thought all you establishment people were uptight."

Taking off his suit jacket, Tom asked, "Who *are* you?"

"Call me Benny." He extended his hand and Tom shook it in an odd three-way handshake.

"Listen, Benny. What's going on here?"

Benny looked around him and smiled. "Power to the People, man—just like the signs say. You ain't never been to a peace rally before?"

Tom shook his head while Meggie continued to stare at the odd gathering taking place right in front of her.

"This should be a good one," Benny added.

"Heard there's supposed to be some draft card burnings, and everybody says Baez is going to put in an appearance . . . *'Blowin' in the Wind,'* man. Ya' know?"

Tom nodded, not sure what to say. He looked behind him and saw his building, run down and far from the glamorous address of his time. In fact the entire park looked neglected. This was an era when the city had more important things to worry about than the condition of Central Park. This was a time when the city, any city, worried about riots and looting and a whole generation of young people that demanded answers to some very tough questions. Nineteen sixty-eight? How old was he? Thirteen?

"Hey, Lilly, my old lady, she says we've got enough beer and sandwiches if you want to hang with us."

"Hang with you?" Meggie's voice sounded frightened.

"He means stay with them. That was an invitation," Tom whispered.

She looked up at him and said in an equally low voice, "Why do some people have paint on their faces—flowers and that strange symbol—"

"It's a peace symbol. All these people are protesting a war. They're called Flower Children because they're peace loving, or, or something . . ." Tom's voice trailed off. "I was just a child when all this was happening."

"But those signs," Meggie asserted, averting her eyes as a teenager grinned at her while trying to draw her attention to his poster.

Tom cleared his throat. "Yes, well . . ." What could he say? In the end he said nothing as Benny introduced his girlfriend.

Meggie shyly looked at the woman called Lilly. She was small and thin with an untamed mass of dark brown hair that fell to the middle of her back. Unlike the women in Thomas's time, this one wore no makeup. She had tiny square spectacles, which seemed old-fashioned even to Meggie, and a warm friendly smile that invited conversation.

"Where are you from?" she asked Meggie.

"Ahh . . . Pennsylvania," Meggie answered after shooting Tom a questioning look. "We're, ummm . . . visiting."

"Right," Tom interjected. "That's right. We're visiting the city."

"Good place to visit, I guess," Lilly replied, "if you got bread. You've got some bread, don't you?"

Meggie's eyes widened and she shook her head. "Bread? Why, no. We don't—"

Tom groaned and muttered, "She means money. But the answer's the same." He reached inside his pockets and felt the monetary relics of another time. "We don't have any *bread*," he pronounced with frustration. "None we can use right now."

Lilly gazed at Benny and shrugged, as if to say she hadn't expected anything else. Looking at Meggie, she asked, "Hey, want to come with me? I have to pick up the beer from Slade's cooler. It's right over there," she said, pointing across the field. "About seventy-five yards."

Meggie glanced at Tom and he shrugged, indicating that it was her decision. She could tell he was remembering their intense argument and the distance they had both wanted to put between them. So then why had he pulled her to him, taking her to this time? Confused, she smiled at Lilly and nodded. "Certainly. I'd be glad to help."

Loosening his tie, Tom watched Meggie walk across a lawn dotted with partying hippies and antiwar protesters. This simply could not be happening to them. Nineteen sixty-eight. He remembered sitting in his living room and watching all this happen on his television. He remembered the discussions he'd had with his parents as they tried to explain this crazy time—

His parents.

It hit him like a wave of cold water, waking him up and making him shiver. They were still alive. Right now. In this time. They were living in Medford, Delaware. In a comfortable white frame house on Oakdale Street. It had deep green shutters and striped canvas awnings on the east windows to cut down on the morning sun and save his mother's rugs. My God. They were here. In that home in Medford. Only two and a half, or three hours away.

What would happen if . . .

Benny interrupted his wild thoughts. "Got a place to stay?"

Tom turned to him, slightly confused. "What? Stay?"

Benny nodded.

"I don't think we'll be here that long." Suddenly

310

filled with a purpose, Tom asked in an excited voice, "Listen, Benny, what's the easiest way to go about getting money right now?"

Benny looked surprised. "You a cop, or something?"

Tom shook his head. "No, I just need money. I want to go home . . ."

"Home, huh?" Benny nodded, while looking over the almost circus scene on the field. Raising his voice to be heard over a Simon and Garfunkel song, he added, "I know what you mean. I'm from Indiana, myself. Sort of feel like Dorothy in the *Wizard of Oz* sometimes being here, but what the hell? Back home everybody paid more attention to the farm report than what was really going on. I'm listening as the body count mounts and they're worried about pork futures. Makes no sense, man." Benny took a deep breath and raised his face to the sun. "Enrolled at Columbia and I'll stay as long as my deferment holds out. After that . . . who knows?"

Tom searched the crowd for Meggie. Finding her and Lilly, he watched as another woman put a necklace of daisies over Meggie's head and kissed her cheek. Everybody seemed so friendly, so giving, so willing to share . . .

"Hey, Benny, how would I go about getting money? Around a hundred dollars."

Pushing his long hair back, Benny said, "Easiest way is to sell some grass, but I can tell that's a little far out for you. Maybe your best bet is to hock something. You got anything to sell?"

Tom thought for a moment, then raised his arm. Rolling up his sleeve he took off his watch. "A

Rolex. Gold. How much do you think I could get?"

Benny took it and said, "I'll ask Soote."

"Who's that?"

Benny nodded over his shoulder. "That's Soote, over by the tree. He sort of runs things, if you know what I mean. Like, nobody pushes nothing without his sayso. He's also the only dude I know that's got a hundred in his pocket. You want me to ask?"

Tom looked at the man who resembled a badly dressed Truman Capote holding court under the wide oak limbs. "Yeah, sure," Tom agreed. "Make sure you tell him it's a Rolex. And it's gold," he added as Benny walked away.

He watched the transaction, saw the way the man called Soote handled the Rolex, holding it up in front of him to see better. Soote glanced in his direction from the corner of his eye and then quickly handed the watch back to Benny. Within less than a minute Benny was back with an offer.

"A hundred and fifty."

"That's it?" Tom asked in disbelief. "Did you tell him it was a Rolex? Maybe I should talk to him."

Benny shook his head. "Listen, man, you can't bargain with Soote. Said he never heard of Rolex before, anyway. Look, didn't you say you needed a hundred? He's offering you that and fifty plus. I wouldn't be turning down that kind of bread, man."

Tom looked at the Rolex, still in Benny's hand. What choice did he have. He had the chance of a lifetime.

To go home again . . .

"Tell him I'll take it."

An hour later the sky darkened with an impending summer storm and Tom and Meggie prepared to leave Central Park, along with a great many others. As the weather changed, so did the carnival atmosphere of the rally. Everyone seemed disappointed as they gathered their blankets and radios. Walking with Benny and Lilly out of the park, Tom and Meggie said their good-byes when all four reached the sidewalk.

"Thanks a lot, Benny. I can't begin to tell you how helpful you've been. Just what are you studying over at Columbia?"

"I'd planned to be an engineer, but that was before the war escalated. Now, who knows . . ."

Tom thought for a minute, then grinned. "Listen to me, do you like games?"

Benny looked confused as thunder sounded in the background. "Games? What kind?"

Excited, and wanting to pay the young man back for his generosity, Tom asked, "Do you ever play pinball?"

"Yeah, sure. Back in Indiana, I was a wizard."

Tom grinned. "Great. Remember video games . . . and computers. Personal computers."

"What are you talking about? I've never heard of video games—"

"Not yet, you haven't. But if you ever do, get into it. Believe me, you won't be sorry. Just remember what I'm telling you."

As Meggie and Lilly hugged good-bye, Tom extended his hand to Benny. Benny clasped it sideways in a sixties handshake. "Strange, man. Who *are* you, Tom Carter?"

Remembering the answer that had been given to him in the past, he said simply, "I'm a friend, Benny. That much you can believe."

Benny shook his head. "Far out . . ."

Looking up to the dark sky, Tom laughed out loud. "Far out," he repeated, though Benny would never know just how true those words were. "Groovy. Right on. Power to the People . . ." Tom couldn't think of any other slogans, so he said, "Thanks again, Benny. Don't worry, you're going to be all right."

As the first drops of rain fell around them, Tom hugged Lilly and then stood out on Central Park West to hail a cab.

After watching their new friends hurry across and disappear up a side street, Meggie turned to Tom and asked, "Where are we going, Thomas?"

A cab screeched to a halt in front of them and Tom opened the door to let her in. Following her inside, he sat back against the leather seat and said to the driver, "The train station."

He looked out the window at a city that was almost foreign to him and added in a low voice, "I'm going home."


The house was empty. No one was at home. Not able to hide the disappointment in his voice, Tom said, "How could this happen? Where could they be?" He'd been so excited, frightened even, to see his parents again. Twenty years from now they wouldn't exist anymore, wiped away in seconds by a terrorist blast on a flight over Japan. The trip to the Orient had been a gift from him, and he'd never gotten over the guilt, or the sorrow, of losing both his parents. Or the anger.

What if he could warn them? Tell them never to go to the Orient? If nothing else, he could do that. He'd write them a note and forewarn them. He tried the door, but it was locked.

"What day is it?" he asked, turning to look at Meggie.

"I think the paper on the train said Friday. Is this your house, Thomas?"

He nodded, running his fingers over his chin while looking up at the screened windows. "That was my room up there."

She looked up at the second floor. Thomas had brought her on this wild-chase and she hadn't complained. He was still angry with her, but seemed more preoccupied than mad. If only he would speak with her, tell her what he was trying to do here? Was he attempting to see his parents? But hadn't he once told her that they had died many years ago? Was he looking for another relative? Why did they come here? What could he hope—

"That's it!" he shouted, startling her so that she jumped at his sudden exclamation.

"What?"

"It's Friday, and it's July. I know where they are. C'mon. Follow me."

And so she did, just as she had been doing all along.


They came upon the baseball field and walked past the rows of parked cars. Tom stopped before

315

a dark gray Buick and smiled in recognition before continuing into the park. Young boys were playing ball, yet Tom ignored them as his eyes scanned the crowd that was seated on the wooden bleachers. He held his breath, searching . . .

There they were!

His mouth dropped open in surprise, shock, and wonderment. His mother and father. Sitting together, just as they always did, to give him encouragement. Why didn't he ever appreciate it then? The two of them, banding together in silent support. Other parents might yell, but not his. Margorie and David Carter would offer a quiet smile if he happened to have looked their way. His dad might wink to take away the butterflies on his way up to bat, but they always let him play his own game. For better or worse.

And why had he never noticed how pretty his mother was? He remembered her graying and tiny. Now she looked young and vibrant, her auburn hair shining in the sun. And when she gazed at his father, he caught his breath in surprise. For a brief moment, when she thought no one else was looking, her face held such love that a thick lump formed at the back of his throat. He never really thought of his parents as ever experiencing that kind of love. Of course they must have, but . . . she looked . . . for a few seconds the look she gave his dad was almost passionate.

And his dad—tall, handsome, just starting to go gray at his temples. Everyone was yelling and shouting, excited by the ball game, and his father was almost laughing. He was looking out to the field with such pride, such happiness, that Tom turned around to see. And it was then that he read the name on the back of the uniforms.

The Harleyville Bruisers.

It all came back to him in a flash. Little League All-Star Game. Bottom of the ninth. Two outs. Two men on. And he was paying right field. Charlie Yansick, the winning run, came up to the plate and Tom had played him deep, having proudly caught two of Charlie's pop flies already. It should have been a cinch, a sure win. And they'd advance in the tournament to win the division.

But that's not the way it happened.

Over how many years had he tried to bury the memory of this day? Even now his belly tightened just remembering that ball rolling over the grass. It was his fault; he'd misjudged, and the Medford Mariners had gone down in defeat. Before this game, Tom had dreamed of playing professional ball, just like every other kid here. Crazy dreams, but still . . . After this day, he never played again. Never even picked up a ball. The memory, even now, was bitter.

He stood by the chain-link fence and looked beyond the infield to the skinny kid out in right field. So intense, so happy to be out there with the rest of the town looking on. As Bill Collins from Harleyville struck out, Tom's fingers linked through the fence as the kid came in off the field at the end of the inning.

"Hey, Carter!" He tried to get his attention. "C'mere for a minute, will you?"

The kid looked preoccupied with his teammates, but made his way to the fence before going to the dugout. When he came closer, Tom had to clench his teeth to keep the emotion under control. Instead, he concentrated on the freckles that spread across the kid's nose and cheekbones, or the sweat as it trickled down from his auburn hair to his sunburned face. Do anything, he told himself, except look into his eyes and see the truth.

"Yeah?"

Tom took a deep breath and managed to say, "You've been playing Yansick deep. Do you really think he's going to chance flying out in the ninth?"

The kid made a face, as if to say "what do you know." Too polite to voice that opinion to an adult, he shrugged instead. "I don't know. I got to go, okay?"

Tom nodded. "Yeah, sure." God, he wanted to reach out and touch him, just touch him to make sure he was real, but instead he swallowed down the sentiment and said, "Good luck."

"Thanks." He was about to walk away when he turned. "Hey, do I know you?"

Tom bit the inside of his cheek and shook his head. "No. Not yet."

But the young man was already returning to his team, too caught up in the excitement of the game to pay any mind to a middle-aged man who's time had long passed.

Turning to Meggie Tom said, "C'mon. Let's watch the game from up there."

He led her up behind his parents, excusing himself as he took the seats directly behind them. He was sorry if others thought him rude, but he needed to be near his parents. Maybe he could touch them, connect, and somehow stop what was

318

in their future. Settled behind them, he stared at their heads, waiting for them to look at each other so he could see their faces. He barely paid attention to the game. Once he interrupted them and asked for a piece of paper and a pen. His skin still tingled where his mother's fingers had grazed his own. She'd looked at him without any recognition. Disappointed, and yet relieved, Tom wrote down his warning and quietly sat behind them, fighting the urge to tell them who he was, and also fighting the need inside of him to hug them both. Either way he'd frighten them, and so he settled for quietly sitting, and staring, and yearning . . .

Charlie Yansick was built like a man. He couldn't be anymore than fourteen but he must have weighed a hundred and ninety pounds. And when he connected at the bat, all that power came whistling right at you.

Tom sat up straighter, along with everyone else. Here it was, that fateful moment. Ninth inning, two men on, two outs. And Charlie Yansick. Tom didn't watch the batter for he already knew when he would swing. Tom stared at the skinny kid in right field, playing him too deep, too far back to —

Wait a minute.

As if on cue, the kid started moving up toward the infield. Everyone in the stands stood as the tension mounted. Yansick fouled twice and the crowd was nervous as he stepped back into the batter's box.

And then it happened. In less than three seconds, Yansick swung at a curving fastball and hit a line drive over first base, only to have it caught by the skinny kid playing right field.

It was a magnificent catch, major league, something to replay over and over in your mind. And he'd done it.

*He'd actually done it!*

The crowd broke out into a cheer and people started congratulating Margorie and David Carter, shaking her hand, slapping his back. Tom allowed himself to place his palms on their backs, while bending down to speak with them.

"Congratulations. That was a great catch." He couldn't believe it—his mom was crying and his dad looked ready to burst with pride.

"Thank you," his father said, quickly turning to shake hands with Mr. Fremancini, their neighbor from across the street.

"He's a good boy," his mother managed to get out, reaching into her purse for a handkerchief. "I'm so happy for him. He was so nervous. This meant a lot." She looked back to her son as his teammates surrounded him.

In that moment, Tom let the tears run down his own cheeks as he quickly slipped the note inside his mom's purse. "I love you," he whispered to them both, knowing neither one would hear. And it didn't really matter.

They knew.

Margorie Carter started talking to a teammate's mother and Tom turned to Meggie. "Let's go."

She stood for a moment and watched him climb down from the bleachers. How extraordinary! These were Thomas's parents, and if that were so, then . . . She looked out to the field, to the young boys jumping up and down with excitement. Hurrying to catch up with Tom, she met him at the fence as he watched the team savor their victory.

The young boy he had spoken with earlier looked his way and waved, nodding and laughing. Tom waved back.

"Who is that, Thomas?" she asked, already knowing the answer.

"It's me," he muttered, and wiped his nose with the back of his hand. Taking a deep steadying breath, he said, "C'mon. We've got a train to catch."

He started to walk away and Meggie took one last look at his parents. His father was helping his mother climb down from the stands when her purse fell, spilling the contents over the ground. Several people bent down to help her retrieve it and all laughed, still happy with their son's victory. Meggie smiled along with them as she turned to follow Tom up the street.

She never saw the piece of white paper blow under the bleachers, the one with Tom's warning to his parents.


"We have to talk."

He stared out the train window into the darkness of the night, not quite ignoring her, just too tired for this conversation. "Not now, all right?" he asked.

"When?" she demanded in an equally tired voice. "I've been waiting all day, and now it's night."

He closed his eyes briefly and then turned to her. "Look, thanks for today—"

"I know it wasn't easy for you. I remember what it was like the first time with Brian. At least you could see them and talk to them—"

"Don't," he interrupted. "Too much has happened today. I need time to sort it all through. Thanks for your patience, for going along with everything, but—"

"Don't treat me like a stranger, Thomas." This time she interrupted him.

He stared at her, a look of intense sadness on his face. "I'm sorry . . ." He shook his head, as if words failed him, and looked back out the window of the train.

How could he ignore her like this? They had been through so much together. "How long are you going to make me pay?" she demanded. "Is your silence and cold treatment supposed to punish me for not ripping open my soul to you and telling you all my secrets? Have you kept nothing from me?"

He didn't answer her.

Frustrated and tired, she moved up in her seat and clasped his arm, trying to force his attention. "What do you see out that window? You won't find your answers there, Thomas." She looked out the glass and into the night. Towns passed by with a blur of lights that became brighter and brighter. Her fingers tightened on Thomas's arm when the dark scenery changed, ever so slightly at first, then becoming more distinct.

The glass window of the train started to enlarge, to frame pieces of furniture, gilt mirrors, antique

322

lamps. Her limbs started to tremble and her stomach tightened with fear.

They were no longer on the train . . .

"Thomas!"

He held her to him in a fierce grip as the white light surrounded them and swept them away.

In her mind she was back in the patch, yelling at Thomas, hating him for hurting her and prying into her life, forcing her to open old wounds and talk about her baby. It was as if 1968 had never happened, and the memory of that time faded along with it. Thomas was shouting at her, looking at her with disgust and disillusionment, demanding answers to questions he had no right to ask.

It was too much to bear again, and she screamed out in horror. *"No! It's enough!"*

And in that moment the window of the train truly and in reality became the window on Madison Avenue.

In New York.

In 1990.

# Chapter 22

"It's gone. Your mother's table, it's—it's gone!"

They stood in front of the antique shop, holding each other, staring into the darkened window. It was Thomas who uttered the words, forcing her to open her eyes and look beyond the glass. Her breath came in ragged spurts; her heart pounded frightfully against her rib cage, and her limbs were shaking. From behind her she heard the sounds of traffic, yet she continued to cling to Thomas, reluctant to release that feeling of security she'd found in his arms. He could have left her, but he didn't. He'd drawn her to him, pulling her along with him into the twentieth century.

She was so confused—one moment angry, hating him with a passion she hadn't thought possible, and in the next she was ecstatic not to have been left behind. Alone. Without him.

". . . right back where we both left," he muttered under his breath. The first of them to speak, Thomas broke the spell and she could feel the muscles in his shoulders again tighten.

She looked into his eyes. "Thomas . . ." She didn't

know what to say, or how to approach him. Just as he had said about her—suddenly, they were like strangers. "I'm sorry, sorry for not telling you earlier."

He turned his head back toward the shop window, as if looking at her was too painful. "I believe you are sorry, Meggie," he whispered in a disillusioned voice. "Don't you understand? It's too late. It's—"

She moved out of his arms and used the window as support. "Wait a minute. I don't think *you* understand. I'm sorry I deceived you about being a nun." She tried to steady her breathing. "I thought it was necessary, and I'd probably do it again if I had to. But you'll never hear any apologies because of what you discovered in that cemetery. You crossed over the line then, Thomas. You went too far."

"I went too far?" His voice sounded incredulous. *"I went too far?"* he repeated, pushing back the hair from his forehead.

She turned away from him, resting her cheek against the cool glass. Her mother's sewing table was no longer in the window, and she found that she couldn't care about its disappearance. Too much was taking place too quickly. Closing her eyes, Meggie said calmly, "And now I'm back here. I have nothing, nothing is left to me any longer—not even my pride. If you would . . . would let me stay with you for a few days until I can find some sort of employment, then I won't bother you anymore. I just need a few days . . ." She took a deep breath, as if coming to a decision. "At least I can be seen and heard in this time. Maybe here I can begin a new life."

"Don't be ridiculous," he interrupted. "What are you talking about?" He didn't wait for an answer as he spied a yellow cab and rushed out to the street to flag it down. "C'mon," he said wearily. "Let's go home."

In the fast-moving automobile, she listened as Thomas questioned the driver about the date. Three days had gone by in this time since Thomas had left it. And in that period her mother's sewing table had obviously been sold. It was gone. Again. For some strange reason, even its loss couldn't summon up her sorrow. Something had closed off inside her; something warm and wonderful was extinguished. Now she only wanted to survive, to stay in this time and begin her life over. There had to be a place where she could belong.

As she watched Thomas instruct the doorman to pay the driver, she swallowed down the growing lump in her throat. It was love that had died. What had happened between them had been fast and furious, like a quick-burning flame. Too hot, too bright, too fiery. And destined to die out just as quickly.

It was for that she felt sorrow.

For the love.


"I don't know what I'm going to do! Kelsey has to be at the pediatrician at three and Toppers has a two forty-five appointment at the vet's. I simply *cannot* be in two places at one time." The well-dressed blond woman glanced at her gold watch and sighed with frustration. "I don't know what I'm going to do."

"Can't you just switch one of the appointments?" her equally elegant companion offered. Both women wore their wealth with a casual ease. From the cut of the fabric, one could tell these women were accus-

326

tomed to the very best.

"You're so naive," the blond woman answered. "You can't cancel a pediatrician, and I've had to wait five weeks to get Topper an appointment with the veterinarian. This is Manhattan, dear, not Scarsdale."

"Well, I wish I could help out," the other woman answered, not too convincingly. "But I'm having lunch with Alexa, and we both know how long she can drone on."

Did she dare? Standing in the corner of the elevator, Meggie said timidly, "Maybe I could help."

Both women turned to stare at her and she refused to look away. Instead, she forced a smile to appear at her lips. It took every amount of courage she possessed to speak up, but now that she had, she wasn't about to back down.

The blond woman scrutinized her, looking over her cream-colored slacks and blouse. Meggie continued to smile. This was too important.

"Haven't I seen you before?" the blond woman asked.

"That's possible," Meggie answered. "I, ah, I'm working for Mr. Thomas Carter." It wasn't exactly a lie, she told herself. She had taken over the role of housekeeper since they'd come back to this time. And it hadn't been easy. Oh, the work was less than she'd done in the patch, but seeing Thomas every day, every night, was more than she could handle. This strained truce couldn't continue. She had to leave. Find her own place.

"Mr. Carter?" the blond woman asked, obviously impressed. "You work in the penthouse?"

Meggie nodded. "His housekeeper, Celia Rob-

327

bins, is on holiday and I've been taking over. My name is Meggie Gillbride."

The blond woman looked at her companion with a pleased expression. "Wouldn't Mr. Carter be upset if you—you free-lanced, so to speak?"

Meggie had no idea what free-lanced meant, yet she shook her head. Mr. Carter, unfortunately, barely spoke to her. She didn't think he would be upset at all. He showed no interest in what she did. "If you would like, I can help you out. Just tell me what you want done."

The other woman, the companion, spoke up as the elevator reached the lobby. "So you do odd jobs, too? Like if I were working late, you could do my marketing?"

Meggie smiled. "And have your dinner warm on the stove when you came home."

"Miss Gillbride"—the doorman caught her attention—"would you like me to call the garage? Mr. Carter said you were to use the car if you went out."

She shook her head. "Thank you, John, but no. I don't need a driver. I won't be going far."

The two women surrounded her and exchanged covetous glances before steering Meggie to a corner of the lobby.

"You would cook?" the shorter, dark-haired one asked.

"And clean, and shop, and do errands," Meggie added, pleased by their interest. Maybe . . . just maybe she had stumbled upon a solution to her problem.

"What about children?" the taller one questioned. "Do you object to children?"

"Object?" Meggie was clearly shocked. "Who

328

would object to children?"

The woman's eyes positively lit with pleasure. "How are you with animals?"

"I like them," she said truthfully. "Not as much as I like children, but well enough."

The woman wet her lips in anticipation. "My name is Grace Easton. I'm in 14C. Do you think you could come down at around two this afternoon and meet Topper. If you like him—I mean if the two of you get along—maybe you could take him to the vet?"

The hopeful look in the woman's eyes almost made Meggie laugh. If this woman only knew how much she needed the job.

"Of course I'll pay you," Grace added before Meggie could answer. "It's worth fifty dollars to keep that appointment."

"Fifty dollars?" Meggie's eyes opened in surprise.

"All right," Grace said. "Sixty."

"Grace!" the other woman looked more surprised than Meggie.

"Well, we are practically stealing Thomas Carter's housekeeper right out from under him, aren't we? And you just wait, Muriel, like I said—this isn't Scarsdale. You actually get used to those dreary supermarkets in the suburbs. Now it takes four times as long just to shop for an evening's meal. The butcher. The vegetable store. The bakery. Who has the time? Last week I needed shallots for a recipe that Jack had found in the *Times?* Seven dollars and forty minutes—that's what it cost me."

The woman sighed deeply, before continuing, "By the time I got back here, I was so angry that we went out to dinner. It's all these little errands that drive me crazy. I ask you: What's the point of moving back to the city if you have to spend three hours shopping and two hours waiting in a veterinarian's office? And she *likes* children, Muriel."

Muriel looked from her friend to Meggie. "My husband's been told to modify his diet. Are you able to prepare high-fiber, low-cholesterol?"

Meggie didn't blink. "Certainly."

Again Muriel and Grace looked at each other. Finally Grace said, "Why don't we all meet again at my place? Shall we say two o'clock this afternoon?"

"But Alexa . . ." Muriel remembered her luncheon partner, then just as quickly added, "Forget Alexa. I'll be back in time." She smiled at Meggie. "Perhaps this afternoon we can work out some sort of arrangement?"

Meggie nodded. "I'll be there. Apartment 14C." She smiled at both women before turning toward the huge revolving doors. Pausing she said to the doorman, "John, I believe I will be using the car at around two-fifteen this afternoon."

"Yes, ma'am."

Thanking the man, she turned and pushed the polished brass that separated the glass doors and walked out into the sunshine. Now what was she going to do?

Her mind raced as she impatiently waited for the traffic light to turn green. Along with a small crowd of people she crossed the street and headed for the Strand bookstalls on Fifth Avenue. She'd bluffed her way through that encounter. Now she would have to prepare herself for the one this afternoon in Grace Easton's home.

*What in the world was cholesterol?* And surely

Muriel was mistaken. Her husband ate *fiber?* She tried to imagine a person eating cotton or wool or jute . . . and burst into nervous laughter while picturing Muriel's husband dining on hemp. No one paid her any attention. That was one thing she liked about New York City. No one seemed surprised by anything.

Within two weeks, Meggie had seven customers. She cleaned and ironed strangers' clothes. She re-taught herself to cook after reading that the way her mother had instructed her was now found to be unhealthy. It wasn't often that she fried, or used anything but olive oil. She learned all about choles-terol and fiber, and Muriel's husband raved about her dinners. From him, she picked up three new customers. All unmarried men, all too busy to lead ordered lives. That was her specialty. Meggie brought order into cluttered lives. She carried a large brass ring with the keys to the homes of her people at-tached. All were within walking distance of each other.

Her days were full. She started with Thomas, making him a breakfast he rarely ate. As soon as he closed the door, she hurried to fill the blessed ma-chine that miraculously cleaned the dishes. Within fifteen minutes she was in Grace Easton's apartment on the fourteenth floor. There Topper followed her around the place as she picked up and attended any errands that Grace would post by the telephone. By ten-thirty she attached Topper to a leather lead and picked up two more dogs on the seventh and fourth floors. It was all very businesslike, those brief walks in the park. She found it distasteful to carry the plastic bags and clean up after the animals, but she knew she hadn't any other choice. This was only a job, not her life's work. By midmorning, she was on to another building to cook dinners and leave them in the freezers, to pick up dry cleaning, to take young Marcy Applegate to her nursery school or tiny Phillip Carsey through the park in his pram.

It was there in Central Park that she'd found out about the large concentration of illegal Irish who made New York City their home. Looking for Gerald, she'd met several people with accents far stronger than her own. She'd become friends and had found out that many had banded together in places called Woodside, Sunnyside, and Jackson Heights. There were thousands of young Irish in Queens, working in Manhattan and the surrounding boroughs as laborers, waitresses, barmen, painters, doormen, carpenters . . . anything where a lot of persistence and a little of the blarney would get them hired. At night they returned to "Little Ireland" in Queens and read the Dublin newspaper that had been flown in the previous day. But that wasn't for her. When she left Thomas, she intended to find a place on the Lower East Side. He would look for her in Queens, expecting her to disappear into the Irish community. Instead, she intended to quietly live closer to her clients. One of her new friends had told her about a building with a vacancy. She had accumulated the phenomenal sum of twelve hundred dollars; every night she took out the bills and carefully counted them. It appeared that the role of wife to both man and woman paid very well indeed. In this age of wealth and time-saving machines, many didn't seem to have the time or inclination to take care of a home and family. And that was the only thing Meggie had been brought up to do, the only training she had ever received. She was finally a wife, with seven different homes. But none she could call her own.

And she had to find a place soon, for it seemed Fate wasn't through playing with her life.

She was almost sure she was pregnant.

Again.

She had seen it on the television that Thomas had installed in her room. She had come home one day to find the glass box there on a small table. She knew why he had done it. Now she needn't come out at night. They didn't even have to see each other at all. Even a poorly timed passing in the hallway was awkward and painful. He was tolerating her in his home out of pity . . . and she'd had her fill of pity in two worlds. No one need pity her ever again.

She'd found a place, a small apartment on the Lower East Side. It wasn't pretty, not yet. The building was rundown a bit and the landlord tended to be surly . . . but it would be perfect. Now, all she needed was the result of this test she'd first seen on the television. What embarrassment she had suffered buying this device. Maybe she was wrong. Maybe her body was only reacting to all the pressures of her work during the day, and the tension of being alone with Thomas at night. Maybe . . .

And then, as the color in the small vial turned a pale pink, Meggie knew her answer.

She was pregnant.

Her gaze remained fixed as she sank to the toilet seat. She couldn't be . . . *pregnant!* Like the dominos the old men played, everything fell into place—why

333

she was so tired, why the tears were always so close to the surface; why her stomach kept churning while she prepared the meals for her clients. And just as suddenly, she recalled the words of the doctor who had attended her after the first time.

*You're not made for children. You're too small for the passage. Some women are like that. Listen to me good, girl, the next time will be the death of ya. No more children for you. Not ever.*

*The death of ya* . . . The words rang inside her brain until she felt dizzy and sick to her stomach. This time her fate was sealed. And again, the father of the babe didn't want her. Well, this time she wasn't waiting around to be told.

She had to get away! The last time she had stayed, had endured the humiliation. But not now! She was older and wiser. She would leave this home of wealth and elegance and suffering. She would give Thomas back his life, the same life he'd had before her. And somehow, she was going to make sure Thomas Carter never knew anything about this pregnancy.

Her fingers trailed down to her abdomen. Another woman would feel joy to create life. For Meggie it was a death sentence that would surely end her own . . .

# Chapter 23

He didn't want to go home.

Leaving his office, Tom ignored the waiting car and decided to walk the twenty blocks; he needed time to sort everything out before he saw her. Meggie. Her name repeated through his brain like a litany as he walked the city streets. If he didn't make eye contact, he could overlook the infrequent stares or signs of recognition from those who passed him. That was the good thing about avoiding publicity. His face was familiar, but most people weren't sure where they knew him from, or what he did. And he needed his privacy now, for he had something very important to work out.

Meggie . . .

Living in the same apartment with her had been sheer torture, and he could never remember being so unhappy, so disagreeable. Everyone in the office steered clear of him unless it was necessary. Even Morris, who Tom had to admit had done a great job of taking over in his absence, tended to shy away. He was making everyone around him miserable. And it couldn't go on. Something had to be done, and yet until this afternoon, he hadn't a clue to solving the dilemma.

It had started with something so simple as a paper cut, one of those annoying results of envelopes that can hurt like hell. This one also bled, making him reach into his pocket for his handkerchief. It wasn't until he was folding it back up that he noticed the tiny corner of heavy white embroidery. It was one of Bridget Humne's, one that she had given to him before he and Meggie had gone to Philadelphia. Meggie must have laundered it and placed with the others in his drawer. And then it had come to him—how much different was he from Meggie?

He, too, had used deception to secure his place in the past. Even with Meggie's invisible help, he still had to fabricate a history, pose as a miner, tell others about a past that didn't exist. And he'd let them all believe those lies, rather than telling them the truth about himself, the truth about where he really came from . . . because that was the one thing they would never have believed.

Anymore than he would have believed Meggie if she'd told him she wasn't a nun, but merely a woman working with the Mollie Maguires in the year 1875. He remembered then how he had first acted around her. She was right, he had treated her differently because of that habit—just as Brian and the others had treated him with respect when he'd convinced them he was Thomas Carter, a miner from Ashland. All lies . . . yet all necessary at the time.

How could he justify his anger with Meggie when he had been willing to do the same thing,

336

employ the same type of deception? Because he had loved her came an immediate answer. Because she had let him fall in love with a lie.

Yet now, maybe he could see why she had done it.

She had felt safe as the nun, safe from him. The stranger. He hadn't taken more cold showers, and suffered more internal guilt, since his teenage years. Tom was willing to admit that perhaps Meggie had sensed that blatant, almost predatory male drive and had retreated behind the safety of the habit. He could accept that. What he couldn't accept was her continued subterfuge after they had made love. He couldn't think about the night in the mountain pool without experiencing a painful tightening in his stomach. Why didn't she tell him after that? He was haunted by that night, reliving it over and over in the darkness of his room. Knowing she was asleep beyond his bedroom wall only added to his anger. How many times did he want to throw open the door that separated them and confront her? Demand to know the truth—who was the father of that child that lay buried beyond the churchyard?

The child.

Why didn't he just admit it to himself? That was at the core of his anger. She had loved someone once, loved him enough to carry his child . . . and still she grieved. But for whom?

How could she not tell him *that*?

When he opened the door to his apartment, it wasn't with the same sense of dread that had plagued him the past few days. He was almost looking forward to seeing her. As he entered, he

337

could smell the aroma of dinner cooking. She was forever cooking, or reading, or . . . or avoiding him. So it was with some surprise that he saw her sitting at the dining room table. Her hands were folded and resting on the edge of the glass, like someone who had been waiting a long while. And he noticed, for the first time, the circles that were under her eyes, the strain that showed in her face. Immediately, he felt penitent for having caused that to appear and resolved to end this quiet war.

"Hello, Meggie." He dropped his briefcase onto a chair and loosened his tie. Taking off his jacket, Tom smiled at her.

She appeared unmoved by his overture, so he tried again. "How was your day?"

She raised her chin to look up at him and he caught his breath. The sorrow that was reflected in her eyes hit him with such intensity that he was immediately contrite. How could he have done this to her? How could he have isolated her in this silence? Never giving her the chance to explain.

"I have to talk to you, Thomas."

He let his breath out in relief. "I want to talk to you, too, Meggie. I walked home today and I had a chance to think about—"

"I'm leaving," she interrupted, without giving him the opportunity to finish. "I'm moving tonight."

His mouth opened in shock. It took a few more seconds for his lips to form the words. "What do you mean *moving?* You can't."

"I am."

He kept staring at her, as if trying to make sense out of her announcement. "Why? Where will you go?" This was not happening! Not today. Hadn't he just decided to see if they could work out their problems?

"I've found a place," she said simply.

"A place?" he demanded. "What kind of place?"

"A place of my own."

Why was she just sitting there like that? Why wasn't she angry? Or fighting with him? Why did she look like none of this really mattered to her any longer? "Where?"

She shrugged. "That isn't important. The reason I'm still here . . . I mean, the reason I wanted to see you was to thank you for letting me stay here with you. I'm . . . I'm sorry if I've made things difficult for you, Thomas. I really never meant . . . that is, you've been very kind."

He took a step closer to her. This could not be happening! "Meggie, let's talk, all right? You can't move out. You belong here."

She shook her head and smiled sadly. "No. No, I don't. This is your home. I never really belonged."

"Stop it." He sat down beside her at the table. "Don't do this. I was wrong, Meggie. I said some terrible things to you. I understand now. Well, sort of —"

Her smile never wavered. "Thomas," she interrupted, "please don't say anything else. I must leave."

He felt battered by her words, by her expression, and her calm acceptance. "Why? *Why?*"

She pushed her chair back and stood up. He could see she was now fighting for control as her shaking fingers reached out and touched his cheek.

He couldn't help flinching at her soft touch, once so familiar and now so absent.

"Because I've finally accepted the fact that I can't control Fate. I've tried to fight it my whole life, but now I know I can't alter it, and neither can you. We just weren't meant to be, Thomas."

He stood up, suddenly angry. "How can you be like this? How can you say these things without any emotion, any feeling? You think you can just walk out of here and forget everything? What about Brian and the others? What about them?"

She turned away from him and walked down the hall. "I can't think about that right now." She reached her room and he saw her pick up the handles of two shiny gray shopping bags. Turning around to him, she said, "I've prepared enough meals to last until Celia comes back. They're in the freezer—"

"I don't give a damn about that," he interrupted. "You can't leave." My God, she had everything she owned in those two little bags. And she was walking around him . . . in the direction of the door!

"I've left instructions on which of them you can put in the microwave. Oh, and please leave your laundry in the yellow bag on your bathroom door. I've arranged for a commercial establishment to come in and pick it up. They've promised me next-day service," she said matter-of-factly, as though he'd never interrupted.

"Meggie, why are you doing this?" he again demanded as she neared the door. "Why won't you even talk to me about it?" He was becoming desperate as she put one of the bags down on the marble foyer floor to open the door. It was too incredible! "Listen to me, this isn't the patch; this is New York City. You haven't the slightest idea what kind of danger is out there. You . . . you're too naive, too nice. Damn it, Meggie, this isn't 1875. This is 1990 and people are different now—"

"Thank you, Thomas," she politely interrupted as she looked at his hair, his eyes, his mouth. He felt as if she were memorizing each of his features. "I want you to know," she said in a low, almost rough voice, "how very much I appreciate everything you've done for me, and for Brian and the others in Lehigha. You were very brave and intelligent. I'm sure they'll work out their problems."

Breaking his gaze, she pushed the elevator button and the doors immediately opened. She entered and turned around to face him. Her lips were trembling as she tried to smile. "I will never forget you, Thomas Grey Carter," she whispered. *"Never . . ."*

Slowly lowering her head, she stared at the carpeted floor, as though she could no longer look at him. Tom opened his mouth to speak, but the heavy steel doors silently closed, blocking her from his view.

*"Meggie!"* It was too late when he managed to call out to her. She was already gone. Feeling powerless, Tom desperately looked around him. He couldn't let her go! He refused to believe that she would walk out of his life. She was acting like a stranger, like they hadn't a past! It was as if they hadn't shared the most incredible experiences together, and survived them. Together. He would not let her leave him. She was his and he'd stop her if

he had to physically pick her up and carry her back here. Cursing the fact that there was only the one elevator which serviced the penthouse, he ran for the stairs. Throwing open the door, he took them two at a time, determined to catch up with her. When he reached the lower floor, he raced for the three elevators that ran the length of the building and used his fist to hit the buttons on all three.

Pacing, cursing, talking out loud to himself, Tom again pounded the elevator buttons and still all doors remained shut. This could not be happening, he told himself. It was like some crazy kind of joke. Meggie was one in a million, one in ten million. He'd been terribly mistaken in the way he'd handled everything. He'd been an ass. But she would forgive him, if only she'd listen. He knew she would. He had to make her listen, make her believe what she had come to mean to him.

Jerking his tie loose, Tom swallowed almost convulsively. He couldn't imagine her on the streets of this city. Alone. That thought caused all his muscles to tighten and his stomach to rebel. My God . . . Meggie. He simply *had* to stop her.

At last the elevator on the right arrived and Tom ran inside, using his fist to hit the lobby button. As he looked up at the ceiling of the car, he actually found himself praying that he would catch her in time.

All he needed was a little luck on his part and a lot of patience on hers.

"Did you see her, Tony?" Tom demanded of the doorman as he raced up to the high desk. "Miss Gillbride . . . did you see which way she went?"

342

"No, sir," Tony answered, surprise showing on his face.

Tom ran outside and stood on the wide sidewalk, his eyes scanning the early evening crowd. People were coming home from work and it was busier than normal. Frantic, Tom looked both ways, desperate to spot her through the crush of pedestrians that weaved around him. His heart was racing and he was beginning to get frightened. She was nowhere to be seen. Terrified that he might have actually lost her, he pushed his way back to the front of his building and climbed up onto the huge marble base of an evergreen. Above the crowd, he searched for her. She should have been easy to find, standing out with that banner of red hair. How could she have disappeared so quickly? How? His heart refused to give up the search, but his mind was telling him the truth.

She was gone.

On the fourteenth floor of the Tower, Meggie knelt on the carpeted floor of the Eastons' apartment and wrapped her arms around Topper's neck. She allowed the dog to lick away the tears that ran freely down her cheeks. Leaving Thomas had been the hardest thing she'd ever had to do. The Westie made a noise deep in its throat and Meggie smiled sadly for the dog actually sounded as if he was sorry for her. Wiping her cheek with the back of her hand, Meggie sniffled.

"Don't I look like the fool?" she asked the dog, and rose without waiting for a reaction. The small

343

white terrier eagerly pranced toward the door. "No," she said, while walking to the kitchen with her bags. She was so tired. Would this night never end? "I can't be takin' you for a walk now. I'm only picking up these keys and then I'm going home." Reaching into her pocket, she withdrew a handkerchief and blew her nose.

Home. Where was that now? she silently wondered as she walked toward the sink and exchanged the keys in her hand for the ones atop the counter. She had told all her people that she would need keys for the service entrance, the back stairs, and the elevator where deliveries were made. It would be safer that way. No one would see her entering or leaving this building, for she was sure Thomas would be looking for her . . . and she couldn't be found. Soon, the reason for her departure would be obvious. Until then, she intended to disguise her condition for as long as possible. But now, right now, she wanted only to leave this building and put the image of Thomas out of her mind.

The tears started again as she pocketed the keys and walked toward the back door in the rear of the kitchen. Without looking again to the waiting Westie, Meggie opened the door and left apartment 14C. As she rode this elevator, so plain, so different from the one in the lobby, she knew she would never be able to put Thomas far from her mind.

She knew with her last breath she would whisper his name and take his beloved image with her.

\* \* \*

It was like a rabbit's warren — rundown, dirty, with more halls and passages than she would ever keep straight. This was her home now. As she wearily climbed the second flight of stairs, Meggie could hear people arguing, babies crying, and dogs barking. She tried to shut them all out as she passed two teenagers kissing in the hallway. They broke apart to momentarily look her over, and then, deciding she was of little consequence, resumed their bold spectacle. Had they no shame? she wondered as she walked past them, not wanting to see where the young boy's hands were traveling. She knew she had no right to pass judgment, but they were so young.

Hurrying to her apartment, she fumbled with the key and then pushed open the door. Immediately, her nose was assaulted by the stale odor of the place. She felt for the switch by the door and blinked several times as her eyes adjusted to the light.

There was one sofa, badly stained and torn in the corner. One chair, not matching and equally dirty. Scarred, dusty tables were scattered about, as if no thought were given to their placement. Depressed, she walked past the tiny kitchen. A filthy stove and a refrigerator not as high as her waist completed that room. She would have to use the sink in the bathroom for water. Inside the last room, she finally put her bags on the bare floor. Walking over to the window, Meggie strained to open it, to let fresh air inside this furnace of a home.

Finally successful, she held on to the windowsill above her head and gasped, desperate to fill her lungs. As she opened her eyes, she looked out over the buildings just like this one and tightened her jaw. She would not cry. Not now. Now she had to think. Her feet ached as she walked back to her bags and, reaching into one, she took out a towel and placed it on the edge of the bare mattress. As she sat down and faced the window, she promised herself it wouldn't always be like this. For as long as she had left, she would take pleasure in finally being on her own. A little hard work never hurt her and she could make something of this place if she really wanted to. Besides, she had no other choice.

Feeling a summer breeze enter the small room, she lifted her face to it and closed her eyes. A picture of Thomas emerged behind her lids and she quickly opened them. She couldn't think about him, or his beautiful home.

Now, this was her home.


She spent the next month cleaning her own apartment, and those of her clients. Although in demand as word spread about her, Meggie did not take on any more people. She found she was able to manage quite well as it was. She cooked and cleaned and found herself enjoying her daily walks with the dogs through the park. She loved being asked to stay with the children and many a night she watched over the wee ones while their parents went out. Those were the occasions when a cab was waiting for her at the back entrance to take her to the Lower East Side. When Mrs. Easton found out where she lived, the woman insisted on including daily cab fare in her pay. Meggie politely thanked her and accepted, for one trip on the subway made it quite plain that mode of transportation was more frightening than she was willing to risk. And the buses only confused her. If you did not have exactly one dollar in coin, the driver refused you entry. Besides, she didn't want to worry about running into Thomas, or anyone associated with him. Thank God he hadn't found out about her business or she would never have been able to leave. She would have had to depend on him when things got . . . when it was the end of her pregnancy. Only once had she wondered whether he had the right to know about all of it, and then she dismissed the idea as selfish. She would not subject him to this. Not to losing her, and the babe. If he didn't know, if he didn't come to love or expect anything, then he couldn't be hurt by it. And if there was only one thing she had left to her in the months ahead, it would be the knowledge that she loved him enough to spare him this grief. But sometimes, alone at night in that small humid bedroom, Meggie wondered at the wisdom of her choices.

Trying to ignore the sounds from the other apartments, she closed her eyes as sleep eluded her. She was exhausted and should have collapsed until morning. But the nights were the worst . . . when she couldn't stop thinking. She tried so hard to be brave about it all, to banish her memories, but on the still, moonlit night when she had felt the first flutterings inside her, the first tiny movements of the child, she had caught her breath in wonder. Too soon that wonder had given way to

347

sorrow and she'd turned on her side and wept for all three of them.

A family that was never meant to be.


Something told her about the danger even before his arm slid around her neck and the knife was pressed against her belly. Holding her packages close to her chest, Meggie felt her knees buckle in terror.

"Just hand it over, Mama. Don't you be stupid."

Meggie tried to speak, but her mouth was dry and no sound came out.

"Don't make me hurt you," he whispered against her ear. The sound was vile and she thought she would be sick.

"Please," she managed to whisper. "Please, don't hurt my baby." She was starting to shake and her lips were trembling in fear. Staring at the flowers in her bag, the incredibly beautiful yellow lilies she had bought from the old woman on the corner, she thought it was impossible to make sense out of the ugliness gripping her and holding her against her will. "What . . . what do you want?"

"What'd you think I want? Gimme your purse." He tugged on her arm, causing her to drop her packages. She watched as the fragile petals of the lilies were crushed and it was as if something inside her cracked along with them.

"*No*." She pulled back on the leather with a fierce resistance. "That's all the money I have," she muttered. "I need it."

He slowly swung the knife back and forth, teasing the air in front of her, and she watched the blade—almost hypnotized by the glint of steel under the dim foyer light.

"Give it to me, you fat bitch!" His voice was a sinister whisper that frightened her almost as much as the knife. Although they had never met, he looked like he hated her. His blue eyes blazed with something beyond desperation, and he was sweating profusely, although it was a crisp autumn day.

He must have sensed her scream, for without any warning, he reached out and sliced the leather strap on her arm. Shocked by a sudden burning sensation, Meggie watched helplessly as the man ran out the door with her purse. He never stopped, not even after bumping into a black woman on his way into the street. And when she looked down at her sweater, she felt more surprise than pain as she saw a bright red stain spreading over the pale pink wool.

The very last thing she remembered as she slid down the wall was looking at the black woman rushing up to her. Wasn't it strange, Meggie thought, not to feel any pain? There was only a vague buzzing in her ears and then that, too, stopped as the darkness enveloped her.

# Chapter 24

"Ma'am? Can you hear me? We have an ambulance coming to take you to the hospital. Does she live here? Anybody know her name?"

"Yeah, she lives up on the second floor. Been here around three months, maybe more."

Meggie heard the sound of a man's voice, a nice voice, and then her landlord's reply. Reluctantly, she tried to open her eyes. The man kneeling before her was young and wearing a uniform of some kind. Her eyes closed and she sharply inhaled at the piercing stab of pain in her arm. Again, she tried to see what was going on around her.

She was lying on the floor. What had happened? Why were all these people surrounding her? Her gaze found the black woman's and held. She came closer and knelt beside her.

"You're going to be okay," she told Maggie in a soft voice. "He got your purse, but all that can be replaced. Goddamn junkies! You're gonna be okay," she repeated, then looked toward the door as several men in white came rushing into the building.

"What's going on?" Meggie whispered through her dry lips. Her mouth felt parched, as if she hadn't had anything to drink in a very long time. "What . . . what are they doing to me?"

"They're taking you to the hospital," the woman said as the men knelt around Meggie. One of them took out a pair of scissors and was cutting the arm of her sweater.

*The hospital!* That's where people died! "No." She tried to sit up. "Not yet. It isn't time. The baby—"

"Not the baby," the nice uniformed man interrupted. "Your arm. Don't move. Looks like a clean cut, but you're going to need stitches. What's your name?"

"My name?" Her eyes finally focused on the metal badge on his chest. Police! "Ah . . . my name is Margaret. Margaret Gillbride." Too soon she realized her mistake. Why couldn't she have thought fast enough to give him another name?

"Where can we contact your husband, Mrs. Gillbride?"

She stared at him. "I don't have a husband," she said simply. Even through the pain she was able to feel the humiliation caused by that statement.

"Is there someone we should call? Family?"

She pictured Thomas and then shook her head. "No one."

"Someone should come to the hospital with you. A friend, then?"

She sharply drew in her breath as another man wrapped her arm in a bandage. It was too tight and she wanted to tell him to remove it. Instead, she said, "No. There isn't anyone."

"Ah hell, I'll go with her," the black woman said, then looked up at their landlord. "Topelki, you've got another key to her apartment. Why don't you take these groceries up there—"

"What'd you think I am? Her personal servant?" the heavyset man demanded. He scratched his stomach and his expression showed his impatience with the entire situation.

"Look," the policeman interrupted, "give her a break, will you? What's so hard about picking up a few things? She just got mugged, remember? And make sure you change that lock." The landlord remained silent. "You hear me?" the officer demanded.

Topelki glared at the younger man. "Who's gonna pay for it? We changed locks for everybody that got robbed, we'd go bankrupt. You'll have to take that up with the owners. Who's gonna pay for it if they ain't?"

Meggie watched as the policeman rose and stood face to face with the landlord.

"The City of New York. You listen to me, you lazy sonofabitch. Your place is right here, right off the front door. How'd that dopehead get in here, huh? Just walked right on in?" He looked around the foyer. "You know, I wonder how many violations we could find if we started looking?"

"All right! All right!" the other man conceded, and bent to pick up a can of soup. Everyone ignored his muttered stream of curses.

Satisfied, the policeman turned and smiled at her. "I'll come with you to the hospital. I'm going to need statements from both of you for my report." He glanced at the black woman, who was standing next to the elevated stretcher. "Miss . . . ?"

"Anne Palmer." She grinned down at Meggie. "Annie."

Meggie lifted her hand to clasp the other woman's. "Thank you. My name's Meggie."

"A hell of a way to meet, Meggie."

Nodding, she let them roll her outside and into a large white vehicle. Everything started happening so quickly that Meggie found herself in some sort of bed fitted along the side of the automobile. One of the men in the white uniform, a doctor, had wrapped something around her uninjured arm and kept pumping it full of air while he checked some gauges. He was asking her questions about her health, about the baby. And it was then that it fully hit her.

She had come close to losing this child to that madman. That was when the shaking began, starting in her legs and traveling up her body. Soon, her teeth were chattering and Annie, who was sitting by the back door, told the man with the gauges to cover her with a blanket. But nothing could help or stop the tremors.

In the last few months she had come to love this child that she carried. It had surprised her. When she had felt its life inside her, she had begun talking to the babe out of desperation and loneliness. Now it was her only friend, and more precious than her own life. She would do anything, anything to save it. "My baby? Is it all right, Doctor?" she asked the young man who sat beside her. Why wouldn't her teeth stop chatter-

353

ing?

"I'm not a doctor, ma'am. They'll check everything when we get to the hospital."

Placing her hand on her rounded abdomen, Meggie closed her eyes and waited to feel the familiar movement. As if in silent communication, the babe kicked and she almost laughed out loud in relief.

Within minutes the vehicle stopped and she was wheeled inside a large building. The policeman from her apartment appeared and asked how she was feeling.

She tried to smile. "Everyone is making such a fuss. I'm sure I'm fine. A little cut —"

He shook his head. "I think you're going to need stitches. Besides, you fainted back there. My wife's pregnant. I know if that'd happened to her, I'd want her checked."

"We're going to need some information," a woman interrupted. She carried a pen and large chart and looked impatient. "Insurance?"

Meggie stared at her.

"Do you have insurance?"

When Meggie shook her head, the woman made a noise of disgust and said, "What clinic do you go to, then?"

"A clinic?" Meggie was starting to shake again. What was the woman talking about?

Annie, who was standing to one side, came closer to the stretcher. "Where do you go for medical help, Meggie? What's the name of your doctor?"

Meggie stared at all three of them. What did they want her to say? The woman in the white coat was looking at her, as if she were a charity case. She was about to tell the woman that she had nothing now. Afraid to leave her money in her rooms, she'd carried her small fortune with her. That horrible man had fled with eleven hundred dollars.

Everything was gone, everything she had worked so hard to save. All of it. Gone, within less than a minute. She was penniless.

"Where are you from? You weren't born here in the city, were you?"

She blinked several times as the policeman's voice invaded her thoughts. She shook her head. "I was born in Pennsylvania."

Annie nodded, while exchanging glances with the policeman. "That figures," she muttered. "Look, have you seen a doctor since you've been in the city?"

She was about to again shake her head when she remembered. Feeling the sharp eyes of the hospital woman piercing into her, Meggie lifted her chin and said, "I've seen Dr. Tankor. Ben Tankor." It was bad enough that they all knew she wasn't married; she couldn't stand this woman's condescension.

Annie looked up at the woman, who shrugged, as if to say she'd never heard of the physician. But she did write down his name.

"You're not going to contact him, are you?" Meggie asked, terrified that perhaps Ben would remember treating the cut at her hairline all those months ago in Tom's home. No sooner were the words out of her mouth than she regretted them. She'd worked too hard to keep herself hidden all these months for something like this to ruin everything.

The woman didn't answer her. She looked at Annie and the officer and said, "They'll take her into emergency now. You come with me. I have some papers for both of you to sign."

As she was wheeled away from them, Meggie heard Annie say, "Look, I was just a witness. I'm not signing anything."


Forty minutes later Meggie found herself wheeled back to the desk where Annie and the policeman waited. Despite everything, she was ecstatic. A doctor, a wonderful woman doctor, did an extensive examination and told her that the baby was perfectly healthy. Even the throbbing in her arm from the stitches didn't bother her. She was alive, and so was her baby. For right now, for this very day, she was grateful that they both had survived. What else could matter?

Before she reached them, she saw one of the many nurses walk up and say something to the unpleasant woman behind the desk. The hospital was crowded with all sorts of people, all colors, all sizes. They hurried past her yelling out for things she had never heard of before and she looked through the rushing blur of white coats to again see the disagreeable woman that had questioned her earlier. She was still listening to what the other nurse was saying. Too far away to hear what was being discussed, Meggie knew it was about her from the sullen looks cast her way.

"I checked out Tankor. A Park Avenue OB-GYN

man, not the kind you'd see around here. Who knows? Maybe she's one of his pro bono cases. Anyway, I called his office and they've never heard of her."

The emergency supervisor glanced at the red-haired woman in the wheel chair and clucked her tongue. "It figures," she muttered. "More damn paperwork."

After stopping at the landlord's for the new key, Annie led Meggie back into her apartment. "Nice place," she remarked while looking around. Actually, it was smaller than her own apartment but this one was furnished with an old-fashioned charm. The lace doilies on the chairs and under the vase of wilted flowers reminded Annie of her grandmother's, and she suddenly remembered how much she missed the old woman and how safe and warm her home had been.

Shaking off the memories, she turned back to the door and touched the shiny new lock. "I can't believe that cop got Topelki to put in a new one," she remarked. "I can't even get him to put a new light bulb in the hallway. I do it myself."

Meggie looked up at her. It was the first time she had ever been alone with a Negro. For that matter, before coming to New York City, she had never even been close to a black person, or an Oriental person, or a Hispanic person. What a sheltered life she had led in the patch. She remembered when a visit from a Southerner had caused quite a stir in Lehigha.

Smiling, Meggie found it fascinating that all cultures seemed to meld together in this exotic city. She had seen Annie before, had passed her in the hallway a few times over the past months. They had both smiled, but neither one of them had spoken. Meggie had always kept to herself and thought Annie was doing the same. Today, the woman had come to her rescue, had stayed with her through the frightening visit to the hospital, had ridden with her and the policeman to the station to file a complaint. Despite her sometimes gruff attitude, Annie Palmer was a very nice woman. And so pretty . . . her short black hair tightly framed her face. A kind face, a little weary-looking right now, but kind. Large, expressive brown eyes easily showed her emotions — whether happiness or anger. And when she smiled, Meggie thought she had never seen a prettier woman.

Embarrassed to be staring, Meggie cleared her throat. "You changed the burned-out light? I wasn't sure how to . . . that is, I didn't know who should do it —"

"Topelki is supposed to," Annie interrupted, annoyance for the landlord showing in her expression. "He probably got a nosebleed when he had to climb the stairs to fix your lock. That was one time I was glad to see some police pressure. Did you see his face when that cop threatened him?"

Meggie shook her head. "Not really. I was . . . frightened at the time about my baby." She tried to smile. It was so nice to have someone to talk to, someone in her apartment after all these months of solitude.

"The baby," Annie said, while glancing at Meggie's rounded abdomen. "When are you due?"

"Around three more months," Meggie answered in a subdued voice. It was very strange the way no one was especially embarrassed by her situation. One would think an unmarried expectant mother was commonplace in this time.

"Around? What's your due date?"

Meggie looked at the woman. "I don't know exactly. I'm sure it will come when it's time."

Annie stared back at her. "You haven't even seen a doctor about this, have you?"

Embarrassed, Meggie clasped her hands on her lap and shook her head. "No. When the time comes, then I'll go. There's nothing a doctor could tell me that I don't already know, Annie."

There was a moment of prolonged silence, then Annie spoke, her voice deliberately cheerful. "Hey, would you like a cup of coffee, or tea?"

Glad for the change of subject, Meggie nodded. "Please, sit down," she said with a smile. "I'll prepare the tea."

Placing her hand on her hip, Annie stared at her for a few seconds before saying, "Will you sit down? *I'll* put the water on and you'll relax."

"But you're my first guest, and you've already been so kind."

Walking into the tiny kitchen area, Annie lifted the teapot and shook it to check for water. She looked around before taking it with her into the bathroom. "Can you imagine not having running water in a kitchen?" she asked, though not really expecting an answer. "Too bad that cop didn't send somebody through this place. They wouldn't have to look real hard for violations." She brought the

359

teapot back and placed it on the gas stove. "I'll just bet one of those rich, and so very respectable, Upper East Siders owns this dump. And they probably couldn't care less that you have no water in your kitchen or that you were attacked because the only security we have is that jerk Topelki."

"I don't think everyone who lives on the Upper East Side is like that," Meggie offered. Seeing the doubtful look on Annie's face, she added, "I work for several people there and they're very nice."

Annie came back into the small living room and sat on an old scarred rocking chair to wait for the water to boil. "Yeah? What do you do?"

"I clean their homes and cook for them. Sometimes, I take care of their children—"

"Wait a minute," Annie interrupted. *"You're* a maid?"

Meggie lifted her chin. "I'm very good at it."

Annie was still shaking her head. "A *pregnant* white woman cleans houses for a living?"

"Annie, please don't say it like that. My people need me and they're very kind. When they found out I was going to have a baby, they increased my salary and told me to work shorter hours. They expected me to quit, but I told them I wanted to keep on working. I'm fortunate to have them, Annie . . . really, I am."

Shaking her head in disbelief, Annie asked, "What about the cab that picks you up in the morning and drops you off in the afternoon."

"They made arrangements with the cab company. You see, they really do care." Meggie ran her fingers through the front of her hair. She felt dirty and tired and the thought of a bath was very appealing. "What am I going to do about tomorrow? The doctor at the hospital said I wasn't to use my arm for at least twenty-four hours. And tomorrow is Kelsey's first outing with his nursery group. All the children are going to visit the zoo. I told Mrs. Easton I would go with them and help supervise the little ones." Meggie looked at the other woman. "Now, I've really ruined it."

"What are you talking about, girl? Ruined what? Some crazy druggie almost kills you and you're worried that little Kelsey is going to miss a trip to the zoo? You've got your priorities all mixed up."

Meggie lifted her chin in defense. "I have no money now. I have to work, and I'm good at it. What do you do, Annie? I've seen you carrying that large thin suitcase—"

"My portfolio?"

Meggie nodded.

"I'm an artist." Annie shrugged. "Actually, a student. Parsons School of Design. My mama was a dressmaker. I intend to take that a whole lot further." She nodded, as if reaffirming her strategy. "I've got plans. After I finish school, I'm going to see if I can apprentice with one of the greats here in the city, maybe even de la Renta or Donna Karan."

She stood as the shrill whistle from the teapot broke through the air. "Who knows? Maybe someday those rich ladies you work for will be wearing an Annie Palmer."

Her mind filled with possibilities and Meggie smiled. "Why don't you get to know them yourself and see what they're wearing?"

Shutting off the tea kettle, Annie peered around the small wall that separated them. "What are you talking about?"

It was Meggie's turn to shrug. "I need someone to take my place tomorrow. I can't just leave my people stranded."

Coming back into the room, Annie put her hand on her hip and stared at her. "And you think *I'd* agree to play maid to those women?"

"Listen to me, Annie. I handle most of the clothes, either handwashing them or sending them out to be cleaned. This could be an excellent opportunity for you to examine the fabric and stitchery firsthand. You could see how they're made. Why don't you find out what these women are buying? I doubt if a day in your school could be as informative as one spent in looking through Maria Costalovia's closet."

Annie's mouth dropped open. "The actress?"

Meggie grinned. "She's so very beautiful, and the clothes . . . Sometimes, I spend almost half a day picking them up off the floor. A very nice woman, but so spoiled. She really needs full-time help, but she doesn't want anyone—"

"If I did it," Annie interrupted, "how do you know I can be trusted? What if something were missing? I'd be the first person who'd be blamed."

Smiling, Meggie said, "I trust you. You didn't have to help me, or come with me to the hospital. That says more about the kind of person you are, Annie Palmer, than you know. If you agree to this, I can telephone Mrs. Easton from the hallway."

"Why would they let just anybody into their

362

homes?"

"You're not just anybody. And I would vouch for you. Believe me, Annie, these people are not as terrible as you're making them out to be. If I say that you are trustworthy, they will accept that."

"And I could spend the afternoon at Maria Costalovia's?" Annie asked the question as if expecting the offer to be rescinded.

"After going to the Eastons'. Topper and the others will be waiting for their walk —"

"Hold it," Annie interrupted. "Topper? Tell me you are not about to suggest I walk a dog."

"Three of them," Meggie answered. "All in the same building. I'll write out instructions. You do like dogs, don't you? And children? Little Phillip is really a sweet child. He just loves his carriage rides through the park."

Annie grinned. "For a chance at Costalovia's wardrobe, I'll turn into Mary Poppins with Soul."

"Mary Poppins?" Joining in Annie's laughter, Meggie was relieved, yet confused. It really didn't matter that Annie never answered her. She had just survived another crisis. Three more months to go. She wouldn't think about it, about the horror that awaited her when that time elapsed. Instead, she would take pleasure in the moment . . . in being alive, with her child still moving inside her.

Smiling at her new friend, Meggie tried to visualize a tiny babe, with a shock of red hair and beautiful large green eyes.

Thomas's eyes.


"Come up for a brandy, Gerald. It's still early

363

yet."

The old man looked back at him and hesitated. Finally he smiled. "Sure. But only one. I'm driving tomorrow. With the weather getting colder, I need my sleep."

"Your hesitancy has nothing to do with the weather and we both know it."

"Thomas, my boy. I'd be the last person to say a man shouldn't enjoy a drop of the grain now and then, but you, son, are becoming a wee bit more familiar with a morning headache than any one person should. And besides, I'm not getting any younger. It's embarrassing that I can't keep up with you."

Ignoring the remarks about his drinking, Tom glanced at the man by his side. Gerald did look tired and perhaps not quite as dapper as he did this summer when they'd first met. But then neither of them were the same. Not since Meggie had disappeared.

He'd done everything he could think of to find her. At first he had thought she'd come back. A day. A few at the most. Then she'd return to him. But she didn't. The silence in the apartment was deafening, and more painful than he could endure. He spent most of his time at his office, even sleeping there some nights, in order not to face that empty bedroom next to his own. No matter where he went, no matter what he did, she was there. In his mind, in his memories. She had invaded his thoughts and took possession of his soul. Finally he had called Mac Weaver from Intercontinental for help. It wasn't long before even Mac had admitted defeat. Meggie was gone without a trace. He wasn't surprised, for Mac was looking for a woman with a past history, and Meggie had none. Not in this time.

Oh, there'd been false hopes. The doormen had claimed to see her in the building, but nothing ever came out of it and it made no sense. Meggie had been swallowed up in the city, just the way she had wanted. Even Gerald thought he had seen her several times in the park — walking dogs or pushing baby carriages. But he could never catch up with the woman he had thought was Meggie. And she, too, had disappeared within the city. That was what ate at him, what caused him to prowl the living room at night and stare out at the lights of New York. She was out there. Alone.

And that was when the drinking started. It was one way to deaden, to numb, his brain. The one way to finally banish images of her and fall asleep. He never let it interfere with his work; he was, in fact, more driven than ever. Reports of his further success circulated up and down Wall Street and he'd already turned down three more offers of interviews by the nation's most prestigious reporters. He found no joy in his business. It was an occupation, a pursuit. A way to convincingly live through another day without her. It was the nights that haunted him. Nights without her . . . wondering what she was doing, who she was with . . .

If he thought she was happy, if he believed that it was for the best, he would try to get over her. But he knew the truth. Meggie left him for another reason. It wasn't that they were never meant to be together as she had claimed. Something had happened to her to change the way she felt. If he could just find her, talk to her—

"Mr. Carter." A woman's voice interrupted his thoughts as he and Gerald entered the lobby of his building. "May I speak with you for a moment?"

Tom vaguely recognized her as a tenant and he hoped she wasn't going to keep him captive with complaints or suggestions. That's why he employed a managing company. Maybe he should move. What other owner lived within reach of his building's tenants?

"What can I do for you, Mrs. . . ."

Smiling, not at all upset that he had forgotten her name, the woman happily supplied it. "Easton. This is really fortunate, you see my husband and I were just on our way out when I spotted you. I hope you don't mind that I stopped you."

Actually, Tom did mind. He really wanted to get upstairs and relax, brandy in hand, with Gerald. "Not at all, Mrs. Easton," he lied. "How can I help you?"

"Well," she began, "I've just had the most distressing news. Several of us in the tower employ the same person and I've just heard that our *au pair* girl, though she refuses quarters with any of us, was attacked tonight right outside her door. As I'm sure you know, she's very special and I've appointed myself spokesperson, so to speak."

She was obviously nervous and he was trying to be patient. What did she think he could do? It didn't happen here. "I'm afraid I don't understand, Mrs. Easton."

"She refuses to move. Several of us have offered her living space, but she is so independent. What

I'm trying to do, Mr. Carter, is provide her with the means to pay any hospital bills that may be coming up. It just occurred to me tonight that I'm sure she hasn't any medical insurance. And with all that money stolen right out from under Meggie's—"

He grabbed the woman's upper arm. "What did you say? What was the name?"

Mrs. Easton looked worried. "Meggie. She worked for you while your housekeeper was away. That's why I thought you would help."

Tom's heart immediately started to race. He had trouble catching his breath. "Where is she?" he demanded. *"Where?"*

"Tom," Gerald said, "calm down and let the woman speak."

Grace Easton was shaken and tried very hard to compose herself. "She . . . Meggie lives on the Lower East Side."

"Where?" Tom thought he was going to explode with a queer mixture of joy and frustration.

"I . . . that is, I don't know exactly. Somewhere in the East Village."

"You're saying she works for you, but you don't have her address?"

Grace shook her head, wishing her husband would hurry up and join them. She was decidedly uncomfortable talking with the famous Thomas Grey Carter. His reaction to her suggestion was bizarre, to say the least.

"What information can you give me about her? Is she all right? Did you say she was attacked?" Please God, he prayed, let him have heard incorrectly.

367

"That's right. But she called me to let me know that someone else would be coming tomorrow to take her place. As if we care about that. As long as she and the baby are all right. Nothing else matters."

For the first time in his life he thought he was going to faint, drop right to the floor and pass out. His throat was closing with raw emotion, and holding on to Gerald's shoulder, he managed to whisper, *"Baby?"*

# Chapter 25

He stood in front of the building on St. Mark's Place, horrified that Meggie had been living there. It was a miracle she hadn't been attacked before this. A group of young men huddled off to one side of the doorway, obviously in the midst of a drug transaction. They eyed him with suspicion as he approached. Too well dressed to be a cop, Tom walked past them without any trouble and tried the door. It was locked. He looked to the side and read the names on the buzzers and mailboxes. Meggie's wasn't among them. Just as he was about to press any in order to gain entrance, a hand reached out from behind him and a small metal pick opened the door in mere seconds.

"Easier than a key. Go ahead, man. Them buzzers don't work no how."

Tom stepped into the foyer, vowing to bodily carry Meggie out of this place. To think that she had probably been dealing with men like that caused a cold shiver to run down his back. He looked around the shabby foyer and realized he had no idea where to find her; she could be on any floor—behind any door. Not knowing what else to do, Tom stepped up to the closest one and knocked.

Almost a full minute later, the door opened to reveal an unpleasant-looking man. Apparently the knocking had awakened him.

"Yeah? What'd you want?" the man demanded, looking Tom up and down.

Tom cleared his throat. "I'd like to speak to the landlord, or the apartment manager. I need some information."

"Yeah? What kinda' information?"

"Are you the manager?"

"Depends. You a cop?" The man's expression became even more challenging.

Tom lifted his chin. "Look, all I want is to know the Gillbride apartment number."

"You are a cop," the man accused. "That woman's caused more trouble . . . You tell that other one, the one that was here yesterday, that I changed the lock—just like he said. What's he got, a pregnant woman thing? He like 'em big, or something? Sending you down here—"

Without thinking, Tom took hold of the man's unwashed shirt and slammed him back against the door. "You sonofabitch, where is she?"

Topelki could smell the raw anger inside the man, like the way the air smelled before a bad storm. Something familiar tugged at his brain, something about this well-dressed man whose face was so close to his own. Whoever he was, Topelki knew he wasn't someone to cross. The green eyes bore into his with a frightening hatred. Swiftly, fear permeated his system, robbing him of breath and making his mouth bone dry. He was forced to lick his lips in an effort to speak, until finally he managed to say, "It's . . . 2C. She's in 2C."

With an expression of disgust, Tom dropped him like a sack of garbage and Topelki nearly collapsed against the door as he watched Tom walk slowly up the stairs.

"You tell her I want her outa' here, you hear me? I don't have to take this shit from nobody. I don't care if you are a cop."

Tom ignored him as he headed for the second floor. This place was a hellhole! Now that he knew where she was, he tried to calm down. The very last thing he wanted to do was show up at her door and frighten her with his anger. Last night after he'd heard about her, he thought he would go mad from worry, and his inability to locate where she was staying. He'd questioned Grace Easton, contacted the others in the building, but no one knew where to find her. If it hadn't been for Gerald, Tom would have called in the National Guard. Gerald very calmly told him to contact the police. After more than a few calls, he managed to get her address. And again, it was Gerald who had held him back from rushing to her at three in the morning.

It was better this way, Tom thought as he reached the second floor. Last night he would have broken down her door and carried her away without questions. This morning, he intended to ask and answer any question, and if she still refused to come with him, only then would he pick her up and leave this place behind.

And the baby. He was afraid to think about

that revelation. It was too incredible to contemplate. Meggie. A baby? How could she leave him and never say a word?

Standing in front of her door, he took a deep breath and raised his hand. He knocked four times.

It startled her. No one had ever knocked on her door, except those soliciting to sell her something, or to bring her to the Lord. She didn't have the money for the first and the strange gleam in the eyes of the second frightened her more than the ruffians on the street. She was content to politely refuse and count herself lucky that the door separated them. Walking over to it, she let out her breath and silently prayed that a fanatic wasn't standing on the other side. Not this morning.

"Who is it?"

Silence.

"Who is it?" she repeated. She had learned never to open her door until the person on the other side was identified. It was almost like warfare, taking chances, searching for identities.

"Meggie? Please . . . open the door."

She moaned at the sound of his voice and held on to the door molding in an effort to steady herself. *Thomas!* My God, how had he found her? Annie? Had Annie told Mrs. Easton and . . . ? What did it matter? He was here!

Closing her eyes, she leaned her head against the door and said, "Go away. Please. I can't see you."

"Meggie, open this door. We have to talk."

As if reacting to the sound of his voice, the baby kicked inside her and she jerked in response.

372

"I'm not leaving, do you hear me? I know everything, Meggie. Either you open this door, or I swear to God I'll break it down."

She looked at the new lock and almost smiled. He would do it. She'd seen Thomas Carter's anger in Fitzhugh's tap room and didn't doubt his word. Feeling defeated, that everything she had worked so hard to build in the last months was swiftly being swept away, she sighed with resignation and unlocked the door.

She quickly moved away from it as it opened to reveal him standing just outside the threshold. She caught her breath and stared. He looked angry, and indignant, and . . . wonderful. It amazed her that the sight of him could still profoundly affect her, make her stomach tighten and the nerve endings of her skin tingle with excitement. Surely, a woman with child shouldn't be feeling these emotions.

As though reading her thoughts, he slowly came into the room and flung the door shut behind him. He looked at her, holding her gaze for a few endless seconds before allowing himself to look down her body. "How could you leave without telling me?" he whispered. "How? I want to know, Meggie. How could you do this?"

Hearing the anguish in his voice, she briefly closed her eyes and then turned away. "Thomas . . . it isn't what you think."

"Then tell me."

She shook her head, unable to face him. Staring out the window, she murmured, "I don't know where—"

"Start when you found out you were pregnant,"

he interrupted, hurt clearly in his voice.

It had all come to this moment, everything they had been through together. Now they were like two strangers in the same room, connected by this tiny human being she carried within her. Since he knew about the pregnancy, it made no sense to continue as before. Now . . . if she could only make him understand.

"That grave in the patch, my son's? It haunts me, Thomas," she whispered in a weary voice. Maybe it was time to tell it all. "I was so young when I carried that babe, caught up with spring and romance and a fool's conception of love. The man, the father, worked for the Reading—a very good job for someone so young. Traveling to different counties on the railroad, checking coal shipments from Lehigha." She shivered at the memory. "Anyway, I thought when I told him about the babe, he would be happy to marry and we'd have this fine house where I could be a good wife and mother and maybe invite Da and Brian for Sunday dinner."

She laughed at her own naiveté. "I should have known when I told him about the babe that he would run, but I was ever hopeful. It wasn't until I'd heard he had asked for a transfer that I knew he didn't care—not about me or the child."

Her throat was burning with unshed tears and she forcefully swallowed them down. "I tried to find him. Embarrassed myself at the Reading offices, demanding to know where he'd gone. They laughed at me. Called me a—" She closed her eyes at the painful memory, refusing to repeat the accusation. "Didn't I know, they said, that Terry Nolan

374

had poked more miners' daughters and left a trail of bastards wider than the Mississippi?" She shook her head in wonder. "It was a joke to them, another notch on Nolan's belt. And my world, as I knew it, was coming to an end. I tried to keep it a secret. I did, but Da knew me too well. There was a fine fight after I admitted he was right. Ahh . . . the disappointment in his eyes. The embarrassment in Brian's . . ." Meggie covered her own in painful remembrance. Finally, she managed to say the words that she had concealed in her heart for all these years. It was a raw, agonized whisper. *"And . . . and I came to hate the poor babe that I carried!"*

Tom reached out and touched his shoulder. "Meggie . . . don't. You don't have to do this."

She jerked away from him. Still looking out the window at the blur of buildings, she said, "Don't touch me, Thomas. For if you do, I'll not be able to finish. And now I see that I must. I've gone this far. It all has to be said, and heard. And . . . and understood."

She tried to gather her thoughts, anxious now to say it, to finally be done with it. "I labored for two days. I wanted to die, to end that pain. I thought God was punishing me for sinning, and I accepted that. I deserved it. But that horrible, endless pain . . . When it came, when that poor child was born, it was without the breath of life. The cord that united us wrapped around his tiny neck and killed him. And—God forgive me, but I was glad he wouldn't have to grow up with the shame. I only wondered why I hadn't died along with him. And I thought maybe, maybe, I had

375

been fully punished; I reaped exactly what I had sowed. But then, even in death, the Church rejected that poor child. Then they could lift their arrogant noses and proclaim it a just reward for straying, for falling from grace and . . . and deny him burial within their sacred grounds. They said he could never enter heaven without baptism. That God would make that pathetic soul pay for my sins was unthinkable! They had to be wrong! That made it final for me. I didn't care anymore, not about any of them. Not even myself."

She was crying, the tears freely racing down her cheeks. Her nose was running and she dabbed at it with the small handkerchief in her hands. "And then the miracle happened. You came into my life and brought such happiness that I thought surely God has granted me another chance. Wasn't I the fool? Even though we argued about this very thing, Thomas, I never thought of my life without you in it. Not until I found out I was pregnant again. And then I remembered. The doctor. He said I couldn't have any more children. He said I was too small. That . . . that it would kill me, and the babe. He said I was never to get pregnant. And now . . ." She could barely breathe for the choking tears and she hugged her stomach as if to protect the innocent within. "And now . . . I remembered the doctor's words to me. I couldn't do this to you—"

Grabbing her shoulders, he turned her around and clasped her to his chest in a possessive hold. "Shh . . ." he kept whispering into her hair. "Hush . . ."

She couldn't be stopped. Grasping him in a tight

clinch, she cried into his shoulder. "But this time is worse. This time the punishment is too great. I love this child, and I'm so frightened, Thomas. I don't want God to take this one, too. I don't want to die!"

*"And you won't,"* he stated in an emphatic voice. "Meggie, listen to me. That was over a hundred years ago." He rubbed his cheek against the side of her forehead, desperate to make her understand. "You can have a child now. There are ways. Maybe even an operation. Millions, and I means millions, of women have babies by cesarean section. Darling, you're going to be all right, and so is the child."

Her sobs had turned into loud hiccups and she covered her mouth before lifting her head. Blinking, she gazed up at him. He was so handsome, so strong, and he seemed so confident. She wanted to believe . . . "They do?" she asked between hiccups.

Smiling, he held her face in his hands and wiped her tears away with gentle fingers. "They do. And so can you. If only you'd told me. Ben Tankor, he'll explain it to you. Where's your phone? We'll see him today."

She sniffled, afraid to hope. But Thomas looked so calm, so confident. "I don't have one. I use the telephone in the hall."

For the first time, Tom looked around him. Deciding not to say anything about the condition of the place, he stared down at her, searching her face. Even with her swollen eyes, she was beautiful, and he pulled her closer to him, relishing the touch of her. It felt so right, as if he'd finally come home. He sensed the sudden roll of her stomach, hard and deliberate against his own, and his breath caught in the back of his throat.

"That was it?" he asked in a voice filled with wonder.

In spite of everything, she smiled. "That was your child, Thomas," she confided, unable to stop sniffling, hiccuping, and now grinning like a fool. Ahh God, could it be possible? Could there be a chance still left to her?

He looked down at her and then softly asked, "Is there anything you want from here, Meggie?"

She looked around, knowing he was going to take her away and she was never coming back. "Just one thing," she said, and broke his embrace. She walked into the bedroom and returned with her crocheting bag. Opening it up, she pulled out a tiny white gown, with delicate embroidered flowers at the collar and cuffs.

"You see, Thomas. I did allow myself to dream."

Feeling as if he was about to cry, he held out his hand. "I love you, Meggie," he said in a cracked voice. "And you are never, ever, to leave me again. Not for any reason. Do you understand?"

She swallowed down her returning tears. "Aye, Thomas," she said meekly. "I will never leave you."

He nodded, attempting to gain control over his emotions. "C'mon, then, let's go home."

Grateful, not thinking beyond the moment, she took his hand and held fast.

"I can't foresee any further complications. Once we get the results of your blood test, I can pinpoint your due date and we can schedule the C-section before that." Ben Tankor grinned at the anxious couple seated across from him. "Congratulations."

Tom and Meggie looked at each other, both overjoyed with the news. Neither could believe their good fortune. It was as if Fate had finally decided they had learned their lessons and were entitled to happiness. And each in their own way silently vowed to treasure the other, never again to be filled with doubt and mistrust.

Hustling her out of Ben's office, Tom stood with Meggie in the hallway. "Before you go any further, I have to ask you something."

Overjoyed, she glanced down at the bottles of prenatal vitamins and birthing literature. She couldn't wait to read everything. "Oh, Thomas. Ben says we're going to be all right! I can safely have this baby, our baby. And I'm not afraid of the operation. Maybe that's why I came to this time. Through you I can have a child."

He kissed her into silence. "Meggie. Will you listen to me?"

Grinning, she nodded.

He looked around the empty hallway before clearing his throat. Suddenly he became very serious. "Margaret Mary Gillbride? Will you do me the honor of marrying me?"

She stared at him in shocked wonder.

"Do I have to get down on one knee?"

Her smile was slow, and sweet, and serene.

"Ahh, Tommy . . ."

When he brought her home to the Tower, he threw open the penthouse door and happily announced to Celia and Gerald that there was a wedding to be planned.

Celia, having heard some of the story from Gerald, warmly welcomed the future Mrs. Carter and hurried to prepare a room.

"No need," Tom called out. "Meggie will be staying in the master bedroom."

In the midst of hugging the bride-to-be, Gerald said, "Really, Tom. Give the woman some room to breathe. I say she should have her own room until the wedding, if she wants." Grinning, he tightened his hold on her shoulder. "What do you say, child?"

Embarrassed, with everyone's attention on her, Meggie tried to smile. "Perhaps, it would be best—"

"Nonsense!" Quickly walking up to her, Tom removed Gerald's protective arm and pulled her against his chest. "If you think for one second that I'm letting you out of my sight until this wedding, you'd better think again." He kissed her forehead. "You can have all the privacy you want. But I just got you back, love. I have no intention of letting you go. Until this wedding you are to be courted and pampered, and your every wish will be granted. All except one. There will be no separate bedrooms."

Unable to suppress her wide smile, Meggie looked at Gerald. "How can I resist this man?"

Grinning in return, Gerald said, "Well, then, it looks like Fate has arranged an early wedding present for you. Mac Weaver called, Tom, to say he's finally located Meggie's sewing table. Everything checks out—initials and all. It was bought by another antique dealer and it's to go off at Sothcby's on Saturday."

Elated, Meggie grabbed Tom's hand. "Sotheby's?"

"An auction house," he answered. "I can easily bid over the phone."

"Oh, Thomas . . . please. I would dearly love to see it all."

He looked down at her and breathed a heavy sigh. "I suppose it's as good a place as any to make our debut."

"Debut?" She smiled. "I don't understand."

Shaking his head, Tom issued a low laugh. "Wait till the press gets hold of this! My dear, be prepared . . ."

# Chapter 26

Nothing could have prepared her for the spectacle that took place. Supremely happy, Meggie walked hand in hand into the foyer of the auction house and up the wide steps that led to the actual area where her Mum's sewing table would be auctioned. Thomas was given a paddle with a number on it to use in bidding and she was very excited as she watched the lovely pieces rotate on a circular stage. She tried to listen as the auctioneer described each piece and quickly called off bids. Truly, she tried to follow when Thomas explained to her that the numbers on a large lighted board told the foreign exchange, the equivalent of dollars in drachmas, francs, yen, and pounds, but it was of no use. She could never keep track of so much money. Imagine, almost twelve thousand dollars for someone's old breakfront! Instead, she patiently waited until her table, her Mum's sewing table, would come up on the block. And it was then that she noticed them.

It had started with a few inquiring stares. Thomas had already warned her about it and she merely smiled at the curious, and looked away. She was proud that he was such an important, famous person, but like him, she was perfectly happy to remain private. Besides, Thomas had reminded her, her false papers of identity were for a proper wedding only. Not to satisfy strangers. Nevertheless, the few stares soon multiplied and before long the area was so crowded that many were standing along the side aisles. The buzz of conversation rose in volume when the sewing table came around to center stage and Thomas raised his paddle.

The show, it appeared, was on.

Lights started exploding in her face and she turned away. "Don't be afraid," Thomas whispered down to her. "They're only taking our picture. If we let them do it now, maybe they'll leave us alone later."

She slowly turned back as Thomas again raised his paddle, upping the bid. She tried to pay attention. Truly, she did, but she was distracted by the flashing bulbs and the excitement in the air. Suddenly, she wondered just why she hadn't let Thomas bid over the phone, as others were doing. Why had she asked him to come here? Because she was impatient, that's why. She couldn't wait to see her Mum's table. Hearing the price exceed the sixty-five hundred dollars that was asked for it in the antique shop, Meggie held her breath. Thomas had said that once he showed interest, he was afraid other buyers, especially antique dealers, were going to compete with him, thinking he had some inside information about the piece. For a few moments, not long at all, several paddles were abruptly raised; all those on the phone checked bids with their anonymous clients and called out counteroffers. It was frantic and frenzied. And quickly over. Finally, when the auctioneer slammed his hand down on his desk, the mahogany sewing table belonged to Mr. Thomas Grey Carter.

Meggie looked up to the exchange board and gulped down her shock. Under dollars, it read: twenty-eight thousand. *Dollars!*

"Let's get out of here," Thomas said, taking hold of her elbow and guiding her through the people who suddenly surrounded them.

"Mr. Carter, when did you become interested in antiques?"

"Who's the lady?"

"What's her name?"

Meggie thought they were rude. She knew they were reporters, but they were nothing like that nice, polite Harry Korson who'd come to the patch.

"The *lady* is Miss Margaret Gillbride."

"Where are you from, Miss Gillbride?"

"Meggie is from Pennsylvania," Thomas answered as he tried to lead her down the stairs and into the foyer. At least twelve men and women were making the trek with them, holding microphones or recorders up to their faces.

"Whose baby is it?"

"Who makes your clothes?"

Meggie could feel the tension in Thomas's arm at the first question. Taking matters into her own hands, she looked at the woman who had asked the second. "Annie Palmer made this," she said with a false calm, referring to the forest green and white outfit Annie had quickly made up for her.

Everyone started to scribble notes, as if she'd just uttered something very important.

"Never heard of her. Where's she from?"

"She's . . . she lives right here in New York City. She's a student at the Parsons School of Design." Thank God she'd remembered what Annie had told her the first time they'd met.

A heavyset man bumped into Thomas's arm. "Now that you've taken over IGL, any truth to the rumor that you're looking toward Detroit?"

Tom forced a smile. "Why don't you ask Mr. Iacocca that question?" He pulled Meggie toward the front door. "If you'll excuse us, please?" he directed to the throng of people as he led Meggie into the waiting car. Within seconds they were speeding down York Avenue.

"Are you all right?" Thomas asked, settling back against the seat. "I told you it could get rough."

Meggie rested her head against his shoulder. "They're so rude, aren't they?"

"Yes, they are. And I'm afraid it will get worse now that they have your name. They're going to go crazy trying to find out any information they can about you."

She turned to see his face. "Will that bother you, if they find out what I did for Mrs. Easton and the others?"

"What? That you had a thriving business going? Hell, Meggie, you were on your way to becoming an entrepreneur."

She smiled. "I take it that means you approve?"

"It means, when I first heard about what you did, I was angry because you didn't need to clean anyone else's home. I would have given you dogs to walk . . . and babies to mind. I wanted you all to myself."

"And now?"

Studying her mouth, he moved his own lips closer. "Now, I still want you all to myself, but I know you have a mind of your own. After the baby is born, you might want to think about starting your own company. You had a very good idea there, my dear. Lease a wife, hmmm . . ."

She could feel his breath on her and her pulse quickened as always in response to him. "Don't even think about it, Mr. Carter. There'll be no leasing taking place here. One week from today there'll be a wedding . . . as long as Annie has the dress finished."

"Will she?"

Meggie knew he was going to kiss her at any moment. "Oh how I hope so," she breathed.

"Me, too." His lips grazed over hers in a sweet, tantalizing kiss that left her breathless and eager for more.

Feeling like a wanton, Meggie summoned up all her willpower and straightened. "The driver," she whispered. "Shame on you, Thomas."

He pulled her into his arms. "Shame on *you*, Margaret," he whispered back into her ear. Shivers of delight ran down her arms. "You enjoyed that kiss every bit as much as I did."

She refused to admit he was right. A lady had to have some secrets. Clearing her throat, she said, "Poor Annie. Do you think I made a mistake by giving them her name?"

Content to have her in his arms, Thomas relaxed next to her as they made their way back home. "I think, my dear, you have just made Annie Palmer's career. She'll be thrilled, believe me. Now, are you sure your dress will be ready by next Saturday? I don't want this wedding delayed, for any reason." His lips brushed her temple. "I've waited long enough."

Meggie closed her eyes briefly and gave thanks for him. Thomas wanted her. It wasn't because of the baby. He truly wanted her with him. Finally, someone loved Meggie Gillbride, with all her faults. It was a very comforting thought, indeed.

"Tommy, I love you," she said simply.

His arms tightened around her.


"I can't believe she's here! *How?*"

Annie shrugged. "I don't know. Just don't get upset, all right?"

Meggie paced back and forth in the vestibule of the church, clutching the small bouquet of baby's breath and violets in her hand.

"Angelica."

Even saying Thomas's ex-wife's name aloud brought a shiver of apprehension. "Why did she have to come back now? Where is she?"

Annie straightened the collar of Meggie's cream-colored raw silk jacket, saying, "She's with Tom." At Meggie's look of horror, she added, "I heard her insist on speaking with him, but don't you worry none. That man loves you. No doubt about that."

Meggie placed her palm over her stomach as her child kicked out. "Of course, you're right," she murmured, looking at a beautiful stained glass window depicting Saint Joan. She must believe that. She and Thomas had been through too much to doubt the strength of their love. Didn't he even arrange for this church wedding? She recalled the argument that announcement had caused. She had insisted they be married in the penthouse, by a judge or a minister . . . anything but face another condemning priest. And wasn't Thomas divorced? Even if his first marriage wasn't recognized by the priests, how could there be a church wedding? She had refused to entertain the thought, afraid something would happen. When she was in need, she had found no comfort in her church. And she didn't want it to darken her happiness now. But dear Thomas had brought a guest home for dinner the next night, a charming young man named John Carey. Gerald joined them and after dinner the three of them had sat around the table and talked for hours about life and the universe. It had been fascinating to sit with men and be accepted as an equal, to have her opinion valued. At the end of the evening, she found herself surprised to learn that the young, intelligent, compassionate man was none other than *Father* John Carey. He was like no priest she had ever met. This man spoke calmly, laughed easily, and seemed filled with a quiet peace. And he wanted to marry her and Thomas in his church.

Thomas had done that for her. He wouldn't desert her now, not even for the beautiful Angelica. Meggie closed her eyes, shutting out the glass artistry of the warrior saint, and offered up a small prayer.

"How did you find us?" Tom couldn't believe his ex-wife was standing before him. He was to be married to Meggie in a matter of minutes.

Angelica smiled as she entered the small vestibule. "Darling, such a greeting! And here I've cut my holiday short just to be here."

"I'll repeat the question. How did you find out we were here?"

Angelica brushed an imaginary speck from the sleeve of her white cashmere coat. Looking up, cool brown eyes assessed him from behind the thin black net attached to her Patricia Underwood hat. She smiled. "If you must know, I called Ben's service and told them it was an emergency."

She turned to the other man in the room. "Sorry, Ben. I was counting on your girls still remembering me."

Ben Tankor shook his head. "Who could forget you, Angelica?" he asked with a sardonic grin. "I take it you'd like me to leave?"

Angelica didn't look at Tom; she merely nodded. "If you don't mind."

"Oh, I don't mind," he answered, seeing the angry expression on Tom's face. Checking his watch, he said, "I'll find Gerald and be back in five minutes."

"Why are you doing this?" Tom asked when they were alone.

Angelica spun around to face him. "Why did you send me that wire? Were you subconsciously hoping I'd try to talk you out of this?"

Tom smiled. "Angelica, you've completely misunderstood my intentions. I thought you deserved to know about my plans. No matter what, we've always been friends."

She saw it in his eyes and her stomach tightened. She had thoroughly enjoyed this man's company throughout the years, to say nothing of his body. But the finality was in his green eyes. It was easily read. He loved another.

"You're really going to marry this little nun?"

Tom laughed. "She's not little, and she's not a nun."

"I thought you said—"

"I was wrong. She's pregnant, Angelica. We're going to have a child."

She felt as if someone had punched her. "I was hoping the picture in the *London Times* was taken at a poor angle. You . . . you're marrying her because she's pregnant? Tom—"

"I love her," he interrupted. "I don't want to explain it to you. I just want you to believe it. She's everything to me. And I can't imagine my life without her."

Angelica felt her mouth go dry and she swallowed several times. Walking up to him, she placed gloved fingers against his cheek in a gentle caress. "Then I'm here to wish you every happiness," she said in a soft, emotional voice. "You are the one man I know that deserves to have it all."

He captured her hand and kissed her fingertips. "You've been a good friend, Angelica. Thank you."

She thought she was going to cry, and tried to cover it with words. "Look what happens when I leave you for a few months. I believe I'm going to miss you, Tom."

They both knew a part of their lives was over. It

was an ending, one that had been postponed for years. They were only friends now, yet it was a friendship that would unintentionally hurt others. And they both had integrity.

"I'll miss you, too, Angelica."

She pulled her hand away and walked toward the door. Opening it, she turned around and forced a smile. "See ya' in the papers, Carter."

It was joke between them because of all the publicity each generated. He nodded. "Give 'em hell, Countess," Tom properly responded.

This time her laugh was genuine. "Haven't I always?"

She didn't wait for an answer.

And none was required.

*The Countess Monteva!* Annie didn't know whether to shake her hand, curtsy, or what. Realizing that she had never curtsied to anyone in her life, and wasn't about to start now, Annie smiled, politely offered her hand, and said hello.

"You're Annie Palmer, aren't you?"

She nodded, ecstatic that this international celebrity knew of her.

Angelica glanced at the red-haired woman who stood behind the designer. In seconds her practiced eyes assessed the cream-colored suit that artfully disguised the woman's pregnant state. Looking back to Annie, she said, "It's lovely. But then I've been hearing good things about you."

"You have?" Annie found herself asking.

"*London Times* ran a picture of Ms. Gillbride and mentioned she was wearing one of your designs." Before Annie could react, she heard the woman add, "Would you mind giving Mrs. Gillbride and I a few minutes?"

Annie looked back at Meggie, unsure what to do. If Meggie needed her, nothing could make her budge.

"Believe me," Angelica said, "I'll not keep her, or delay the ceremony."

Meggie nodded to her friend, yet felt unsure of her decision as soon as Annie closed the door behind her. What did Angelica want? The possibilities terrified her.

"I've just come from speaking with Tom. I thought I would tell you before someone else blew it all out of proportion," Angelica began. "And I might as well add that he spent most of that time talking about you."

Meggie felt an immediate relief. Still, what did Angelica really want? "Thank you for telling me that."

"I don't know what he's told you about our marriage, and the relationship we've had since the marriage ended."

Meggie tried not to flinch as the baby issued an exceptionally strong kick. "We've discussed it," she said, trying to stay calm. "Thomas and I have no secrets."

Surprisingly, Angelica smiled. "I'm here, Meggie, to offer you my congratulations. He loves you very much."

"I know," Meggie said softly, relief and gratitude washing over her.

Angelica came closer, standing directly in front of her.

"Then take care of him. Promise me that. He'll be a good husband and a wonderful father." She stopped speaking and swallowed deeply, as though to gain control. "You see, Tom has always wanted children. I didn't. I didn't want that kind of a commitment. Motherhood would never have fit in with my lifestyle." She forced a smile, but it contained a hint of sadness. "And I don't regret it, not really. Maybe someday, when I'm old, but not now." She shook her head. "Not now."

Meggie nodded. She couldn't picture the beautiful Angelica doing the many thankless, unglamorous jobs of a mother. "I don't believe there's anything wrong in being honest with yourself. I think it's an admirable quality."

Angelica smiled. "I'm not quite that noble, Meggie. I'm actually a very selfish person, and there aren't that many people that I really care about. Thomas Grey Carter happens to be one of those that I treasure. So, please . . . take care of him."

Meggie looked into the eyes of Angelica and saw a warmth that couldn't be false. Lifting her chin, Meggie said, "I will, Angelica. I promise, no matter what, I'll always look after him. And I'll try very hard to make him happy."

Nodding, Angelica said, "I won't lie to you, when I came here this morning I was jealous. I didn't want to share Tom with anyone. And I wasn't sure why he was marrying you. If you remember our last meeting, you were a nun . . ." She took a deep breath. "Now I know why."

"I never thanked you for those clothes," Meggie said, a lump forming in her own throat. She smiled. "That was very kind of you, Angelica. I don't believe you're as selfish as you'd like everyone to think. You wouldn't be here talking to me, if you were."

She leaned toward Angelica and kissed her cheek, briefly feeling the netted veil under her lips. "I'll take care of him . . . for both of us."

Without saying another word, Angelica quickly turned and left.


They were married in a small quiet ceremony. As a wedding present, the groom had asked those in attendance to grant him and Meggie their privacy and not reveal anything to the press. Gerald had stood next to him as his best man, along with Ben Tankor. Annie had proudly assumed the role of maid of honor, with Grace Easton as an attendant. Standing behind them and witnessing the occasion had been a strange gathering, consisting of Celia, Mac Weaver, Meggie's clients and their guests, and Morris Lowden from Carter Enterprises.

Odd, indeed.

But once Meggie walked up to him, Thomas could think of nothing else, save finally making her his own. He held her hand and could feel how nervous she actually was. Yet about halfway through the ceremony, he glanced at her and saw tears in her eyes. She was staring at John Carey as the priest spoke to them of love and fidelity. And he knew then that he'd been right about marrying in the church. It meant everything to her. She just hadn't known how much at the time. He knew, without her ever saying the words, that Meggie

Gillbride was finally at peace with herself.

The wedding dinner at Maxim's was a total success. When their party entered, the sweet sound of violins greeted them. Five men stood on the landing and serenaded them as they walked upstairs to a private dining room.

They sat under a brilliant stained glass ceiling and lunched on lamb and poached salmon. On each table was a magnificent floral arrangement as exquisite as any work of art. The service was impeccable and the guests properly impressed. Personally, Tom thought all the rosewood and gilt reminded him of a first-class, turn-of-the-century bordello. It was lush and opulent, and everyone seemed in awe.

Leaning toward his wife, Tom whispered, "How do you feel, Mrs. Carter? Are you tired?"

Her smile was serene as she gazed down at the wide gold band on her finger. "We're really married, aren't we?"

He grinned. "We'd better be. In fact, I can't wait to show you how married we really are."

Shaking her head, she laughed. "Our guests," she quietly protested.

Tom stood up, getting everyone's attention. "Meggie and I would like to thank all of you for being with us today. Thank you for celebrating with us. But now, I'm afraid I'm going to be taking Mrs. Carter home. It's been a very full day."

Meggie made a noise of protest, but Tom ignored it as he continued. "Please stay and enjoy yourselves. There will be cars waiting for you and the drivers each have tickets for several Broadway plays. Gerald has volunteered to organize, so the party needn't cease because of us." He looked around to his guests and smiled. "We would be pleased if you'd continue to celebrate our wedding."

He tried to be patient as Meggie insisted on kissing every single person in attendance. For a moment he thought she might go after the violinists, but she stopped short of that and, instead, spent a full five minutes giving them lavish praise.

He looked at his watch. Exactly twenty-three minutes had elapsed since he'd made the announcement of their departure. He could not wait to get her alone.

And then he would show her how much she meant to him . . .

He was fascinated with her.

The sight of her, swollen with his child, created an almost unbearable pleasure within him. Together, they had created this miracle of life, this tiny being. Looking at Meggie as she gazed out the window, he came up behind her and slipped his arms over her shoulders. She leaned her head back against his chest, allowing his hands to rest on her belly.

It was dark, the middle of the night. He was used to her frequent trips to the bathroom, but tonight she had not returned. And he had found her, silhouetted in moonlight that poured in through the glass wall facing the park. It was a sight that he would never tire of seeing.

"I was worried," he whispered down to her.

"You shouldn't have been. I was just thinking."

"Thinking? About the baby?"

She nodded. "About the baby; about you. About us, and how fortunate we are. About everything we've been through, how far we've come."

His hands became more possessive. "Everything's going to be all right now. We have each other. We'll leave on Monday for the house in Connecticut and spend some time together—out of the city and away from the press. I think you'll like Darien, and the house is right on Five Mile River. You can even see Long Island Sound. It's very pretty, and quiet."

She nodded. "It sounds lovely."

"But? I hear a hesitation."

She laughed. "I have no secrets from you, do I?"

"I hope not. Now, what's wrong?"

She sighed. "It's so foolish, I know, but I'm going to miss the park."

"The park?" He looked out the window and down at Central Park. It was laid out beneath them like nature's patchwork quilt. "It'll be here when we come back. Ben wants you in the city a full month before your delivery date. The park isn't going anywhere, Meggie."

"I knew you'd think it was foolish." She resettled herself in his arms. "I've spent a lot of time there, walking children and dogs. Exploring. I love it. I even liked the rainy days when you could smell the dirt and the grass. And don't forget that's where we met Gerald." She paused, as if considering something. "Doesn't he seem happy to be a carriage driver? And doesn't that seem odd?"

He rested his chin on the top of her head. "It does. But don't try and figure him out. It's useless. I gave up months ago. He's the most philosophical man I have ever met. The fact that he enjoys driving a carriage through Central Park only makes him more quaint. I've even offered him a job, and he turned me down flat."

"Good for him," Meggie said. "A person should be happy with what they do. You can tell he loves the park. It's a part of him."

Tom sighed deeply. "I can see I'm outnumbered."

She turned to face him. "Thomas, no one's against you. It's just a feeling I have about the place, and Gerald shares it. He'd never be happy working inside, shut off from the sun and fresh air."

"Well, what about the winter? It's coming, and I hate to think of him out there freezing."

She touched the side of his face and could feel the slight stubble already growing on his cheek. "Sweet man. Don't you know he doesn't want your help? Gerald doesn't value the same things as you. He's found his peace. He's content with a hot supper and a few pints of beer, and a warm comfortable room to sleep in at night. It's his friends that count. Why, I've seen plenty just like him back in the Lehigha. In the patch alone, there'd be old Brandon Haggerty who'd—"

*"Meggie!"* He grabbed her shoulders and held tight.

She stopped speaking and stared at him.

"Meggie, remember . . . you can't think about that anymore. Put it out of your mind. I know it's

398

hard, but let's talk about something else, all right?" His brain scrambled to find another topic. "Do you remember us standing right here, looking at the fireworks? I loved you then, only I was too scared to admit it. Of course, I thought I was in love with a nun. Remember?"

She nodded, suddenly frightened. "Hold me, Thomas," she whispered in a fierce voice. "Please. Keep me with you."

"Always, love. Always . . ."

## Chapter 27

It was a small village, charming and quaint. Its homes were a tribute to old money — large, stone structures with wide grassy lawns rolling down to Five Mile River. The people who lived in them were for the most part quiet, unassuming, and comfortable with their wealth. No one paid much attention to the Lindburg house and its famous history, or to the Carters who lived next door. Though everyone was aware of them.

Everyday she walked by the river. It filled her with peace to listen to the birds and the gentle lapping of the water against the bank. They were so fortunate, she and Thomas, to spend these past months in this beautiful house. Not for the first time Meggie wondered why she had ever been hesitant to leave New York City. She would miss this large Victorian home with its wide porches and comfortable rooms. Only two more days before they went back to the city to await the birth. Two more days of this peace, this quiet life.

She shook her head, as if dismissing the thought as she headed back to the house. They had been so happy here. Here, in Darien, Thomas had shown her how perfect married life could be. He'd been the attentive husband, at first waiting on her, seeing to her every need, until she thought she was going to scream at him to stop. Instead, she had calmly told him that she wasn't suited for the life of leisure, and if he didn't go back to work, she was going to start up Lease a Wife, right here in Darien. He'd compromised. He installed a complete office in the study. Before long they drifted into a comfortable routine. Mornings were work. Afternoons and evenings were for each other. He left her alone while she supervised the redecoration of the nursery, and she was free to observe him conducting business until early afternoon. And then he was hers.

She looked at the side of the house, where Thomas was talking with a gardener, and smiled. Once last week she had made a casual remark about starting a garden this spring. She should have learned to watch what she said around her husband. He took every wish quite literally. Shaking her head at his indulgence, she continued walking back. The babe was going to be terribly spoiled. There'd be no helping it, for Thomas was like a child himself when it came to his new family. Hardly a week could pass before he would show up with a new cuddly animal or toy to add to the growing collection in the nursery. She knew he would do anything to ensure their happiness, and sometime soon she was going to have to talk to him about it. But not now. Let him enjoy himself.

As her gaze returned to the house, she stopped

short and caught her breath. Her palms covered her belly in a protective gesture and her heart started pounding. The woman had returned . . .

Again.

She stared in wonder at the scene taking place before her on the lawn. It wasn't the first time she had seen the woman. The first time the red-haired woman had run across the lawn Meggie thought she was seeing the ghost of her mother. The image wasn't clear, not completely, almost as if there was a film over her eyes. She hadn't said a word, only quietly observed as the laughing woman had run in front of her, and then quickly faded. It was so brief, so hazy, she wasn't sure she had really seen anything at all.

Each time the woman and her surroundings became clearer. It was as though Meggie were silently observing a part of someone else's life. And that life was taking place in Ireland — she was sure of it. It wasn't her Mum, for behind the pretty woman were automobiles and things from this time.

Now the woman was sad, looking back at her small home, and a dozen or more people standing in front of it that Meggie felt must be her family. She could feel an intense sadness, and something else, something pulling the woman away from her land, from these people.

Meggie covered her eyes with her hands and breathed deeply and quickly. The scent of lavender surrounded her — as always at these moments. She was foolish to allow these thoughts. Surely it was just a pregnant woman's fanciful imagination. She peeked over the tops of her fingers and was relieved to see only the long expanse of early spring grass. She mustn't allow herself to think of these things, yet they came upon her without any warning. If she could put Lehigha behind her, then she must learn to do the same with this. Yet there was something in Meggie that longed to reach out and comfort the young woman who looked so much like her mother, to put an arm around her and touch her lightly freckled face. Perhaps she was a distant relative, still living in Ireland. A strain of her Mum's people must surely still be there. Perhaps . . .

Yet, to be honest, maybe she held back and stood outside the vision for a different reason. Somehow she felt that to assist the sad woman would be to admit that the vision was real, that any of it was actually happening. She had learned to accept the unexplainable, for her life with Thomas in this time was the reward.

But this? These unexpected daydreams were becoming more real. And a tiny part of Meggie worried for her own sanity. She had Thomas and the babe now to think about. She mustn't allow anything to endanger the life she was building with them.

Returning Thomas's wave, she hurried to the house yet stopped short as a vague heaviness settled in the small of her back. She shouldn't have kept walking, just because it was a beautiful spring morning. Now she was going to be sore, and probably cranky. When Thomas found out he would lecture her, and she would more than likely cry. Not that she didn't fight her emotions, but they rose to the surface so easily now. She felt large and awkward, and decidedly unattractive.

Dear, sweet Thomas, he had put up with so many different moods in the last few months. Surely the man was a saint. Imagine—a man insisting on being with her during her childbirth! Together they had watched the television and seen a Cesarean birth and a normal birth. Neither had been easy to watch, yet Ben and Thomas assured her that she wouldn't feel the pain of the operation. It was a commonplace procedure in this time. She kept telling herself that she mustn't be afraid—that it was only fear of the unknown. Thomas kept telling her that she could do this. She wanted to believe him, to be strong for him. And in her heart, she knew she would risk anything for the safe delivery of this child.

She entered the house from the back, and as always, she was filled with peace. There was something about this house decorated in comfortable country furniture that was far more welcoming than the stark white decor of the penthouse in the city. This was where she would like to raise their child. Out here where you could smell the clean scent of the river and the lavender— No, she reminded herself as the telephone rang, the scent of lavender came from the ethereal guest on her back lawn. And wasn't that odd? That she could smell the fragrance of the woman?

Anxious not to think about any of it, Meggie walked into Thomas's study to see what was being transmitted over the FAX machine. She was fascinated with the invention. To think that someone anywhere in the world, could send pictures of just about anything to right here in her home. She loved to read the names of the cities and countries, and find them on the huge world map hanging over her Mum's sewing table. Names like Sydney and Brussels and Singapore sounded so exotic to her. And to think that once she had thought Philadelphia was nearly foreign.

Smiling at the memory of that poor country girl, Meggie looked down to see where the message had originated. She sighed with disappointment. It was only from Mac in the city, yet she decided to wait and bring Thomas the material. She leaned her hand on the desk, casually reading.

Suddenly, Meggie straightened while looking at Mac's message:

Finally located some information on Brian Gillbride. Thought you'd want it right away. Copy of 1875 newspaper following.

She couldn't breathe. She couldn't think. She kept staring at the machine, impatient for the next transmission. Her brain kicked in and a hundred questions whirled around inside. Brian. Why was Thomas doing this? Somehow she knew he was doing it for her, to let her know her brother had made it through that crisis, to put her mind at ease. She heard the two beeps and the steady hum that indicated something was coming through the machine.

She saw it immediately. The circled words in the newspaper article.

Among those killed in the bombing was Brian Gillbride, negotiator for the miners.

She was stunned, unable to move. Her eyes kept reading those same words, over and over again. It couldn't be! Of course Brian wouldn't be alive in this time, but . . . he was killed in a bombing! *Killed!* She felt dizzy as her entire belly tightened in protest against the horrible thought. It was James Roarity. It had to be! That bastard was responsible for her brother's death. She had to warn Brian. This time—

"Meggie?"

She spun around to face him. "Thomas, you must help me! Brian . . . Mac sent a message that says he was killed—"

Hurrying up to her, he held her in his arms and looked down to the machine. "Damn! Why did he send it here?" He quickly expelled his breath. "I'm so sorry, Meggie. I had asked Mac to do some research for me, to find out what happened to them. You shouldn't have to go through this now." He kissed the top of her head. "I should have told him to send it to the office in the city!"

She pushed away from him. "You weren't going to tell me?" She was desperate to ease the terrible ache in her heart. Brian . . . his name rang through her head, like a soft litany.

"Not now. I would have told you after the baby was born. We've had so much to deal with already."

"We have to go back."

*"No!"*

"Thomas, listen to me. You can warn him. You can stop this—"

"I can't, and I won't. That's in the past. It's over and done with. I'm sorry. I feel like I've just lost a good friend, but I can't do it, Meggie. We have a life here, a good life. Nothing's happened for months; you've been happy here. Don't think about the past. Don't think about any of them." She looked desperate, frantic, and he slowly walked over to her. "You belong here, with me."

She had backed up against the sewing table. Clutching the edge of the smooth satinwood, her fingers touched her initials, scratched into the wood when she was but a young girl. So many years ago . . . in that tiny house . . . in the patch. Her Mum scolding her. A youthful Brian laughing at her troubles.

*"Meggie!"*

His warning was too late.

She was already gone.

His first sensation was of cold. It was dark and cold, and he could hear the annoying trickle of water, like in the—my God, he was in a mine! Fear ran down his spine as he heard the voices of men around him. Angry voices. His pupils were still adjusting and he blinked several times while staring at a tiny flame across from him. Meggie! Where was she? He'd grabbed her . . . touched her arm . . . and then he was here in this mine.

Without her.

"Jimmy, this is foolishness. You'll not be blowing this shaft. We've come all this way without violence, and we're too close to a settlement now. Tom and me'll stop ya, if we have to. Won't we, Tom?"

To fill in the silence, Brian quickly continued,

"From all the articles appearing in the newspapers, we actually have public support. For the first time, people all over the state and beyond are hearin' about our troubles." Brian sounded frantic. "The Reading's gettin' desperate to settle it all and get back to work. They look bad enough as it is. You do this, Jimmy, and the support will swing right back to Nate Gowen. We can't allow it. Right, Tom?"

As the small area grew brighter with the light from the oil lamps, Tom looked at Brian standing next to him. "I have to leave," he somehow managed to say. "I have to find someone." He felt as if he were drunk as he pushed off Brian's arm and started to walk away from him. Meggie! Where was she? Pregnant. In this time! He *had* to find her and get her out of here. Maybe she was back at Bridget's, or at the cemetery. He'd tear the town apart until he found her.

"Tom?"

"Oh, and by the way, Brian," he said, turning around and pointing to Roarity. "That sonofabitch over there is a traitor. I told you before about him, but you didn't want to listen. He works for the Reading. They brought him in from Chicago to infiltrate the Mollies. He told them everything you were planning. Gowen owns this town." He barely glanced at Roarity's shocked expression. "So don't go to the police. Not here, Brian. Find help outside Lehigha. And I think you can get Gowen on tampering with the U.S. Mail, if nothing else. They intercepted every single letter we sent *The Gazette*."

He turned once again to leave, to find Meggie,

but a voice, cold and sinister, stopped him. "You're not goin' anywhere, Carter. Why don't you come on back here and tell me where you got all your information?"

A sixth sense told him James Roarity was holding a gun on him, and would shoot him in the back if he tried to walk away.

Tom turned around.

He was.


What had she done? She was here. In Bridget's home. Without Thomas. But he had touched her! She had felt his hand on her arm. She couldn't be alone here . . . she couldn't! Hugging her hard abdomen in protection, Meggie refused to think about the consequences of being back in this time. Alone. She tried to think calmly. She would never be able to figure this out if she didn't collect herself and quietly go over—of course! He must be wherever . . . wherever the Thomas of this time was. She just had to find him. Was it morning? Afternoon? What day? Was he working?

Seeing a newspaper on the table by the window, Meggie rose and walked over to it. Unconsciously, she rubbed the small of her back as she read the headlines.

READING DEMANDS THE RE-OPENING OF TUNNEL #18

In smaller type underneath it:

MINERS REFUSE TO NEGOTIATE ON ISSUE,

She remembered. Tunnel #18 was where eleven men had died when she was a young girl. She'd grown up hearing stories about water leakage and pockets of natural gas that could explode at any time. It had been closed off for years because of the danger. How could the Reading even think of reopening it now?

She started to pace back and forth in front of the window. Where would Thomas be right now? And how—if, God forbid, he didn't follow her here—was she to warn Brian? Somehow—

A loud knock on the door followed by its being flung open. "Thomas? Are ya in here? I thought I'd heard . . ." Bridget anxiously looked around the room before her shoulders slumped in disappointment. She shook her head and Meggie could detect a worried expression on her face.

"What's wrong, Bridgi?" she whispered, even though she knew the old woman couldn't hear her. Something about Bridgi's face made Meggie follow her when she left the bedroom. She took the stairs slowly, for the heaviness in her back had returned and a pulling sensation had begun to run down her legs. She watched Bridgi walk into her kitchen. She looked agitated and nervous as she tested the kettle for water and then, just as quickly, slammed it back onto the coal stove.

"Damn them," Bridgi cursed, and Meggie's mouth opened in surprise to hear it. "I must do *something!*" Untying her apron, Bridgi threw it over a kitchen chair and opened her back door. Intrigued, and more than a little frightened, Meggie followed.

By the time they reached Liam's house, Meggie's legs felt weighted down. She was getting too big to be running after anyone. Running? Hah! She was near out of breath just trying to follow and keep up with old Bridgi. Passing through the town, she saw several strange men with rifles across their chests, as if the patch were in a state of war. Her anxiety increased as she observed them standing on corners, glaring at anyone who passed. Bridgi ignored them as she rushed to Liam's. Meggie tried very hard to keep up, but the soreness in her back had increased, drawing and pulling her muscles in the strangest way. She was ready to find the nearest chair and collapse. Lord, but her body had undergone a severe change, she thought, as she rested against Liam's house while Bridgi quickly knocked on the door.

Immediately, the door opened and Meggie barely had a chance to slip inside with Bridgi as Liam shut it behind them. "Bridget. What's wrong? Were you stopped?"

Bridgi made a sarcastic noise with her mouth. "What? By those bullies Gowen's hired? His private police? Hah! Private army is more like it."

Nodding, Liam looked up as his daughter, Noreen, entered the front room. "Put on a pot of tea, child. Mrs. Humne has come to visit."

"No time for that, Liam," Bridgi abruptly announced. "I don't know who else to tell." She pulled her shawl more tightly about her shoulders. "You know I bring lunch to the guards. Well, they pay me no mind, as if I weren't there sometimes." She looked around her in a secretive way. "I heard

Gowen himself talkin' to three of them fancy city men that he brought here. He was saying how Roarity had fouled up twice before and that he'd better get it right this time. Then he said Roarity was going to make it look like Brian and Thomas blew the tunnel. And if they were both blown to hell and back in the process, all the better. He went on ranting about what the two of them had already done to thwart him. What'll we do, Liam? Where are Brian and Thomas now?"

Liam's face turned ashen. "Sweet Mother of God," he whispered. "They're with Jimmy."

"The traitorous bastard!"

Everyone turned to look at Noreen. The pretty young woman appeared ready to do battle herself. Liam was about to say something when the front door suddenly blew open. Everyone in the room stared at the swinging door, and Bridgi crossed herself while Noreen looked out the window.

There wasn't any wind.

Meggie stood at the Monroe colliery. She was right all those months ago when she'd compared it to a wooden monster. She hated it and was terrified to enter. Ever since she was a child, she'd had an unexplainable fear of the place. Her breathing quickened and her mouth became dry with panic at the thought of going down there. Thomas had told her the name for it, the fear of closed places. But she knew it was more than that. Somehow, everything she had gone through had brought her to this moment. Thomas and Brian were down there, with that sonofabitch Roarity. She could help them, for she was the only one who could make it down there undetected.

412

There was no warning, not even pain. Even as she watched the water drain from her body into the dark clay beneath her feet, Meggie knew there really wasn't a choice.

She could have her baby, or she could have Thomas.

Maybe, just maybe, she could have both.

What she didn't have any longer was time.

# Chapter 28

It was a nightmare with three participants.

Keeping his distance from the men, Roarity took out a pocket watch and glanced down at it. Satisfied, he put it away and smiled at the men he held at gunpoint. "It didn't have to be like this, Brian. I want you to understand that. You chose to listen to this one, over there," he said, nodding to Tom. "And he put those grand ideas into your head about peaceful negotiations."

"Jimmy, put the gun away," Brian said in a strong voice. He was moving closer to the man he had once trusted with his life.

"Stay where you are, Brian," Roarity commanded. "If you think I won't shoot you, you're wrong."

"What are you going to do," Tom demanded, "kill us both? Give it up, Roarity. How will it look when our bodies are discovered? Your boss isn't going to be too happy to be the center of attention again. There will be an investigation."

Roarity grinned. "My boss is the one who ordered this. And nobody's going to discover anything. You see, my friends, in approximately five minutes the opening to this tunnel is going to be closed off with the two of you inside it."

Brian and Tom looked at each other. Tom could think of nothing else save Meggie and how to get out of here alive so he could find her. He saw the flash of desperation in Roarity's eyes and knew he had to keep the man talking until he or Brian could figure a way out. *Five minutes!*

"I never trusted you, Roarity—if that's your real name. What kind of man does it take to become a traitor? To deceive men into thinking they're your friends? Who are you?" Tom asked in a deceptively calm voice as he looked around the small opening in search of a weapon. A shovel, a pick . . . anything. There was nothing.

"You're one to talk, Carter. You're more mysterious than I am. But I've always used my real name. Saw no reason to change my policy just because I was infiltrating a band of murdering thugs."

Brian straightened. "Then you never really knew us, Jimmy. We didn't kill; we retaliated. And only after being backed into a corner with nowhere to go. You'll never know how heavy that weighs on my heart."

"Oh, I'm sure, Brian. Not that I didn't find myself sympathizing with your cause. Gowen's a coldhearted bastard if I ever met one. And you're right, he's desperate now. Nobody ever thought it would get this big, or last this long. But I'll finish the job I'm paid to do. And I'm paid quite well."

He glared at Tom. "And all of it would have been over if Mr. Carter, here, hadn't come upon the scene. Nothin' went right since the time he showed up in Fitzhugh's. Then you didn't want to listen to me anymore. Only him. That's why I knew if I said I was going to blow this tunnel, both of you would try to stop me. Finally, I can get rid of you . . . and him."

"Tom offered us hope," Brian said. "You only wanted to instigate more violence. You were counting on me getting caught. Was I supposed to hang? In place of Connon?"

At the mention of Connon Rafferty, Roarity seemed to stiffen. "I was sorry about Connon. We needed to make an example out of one of you. Connon was easy; he was too far in debt. It was almost child's play to set him up. You never should have left him in, Brian. That was a mistake. Connon was your weakest link." He pulled out his watch and checked it. "Enough of this. It's time for me to bid you farewell."

As Roarity talked, Tom had heard low moans in the distance, and the sound made the hair on the back of his neck stand up in dread. He squinted, trying to see up the darkened tunnel. And when he did, his heart stopped for an agonizing moment.

It was Meggie.

She looked terrified. Holding on to one of the wooden timbers that braced the wall of the mountain, Meggie appeared in pain. Her tan and white maternity dress was stained from the coal dust and she looked exhausted. Seeing her move toward

416

Roarity, he called out, "Don't do it!"

Roarity stared at him. "You have no say in this, my friend." He appeared nervous when he added, "I have to get out of here and leave you two gentlemen now. Any preference which goes first?"

Tom watched as Meggie's knees almost buckled and he called out to her. "Meggie!"

Brian and Roarity turned to look. Roarity tried to regain his composure while pointing his gun at his prisoners. "Nice try, Carter." He looked at Brian. "I might as well tell you. Everything would have been fine if Liam hadn't moved the time of the explosion up an hour. The plan was for us to be waiting when she came into the Reading building and catch her red-handed. I could have diffused the bomb, so don't blame me for your sister's death."

"You sonofabitch!" Brian cursed. "You made the suggestion to use her in the first place. You set her up, just like the rest of us. You would have had her hang! Why? What did she ever do to you?"

Roarity's mouth twisted in an evil expression. "She thought she was better'n any of us. Always acting high and mighty, as if no one knew about her sullied past."

"Shut up," Tom growled. "Don't you dare talk about her." He watched as Meggie picked up a broken shovel handle.

"You didn't even know her," Roarity countered while backing up toward the entrance of the tunnel . . . and Meggie. "A fine-lookin' baggage if I ever saw one. Meant to have her, too, after her arrest, but Liam messed that up good."

Enraged, Meggie seemed to summon her strength as she reached out and brought the handle down on his arm. Roarity looked too shocked to yell out his pain.

It appeared so odd to see Roarity's hand swing out and the gun fly through the air that Brian was momentarily immobilized. Where had the handle come from? It wasn't until he saw Tom rush up to Roarity that Brian was able to join him.

By then Tom had grabbed the man around the collar and was turning him around. Tom's fist was pulled back, ready to smash into Roarity's face, when Brian caught it in his own hand.

There was no need to speak. Tom moved out of the way as Brian slammed his huge knuckles into Roarity's cheek. "That's for my Meggie," he hissed. His fist came back again and again, connecting with the man's nose and eyes. Skin tore under the angry blows and blood flowed. Roarity was barely conscious and Tom had to pull Brian away.

"And that," Brian whispered as he gulped for air, "is for disgracing the honor . . . of the Mollie Maguires." His voice was filled with emotion as he watched the man sink down to the floor of the tunnel. No one heard, nor would they have cared, that Roarity's head hit a large chunk of discarded coal. And somehow it seemed fitting that the final blow, the one that took the traitor's life, was brought about by nature itself.

"Thomas . . . the dynamite . . ." Meggie reached for him, gasping with the ripping pain that slashed up her legs then down across her belly. "Bridgi heard. Get . . . get Brian out. You, too!"

Holding her to his chest, Tom tried to support her. "You have to get out of here, Brian. This place is going to blow any minute."

"What do we do about him?" Brian asked, looking at the broken body of James Roarity.

"Leave him," Tom answered in a cold voice. "Get out."

"What about you?" Just noticing the way Tom's arms were, Brian moved closer. There was something about it, something odd and almost frightening. Maybe it was the light that was playing tricks on his mind. Maybe . . . It was as if he could see a form, the faint outline of a woman in Tom's arms. A woman . . . that looked like his sister.

*"Meggie!"* He breathed her name in a voice mixed with fear and awe.

Tom turned to him. "Brian, she never blamed you for anything," he said urgently. "She loves you. That's what brought her back here. Now get out before it's all for nothing."

"I don't understand, Tom. How can . . . ?" Brian looked stunned, even as the brief vision faded.

"You must get out of here. We don't have much time. Go into hiding, Brian. Let them think you were caught down here." Tom struggled to hold Meggie upright. She was clinging to his shoulders, her head buried against his chest.

"Tell him I love him again. And—and to protect

419

himself. They'll try . . . again . . . Thomas. You know they will. Please help me, I can't walk. The baby . . . !"

"Protect yourself, Brian. Now get going. *Go!*"

Confused, Brian asked, "What about you, Tom? What's happening?"

"I'll follow. Just go!"

Brian reluctantly disappeared up the shaft. He turned back only once, as if undecided, then ran.

Knowing she could never walk, nor could he carry her, Tom gently lowered her to the ground. He ripped off his corduroy jacket, rolled it into a ball, and placed it under her head. "You're going to be all right, do you hear me?" He refused to look at the dark stain covering the bottom of her dress. She was going to be okay.

She had to be.

When it came, there was no warning. The noise was deafening as it swept over them like a monster unleashed from the belly of the mountain. Holding Meggie in his arms, Tom barely had time to throw himself across her for protection. The mountain trembled and moaned, as if being torn apart, and debris fell around them.

And when it settled, when all the noise quickly disappeared save a few groans of weighted timbers, they were left with a silence that was almost as frightening. It was as if they were closed off from the rest of the world—entombed below it.

Lifting his head, Tom blew coal dust away from his eyes and wiped it from his face. He looked down at her. "Meggie? Are you all right?"

She moaned then gasped in pain. It seemed an

eternity until she was able to speak. "Oh Tommy, what have I done to you? What have I done to us? This poor babe . . ."

"You're in labor, aren't you?" he asked, already knowing and dreading her answer. She nodded and brought her hand up to cover her eyes.

"How? How can that be? Ben said you weren't due until next month."

"Dear God, I don't know how to measure time anymore. One day in your time could be three weeks in this. All I know is it's coming now. What are we going to do?" she cried, beginning to again gasp as the pain returned.

He didn't know the answer. He only knew he had to get her to his time, to a hospital where she could have the Cesarean. Otherwise . . . He refused to think about the alternative.

"All right. Listen, Meggie," he demanded, unbuttoning his shirt and pulling it off. "We're going to have to work together. We have to get back." He shook out the shirt and turned it inside out. Without saying anything to her, he gently lifted her and placed it underneath.

He felt dizzy when he saw the amount of blood she had already lost. This had to work. It had to!

"I'm so cold, Thomas. I'm sorry I did this. I had to help Brian. Do you think he made it out?" The questions were asked one after the other, as if in a rush. As she reached for him, her next labor pain quickly followed.

He held her hand, feeling her nails dig into his skin, and he welcomed the pain—anything to take part of it away from her. "I know you're cold," he said over the contraction. "It's the mine. It's always cold down here." He rubbed her forearm, as if it might bring warmth into her body. "Sure, I think Brian made it out. You did it, Meggie. You saved him."

She labored for breath. "You think?"

He nodded. "Yes, I do. Who knows what Brian will go on to become?" He'd say anything to get her mind off her suffering. Who knew what would happen to Brian. Brian was no longer his concern. Now it was Meggie, his beautiful, brave, stubborn wife. He settled himself behind her, holding her upper body against his chest, and wrapped his arms around her.

Swallowing several times, Meggie wiped her mouth. "I . . . I can feel your warmth. You, you must be freezing. Your shirt? Where's your shirt?"

He ran his fingers through her hair. "Don't you worry about it. Now, listen to me, Meggie. You're going to have to concentrate. I want you to think about Darien, okay. We'll both do it. Remember the sailboats on the Sound, and the river? Picture them in your mind—just like you were standing on the porch and watching them."

"Thomas? I never told you about the woman I keep seeing on our lawn." She was panting, like an injured animal, and he held her hand as another contraction began.

"Tell me about it, Meggie," he urged. "What does she look like?" He could actually feel the muscles of her body constricting as the pain moved over her.

"Like . . . like my Mum, or . . . me. But she's

so sad, and confused, I think . . . *My God! The pain!*"

He started to shake, and he wasn't sure whether it was from the cold, or his own fear. He didn't know what to do to help her. He tried to remember the films they had watched together about the birth process, but his brain refused to concentrate. And then he realized that her labor was progressing too fast. The baby must be moving down the birth canal. Or trying to. She was too small. Ben had told him that Meggie was too small to successfully go through another delivery, or a prolonged labor. Unless the baby was tiny, or underweight, it would become lodged in the birth canal and both Meggie and the child would be at risk. From her last checkup with Ben, they both knew the baby was going to be large. Or they had thought it was large because she was still a month away from delivery. But it was at normal birth weight right now. Without wanting to, Tom remembered what had happened the last time Meggie had tried to deliver a child. They had to get back to a hospital, to help!

"She smells of lavender," Meggie whispered with difficulty. "I don't know why, but there is always the faint"—she paused to catch her breath—"the faintest scent of lavender around her. I like her, Thomas."

"Darling, try to concentrate on me," he murmured. His lips were near her temple and he lightly kissed her. She was so cold. "Think about her then. Try to imagine this woman on the back lawn and you with her. We'll both try, all right?"

423

But she was already in the throes of another contraction. The pain robbed her of concentration, and Tom feared that without Meggie's help they would never get back.

*"Please,"* he begged, while rocking her back and forth, "please help me, Meggie."

"I love you," she breathed. "I would do anything, anything for you. But I'm so frightened. I don't know . . ." She gasped for breath as the contraction eased. "And, and I'm so cold."

"I know." He wrapped his arms more tightly around her, hoping to give off any remaining body heat. "But you must concentrate, Meggie."

"Promise me you'll take care of the baby if . . . if anything should happen. Don't let anything happen to the baby, promise me."

"Nothing's going to happen. We can get back. I know we can. Now—"

*"Promise me!"* Another contraction took her under its control.

"I promise!" He was desperate and felt she was giving up. "Meggie, please try to help me. I don't know how else to get us back. We can't stay here. You have to get to a hospital. Please . . . help me."

He had no idea how much time passed in that cold, ever-darkening cave. He thought perhaps he had died and this was his hell, to be holding someone whose life meant more than his own, and to watch her suffer. There wasn't anything he could do to make it go away. It was hopeless. His money, his power, meant nothing, were nothing, when presented with this situation. No amount of

424

money, no degree of influence, would change the fact that they were buried alive, and quickly using up the precious air that was trapped along with them. He had nothing left to do, but pray. And it had been so long since he'd done that.

"Tommy, let me see your face." Her voice was growing weak, almost a faint whisper.

Turning around, he held her in his arms so that her cheek was against his chest. He thought he would lose control and break down when he saw the pain in her face. When he moved, he also saw the ever-widening circle of blood underneath her. "Margaret Mary Gillbride, you'd better pull yourself together," he said roughly to hide his own fear. "I don't know anything about children. You're the expert."

Licking her dry lips, she smiled. "You'll be a wonderful father. And I'll . . . always be with you."

"Promise me that," Tom demanded.

Again she smiled, a feeble, weak movement of her lips. "I promise." Her body straightened with the impact of another contraction and Tom could do little more than hold her and whisper to her through it.

When it ended, she seemed to melt into his arms; she was that fragile, that weak. "Meggie?"

It took her a few moments to answer, to gather her strength. "How did it all happen, Tommy?" she asked in a hushed voice. "How could we have . . ." Her breathing was labored. "I think fate must be laughing at me now," she whispered. "I thought I had made my peace with it."

"Hush." His arms tightened around her. "We're going to get out of this. Somehow . . ." If only he believed it.

"Is it getting darker? I can't see . . . you." She tried to raise her hand to his face, but it fell back from lack of strength.

He couldn't stop the tears. They ran freely down his cheeks and into her hair. This could not be happening. Nothing in his life had prepared him for this. "Yes, darling," he murmured as he picked up her hand and kissed her fingers, "we are losing the light. The oil in the lamp is down." He gulped back the acid taste of his tears and raised his head. He wouldn't tell her that they had little air left. Already he felt light-headed from the lack of oxygen.

*"Tommy?"*

He looked down at her and held his breath.

"Tommy, are you still holding me?" Her voice was so weak that he had to strain to hear it.

He bit his lip to stop from crying out. Instead, he breathed, "Always, love. You'll always be with me."

She smiled. "Ahh, Tommy . . . don't I know?"

Her head fell to one side, limp, lifeless, like a sleeping doll. Not real. She never heard his blood-curdling yell of frustration and pain.

*"Nooo . . . you can't do this to her!"*

It took the last of his breath, the last of his oxygen, for why else was he surrounded in a blazing white light, the heat of it taking away the cold and chill? Holding on to Meggie, he felt it enter him, filling every inch of his body and seeping out again through his pores. It wrapped around them like a soothing, protective blanket of warmth, moving them, carrying them back.

All they needed now was time.


He stared at the coffee grounds in the bottom of the cup, almost as if he might see the future in that murky dark mass. What would it tell him? And did he want to know? Standing, he walked over to the long expanse of glass and looked down to the hospital parking lot. Neat lines of cars covered the asphalt, like soldiers at attention. And all carried Connecticut license plates. He watched with a vague interest as an ambulance raced into the parking lot. It stopped somewhere below him, out of his line of vision. Probably Emergency, just like with Meggie. Rubbing his eyes to stop the tired burning and fatigue, Tom was never so glad to see an automobile or to hear a siren as he had been forty-five minutes ago.

Once back in the study in Darien, Tom had immediately called for help. He'd raced through the house for towels and blankets and pillows. He couldn't explain why he'd packed the towels between her legs and then elevated them. Some inner voice had guided him. Or he must have read it somewhere. If he could keep her warm, if he could stop the bleeding . . . But she had looked almost gray and her lips were tinged in blue. She had lost so much blood. He'd stayed with her, holding her hand, talking to her, stroking her hair. Anything to let her know he was still there. Somehow, though she'd never regained consciousness, she would know his presence. And he hadn't let her go, not even in the ambulance. He'd remained at her side until they took her away behind the closed doors. He'd told them about Ben, about the Cesarean, and begged to go inside. He was frantic to make them listen. He was supposed to be able to be with her. Ben had said . . .

But that was before their world was turned upside down. That was—

"Mr. Carter?"

Tom spun around to face a young man dressed in operating room green. His surgical mask was pulled down to his neck, and he looked tired and . . . and something else that scared the hell out of Tom. "Yes?"

"You have a son, Mr. Carter."

Tom's heart raced with a sudden joy. A son! "And Meggie? My wife?"

"Why don't you come with me?"

Starting to walk alongside the man, Tom stopped. "What's wrong? Where's my wife?"

The doctor sighed loudly. "I'm very sorry. She'd lost so much blood. By the time we got her into surgery . . ."

His eyes widened in denial; a heavy heat settled on his chest, almost strangled him. "What are you saying?" he demanded. "Where's my wife?" He heard the hysteria entering his voice, yet that didn't stop him from grabbing the man's shirt. *Where is she?*

The doctor removed Tom's hands. "I'll take you to her. She died during surgery. We were lucky to save the child," he added, as if that were a consolation.

What did he know? Tom thought as he followed the man beyond those forbidding double doors. He was too young to be a good doctor. Ben would come and straighten all this out. He had to stay calm, that's all. Meggie wasn't like ordinary women. She wouldn't die and leave him. She'd promised! He almost felt like laughing at this man of medicine. How little he understood. He couldn't even begin to comprehend the miracles that he and Meggie had experienced. Meggie didn't die. Wouldn't she laugh, too, when all this was over? When they were back at the house together? Wouldn't she?

The man opened a door and Tom felt his legs almost give out as he entered the pristine white room. She was there, lying on a narrow bed, with a white sheet tucked neatly under her chin.

She looked like a fine porcelain doll.

He heard the swoosh of the closing door and realized he was alone. Walking up to her, he ran his fingers through her hair.

"Megs? You're not going to believe this," he whispered through the painful tightening of his throat. "They think . . . that young doctor thinks . . ." He stopped speaking and stared at her beautiful face — so peaceful, so serene, as if she'd just found out the answer to a secret and had been right.

Slowly, giving in to the tears, he bent his head and kissed her lips. They were cold, unresponsive, passionless.

It wasn't his Meggie at all.

He gazed at her, a mixture of confusion and sorrow in his expression. "Why did you do this? What am I going to do without you? What am I going to do?" he mumbled, cradling her face.

Everyone on the OR floor stopped what they were doing as a howl of anguish and grief was heard. It flooded each corridor, each room, making the listeners shiver and count their blessings.

*"Nooo . . . You promised me!"*

He stood at the nursery window, looking down at his son. An older woman, a nurse, was holding him up to see. She looked as if she expected some reaction from him, some sign of pleasure.

He had none to give.

"He's a fine-lookin' lad."

Gerald put his arm around Tom and squeezed his shoulder. "You're looking at innocence there, Tom. That little one was created by your love for Meggie, and hers for you. He's yours now. Your responsibility."

He had no comment. He was numb, without feelings. All he wanted to do was leave, go back to the city, and drink until he passed out. He didn't want to think, or feel, anything.

Not now.

Ben walked up to him and stood quietly for a few moments. "Tom, I don't know how to tell you this."

He didn't even look at his friend who'd driven up with Gerald from the city. No one could help

430

now.

"They . . ." Ben cleared his throat. "Damnit, I can't believe this, but . . . well, they've lost her. They're going crazy looking, but no one seems to know anything. I'm sorry. I never heard of anything like it. These things just don't happen. I'll go back and—"

"Doesn't matter," Tom interrupted in a dull voice. "She's gone." Staring at the infant, he mumbled, "Just doesn't matter . . . none of it does."

Gerald motioned Ben away and the obstetrician quietly went back to do battle with the hospital staff. When they were alone, Gerald leaned closer to Tom and said, "You'd better listen to me, son. I know just what you're thinking, and maybe you're right. Maybe she was taken back, back where she really belonged. Maybe they'll never find her. But she didn't leave you alone. You need to take a better look at that babe in front of you."

Reluctantly, Tom's gaze moved back to the baby. He was tiny and his skin alternated between a startling red when he squirmed to a pale, pale pink. When he opened his mouth, he looked like an old man, weak and defenseless. And on top of his head was a patch of golden red hair, not as red as Meggie's, or as dark as his own. But still . . .

And then the baby opened his eyes. Blue eyes. Somewhere he's heard most babies were born with blue eyes, but not like this, he thought. They were just like Meggie's—a startlingly blue sapphire. He pressed closer to the glass and Gerald motioned to the nurse. The woman grinned and nodded before bringing the wrapped bundle to the door.

Swallowing several times, Tom felt almost frightened as he and Gerald walked over to meet his son.

"I thought it would be easier this way. Now you can look at him all you want." The nurse had put the infant into a small rolling crib made out of clear plastic pushed it to the open doorway. She smiled and left them staring.

"Wouldn't Meggie be proud?" Gerald whispered, bending down to see better.

Tom sniffled, trying so hard to fight back the flood of emotions that threatened to overwhelm him. He didn't want to care, to feel this . . . "Yes," he managed to say. "She would."

He looked at the tiny child. He was making mewling sounds, like a hungry kitten. His hands were clenched into miniature fists and he tried to bring one into his mouth. Capturing his first two fingers, the child sucked loudly. "She . . . she wanted him. I think . . . maybe, to take the place of the one she'd lost. She never really got over that, you know?" Tom felt his lips tremble when he heard the infant cry out in frustration after his fingers popped out of his mouth. Without thought, Tom reached down and touched him, moving his tiny arm and helping his son recover his fist.

Neither he nor Gerald cared that tears brimmed over their eyes as the babe again sucked in contentment. Taking out his handkerchief, Gerald roughly swiped at his nose before muttering, "Well, now, what are you going to do about that?"

He impatiently pointed to a card taped to the bassinet. The top of it read: BABY BOY CARTER.

"A child needs a proper name. It's a big responsibility you're undertaking here. Have you given it a thought?"

Tom stared at the child, his child . . . and Meggie's. She hadn't left him, not really. Even now, he could feel her love as he looked at the baby. And he could imagine her impatience. She would scold him for not thinking first of the child. *Grieve later, if you must, she would say. But now, name my babe!* He took a deep steadying breath.

"How does the name 'Patrick' sound?"

Smiling, Gerald nodded his approval. " 'Tis a fine choice."

# EPILOGUE

Central Park was celebrating spring with a profusion of tulips and crocuses that lined the carriage walks. Buds appeared on naked tree limbs, ever ready to burst forth with restored life. It was a season of renewal, and always a painful time for Thomas Grey Carter.

Walking behind his three-year-old son, Tom glanced at the man by his side. Gerald looked so much older than when he'd met him. He seemed more tired than ever after this past winter, and he was still a stubborn old fool, refusing to give up his independence and move into the penthouse. And now Tom really needed the help. Celia had announced last month that she was retiring to live with her daughter. In the past three weeks he had interviewed more housekeeper/nannies than he would have believed existed in this city. He'd found fault with every one and refused to entrust his son to their care. Patrick was passionate about his love for Uncle Gerald, telling his little nursery friends that he had his very own Santa Claus. Gerald would be perfect until he found the right replacement. But to Tom's surprise, Gerald had firmly refused, saying he would take on the job of finding the right person himself. And that's what they were doing in the park. The park, no less! It was incredible what this old man could talk him into.

"You're saying I'm to interview this person here? Why not conduct this in the proper place? Like where they'll be working, maybe?"

Gerald made an impatient sound. "I told you, this one's different. She doesn't have her green card. She's here illegally—"

"Oh no," Tom interrupted. "Not another flower of Ireland. I can tell you right now this is a waste of time. It won't work. Do you know how much trouble I could get into for employing an illegal alien? Besides, I don't want that kind around Pat."

"And what kind is that?" Gerald demanded, an indignant gleam in his eye.

"You know. Look, if she didn't go through immigration, I don't want anything to do with this. That's all."

"Maybe I should leave, too."

Tom looked at his son. "Patrick, be careful with that ball. We'll be there in a few minutes." He turned to the old man. "What are you talking about? Leave?"

"I don't possess a green card, either. Maybe I'm not fit to be around your son."

Tom's mouth hung open in surprise. "Why didn't you ever tell me? Maybe I could help."

"And maybe you can help this woman. She needs the job. She's been in the city for a few

435

years, working odds and ends, so to speak. She has a degree from Trinity College in child psychology, but can't use her knowledge because she's here illegally. Why don't you just meet with her and then make up your mind?"

Tom smiled. "You're a real mystery, Gerald Kane. Monday morning I'm calling immigration and finding out what can be done about you. By the way, where are we meeting this latest candidate?"

Gerald smiled. "At the zoo. She said she would be at the seal pool."

Tom's stomach tightened. "Meggie loved the zoo." Even after three years the ache and loneliness hadn't disappeared.

"You know," Gerald said without acknowledging Tom's statement, "I think you've done a fine job bringing up that boy. I think she's proud of both of you."

Annoyed, Tom answered, "You know, old man, for over three years I've listened to what you think. You have some of the craziest ideas running around in that head of yours. I understand your role of teacher. I accepted that a long time ago, because I needed it. I needed someone to remind me of my responsibilities, to give me some answers to the insane things that were taking place in my life. But that never took away the pain of losing her. Can you understand that?"

As they neared the entrance to the zoo, Tom took hold of Patrick's small hand and smiled at his son's excitement.

"The monkeys, Da! Can we see them?"

"Of course we can," Tom answered with a smile. No matter what he did, Pat refused to finish the end of Daddy. He shortened it to Da. At first Tom had thought the child was just a bit lazy, or stubborn. Now he knew better.

"And the seals, too," his uncle Gerald added with a grin.

"Yah, the seals," Pat chimed in, actually bouncing on the balls of his sneakered feet with excitement.

They stood in a long line, waiting to pay. Still annoyed, Tom turned to Gerald. In that moment he saw the many fine wrinkles that seemed carved into the gentle face. How old was he? And when had he aged so? Tom quickly lost his anger as a rush of affection washed over him. "Seriously, Gerald, what do you believe, really believe?"

Looking at Patrick's impatient little body pull on Tom's hand, Gerald said, "I believe that Margaret Mary Gillbride had to complete a cycle in her own time. She cheated death because something important, something vital, was left unfinished. I think you're holding his hand." He sighed, as if tired. "Did you ever hear the expression, 'To get to the future, you must go through the past'?"

Tom shook his head.

"I believe the seeds which we have sown in the past grow in the present and influence the paths we take in our lives. I believe that there is a soul, a consciousness within each human being, that has accumulated all these experiences." Gerald waited as Tom paid their admission.

Following those in front of them through the

stone walkway, Gerald continued. "You see, Tom, you still think of time as linear, but I believe it inhabits all four dimensions, including its own. Haven't you ever wondered why you felt such a powerful and compelling attraction to Meggie? Could you have met before? In another time? Why do we each seem to have a built-in ability for certain physical or mental endeavors? What about our strengths and weaknesses, our likes and dislikes, our prejudices and fears? Where do they all come from? And why can't we explain them all?"

Shrugging, Tom found it hard to believe that they were having this conversation in the park. Usually such deep metaphysical discussions took place late at night when both of them had had more than their share of smooth whiskey. "You mean like how lucky I've been in business?" He tried not to laugh out loud. "Are you saying I was a clerk to Jay Gould, or something?"

"Listen, boy. Luck has had little to do with it. You've worked hard. But I'm willing to bet that more than a few times you were in the right place at the right time. And made the right choices, or took a chance when others wouldn't have."

Tom nodded. Gerald had just about described his career. "Sometimes, Gerald, you scare me. All I asked was what you really believed in."

Shaking his head, Gerald laughed. "Ah, but I didn't tell you my most firm belief."

Tom grinned. "I'm afraid to ask."

"I believe we're all angels." At Tom's look of impatience, Gerald defended his statement. "I do. Not all of us can remember, but I believe we were

438

sent to each other to help. Guardian angels don't always have wings, you know."

"And you know this, of course?"

Gerald touched Tom's shoulder in a show of affection. "Everybody is an angel, lad. We all start out good, pure, if you like. And then as we age, the choices are made. Good versus evil. Kindness versus greed. If you remember nothing else about our years of discussion, remember that. We're all out here, in this time, for a reason. When we find it, we'll find happiness."

Tom was about to say something when Pat dropped the green ball he was carrying and pulled away to run after it. Always frightened to let go of him, Tom turned to follow.

"Patrick, come back here!"

The ball rolled down toward the stone wall in front of the glass tank of water, where the seals played to the delight of the many onlookers. Tom watched as it came to rest at the feet of a woman. A woman with red hair as bright and shining as . . She bent down to pick up the ball and Patrick stood next to her, holding out his hand. She looked . . . From the back she looked so much like Meggie that his heart started to pound and despite the cool weather he broke out into a sweat.


"You have hair like mine."

Handing him the ball, she looked at his patch of red and nodded. "That I do. And what's your name, may I ask?"

The adorable toddler smiled. "Patrick."

439

Kneeling to his level, she said, "Patrick. Now isn't that a grand name? Like the patron saint himself."

The child nodded, laughter showing in his eyes. "You sound like Uncle Ger."

She didn't answer. There was something about his eyes. This little child with startlingly blue eyes. Something so familiar . . . it was . . . it was . . . The answer fluttered around in her brain, like an elusive butterfly. But then perhaps she was just afraid to name it.

She couldn't stop staring at the child, so beautiful, so precious. She wanted to clasp him to her chest, yet knew the action would frighten him. Dear Lord, what had brought her to this place? What had made her leave Ireland three years ago? Something had pulled at her, drawing her across the Atlantic to this city. The family all thought she was daft, but she had known all those years ago that she belonged here. What wasn't clear, for she had left university to work in menial jobs in this country. And now, she was to interview for another. Maybe she'd make enough this time to go home, for her patience was running out. She was ready to admit her mistake.

"Pat, come here."

She heard a man's voice calling the child and young Patrick smiled at her before running back. She straightened and turned her attention to the playful seals, ignoring the strange pull of the child. If Gerald didn't get here in five more minutes, she was leaving. The old gent meant well, but maybe he forgot.

There was a saying her grammy used to repeat: A man'll touch you with his eyes before his hand. She felt like that now. Her shoulders started to tingle, as if someone had gently caressed them. She wanted to spin around, to face him, but she was unaccountably frightened.

Slowly, fighting that fear, she turned.

He was standing with the child in his arms. Gerald was far behind him . . . smiling. She felt her heartbeat increase as the man and child came closer. Something was happening, something was making her almost dizzy with happiness.

And then it became clear. In what seemed like a timeless flash of insight, she knew who he was. She knew where he lived, his favorite color, what he liked to eat, to read, the soft and sometimes demanding taste of his lips. She knew every detail of his body and the astonishing, breathtaking passion they had once shared. Tears started to pour down her cheeks as another's memory flooded her mind and mingled with her own. And the child . . . that, too, was so obvious, for it was no more than looking into a genetic mirror filled with precious, timeless memories.

He was a part of her. They both belonged to her!

It couldn't be!

She was . . . and she wasn't.

But how?

When she'd turned around, Tom felt his heart stop, felt the heat of fear press down on his chest. How could this be? She looked like Meggie. This woman. This stranger in the park. How could she look like his Meggie? He spun around to find Gerald, to make the old man explain.

But Gerald was shaking his head and laughing at them. It wasn't a cruel laughter. Although for some reason Tom couldn't hear it, he knew the sound would be filled with love. And then something equally frightening happened.

Gerald, his dear friend, started to fade. *Fade!* Like some silly caricature of a leprechaun receding into the woods. Tom opened his mouth to call out, to call him back, yet before he could, the old man's image broke into hundreds of tiny white lights. Like miniature fairy lanterns the lights danced up beyond the naked limbs of the trees and into the sky.

It was incredible. Was he the only one to see it? No one else seemed affected. Why didn't anyone else say something? Why—

Feeling the hesitant touch of her hand on his arm, he turned around.

"My God! How can it be?"

Clutching Pat to his chest, Tom stared in wonder at her. There was something different, something more calm in her eyes. They were shiny and bright with tears. Her mouth trembled with emotion. Those lips . . . her lips, her smile. Even the freckles that danced across her cheekbones. Everything . . . so similar. But it was her eyes. He would know her anywhere—in any time. And suddenly, unbelievably, his heart filled with joy and renewed hope.

"Meggie?"

She smiled and reached out a hand to touch Patrick's arm. The other she slowly brought to his face, running her fingers so very softly across his cheek and into his hair. Inhaling deeply, he detected the faint, flowery scent of lavender on her skin.

"Ahh, Tommy, now did ya think I wouldn't know ya?"

# ꓮꓞꓕꓰꓣꓦꓳꓣꓓ

You are a child of the universe, no less than the trees and the stars; you have a right to be here. And whether or not it is clear to you, no doubt the universe is unfolding as it should.

Therefore, be at peace . . .

*Desiderata,* from **THE POEMS OF MAX EHRMANN.**

# ROMANCE FROM JO BEVERLY

DANGEROUS JOY           (0-8217-5129-8, $5.99)

FORBIDDEN               (0-8217-4488-7, $4.99)

THE SHATTERED ROSE      (0-8217-5310-X, $5.99)

TEMPTING FORTUNE        (0-8217-4858-0, $4.99)

*Available wherever paperbacks are sold, or order direct from the Publisher. Send cover price plus 50¢ per copy for mailing and handling to Kensington Publishing Corp., Consumer Orders, or call (toll free) 888-345-BOOK, to place your order using Mastercard or Visa. Residents of New York and Tennessee must include sales tax. DO NOT SEND CASH.*

# ROMANCE FROM JANELLE TAYLOR

ANYTHING FOR LOVE　　　　(0-8217-4992-7, $5.99)

DESTINY MINE　　　　　　　(0-8217-5185-9, $5.99)

CHASE THE WIND　　　　　　(0-8217-4740-1, $5.99)

MIDNIGHT SECRETS　　　　　(0-8217-5280-4, $5.99)

MOONBEAMS AND MAGIC　　(0-8217-0184-4, $5.99)

SWEET SAVAGE HEART　　　　(0-8217-5276-6, $5.99)

*Available wherever paperbacks are sold, or order direct from the Publisher. Send cover price plus 50¢ per copy for mailing and handling to Kensington Publishing Corp., Consumer Orders, or call (toll free) 888-345-BOOK, to place your order using Mastercard or Visa. Residents of New York and Tennessee must include sales tax. DO NOT SEND CASH.*

# ROMANCE FROM FERN MICHAELS

# ROMANCE FROM ROSANNE BITTNER

CARESS                          (0-8217-3791-0, $5.99)

FULL CIRCLE                     (0-8217-4711-8, $5.99)

SHAMELESS                       (0-8217-4056-3, $5.99)

SIOUX SPLENDOR                  (0-8217-5157-3, $4.99)

UNFORGETTABLE                   (0-8217-4423-2, $5.50)

TEXAS EMBRACE                   (0-8217-5625-7, $5.99)

UNTIL TOMORROW                  (0-8217-5064-X, $5.99)

*Available wherever paperbacks are sold, or order direct from the Publisher. Send cover price plus 50¢ per copy for mailing and handling to Kensington Publishing Corp., Consumer Orders, or call (toll free) 888-345-BOOK, to place your order using Mastercard or Visa. Residents of New York and Tennessee must include sales tax. DO NOT SEND CASH.*